Winter Women, Midsummer Men

'Imogen, aren't you happy?'

'Sure.'

He raised his eyes, then flicked at some imaginary speck on his black jacket, waiting for her to continue.

'You see, I feel guilty, Ira. I've got everything I ever wanted. Everything my grandmother ever wanted for me – and worked so hard to get. I've got money, a lovely home, a baby, and a great husband –'

'So how come he came last?'

'What?'

'If Giles is so great, how come he came last?' Ira repeated.

Imogen's eyes narrowed. She adored Ira, but at times she found him taxing; too clever by half.

'I love Giles.'

'I know.'

'We have a good marriage.'

'I'll take a dozen.'

She frowned. 'What?'

'Sorry, I just got carried away with the sales pitch.'

ALEXANDRA CONNOR

Winter Women, Midsummer Men

Mandarin

A Mandarin Paperback
WINTER WOMEN, MIDSUMMER MEN

First published in Great Britain 1994
by Mandarin Paperbacks
an imprint of Reed Consumer Books Ltd
Michelin House, 81 Fulham Road, London SW3 6RB
and Auckland, Melbourne, Singapore and Toronto

Copyright © Alexandra Connor 1994
The author has asserted her moral rights

A CIP catalogue record for this title
is available from the British Library
ISBN 0 7493 1418 4

Typeset by Deltatype Ltd, Ellesmere Port, Cheshire
Printed and bound in Great Britain
by Cox & Wyman Ltd, Reading, Berks

This book
is dedicated
to H.

Life is a jest; and all things show it.
I thought so once
But now I know it.
John Gay

Prologue

'You heard the one about two Jewish women who were walking along minding their own business? Well, a flasher stops in front of them, opens his coat to expose himself, and then walks on. Stunned, the woman turns to her friend and says, "Did you see that *lining*?" '

Ira burst out laughing at the other end of the phone. 'How come I'm the one's whose Jewish and yet you have all the best jokes?'

Imogen shrugged nonchalantly: 'I save them all up, just so I can amuse you when I call.'

'You don't have to amuse me all the time.'

She heard the old tone in his voice and fielded it: 'I know I don't, but you'd soon hate it if I rang up to moan, Ira.'

He leaned back in his office chair and tucked the phone under his chin, his hands fingering his mail. 'Okay, so now I know you're not going to moan – but why the call?'

'My husband is having an affair.'

The words made him take in a deep breath. 'How does that make you feel?'

'Like celebrating,' she retorted hotly. 'Oh, for God's sake, Ira, how do you *think* it makes me feel?'

'He must be mad.'

Imogen's voice was momentarily wistful. ' "I am but mad north-north-west; when the wind is southerly, I know I hawk from a real whore –" '

Smiling grimly, Ira corrected her; 'Shakespeare actually said "I know I hawk from a handsaw".'

'Shakespeare wasn't married to my husband,' she snapped.

'I can see you're taking this well,' Ira said slyly, provoking

1

her, wanting her to talk, to confide in him, to open her heart. To turn to him.

'It hurts,' she said simply. The admission was heartfelt, dreadfully simple.

Oh God, Ira thought, after all that's happened to you, why this now? Why did this have to happen? I thought you'd made it, left all the bad times behind. But they keep catching up with you; how they *keep* catching up. . . .

Ira's voice was quietly sympathetic. 'Tom will come round.'

'He's in love, not in a coma.'

The joke sounded sour to both of them.

'Imogen, you are the most incredible woman I have ever met, no man could leave you. He'll come home, honestly he will.'

'Ira. . . .' She said his name quietly, with no intimation of emotion. Was she about to ask him for something? Or confide? 'Ira . . .' Imogen repeated. 'I want to teach my husband a lesson.'

Ahhhhh.

'. . . I don't want to publicly humiliate him,' she went on carefully. 'That would humiliate me too, and the family, and that's not on. No, I just want to show him the error of his ways. I want to make my point.'

'With a stiletto between the shoulderblades?'

She smiled fleetingly. 'He asked for it.'

'And I feel sure he's going to get it,' Ira responded wryly. 'But remember the old saying – "People of any breeding take their revenge cold".'

'Which means what exactly?'

'It means, don't do anything in haste that you might have cause to regret at leisure.'

But her tone was certain, immovable. 'I've thought it all out. Tom will never know it was me, he'll never guess; he wouldn't think me capable of it. But a little piece in your magazine – without naming any names, but pointing out some of his little proclivities – should bring my husband back into line.'

Ira was torn between two emotions: a desire to create mischief and a desire to protect Imogen.

'Your husband, in case you had forgotten, is an MP –'

'. . . which is why he has a lot to lose,' Imogen countered. 'The article would name no names, Ira, but he would realise that someone was on to him and that would make him think. He doesn't know that I know about his affair, so he would never suspect me. But he would run very scared, Ira.'

'Right back home?'

She nodded. 'With any luck . . . you see, I love him . . . Okay, so now laugh.'

'I wasn't laughing,' Ira replied carefully. 'But an exposé seems a little savage, especially an exposé in my kind of magazine.'

'A soft porn magazine?'

He raised his eyebrows, mimmicking horror. 'S'*Expression* is for the man about town –'

'Especially if that town happens to be Bangkok,' Imogen said, laughing despite herself. She had known Ira for years, watched him and his bewildering lifestyle, remained close to him, even after she married an up and coming MP – or was it up and running? She adored Ira and she was grateful to him. He was too glamorous for words, just as she was; too glamorous and too clever; too adept and too kind. Ira Mazan, she thought desperately, I know you and you know me, so help me now.

'Ira, please. . . .'

'Okay, okay, Imogen. You write a piece anonymously and I'll put it in the magazine. I just hope it won't rebound on you.'

'I don't want revenge,' she said genuinely. 'I just want my husband back, and a little piece about an MP, outlining his sexual dalliance, might just do the trick.'

'And what are we going to call it?'

Imogen smiled grimly. 'Oh, I've already got the title, Ira. "Private Members", what else?'

PART ONE

Know you what it is to be a child?
. . . it is to believe in love, to
believe in loveliness, to believe in
belief; it is to be so little that the
elves can reach to whisper in your
ear; it is to turn pumpkins into
coaches, and mice into horses,
lowness into loftiness, and nothing
into everything, for each child has
its fairy godmother in its soul.

('Shelley', Francis Thompson)

Chapter One

'I've got to take under my wing,
Tra la,
A most unattractive old thing,
Tra la'

She sang the words over and over again, bouncing the baby in time to the 'Tra las' and planting a smacking kiss on the top of Imogen's head at the same time.

'Tra la', (kiss) 'Tra la' (kiss).

' "And that's what I mean when I say, or I sing,
Oh, bother the flowers that bloom in the spring." '

The baby laughed on cue, looking up at the woman holding her. The words meant nothing, Imogen was only seven months old at the time, but the tune and the manner in which the song was sung conveyed the extraordinary love between the two of them. The small kitchen was crowded with furniture, the coal fire crackling in the grate, the dated appliances well worn, underlining poverty. Through the net window came the sullen sunshine of late summer, the laundry basket on the table beside them bulging with unpressed clothes, the iron balanced pre-cariously on the top of a pile of towels. At fifty-four, Elizabeth Forest had every reason to hope that her life might become less demanding; that the steady work routine of her previous years might lessen, her husband's retirement

7

holding out the tantalising hope of late rising in the morning and holidays in Southport or Lytham St Annes. She had been careful with the money, and even more careful with her husband; the war years were starting to recede, and with them some part of his crippling melancholia. He would even whistle now – well, occasionally – but it was a good sound and it reminded her of other times. Better times, before Graham had gone into the Army, and gone off to fight. He had not minded the life too much at first, had written home often to his wife, and she had longed for the letters, hoping against hope that he wouldn't meet someone else.

He was four years younger than her – not that he said it mattered – but although she believed him when they married, as time passed those forty-eight months seemed to swell, to age her more rapidly than him, and Elizabeth knew that the four years, the four little years, seemed woefully more as she left her twenties and moved into her fourth decade. She gave birth then, at the age of thirty-five, to her only child, Julie. A maudlin little baby, bleached of colour, lacking her own fierce dark looks or any of Graham's delicate features. A baby raised in air raid shelters as the bombers passed overhead, aiming for Manchester. An early baby, picking the worst time to exit the womb; a baby whose birth exhausted Elizabeth and whose silence alarmed her. Not that there was any reason to worry, the doctor said she was healthy; but later they asked if Elizabeth could take her to relatives, away from the city and the war raids. But there was nowhere to go. There were no relatives, only Graham's mother and she lived with them, bedridden in an upstairs room. So Elizabeth and her baby and her mother-in-law stayed in Little Lever and Elizabeth saw the ageing effect of motherhood and worried, not for her loss of appeal, but for the effect such a loss might have on her husband.

'He might leave me now I look different. Older . . . after all, he could have anyone,' she'd say to her friend, Cathy. 'Oh, I know he doesn't look at other women, but you know men – they don't have to, it just sort of happens. Women move in on them, and before they know what's hit them, well, it's done.'

Cathy was unmoved. Graham Forest might be a good-looking sort of a chap, but he was too quiet to make a girl's heart flutter with unbridled passion. And he was too serious . . . bookish, almost. Well, if you counted Zane Grey as a writer, he was bookish. Always reading something. . . . He never noticed women, at all – all his female fantasies remained firmly between the covers. Hard covers, that is, with 1/9d. written on the front.

'You've nothing to worry about,' Cathy said confidently. 'He's a good man.'

Elizabeth was unconvinced. And remained unconvinced throughout the war. His letters were lengthy, well written, considering Graham had had only a scant education, and tender. More tender than he ever was in life. His feelings adapted well to paper; the distance relieved him of the embarrassment of face-to-face contact. In a letter he could express love and not have to suffer the immediate response to his affection, the postal service performing an effective and extended foreplay to their intimacy. Separation allowed a redevelopment of their love, and when he came home on leave, that love was physically expressed without words. Because who needed the words then? They had been said, been written, lay under the mattress, a bundle of sentiments seeping through the bedclothes, scenting every midnight thought.

And then Graham Forest, husband of Elizabeth, father of Julie, returned to war and entered as a soldier with the Medical Corps when the Army went to relieve Auschwitz and Dachau. He changed then; no more Zane Grey, no more Graham Forest with his head in a book; no more goodness coming like a postscript to every letter. He never spoke of what he had seen, never mentioned the atrocities, never expressed by a word or look what had damned him, but the experience took him away from Little Lever; from the cramped kitchen and the narrow terraces; away from the comfort of the old bed and the familiarity of a home whose image he had carried in a photograph. Some better man went through the concentration camp gates, and that man stayed after the Army left; the ghost of Graham Forest's tranquillity for ever haunting the German soil. In body, he returned to England, in body, he returned to the role of

9

father and husband; but his soul remained winded in another place and his heart closed.

The doctor called it depression, shock, but the words meant nothing, Elizabeth knew that. She had fallen in love with the man who had gone away and now a melancholic impostor had taken his place. Sympathy was misplaced and unasked for; Graham wanted neither to confide nor to weep. There was no means of renewal, no recovery, no period of convalescence. He had gone, and she was, from that time onwards, forced to live with another man.

Yet her own temperament was strong enough to resist despair, and she turned to her child for love, giving enough affection for two, to one, expecting in this way to receive a second-hand comfort. But it was not to be so simple. Julie was a still child, and sensitive. Her long silences, usual since her birth, now worked in time to her father's moods, and she would resist Elizabeth's ebullient loving and sit on her father's lap instead, resting her head against his shoulder. He smoked and sat silently, and she sat with him, the kettle on the grate singing, the firelight lighting the worn kitchen.

A jealous woman would have resented such cloistered affection; but Elizabeth did not. She had love to spare, but little imagination, and decided early on that if her child could comfort her husband, then so be it. Perhaps Julie's need might draw her father back. So as Graham slid further into melancholia, Julie took the long walk with him, and left Elizabeth to run the normal day-to-day business of living.

'He just sits there –'

'He should be at work,' old Mrs Forest said sharply upstairs, her wasted figure tight in the narrow bed. The walls were thin – you could hear anything through them, Elizabeth said often. Everything – a cough, a movement – you could hear someone changing their bloody mind, she told Cathy. Thin walls, forbidding secrets.

'He's back at work now, you know that.'

The old woman raised her eyes upwards, tightening a bed-jacket around her shoulders. A stroke had partially immobilised her two years before – 'a stroke of luck,'

Elizabeth said drily to neighbours – and now she was where she had always wanted to be, in the middle of her family. In the core of it all, meddling and fretting and listening.

'He'll come round, I know my son,' she said fiercely.

Elizabeth studied her carefully. Only seventy-four, Maggie Forest looked well into her eighties, her hair plaited and drawn over one shoulder, as white as a candle. Her face had sunk, her false teeth over-large, her eyes quick with curiosity. You'll live for ever, Elizabeth thought, you'll sit on this bed until the Last Judgment and then what? She glanced at the crucifix opposite. The only person Molly Forest never had a harsh word to say about was God, Elizabeth thought wryly – and that was only because she hadn't met him yet.

'He's really upset – but he still won't talk about what happened,' Elizabeth persisted.

'Oh, men don't feel, women do. He'll get over it,' the old woman replied, losing interest. 'When's supper?'

Elizabeth should have known better than to expect any type of comfort or advice. The problem was hers. Not her child's, or her husband's. The others could cope with the changing of Graham, only she mourned for the lost man. Slowly she walked back into the kitchen and watched her child on her husband's knee. He stared, immobile, into the firelight. : . . What do you see? she wondered. What do you see, and where do you go to? . . . The room chilled her, the loss magified and momentarily unbearable. If you had died I would have visited your grave and bought flowers. I would have *kept you*, Graham Forest, kept you whole and safe in my heart. . . . Elizabeth's eyes misted over, but she continued to watch him, a sudden and unfamiliar resentment burning inside her. I want my husband back, she thought helplessly, Oh, God, give me back my man.

Graham turned then, almost as though he sensed her thoughts, and for a long instant his eyes fixed on hers. The room hummed suddenly with memories, words spoken, laughter muffled in the old bed. The walls swung to the sound of familiar songs, and the quick rap on the door. The very floor shook to the memory of his step, and the welcome slap of war letters landing on the mat. Sweet memories

11

flooded them both, remembrances tearing into each of them as steadily Graham continued to stare at his wife, almost pleading with her – and yet she could not read his expression; the ease with which she had followed his written words was denied her, and she floundered. Unable to understand what he was trying to express, Elizabeth no longer saw her husband sitting there, but some other man, a stranger who had taken her husband's place by the fire, a man who had stolen his place in her bed, a man who had taken his food and his clothes. A thief who had taken away a good man and come dishonestly in his stead.

And it was then that she realised she hated him.

Elizabeth's thoughts returned to the present and to the child on her lap. Little Imogen – what a name, how typical of Julie to pick a name which jarred uneasily in Little Lever. And yet it was a name the child might well live up to. Oh yes, Elizabeth thought, this was some special kind of baby. Almost on cue, Imogen looked up at her grandmother and smiled easily, charm as potent as birdsong. She creeps into hearts, her grandmother thought, creeps right in and lodges there. At first she had thought that she was biased; all grandmothers think their ducks are swans, she had said to Cathy. But it wasn't wishful thinking; *everyone* thought this little scrap had the making of something extraordinary.

But from where had Imogen got the magic? Elizabeth wondered for the hundredth time. Not from Julie, or from Les Mallinson, her son-in-law. They had met when Julie was eighteen – a solemn girl who went to work for the council; a girl who wore her hair short and her clothes long; a girl without any noticeable desire for love. Except for her father. For Graham Forest, Julie had all the love in the world.

Perhaps Elizabeth should have tried to limit that love. Perhaps that had been her mistake. But she wasn't a clever woman and she had quite genuinely believed that her daughter might help her husband back to life. Instead they both withdrew from life, the years wedging them into a kind of permanent role play. Graham Forest was forever the man who had returned from the war, and Julie was forever the sombre comforter. There was no room for advancement. No need for progress. Both found their allotted parts easy to play, and impossible to leave.

So as Graham's melancholia increased, his daughter's natural reserve fell into line with the maudlin shadow of her father's depression. She played Dr Watson to his Sherlock Holmes willingly, the supporting role adopted and treasured. But the lead player was not Graham; it was something altogether more subtle. His depression and withdrawal became the star of this peculiar private screening – and haunted them both. Long, listless periods of time passed, Graham still in the crowded kitchen, Julie doing her homework on the table by the fire. He read little, preferred to think. But of what? Elizabeth wondered. How could anyone find that much to think about so constantly? *Was* there that much to think about? . . . She had allowed him plenty of time to recover, been tolerant, waited patiently for the time when he would open up and confide in her. But it never came. Neither to her, nor to Julie.

But Elizabeth *minded*. Her daughter might not resent the silent reserve, but she did. She minded it after the first couple of years had passed, and later, when Graham lost his job at the factory and slid ignominiously into menial work, she raged about it.

'Just tell me what's the problem,' she pleaded. 'Just open up. For God's sake, Graham, you used to want to do something with your life.'

But he didn't even want to live it any more. That much was obvious from the solidly detached look on his face.

'Elizabeth, let it rest –'

'Let *what* rest?' she howled with frustration. 'You've rested for bloody years, Graham Forest, it's time to get moving again. I can't live like this.'

She couldn't; he could. What was the solution? Not divorce, no one divorced then. Besides, she felt honour-bound to stay with him. For better or for worse; in sickness and in health. Or, to put it another way, she wasn't prepared to kick someone when they were down.

So she went down with him. And the house changed, the seeping melancholia affecting Elizabeth's high spirits until she found herself working at life, without any hopes for the future. She dreamed of Julie getting married, of course, but the girl seemed indifferent to men, and uninterested in boyfriends. And she had neither the looks nor the personality to draw suitors; indeed, she seemed to have inherited her father's depressive streak. Not that Julie had suffered; there was no cause for her malaise, no event like the war to mark her decline. Her nature was simply despondent, and with the ever-present example of her father before her, her natural inclination became fixed.

'Can't you see that all this mooning about's not good for the child?' Elizabeth demanded of her husband when Julie was ten. 'You have to try and cheer up, Graham. If not for me or for yourself, do it for her.'

His expression was wiped clean, without understanding. it chilled her, as did his nocturnal habits. They had long since stopped making love. She never questioned that; was too embarrassed to raise the subject and preferred to think that it was due to what he had experienced in the war, rather than her own lack of appeal. So instead they lay like strangers in the old bed and if one accidentally touched the other they apologised and moved away. The cold inches between them were occupied by Graham's torment and Elizabeth's dry anguish, the war letters under the mattress mouldering like a guilty corpse.

He never slept through the night. In the early hours Graham always woke and sat on the side of the bed with his head in his hands. At first, Elizabeth had tried to comfort him, had wrapped her arms around him and tried to soothe him. But the rigid detachment with which he responded chilled her, and after a while she merely looked on – helplessly.

'He needs a hobby,' Mrs Forest said firmly. 'All men need a hobby.'

'Like what?' Elizabeth replied tartly. 'Pigeons?'

'No, he never liked birds,' she responded. 'Maybe cards would help. Cards are a nice quiet pastime.'

But cards didn't help. Neither did walking, betting, or having a beer with the few friends Graham still possessed. And then, early one November, Julie came home from school with an idea. She was animated, unusually so.

'Can we have fireworks, Dad? Like the others in our street?' she asked him keenly. 'We could let them off in the back yard.'

If Elizabeth had suggested it, he would have resisted – but this was Julie, and Julie he loved.

'We could get a few . . .' he murmured half-heartedly. 'They're dear though, so it'll not be many.'

So the fireworks were bought and duly set up, and on the 5th of November they were lit. Under a glowering northern night the Catherine wheel spun, the sparklers flared, and for an instant Graham looked up at the transformed sky and something faint, something ephemeral, spluttered to life. His eyes lost their vacant look, and he smiled once, briefly, the gesture fading as quickly as one of the cheap fireworks. But some little peck of vitality had fluttered through the mire of anguish; some tiny spark of life had flared under the artificial gaudiness and in that brash instant Graham Forest had forgotten the past.

From then onwards his hobby was fireworks. All kinds of fireworks, and in the winter the solemn skies over Little Lever spluttered with quick flashes of light, the unexpected magic calling the neighbourhood children to watch over the back-yard gate. Graham never acknowledged them, but he never shooed them away either, and side by side, father and daughter lit the blue touchpapers and retired for an instant in the fleeting and spectacular glory which took them both somewhere away from pain. The fireworks ripped into the darkness; they punched a hole in the melancholia; and while they burned and twisted and flashed their energy and colour, they drew Graham Forest into life. And when they died, he closed down again.

The hobby became obsessive and expensive, until Graham began tentatively to make his own fireworks in the mouldering little shed. Soon overtime assured the money to support his continued passion; the same overtime which kept him longer away from home and meant that when he was home, he was in the shed.

Fascinated by the turn of events, Elizabeth turned to Cathy. 'Fireworks, at his age! Would you believe it?'

'It's his second childhood, all men go through that,' she

replied phlegmatically, resisting the temptation to repeat the neighbourhood gossip. Graham Forest was mad, they said, stark staring mad. God knows what happened to him in the war, but whatever it was, it knocked him off his trolley. 'Still,' Cathy said wryly, 'with all the banging and the lights, at least you always know where he is.'

In the end, Graham's passion was brought before the police, the local bobby warning him that he could only set off fireworks before nine o'clock as the noise kept some people awake. Graham listened impassively, but although he obeyed in the winter, in summer the curfew was unendurable. At ten o'clock in July the sky was too light to show up the beauty of the colours, the display swallowed up in the indifferent twilight; so he began to wander, seeking out parkland or bomb sites, a solitary figure lighting fireworks in the war-wasted ruins. Many a summer light kept him out until after twelve, his boots sounding on the street when he finally returned, his hands smelling of powder, and stained by the cheap products he used.

As she grew up, Julie grew out of the firework hobby and spent more time reading, although Graham continued as before and hardly seemed to notice that she was no longer with him. All his mind could comprehend was that for the few glorious instants that the firework blazed, he lived. In those moments there was a release from the memories, his spirit lifting with the cheap wood and powder, his despair riding the back of the soaring display. The fact that the fireworks returned to earth, dead and finished, was not lost on him. The soul might triumph, but the dead weight of recall brought it back to reality. And so, as the last firework landed, burnt out on the bomb site, Graham sighed and returned home.

True to Elizabeth's prediction, old lady Forest continued to flourish in the back bedroom like a sick plant which somehow still managed to mooch throughout long summers and inhospitable winters. Nothing destroyed her; nothing was meant to; and as Elizabeth aged and Julie grew up, she became the one unchanging and dependable feature in Elizabeth's life.

'She should be courting by now,' Mrs Forest said, jerking her head towards the closed bedroom door as Elizabeth sat by her bed and stitched the frayed edge of a sheet. 'A young girl should be out having some fun. She's seventeen, I was married at that age.'

'Julie's not interested –'

'She should be!' the old woman snapped. 'It's not natural.'

'I don't think she's comfortable with boys,' Elizabeth suggested.

'You're not supposed to feel comfortable with them, you're supposed to marry them.'

Elizabeth kept her head down, stitching the sheet. Julie was working for the council, a typist in an office with three other girls. She seemed content there, as content as she ever did, and had even talked of rising to secretarial status in due course. It seemed a grand ambition to Elizabeth, certainly one up from the neighbourhood shopgirls, and yet what was the future in it? A secretary earning a good wage was something to be proud of, and yet without a man and a home and family of your own, what woman *could* be happy?

An image of Julie came before her eyes. A wan child grown into a wan seventeen-year-old, wearing sombre colours which made her sink into the background. In the summertime when all the other girls pulled on their finery and walked into town, she stayed home. While they giggled at the boys who wolf-whistled after them and flirtatiously accepted invitations to the cinema, Julie remained home. Long white summer nights which drew the young out, startled her and made her bolt for the security of the kitchen or the cool front room. While the other girls strutted like luminous mayflies in their new clothes, she hid away, and the boys passed by the window on their way to meet other, happier, girls. They relished their youth and the lusty feelings which swamped the northern summer; they ran after the opportunities which were so brief; they flirted with the world as it flirted with them, before marriage and children and the mundane routine bolted them into old age.

Go out, Elizabeth willed her daughter. Go out as I did and find a man. Go out and let them look at you, because before too long men look away. Faces age, good looks die, and other pretty birds come out in the summer sunshine. Take a chance, she willed her daughter, while you have time on your side, take a chance. . . . But she never put her thoughts into words. There was something too distant, too aloof about Julie to invite confidence.

Critical and envious by nature, Julie had longed to escape from Little Lever and had moved into Manchester for her council job, and there she had seen a different kind of existence. There she was respected for her work and progressed quickly; and there she was far enough from home to create a different backdrop for herself.

Little Lever was never mentioned; and Julie soon realised that in order to avoid lying she had to distance herself from her fellow workers. If she was aloof, no one asked questions – and then she could skilfully manipulate the truth to appear more attractive. She wasn't going to marry to escape; she was going to work her way up. Her ambition came from a deep bitterness with life. Having grown up with her father's example before her, she resented his sensitivity while sympathising with it. But her mother she could not under-stand – Julie chose to see her mother's stoicism as defeatism and daily withdrew further away from Elizabeth.

But there was a deeper animosity which wriggled under Julie's skin, and that was directed not at another person, but at herself. She knew without being told that she was plain, unattractive, without sex appeal. Her body underlined her barrenness of spirit. Flat-chested and thick-waisted, Julie had none of the female roundness of figure, her torso reiterating what everyone knew – she was undesirable. So she had decided early on not to attempt the impossible. There were never any hesitant make-up sessions, her fingernails were never varnished, and her hair remained short and uncurled. Beauty was out of her reach, beyond her.

In disliking herself so thoroughly she could never see anything good in the mirror, and after a time that feeling of disappointment and resentment spilled over into the world. Embittered, Julie could see little to value in anyone or anything; the only interest in her life was her father and her career. Nothing else mattered. Bitterness burned brilliantly, hotly; it took her through the long days and kept her working long after others had gone home from the council offices.

She was often the first to arrive and the last to leave, unnoticed and unremarked. The late buses – so often a hazard for other girls – only took Julie home. There was always a tray laid out for her, a sandwich and a mug of tea waiting, Elizabeth oddly diffident in front of this changeling daughter. And then, reluctantly pressed into conversation, Julie would tell her mother about work, emphasising her own progress, casting quick glances at Elizabeth to see if the requisite approval was offered.

And Elizabeth watched Julie and thought of her husband and wondered when the two people she loved most in the world became strangers. Who stole Graham? And which greedy demon returned for my child? she asked herself as a fathomless ache lodged under her heart. I only ever wanted a family, and instead I was given shadows. Their griefs, worries and resentment sat around the table, their anguish more substantial than themselves. What they were, and could have been, and what they had lost, stood solemn and unyielding witness to their remains.

I am dying amongst ghosts, she thought hopelessly, longing for something, or someone, to give life to her heart again.

Chapter Two

Imogen was born in answer to Elizabeth's wish. Imogen, a name out of touch with Little Lever, out of touch with Elizabeth. But not Julie. She had wanted to get on and when her ambition was thwarted she changed tack – if she couldn't be a career woman she wanted to marry, and then she wanted a special little girl. Her professional ambition had floundered when another woman was promoted over her head. She decided, illogically, that the council had turned against her. Elizabeth tried to reason with her, told her: stick it out, in time you'll get promoted, but Julie didn't want to know. She had given her best to the council, and they had turned on her. So now she was going to find another life.

But her marriage to Les Mallinson came as a complete surprise. They met, they married. They had a child. Imogen. He was too soft to argue about the name. He thought his wife was right in everything, or if he didn't, he never said so. Julie had been spinster material, old for her age. But then Les Mallinson had crossed her path and, dull-witted and unsure of himself, he'd allowed his future to be dictated by a woman whose determination flattened any objections he might have.

A thin man with a gap between his teeth, Les wore glasses with fingerprint smears on the lenses and talked quietly, always allowing Julie to have the last word. The first and the last. He worked for the council too, in some obscure office which he never talked about. All three of his brothers had married before him, and he had, at forty, given up hope of having his own family – until Julie sighted him. He was her first and last chance. Not handsome, not clever, not ambitious. But available. She won him over, and he was too malleable to resist.

Julie's contempt for him was boundless. Her voice when she spoke to him, curt; her expression pitying. But he didn't resent it. He hadn't expected more, and was in his own way as morose as she was. In that sense they were admirably matched. But having been happy once in her marriage, Elizabeth found their relationship chilling. She might now be distanced from Graham, but once they had adored each other, had loved and longed for each other. To begin married life in the bitter coolness of indifference unnerved her, and she tried repeatedly to reason with her daughter.

'Julie, you should marry for love –'

'Why?' she countered, her rigid face turned away. 'You did, and look where it got you. Les and I understand each other. We don't expect much.'

The tone in Julie's voice unsettled her. 'But you shouldn't marry just for the sake of being married –'

Her daughter turned on her, anger obvious. 'I'm going to take what's on offer, Mother, and what's on offer is Les Mallinson. Think what you like, but it's the way it is, and I'm going to marry him.'

Her eyes were dilated, mad with bitterness. For one instant, she was almost frightening.

She calmed down though and married Les, and for a while they seemed reasonably content, their home over-tidy, the food marshalled in rows in the cupboards, the towels folded in exact ranks along the side of the bath. The terraced house they had bought was tight with Julie's animosity, her meticulous tidiness making visitors un-comfortable. Not that there were many callers. The few friends she had made at the council soon fell off, baffled by her repeated accusations that she had been persecuted at the office. The truth was altogether different; Julie had been overlooked for promotion and had reacted violently, ripping up her boss's files and throwing his jacket out of the window into the car park below.

Her outburst had astonished everyone, and when she was called in to explain, her employer had accepted her resignation with barely disguised relief. From then onwards

Julie told everyone that she had been fired, and that her shorthand had been constantly altered, her letters scribbled over, other people supplanting inferior work in place of her own. No amount of reasoning could rid her of the obsession, so she retired from the council at twenty-four and slid into the quiet anonymity of a terraced street in Little Lever, just round the corner from her mother's.

Elizabeth never knew about the brouhaha at work as Julie never confided in her, but she did see a change in her daughter and wondered uncomfortably about Graham. Had melancholic, silent Graham passed down his genes to his child? Maybe the concentration camps hadn't been all the reason for his depression, maybe he had always carried the fault within him and the war had simply escalated his decline. And maybe, just maybe, Julie carried that fault too.

The idea unnerved her. No, not her child, she thought, not Julie.

'She's strange,' Elizabeth confided to Cathy. 'Really strange.'

Her neighbour looked at her hard. People had talked about Graham, now they talked about his daughter.

'She'll settle down now she's married. You'll see, love, she'll change. Once she has a family to look after she'll be another person.'

The words were prophetic. Throughout a long wet northern summer Julie carried her child with stoic, rigid, breathless calm. The house was cleaned from top to bottom, the tiny box room converted into a nursery, the yard whitewashed. Rainy June limped into rainy July and then on to a drenching August, with Elizabeth visiting her daughter daily.

'You've made the house lovely –'

'Mind the seat, Mother!' Julie snapped, readjusting the plastic covering on the new settee. 'I want to keep it nice.'

'It is nice, love, but you can't expect to keep it as a showplace when the baby comes. Little ones cause mess, they can't help it.'

'I don't like "mess", Mother,' she retorted acidly, laying down two china cups of tea on the table between them. 'A child doesn't have to have the run of the place, you know.'

Elizabeth's hand shook when she picked up the cup and she hurriedly laid it down in the saucer again. I'm nervous in my own daughter's home, she thought incredulously, her eyes straying towards the window. The cleaned panes were flat, blank, the sun without warmth, a bunch of artificial flowers fanning out from a cheap glass vase. She knew that upstairs the bedroom would be cool, the bedspread ordered, neat, the two dressing gowns hanging rigidly behind the door. Even the back yard was tidy, a whitewashed arena, sterile and unwelcoming, without grass.

'Not long to go.'

Julie looked at her mother, wondered when she was going to leave, wondered how soon she could begin to clean up after her. She was squashing the cushion, wrinkling the nice clear plastic, making things messy.

'You're not worried about the birth, are you?' Elizabeth asked gently.

'No.'

'Oh.' Her voice lapsed, the tea settling in the cup, a skin forming. 'I could help after the baby's born. You know, pop round and do your shopping.'

'Les will help.'

Elizabeth wondered why she was being shut out, and experienced that winding of the heart she had endured for so long with her husband. But perhaps Cathy was right, she thought eagerly, perhaps Julie *would* change after the baby was born. Soften up, relax.

'If there's anything I can do –'

'I'll let you know, Mother,' she said. 'I'll let you know.'

The summer was doused with rain, slippery underfoot, the streets greasy. While others sweated under the dour humidity, Julie wore three cardigans, her hands cold, her skin waxy. She carried the baby high, out of reach, tucked under her breasts. From the back she looked thin; only when she turned was the pregnancy obvious. Not that she ever referred to it. She might buy baby clothes and make the stuffy top room a nursery, but to all intents and purposes she carried her child as another woman would carry a bag of laundry. Pregnancy was a necessary chore, no more.

Then in the final week she took to calling the council offices, asking for the woman who had replaced her. Her abuse was thick, her voice guttural, the language shocking. Only her condition prevented anyone taking further action. She was pregnant, they said, and some pregnant women go a little odd. . . .

And some stay a little odd. Like Julie. After the birth she sat stiffly in bed, the cot beside her. A baby girl, they told her. She called her Imogen. That much was easy, but she didn't breast-feed her, or pick her up. Les did. Clumsily, good-naturedly, handing her to Elizabeth, while Julie glowered from the bed. Silent, her face a white disc of loathing.

'You think I don't know,' she began, her mother turning to her, her expression hovering uncertainly. 'You're going to swap her, aren't you? Swap her for the one you had last week.'

Les looked at his wife, his face stupid, unravelled.

'Now, love –'

'Julie, what are you going on about?' Elizabeth asked, her arms automatically tightening round the baby.

'You think you can exchange that pig child of yours for my baby.'

Her face boiled with colour and the lobes of her ears flushed, filled with blood.

'Julie, what *are* you talking about?'

'You!' she screamed, lunging forward towards her mother, and gripping the iron rail at the foot of the bed as she looked up at her. Her face was only inches from Elizabeth's, her pupils dilated.

'Did you bring it in under your coat?' she asked, tugging at the front of Elizabeth's jacket, her hands jerking the thin material. 'Well, where is it? In your bag?' She skittered off the bed so quickly that Les jumped back, startled. 'I'll find it, Mother!' Julie cried, her voice singsong, 'I'll find it! You can be sure of that – I'll find it!'

Her hands wrenched open the bag, tipped it upside down, Elizabeth's trivial possessions clattering on to the lino, a hairpin cantering under the bed. Startled, Les mewled once, almost like a child, his fear regressing him as Elizabeth turned hurriedly towards the door.

Seeing her move, Julie grabbed hold of the bottom of her dress, her fingers twisting the cloth.

'Give me my child back!' she said violently, her eyes narrowed, feral. 'I want her!'

Elizabeth continued to back away, holding Imogen and keeping her eyes fixed on her daughter. A heat and a smell seemed to come from Julie, even the room took on the force of her madness, and in that one palpable instant Elizabeth waited for her daughter to spring.

Old lady Forest was Elizabeth's strongest ally. Separated from the family for years in her attic bedroom, she could see situations once removed, with a detached perception. Over the years she had suspected the lovemaking, feared the news from the war, heard the rows, and finally recognised her son for what he was. Graham Forest, her only child, depressive, withdrawn, but not mad. Not really. Not quite. She had seen the fireworks come up from the back yard, little puffs of starlight peeking in at the bedroom window, his moods trailing on the tail of a rolled-up tube of gunpowder. Up and away – then down, back to life, and the salt-water sting of reality.

So to old lady Forest it was no surprise to hear about Julie. Like father, like daughter. It was sad, embarrassing, but it was bloody life. Just like being bedridden. There was no sense to it. Who said there had to be? Who expected justice? Not her.

She told Elizabeth the same. 'You've got to make the best of it.'

Her daughter-in-law was quiet, her upper body bowed over the baby on her lap. Imogen was smiling. A doll.

'I said, you've got to make the best of it, Lizzie. Think of the little one.'

Elizabeth glanced up. Her eyes were steady, but there was a skimming of something over them. Not tears, something deeper.

'Les has gone. Cleared off,' she said quietly. 'The council said he'd been in Monday but they hadn't seen him since.'

'Useless bugger,' old lady Forest said thoughtfully, wiping the side of her eye with a handkerchief. Not tears.

Just random northern pollen blown in on a hot wind. 'I always thought he was spineless. Bloody men, they're all the same. Useless. You can rely on women, but men you need like a fish needs a bicycle.'

Elizabeth had heard it all before and closed her eyes momentarily. 'Graham's no good to us,' she said.

'Never was, even as a boy.'

'Listen to me!' Elizabeth snapped suddenly.

The old woman raised her eyebrows. 'Well, get on with it then,' she said.

'Julie isn't going to be coming home.'

'That bad?'

Elizabeth nodded. 'That bad.'

'So you'll look after the baby?'

'Of course. Who else?'

'What about Les's family? Won't the other grandparents have something to say about this?'

'They're not interested. There are more than enough Mallinsons to worry about already,' Elizabeth said flatly. 'I've spoken to them and they're more than willing to let me bring the baby up.'

'Without offering any kind of help? Money, I mean.'

'Nothing.'

The old woman blew out her cheeks. 'It's a mess.'

'No.'

'Oh yes it bloody is!' she snapped. 'You're stuck with Julie's baby, no help from Graham and I'm no good either. It's too much for you, Lizzie.'

'I can do it. I have to,' she said slowly, then looked at the old woman. 'I need help, though.'

Her interest was tickled. 'What kind of help?'

'I want to get the baby away. I don't want Imogen to know about Julie. My life ended a while ago, you know that. Graham doesn't need me, and Julie . . . well, she's looked after.'

'She might recover –'

'No,' Elizabeth said evenly. 'The doctors have told me that she won't. She's a danger to herself. She doesn't understand anything, and she couldn't possibly look after her child.' Elizabeth swallowed painfully. 'In time, maybe

26

with new drugs, maybe then she might get better. But not now.' Elizabeth's face was flat. Dummy face, nightmare words. 'We only have a chance away from here. If we take the baby –'

'We?'

'I'll take you with us.'

'Why? What can I do?'

'Just do what I say!' Elizabeth snapped. 'We'll go away from here, somewhere healthy. Bring the baby up strong. No Graham, no Julie. She'll never know about them. She mustn't find out. Her parents are dead, that's the story. No truth. No need of it. If we cover our tracks she'll never find out.'

'She will. Secrets only hibernate for so long,' the old woman said cautiously. But she wanted to go, to be off from the top room, away from the same dull view of Little Lever. And besides, she had a little money put aside. It wasn't much, but there was no point waiting until she was dead for Elizabeth to have it. She needed it now. They all needed it now.

'What about Graham?'

'We leave him here,' Elizabeth said. 'He can cope. He has a pension and the house.'

'You'll have to go out to work.'

'I know.'

'At your age?' Mrs Forest countered. 'That's not going to be so easy.'

'People want their houses to be cleaned and their meals to be cooked – I'll find work.' Elizabeth paused, looked hard at the baby on her lap. 'This child is going to succeed in life. God knows, I didn't, and neither did Julie. But this one will. As I live and breathe, whatever it costs, this one will.'

Chapter Three

1969 – Ten years later
Brighton

She was sick of the sodding pier. There was only so much pleasure anyone could take from a strip of metal reaching out into a slab of water. Seagulls, rocks, salt smell, palmist –the images were grindingly familiar, tourist bait; the Grand Hotel wedged between buildings like a fat lady in a white dress. Suzanne Jacobs breathed in carefully, rationing the amount of ozone entering her lungs, her eyes wrinkling against the sun.

The water glubbed under her feet, flickered in between the wooden slats of the pier as she traced a crack with the toe of her shoe.

'Jaco! Jaco!'

She turned her head. Smiled. Bent at the knees.

'Jaco,' Imogen said happily, hugging her and then turning back to the woman who followed.

She was different now. This Elizabeth. Heavy, weighty, bad on her feet from being stout. But she smiled from right down in the stomach and held it. Happy.

'I said she'd be here,' Imogen went on cheerfully. 'I just knew she would.'

' 'Lo there,' Elizabeth said easily as she drew level with them. 'Doing what the doctor ordered, then?'

'Only under protest,' Suzanne replied, walking over to a nearby bench and sitting down, Imogen beside her. Elizabeth stood by the rail, gazing out to sea. There was a boat on the horizon and a child's hat bobbing on the water under her feet. That's careless, she thought, I bet someone's mother's looking for that right now.

Not that she was worried about money any more. Old lady Forest had coughed up her savings when they moved down to Brighton and within a week Elizabeth had a job and a flat. Within a month she lost both. No one wanted old ladies. No one wanted babies. No one much wanted Elizabeth. Alone she had a chance, but not as a trio. She didn't tell them that. No way. They were together and somehow they would stay together. But the weeks passed and even the cheapest accommodation ate hopelessly into their funds, and soon Elizabeth found herself working two part-time jobs just to pay for a babysitter and keep a roof over their heads.

The roof fell in a week later. Old lady Forest took ill and Elizabeth spent her time moving between hospital, nursery and work. No one could have done it. She couldn't. She failed. She realised it the day she stood on the pier and looked out at sea with Imogen in her arms. Dear God, she said, this is it. . . . Her stomach ached with distress, a feeling of homesickness thundering over her. The day was mottled with rain. Warm rain; not northern rain, southern rain which bruised nothing. Not even earth. Dear God, she said to herself again, this is enough. I can't take any more. Someone's got to help.

Someone did. A woman of about thirty came down the pier and leaned against the rail only a yard from Elizabeth. She had a mass of dark hair and a beaked nose, her eyebrows violently arched. In a red dress she seemed exotic, out of place, and when she turned to Elizabeth she stared at her fiercely.

'What are you looking at?'

'Sorry,' Elizabeth said automatically, glancing away.

The woman walked towards her, extended her hand and touched the side of Imogen's head. Darkly asleep, she never moved.

'Is she yours?' Her voice teetered uneasily.

'My granddaughter,' Elizabeth said evenly, ashamed of the faded, overwashed shawl wrapped around the child. 'She's called Imogen.'

'Fine name,' the woman replied, her voice oddly plaintive. 'Fine face. Where's her mother?'

'Dead,' Elizabeth said calmly. The words were well used now. Almost easy. 'Both her parents are dead.'

The woman stopped looking at Imogen and stared at Elizabeth. She fixed her unusual dark eyes on her and studied her, considered her, weighed her up.

And Elizabeth held her ground. She knew how she looked. Hair badly cut, clothes shabby, shoes down at heel, complexion waxy from bad food. Even the scent of her clothes embarrassed her. Mothballed, cheap, common.

'Have you got work?'

Elizabeth tried to sound composed. Not desperate. Desperate makes people uneasy.

'Not just at the moment.'

'But you need work?'

'Yes.'

The woman frowned, then touched the side of Imogen's head again. She felt the child's hair and then ran her index finger along a blue vein in her temple.

'Come with me.'

Together they had walked back to Royal Terrace, where the woman unlocked the front door of a three-storey house in the Georgian crescent. Timidly Elizabeth walked in, clutching Imogen. The hall was painted dark green. A selection of semi-erotic prints adorning the walls, and a huge bronze statue of a naked man facing them. Quickly the woman threw open the double doors on her right and beckoned for Elizabeth to follow. The bay window looked out over the afternoon sea, the walls were blanketed with rugs, and the furniture was unlike any Elizabeth had ever seen. All the colours were hot – reds, purples, yellow – and all acted as a heady backdrop to the woman herself.

'Sit down,' she said easily. 'I'm Suzanne Jacobs.' Her hand extended, Elizabeth took it as Imogen woke up. She stared around her, blinked and then yawned. Suzanne watched her, amused. 'A critic! I don't think she likes my taste,' she said, laughing.

'Oh, no, she's just tired, that's all,' Elizabeth said hurriedly.

'It's okay, I was only joking,' Suzanne replied, getting to her feet and walking out. A minute later she returned with coffee, laying a cup before Elizabeth and a beaker of milk in front of Imogen. 'Is that all right? I mean, I don't know much about babies, but they all drink milk, don't they?'

'It's fine,' Elizabeth said gratefully, feeding Imogen and then sipping her coffee. It was bitter, thick.

'You looked so desperate on the pier. I mean, I hate this town, but you looked at the end of your tether,' Suzanne said, leaning back and crossing her legs. Her shoes were red silk, heels three inches high. Expensive, unworldly shoes, in an expensive, unworldly house. 'I need someone to look after me,' she shrugged. 'I need a housekeeper.'

Elizabeth tried to breathe normally. She could do it. She could do whatever this woman wanted. Clean, cook. But what about Imogen? And old lady Forest?

'I go away sometimes. You know, I travel . . . buy stuff. I don't sell it, though. Not much of it. It's more a hobby than a business. Something I do to fill in the time. You see, my husband lives abroad.' Suzanne's left foot swung in the sunlight. 'Listen, to tell you the truth, I'm a bitch. That's a fact. I can't keep staff because I don't treat people right.'

Nonplussed by the woman's honesty, Elizabeth didn't know how to respond for an instant. Then her confidence lifted, inched into life. This woman needed just what she needed. Security. She needed emotional security; Elizabeth needed financial security. Simple.

'Listen, it's not just me you'd be taking on, Mrs Jacobs. I have Imogen to look after and my mother-in-law. She's in hospital, but she'll be out soon, and she's virtually bed-ridden.' Elizabeth paused, watching Suzanne's face, waiting for the flat look of rejection to skim into place. 'I'll make your home run like a dream – in return for their security. And a wage.'

Now it was Suzanne's turn to be nonplussed. But she was impressed too; fascinated by Elizabeth's courage when she was on her uppers.

'Where do you come from?'

'Up north.'

She nodded. 'I'd heard they were blunt up there.'

'Where do you come from?'

'Israel.'

31

Elizabeth smiled. 'I've heard nothing about your lot.'

Laughing, Suzanne leaned forwards. 'Okay. There's room for your mother-in-law and you, and the baby.' Her eyes fixed on Imogen and then turned back to Elizabeth. 'What's your name?'

'Forest. Elizabeth Forest.'

She nodded once. 'I can't have children, Elizabeth. I found that out this morning and when I went down that pier I was cursing God and everybody and everything. But, do you know something? I was still hoping that somehow I'd have a child, believed I could make it possible. After all, it couldn't be impossible, not when I had money, everything a child needs.' Her eyes moved back to Imogen. 'She's not mine, I know that. And I'll never try to take her away from you. But someone answered that prayer and sent her.'

Elizabeth couldn't reply. Two prayers in one day. Two answers. Too good to be true.

Beware of things too good to be true. But then again, don't look a gift horse in the mouth or it might bite you. So Elizabeth told old lady Forest in the hospital that night. I've got a job and a home for all three of us. Where? A nice Israeli woman's house. Foreigners! she sniffed. But she looked pleased. Warmed up too, circulation coming back. You'd have died to let me off the hook, Elizabeth realised suddenly. Thanks. But no thanks. You're going to live and we're going to see Imogen succeed. With Mrs Jacobs's help. Bitch or otherwise.

And she *was* a bitch. A real hundred per cent cow at times. Particularly times when her husband didn't come home and cancelled a trip, or when she was bored. Then she was a shrew, a violent, unattractive, maudlin, self-pitying shrew. With bad habits. Like staying in bed and smoking; like leaving the bath full of dirty water; like throwing tantrums at the slightest provocation. Her temperament was unstable, capricious, greedy, fierce.

'I don't like things done like this,' she said only days after Elizabeth had begun working for her. 'This has to stop!' Her left hand swept across the table, the china smashing to the floor. A glass rolled on to the wooden surround, the white and green plates bellyflopping on to the Chinese carpet.

'You liked it well enough the other day –'

'I don't like it now!' Suzanne snapped. Her hair was tied back in an elastic band, her face bald without make-up. A heavy towelling robe fell to her thin ankles and slid sluttishly off her right shoulder. In her whore's mood, Elizabeth thought grimly.

'Calm down.'

'Don't tell me to calm down!' she blared. 'You work for me, you should show some respect. I gave you a roof over your head. You owe me.'

'Keep the bloody roof and the bloody job,' Elizabeth replied violently, taking off her overall and walking to the door. 'I'll survive.'

'Oh yes? Like how? You were down and out when I found you.'

Elizabeth swung round, facing her employer. 'Listen, no job is worth this.' Her eyes scanned the room. 'You're a ridiculous woman.'

The words shocked both of them, but Suzanne was the first to respond. Her tongue ran over her lips and she hitched her dressing gown up over her shoulder. There was a look in her eyes which hovered between irritation and anxiety.

'Okay, I'm sorry,' she said, glancing down. Elizabeth knew the gesture was false. The penitent Madonna now. 'Sorry, don't go. Don't go, Lizzie.' She crossed over to her employee, touched her arm hesitantly. 'Busy Lizzie, sorry, don't go.'

Her moods shifted every few hours. Pitiful, angry, shrewish, charming. On and on they went, a pop-up book of roles. One on, one off. For a while Elizabeth was worried that she was unstable, the disturbing memory of Julie coming back to her when she looked at her employer. But after a while she realised that Suzanne Jacobs was merely spoilt. Over-indulged, over-wealthy, over-bored.

So she decided on her own tactics to keep both the job and the security. Suzanne cared about no one and nothing but Imogen. She had hired Elizabeth because of Imogen, and now Elizabeth would control her through her grandchild.

'I can't have the baby upset,' she said one day. 'It's not good for her. Perhaps this wasn't such a good idea. . . .'

'Listen, Lizzie,' Suzanne said eagerly. 'I'm just not used to having a baby around. I'll get used to it.' She gazed out of the window to the small enclosed garden where Imogen lay in her pram. 'We'll take her out. Get her some new clothes.'

Elizabeth hesitated. She wanted the best for her grand-child and knew that this woman could provide it. But at what cost? The atmosphere of the house was highly charged, the furniture, paintings and whole demeanour of her employer wilful and sensuous. Should a child be brought up in such an environment? she wondered. Oh yes, Imogen was a baby now, but in a few years what would she make of the nude statues, the heavy theatricality of the house? There was nothing English about this home. I might be set in one of the most outwardly traditional towns in England, but the atmosphere was foreign, strange. Even the scents were heady here, the flowers full-blooded gardenias, the food kosher. It had seemed the answer to a prayer, and if God had put her here with her family, she would accept it. But only God knew why – she didn't.

Yet old lady Forest thrived when she came back from hospital. This was more like it, she told Elizabeth. . . . She revelled in the arguments, the door-banging, the Yiddish or Turkish music played in the early hours. This was living, she said. It made you feel alive.

'But what about Imogen?'

'What about her?'

'Do you think it's good for her?' Elizabeth pressed the old lady.

'No, I think that living in a stinking bed and breakfast without enough money to pay for food was better,' she replied bitingly. 'God, Elizabeth, count your blessings. You wanted her to get on, well now she has a chance. Mrs Jacobs likes her, and if she goes on liking her your grandchild will have a start in life few kids ever get.'

And Suzanne did go on liking Imogen. She never changed her character, but she modified her behaviour around the child, allowing the best of herself to show through. She also educated Imogen in the most natural way possible. No lessons, no lectures, no pressures. But babies watch and they copy, and Imogen was more alert than most. She was allowed to look at the art books, allowed to play with Suzanne's clothes, allowed to be precocious and funny, and because she was surrounded by three women who adored her, she grew up quickly and with devastating confidence. Upstairs, old lady Forest told her about the North and about her past. She recreated the mills and the little pulleys, the dank smell of the streets and the war years. Imogen listened, remembered. In the kitchen she also listened, this time to Elizabeth. From her she learned about cooking, cleaning, morals. And love. Oh yes, especially love.

The truth was adjusted. Cut down to size like an overlarge print cut to fit a frame. Her parents were dead, and Elizabeth's husband was dead too. No grandfather, love, just us. . . . Imogen believed her, of course, she had no reason not to, but at night when everyone was in bed, Elizabeth wrote the first of her letters to Graham and told him they were fine. Doing fine. How's things? Are you coping? Have you heard? Well, *have* you heard from Julie?

His replies came back addressed to a Post Office box number – which was all Elizabeth ever gave him. No address, no telephone number. No closeness. I did my best with you, Graham, and it wasn't enough. Sorry. . . . But she needed to keep in touch to know how he was, if he was coping. Living. He replied as he always did. He was fine. Julie was the same as ever. No change. . . . He never said he missed his wife, just mentioned the fireworks and said – around November – that he'd named one after her.

Elizabeth liked the idea of that. A high white light called Elizabeth skipping over Little Lever like a comet. Thanks, Graham, she wrote back. I could send you one, he replied. . . . Yes, she said, that would be nice. . . . But it never came. Maybe he'd run out of materials, maybe it never existed, but she liked to think about that firework when it was dark and she lay in bed alone.

Not that there was much time to be lonely. There was too much work for that, and when the fourth year at Brighton came round old lady Forest died suddenly. Went out. Ended. One day there, the next gone. Elizabeth wrote home to Graham and told him, and asked if he wanted to come to the funeral. But he didn't. He couldn't face it. He never could face things. So Elizabeth faced it alone and coped. She coped with the house on the seafront and her Jewish employer and was winded with the distress of Suzanne's divorce and Mr Jacobs's remarriage, and the grim spectre of hysterical illness which followed.

Because Suzanne couldn't cope. Hadn't had to, you see, had been given things too easy and hadn't the emotional make-up to fight. She became ill instead, and ran through a variety of Harley Street specialists, none of whom told her that her husband's remarriage was the thing sticking in her gut like a growth. Only Elizabeth realised that – and she couldn't say anything. She left the comforting to Imogen, and the four-year-old rose to the challenge like a professional.

Clever, quick, charming, she mimicked and skipped her way around the house, jumping on to Suzanne's bed in the morning and hauling her out of whatever greasy nightmare she wallowed in. Her protests were half-hearted.

'Go away.'

'No,' Imogen countered, snuggling up to Suzanne and laying her head next to hers.

'I'm not well,' she insisted, turning away, but still feeling the small body against her back. The room was stale with smoke and wine, her curtains drawn, her dressing gown dropped by the side of the bed where she had left it. Drawers, half opened, spilled out their contents, a handbag discarded on the table, a vase of dying flowers smelling foully.

'Go away,' she repeated, although her hand snaked out from under the covers and stroked the little head next to hers. 'Shouldn't you be at school?'

'No school, it's Saturday,' Imogen answered, encouraged by the gesture. In another minute she would have effected her miracle. Suzanne would get up and soon she would take her out.

Suzanne turned heavily, her eyes streaked with old make-up. 'Where's Elizabeth?' she asked.

'Washing.'

' "Busy Lizzie",' Suzanne mumbled, sitting up. Her hair

was wiry, sticking out from her face, her hand lifted to her left ear. 'I've lost an earring,' she said petulantly. 'Shit.'

Imogen slid off the bed immediately and on to all fours, rooting around the bedroom for the lost gold hoop. Her little figure was sturdy, small for her age, her hair rubbed up at the back where she had lain on it. Grudgingly amused, Suzanne leaned on one arm to watch her, and smiled when the child found the earring and held it up triumphantly.

'Found it!' she shouted, adding more softly, 'Now can we go out?'

The ploy worked, just as both of them knew it would – just as Elizabeth knew it would.

So Imogen slid under Suzanne's defences; curled into her rigid heart and found a permanent place where no other human being ever had. Elizabeth felt no jealousy watching the bond between the two of them; she had wanted to give her grandchild the best start in life, and if this woman was to be the means to provide that, so be it.

But as Imogen grew, intelligent and strong-minded, and was sent to the best school in Brighton at five, her progress underlined that sad other child. The one no one knew about, the Julie who remained up north. Graham said little in his letters, only that there was no progress, and later, that there was no hope. The drugs kept Julie calm, but unresponsive. Blindly forgetful, she wallowed foggily in her own sickness and never remembered her husband or her child. As Imogen began to find her place in the world, Julie dropped off the edge of the same globe and wandered blearily into a vacuum.

Once settled, Elizabeth occasionally begged time off. Only a couple of days at first, then later a little longer. She never took Imogen with her, leaving her instead in Suzanne's erratic care, but as time passed and she began to trust her employer, Elizabeth went alone. She travelled up on the train. Suzanne never asked her where she went and she never offered any confidences. She simply slid away from Brighton and up to the hospital on the outskirts of Manchester.

Elizabeth never knew why she went. Never expected to

be cheered by the visits, or to find hope reawakened. She went because Julie was her child.

The hospital's day room depressed her. It was raining and the busted half-opened blind looked out on to a barren courtyard. There was no smell. But far away someone sang a Beatles song.

'Julie?'

She came in silent, unresponsive. Looked at her mother without recognition.

They took care of her, that much was obvious. She was fatter, not at all the bitter wand she had once been; she even smiled distantly. Elizabeth wondered about that; wondered how the drugs managed to elicit a sweetness that love and motherhood never had. What an impostor this Julie was; and what had they done with the real one? Or maybe this *was* the real one? Maybe under the sour scum of her illness medication had tugged out some sweetness of soul. Julie, Elizabeth thought, reaching out her hand and taking her daughter's, oh Julie.

'How are you?'

Julie's eyes focused slowly. Drugged. Medicated into life. 'Fine.'

'You look nice,' Elizabeth said, her mind throwing up an image of her as a child in Little Lever. Watching fireworks. A little girl who had been company during the long war, one who had heard the night planes going over and run to the mat to pick up her father's letters. Look Mummy, look, it's for you. . . No, it's for both of us, love. . . .

'Is the food nice?'

'We have ice-cream.'

Ice-cream in winter. Vanilla ice-cream. Like Granelli's used to be, the old cart coming round Little Lever at four on a Sunday afternoon. Only Julie hadn't liked ice-cream then.

'That's good,' Elizabeth said woodenly, stroking her daughter's hand. I want to tell you about your child, she thought. I want to tell you that she's clever and that she's going to surprise us all. Don't you remember, Julie, don't you *want* to remember? . . . But she never said it, and after another few minutes, she left.

She came back to the moneyed house and the Yiddish

38

music and found Suzanne cutting out pictures of the models in the magazines, pasting them on to a piece of board for Imogen. Fascinated, she watched them; watched the strange, foreign woman standing in Julie's place; watched her blonde grandchild take without question what love was offered. The room hummed under the scent of perfume and exotic food, the phone ringing in the hallway outside, Suzanne's Burmese cat sunning itself on the window ledge. An expensive life, full of its own traumas, taking in the foundling child.

If she had had doubts at first they were soon squashed. Suzanne Jacobs might be neurotic and wilful, but Elizabeth realised that she was needy. As needy as Imogen was. If anything happened to her, her granddaughter was safe. Of that she was sure. There was money here, enough to cushion any problem; there was education here; and confidence and an entrée into a life she could never have provided. Little Lever meant nothing to Imogen. Her world was the Brighton seafront, the expensive school. Her accent was free of northern vowels and her memories free of northern recall. She had no parents that she knew of, and no responsibilities. Her life was to be sweet – and even then Elizabeth knew that the time she could share it with her was limited.

There was too much to hide. Too many ties to cover up. Too many lies. She might have grown used to watching what she said, used to putting her thoughts through a mental sieve before she spoke; that she didn't resent. No one needed to know about Graham, or about Julie and Les. Only she needed to know that, and she was more than prepared to keep everyone's secrets. But time would pass. It always did. It would creep on and Imogen would grow up and all the tenets by which Elizabeth lived would have less and less influence on her granddaughter's life.

I am an old woman with a northern accent and little education. A working woman, she thought without pity. I can choose to make her love me and pity me and in that way keep her with me, or I can let her slide into Suzanne's world. The thought wedged under her ribcage and she leaned against the wall heavily. I have done what I can for her,

Elizabeth decided brokenly. From here on in, I can only step back.

So she did. She did not withhold affection, but rationed it. Her love for her grandchild was so powerful, her ambition so fierce, that she allowed another woman to take what any other grandparent would have demanded and fought for – the love of her own flesh and blood. Bravely Elizabeth stood back and subtly allowed Suzanne to take centre stage; allowed her to spend time with Imogen, to spoil her, to take to the theatre and up to London.

The jealousy scalded her at times, but how could she compete? She had neither the money nor the knowledge to be able to educate Imogen; she didn't know which were the best shops, or how to hail a taxi, or how to order from a menu in French. The world she wanted for her grandchild she could see clearly enough, but it was out of bounds to her. I want you to have it, but I can't come with you, she thought. If I'd kept you home, I could have managed. I could have told you about Little Lever, encouraged you to get a secretarial post working for the council. But what else? What else? . . .

Standing by the door, Elizabeth watched Suzanne spray a little perfume on her granddaughter and saw Imogen laugh, sniffing the scent as she had seen her mentor do. What places she can take you, Elizabeth thought, what things she can show you, what dreams she can inspire in you. Without effort, without struggle, what a life she can lead you into, and what miracles you might achieve there.

And me, she thought, what can I do? The answer made her tip back her head, fighting tears. I can let go, Elizabeth thought, and the realisation was almost a grief.

Chapter Four

Imogen was swinging her legs on the bench, her eyes focusing somewhere on the horizon as Elizabeth's thoughts came back to the present. At ten, she was average height, average weight, average intelligence. An average child – until she spoke. Then she was something way beyond average. Her character was formidable, her charm immense. Without effort Imogen had assimilated everything Suzanne had taught her; secreted it in that hurrying little brain; nurtured it along with her powerful memory – and honed it to perfection.

You looked at her and thought, what a nice child, Elizabeth realised – then you spoke to her and she replied and you were intrigued. This was no ordinary child. By some process of nature she had inherited something from all her relatives, her blood carrying the good soul of each of them. That melancholia, so dangerous in Graham, was intensity in Imogen; that ambition, so thwarted in Julie, was curiosity in Imogen; that hardiness, so selfless in Elizabeth, was resilience in Imogen. And from old lady Forest, Imogen inherited the one blessed gift which enchanted everyone – her humour.

She could mimic anyone. Copy an accent, memorise an expression, then turn and look over her shoulder and raise an eyebrow, both hands on the hips. Saucy. Go on, laugh, I dare you, the expression said. Her northern roots, coupled with the exotic atmosphere in which she had been brought up, lent her a unique insight. Her mind worked differently; she saw the potential in people and situations with a rapidity which was stunning. She was old for her years because she seemed already to know that she was living in a hurry.

41

Graham Forest had given up, Julie had dipped into madness, and Les Mallinson had stepped back; and yet Imogen, knowing nothing of them, seemed to live for them all. They had retreated or been cowed, their lives diminished, limited; but in her they continued, achieving through her what they could not achieve themselves. She knew nothing of her grandfather or her parents, but what they lacked, Fate had given in recompense, to her. Her hugeness of spirit, her will, her downright joy carried them all on.

Julie did not know her child, Graham did not know his granddaughter, but their blood flowed in hers, and their losses were overshadowed by her successes. Elizabeth watched Imogen in astonishment. An expression was Julie's without her daughter's dead heart; a gesture was Graham's, without his terror of the world. In Imogen, all their lives enfolded, intermingled and continued – in a child, all their fears became hope.

Oh, thought Elizabeth, when she visited Julie again, what you would think of your child. The gods love her, they love her. Julie was unresponsive. Do you remember the plastic seat covers and the tight little house? Elizabeth wondered. All the bloated terror of madness that struck you has missed her, thank God. It's missed her.

'I'll come again soon.'

Julie looked up. Dead eyes.

'I love you.'

Nothing.

But I can bear it, Elizabeth thought. I can bear it now. Because of Imogen. Because of her I can look at you and not want to shake you.

Remarkably, Graham asked after Imogen when he next saw his wife. Surprised, Elizabeth hesitated, wondering what to tell him. He was old now, wearing glasses – National Health – and there was a selection of medicine bottles on the fireplace.

'Is she . . .' he started tentatively, 'is she pretty?' he asked, holding out his hand for the photograph. The Little Lever house was unchanged, the fireworks still outside in the shed. He took the print and stared.

You can't see it there, Elizabeth thought, no one can photograph magic.

'She's blonde.'

'Her hair goes white in the summer,' Elizabeth answered. Brighton sun, bleaching away the blues.

He passed the photograph back to her: 'She doesn't look like us.'

No, she doesn't, Elizabeth thought with relief. She can't ever give herself away by a resemblance; can't ever be spotted by some interfering day tripper who might say, 'Ooh you look like a girl up north I used to know. Julie, she was called. You're a dead ringer for her.'

Imogen was a dead ringer for no one.

Elizabeth cut him off: 'No, I don't think so, love, best not to.'

No fireworks, no new office buildings built hard on the old bomb sites; no gloomy front rooms, smelling of damp. Not for my grandchild, not for Imogen. I don't want her walking down past the council offices, picking up old smells, old memories, taking away the southern tan and the southern confidence. Not now, not ever.

'I could come down,' Graham ventured.

And I could come back. Elizabeth thought.

But neither of them would, and they knew it, and when Elizabeth walked to the end of the street, she did not look back.

Suzanne's life changed after her divorce. For a while she resisted the idea of getting involved, but soon her vanity and loneliness forced her out again. At weekends a BMW was parked outside the house, a thin man in a dark suit coming down from London. A friend of her father's, she said at first, a solicitor. There were others. A doctor, an accountant. None lasted. Uncle James and Uncle Monty swept into the hall at Brighton and sniffed out the territory. Suzanne had money. A Jewish woman, albeit divorced, and not that old. Not a bad catch, really.

She wanted company and she liked sex, so she endured these men. But her intelligence railed against the absurdity of her situation, and her hope was limited. Glyndebourne would be nice, she'd say. Oh yes, I like Wimbledon on the day of the finals. Tickets for *King Lear*? Great. St Tropez, okay. . . . The full promise of the sixties came into bloom, and Suzanne, the disaffected and dissatisfied Suzanne, hitched up her skirts and danced all night with – if not the best of them, at least the rest of them.

Parties went on until the early hours, prople driving down from London, some staying in the spare bedrooms, some at the Grand. She was a willing hostess, a generous, if detached, friend. Her circle increased, the volume of visitors presenting a never-ending spectacle to Imogen. Writers, painters, models, filmmakers – some successful, some sensing that Britain was coming into its own and ready to make a killing. Suzanne's was the house they came to, hers was the bank account they borrowed from, hers was the car they borrowed too. They were living rough, fast, without responsibility. When one man borrowed the Jaguar Suzanne waited all the following morning for it to be returned, but it wasn't. It was found instead, wrecked in Fulham, a lipstick message on the front window: 'Sorry.'

And yet while her social life was chaotic, at home Suzanne was constant. She had the ability to step back mentally, and was not liable to be fooled. She needed those people at that moment, but she judged to a nicety her involvement. Drugs were for others, promiscuity was for others. Not her. And nor her family. So she carefully measured Imogen's exposure and saw to it that she saw only the charm. Not the dirty sheets, not the amphetamines, not the wheedling for money. What Imogen saw was the guests' arrival. Beautiful women in expensive dresses, sweet and attentive before the second and third drinks turned them all into blathering hags. Fights were conducted elsewhere; no one made love in Suzanne's house, or slept over, rising unshaven and bumping into Imogen in the early hours.

It was a full-time job, but worth it. But it was also dangerous. Imogen saw the best of these people and never the worst, and so she had no fear of them. They were her montage come to life; breathing, glamorous idols to be adored. And emulated. Aware of her own growing charm, she talked to them easily, amusing them and feeling for the first time the heady power of an audience. In the drawing room she was trotted out, her mimicry encouraged, her wit blossoming under the praise. Suzanne watched her, leaning against the fireplace and seeing how she held a dozen people spellbound. She had no jealousy of Imogen, only a fleeting surprise that a child could be so confident.

'She's a jewel,' one said.

'She'll go on the stage,' another man, an actor, replied, leaning towards Imogen and taking her hand. 'Let me look at you.'

'Don't give her ideas,' Suzanne said suddenly, watching as Mike stared into the girl's face. 'She's not going into the theatre.'

'But she has talent,' he said eagerly. 'You should want the best for her.'

Suzanne moved away from the fireplace and rested her hand lightly on the actor's head. 'Oh, but I do, my love. Enough to know that she can do better for herself, I mean, how long is it now since you had a part?'

He brushed her away, stung by the remark.

Imogen listened, but she wasn't in any real danger. The theatre, for all its glamour, did not entice her. Other things did. Writing, talking. But not acting. Her head tipped to one side, her thoughts wandered. How long before she could slip out of the room and go downstairs? she wondered, thinking of Elizabeth in the kitchen. The voices hummed round her, someone dropping a glass while someone else drummed out a Nat King Cole song on the piano. She turned, caught the eye of a woman on the settee and smiled automatically. The woman returned the gesture.

'Sit by me,' she said, patting the cushion next to her.

Imogen did as she was told.

The woman was quiet, removed from the rest of the party. Her dress, riding high over her thighs, was the colour of burnt sugar. Her hands, holding her glass, shook.

'Could you get me another drink?'

Imogen dutifully did as she was told, then regained her seat.

'Thank you,' the woman said, draining half the wine in

45

one swallow. Her voice was low, far off, and she fascinated the child.

'What do you do?'

'I'm a singer,' the woman said without animation. Her hair was piled high on her head, leaving her neck and ears exposed. 'Penny Redling. I've got a recording contract and my single comes out next week. They say I'll be a big success. Number One.' She said the words flatly, without believing them. Imogen pitied her instinctively.

'I'll buy it! What's it called?'

Penny looked at her for a long instant. ' "Two Can Play at This".'

' "Two Can Play at This"?' Imogen repeated, committing the title to memory. 'I'll tell everyone at school to buy it,' she went on eagerly. 'Will you be on television?'

Penny nodded, but the thought seemed not to please her. 'Next week.'

'That's good,' Imogen said, surprised by the woman's lethargy. 'Aren't you pleased?'

In reply, Penny leaned her head back against the settee. In the same instant Mike's voice rang out: 'Penny's pissed, Penny's pissed.'

'Not in front of Imogen!' Suzanne said hurriedly, hustling the child out of the room.

Grateful to be banished, Imogen wandered downstairs to find Elizabeth padding about barefooted on the tiles, her stockinged feet swollen, a smile ready as her granddaughter walked in.

' 'Lo, love.'

'Hello, Gran,' she said, sliding on to a kitchen stool.

Elizabeth jerked her head upwards 'They seem to be having a good time.'

Imogen nodded, unusually subdued. Alerted, Elizabeth stood in front of her. 'What's the matter?' she asked.

'There's such a sad woman up here,' Imogen said quietly. 'She said she was a singer . . .' her voice trailed off, tears threatened.

Surprised, Elizabeth wiped her hands and sat down. 'Why?'

'She seemed kind of . . . lost.'

Imogen's perception made Elizabeth pause. She was a happy child, encouraged and safe. Sadness was unlike her.

'Some people are lost at times, love. She'll be okay.'

But Imogen was not to be consoled so quickly. 'Why is she like that?'

It took Elizabeth a moment to respond. 'She's unhappy, perhaps. Grown-ups get unhappy sometimes.'

A long moment bleeped out its seconds.

'Gran, what was my mother like?'

It was the first time Imogen had ever asked the question and it left Elizabeth floundering, suddenly rocky with unease. What had happened upstairs, she wondered, for such a thought to come to her? Why had one woman's sadness brought her mother to mind?

'She was . . .' Elizabeth paused. She *was* no, she *is*. But Imogen couldn't know that. She was about to lie, to look into her granddaughter's face and tell her about her dead mother. To deceive her. But what was the choice? To tell her the truth? Your mother sits by a broken window blind without looking out, just dribbling. She thinks of nothing and never asks about you. She is sick and can never get better. She is the reason I brought you here; she is my child; and my secret. She is dead to everyone except me. She is off limits. She is gone.

'She loved you very much.'

Imogen glanced at her grandmother. 'But what was she *like*?'

'Sad, love.'

'Oh.' Imogen had half expected it. 'Why was she sad?'

'Life didn't turn out the way she expected.'

'And my father. What was he like?'

'Good. But weak.' Elizabeth kept the descriptions short. Limited lies.

'What happened to them?'

'They died.'

Imogen sat still for a long moment. The lie was enormous. It grated against Elizabeth's heart. I'm sorry, but I have to lie to you, I have to. . . . She had told her grandchild of their death before, but this time there was something different. The lie was accepted, but not believed. Not wholly. Imogen was growing up. She knew something. . . . I never wanted to deceive you, Imogen, but what good would the truth serve? To make you curious? To make you force me to take you up north and show you the ruin of your mother? What possible good could come from you knowing that your father rejected you? And worse, if you knew of your mother's illness, would you worry, expecting any day for her sickness to strike you? No, sorry love, but no. A lie is a lie, but it stands.

'Mrs Jacobs has a visitor coming tomorrow,' she said.

Imogen looked up. 'Who?'

'Her nephew, Benny. He's a little older than you and he's coming to stay for a while.'

Imogen liked the idea and brightened, all thought of her parents apparently dismissed. 'Is he staying here, with us?'

Elizabeth nodded and got to her feet. The danger had passed. For now at least, the past was safe.

'His mother and father are going to Europe for a month, so Mrs Jacobs said he could stay here.'

The idea was becoming more appealing by the moment. The long summer school holidays had begun and Imogen was already bored. She had a number of girl friends, but had longed for someone different, and now this boy, Benny, was coming. It would be fun.

'I don't want to!'

Suzanne frowned, suddenly irritated, her hand resting on the door handle as she watched a small, dark-featured boy argue vehemently with a stocky woman standing by a red Jaguar. The day was clouding over, Brighton rain threatened. Nonchalantly Suzanne blew on her newly painted fingernails and listened.

'I want to go with you!' he screeched, aiming a kick at his mother's shins.

Suzanne's eyebrows rose, her lips making a crimson O shape.

'. . . I want to go too! I want to go! I don't want to stay here!'

'Now, Benny, be a good boy, we've been through this. It's Daddy's business trip, you can't come. It won't be for long.'

His foot flicked out again quickly, just missing her. The gesture was ludicrously petulant for a twelve-year-old.

'Benny, don't darling. Please, be good. I'll bring you plenty of presents back.'

'He'll settle,' a voice said behind Suzanne.

She turned slowly and studied her brother. 'You said he was quiet, Malcolm. He looks a little bastard to me.'

He flushed quickly. Not so cool in his business suit.

'He's just highly strung.'

'He should be,' Suzanne retorted acidly, her gaze turning back to the harassed woman outside. 'Listen, Ruth, either bring him in or throw him over the bloody cliff – but do something, for God's sake.'

Embarrassed, Ruth tugged at her son. He half stumbled, half limped, towards the door.

'He'll settle –'

'We've been through that,' Suzanne replied, shutting the front door and walking into the drawing room where Imogen stood waiting.

'This is Benny,' she said drily.

He stuck out his tongue immediately.

Imogen stuck hers out.

'I think they'll get on,' Malcolm said inanely.

'I'm sure; they'll probably even be engaged by the time you get back.'

'I want to go –'

'Oh, dry up!' Suzanne snapped suddenly.

The boy regarded her in astonishment. 'You look like a witch.'

Her long dark eyes narrowed and she moved towards him slowly. 'I *am* a witch, little boy,' she said menacingly. 'And I can turn you into a frog any time I like. So watch it, or you'll spend the next month in the pond outside.'

The words had the desired effect. Benny, suitably cowed, stepped back, his parents beating a hasty retreat to the door.

'We'll come for him on the 31st,' Malcolm said gratefully. 'Honestly, he'll settle.'

'If he doesn't, where will I have the body sent?'

A strangled cry came from Ruth's throat.

'Suzanne's just joking, darling,' Malcolm said hurriedly.

'It's her sense of humour, that's all. She was always a scream. . . . Trust me, Benny will have a lovely time here.' He guided her eagerly towards the door. 'It'll be good for him, to be away from us for a while. You spoil him too much. He'll love it here.'

He didn't. He hated it. He wouldn't eat lunch or dinner and sat by the window, pining. His hair, thick and dry, sprang out wide from his temples, his eyes deep set and suspiciously red rimmed. He was tall, with big feet and big-knuckled hands, and he moaned constantly.

'Fun, isn't he?' Suzanne said to Imogen.

'Does he *have* to stay, Jaco?'

She glanced at the boy through the drawing-room door. This was no joke, some big gangling boy who couldn't stop snivelling. And he was staying for a month! One whole month.

'Couldn't he go somewhere else?'

'All the boarding kennels are full,' Suzanne said, turning away in disgust. 'He's just like my brother used to be when he was a boy. Always crying.'

'I hate boys who cry,' Imogen said vehemently. 'He won't even talk to me.'

He wouldn't. All her attempts at conversation had been met with either a poked-out tongue, or a turned back. His misery saturated the house, dampening everybody's spirits as the day wore on. Imogen turned to Elizabeth for advice, but was told to be patient. He'll come round, Elizabeth said. . . . But she doubted it. She saw him as a spoilt kid, a boy who would have had the softness knocked out of him up north, a boy who behaved like a girl. Not even that – Imogen hardly ever cried.

'You'll see, he'll come round. No one can keep this up for long.'

Benny could. He kept it up all that day and that night he wandered around the house and into the kitchen after one, making himself a sandwich and leaving a mess for Elizabeth to find in the morning.

'Listen, love,' she said patiently, 'just tell me if you want something, I'll make it for you.'

'I'll do it myself!'

Her hand itched and she tried to control herself.

'Benny, don't be silly –'

'You're the help, you can't tell me what to do.'

She clipped him round the ear without thinking, his eyes widening in shock. For an instant he stood speechless before her and then began to howl.

Imogen ran into the kitchen.

'What happened?'

'She hit me!' he wailed.

A slow smile crept over Imogen's face.

'You all hate me here!' he went on, hysterically. 'And I hate you! I hate you all!'

He kept it up for three days, skirting round Elizabeth, ignoring Suzanne and moaning fitfully to Imogen. All attempts at consolation were rebuffed. No, he didn't want to go out; no, he didn't want to go to the shops; no, he didn't want to play Scrabble, listen to records, or meet her friends. No, no, no!

Elizabeth was at a loss what to suggest. 'Perhaps you could take him out to the country?'

'And leave him there?' Suzanne countered, walking round the kitchen in her Carmen rollers. By the window she paused, covering her right eye with her hand and squinting out into the small garden. 'I think I need my eyes testing, everything's blurred,' she said, covering her other eye and repeating the process. 'God, I must be getting old.'

Elizabeth glanced over. 'We could take him down the pier.'

'He wouldn't go.'

'He might. He can't keep this up for a month.'

Suzanne looked at her evenly. 'He's like his father, troublesome. You know, when he was a boy Malcolm was always running away from school – maybe we should leave the door unlocked when we go to bed?'

Elizabeth ignored the sarcasm. 'He'll get ill if he carries on like this. Besides, it's not good for Imogen.'

That was all that was needed. Suzanne, suddenly aware that her charge might be affected, decided on immediate action. Barging into Benny's room, she stood with her hands on her hips and faced him.

51

'Grow up.'

He sniffed loudly.

'Benny, you and I have to come to an agreement.' She racked her brains for a threat that would galvanise him. The solution came readily. 'You either cut this out, or I'm sending you to your Aunt Lyla.'

The effect was extraordinary. Lyla Stein lived in Manchester, a pinched, vile-tempered woman who had outlived two husbands and ran the local Jewish Women's Guild. She was loathed by all members of the family. An Orthodox Jewish woman, she followed her religion obsessively and allowed no television or outside amusements. Synagogue was all she lived for; synagogue and good works. She wore her hair in a bouffant with a veil to keep it in place. A veil stitched with tiny coloured beads. Technicolor dandruff, Suzanne called it.

'Aunt Lyla?' Benny said with dank horror.

Suzanne nodded. No one in the world ate half a boiled egg. But Lyla did. Making an issue of it, eating half and then dabbing her mouth with her napkin and looking around at everyone else.

'You can eat a *whole* egg?' she'd demand, with the same astonishment someone else would have said, You can eat a *whole* turkey? 'Myself, I can only eat a little. A small stomach is a sign of breeding.'

'Aunt Lyla?' Benny repeated, the full horror sinking in.

'You have half an hour to make up your mind,' Suzanne said. 'You can either stay here and have a good time, or go up to Lyla's and learn how to be a rabbi. Your choice.'

There *was* no choice. Benny made up his mind in twenty minutes. Grudgingly he allowed himself to be persuaded out and grudgingly he followed Imogen and Suzanne round the Lanes, stopping frequently to look into the windows, dragging at their heels.

'He's stopped crying.'

Suzanne glanced at Imogen and raised her eyebrows: 'Thank God for small mercies. D'you want to go to the cinema tonight?'

Imogen stared at the figure lumbering behind them. 'With Benny?'

' 'Fraid so.'

They went to the cinema and the next day Benny agreed to play Scrabble. Having been threatened with banishment he was now unnervingly agreeable, totally compliant, and amenable. If Suzanne stretched out her hands, he passed her cigarettes; if she reached for her drink, he was on his feet, getting it for her. His attentiveness, at first a joke to Imogen, soon began to unsettle her. Having monopolised Suzanne's attention for so long, this interloper came as an unwelcome threat to her stability.

She knew that Suzanne wasn't her mother, but she was the closest thing she had. And more, she was a friend. Along with Elizabeth, she was the one real certainty in her life – and Imogen had taken it for granted.

Until Benny. Now this overgrown cuckoo had blundered into her nest and taken over her place in Suzanne's affections. It might be temporary, but it hurt. What if Suzanne really began to like him? What if he stayed? . . . The thought plagued Imogen; it kept her wakeful and made her quiet and when Benny tried to ingratiate himself with her, she resented it.

'Let's go down to the beach.'

'I'm working.'

He looked over her shoulder. Automatically, Imogen shielded the page from him.

'What are you doing?'

'Mind your own business.'

'Let me look!' he shouted, pulling away her arm and picking up the paper. He stared for a long moment at it and blushed. The crude caricature was of him: it was rough, but accurate, his hair sticking out, his eyes narrowed and shifty as he wrung his hands together. He recognised himself and his faults and hated her for it.

'Bitch!' he said simply, ripping up the paper and running out.

War was declared, the two children avoiding each other from then on. Benny resented Imogen's skill and her perception; Imogen resented the needling closeness he was developing with Suzanne. Like opposing armies they plotted and weighed each other up, waiting for an opportunity to put each other down. When Benny was agreeable, Imogen was clever. If he offered to help Elizabeth in the kitchen, she would turn her attention to Suzanne, making her laugh when she mimicked Benny's unbroken voice. But then Benny would talk to Suzanne about their family and Imogen was left out. He knew that she was smarter than he was, and that made him antagonistic, but he also knew that she was the granddaughter of his aunt's housekeeper, and that made him feel superior.

Before long Imogen felt that *she* was the interloper, her secure place in the house usurped by the rightful heir. Upset and suddenly insecure, only she knew the mean nature Benny succeeded in hiding from the adults – the way he stirred up the fish in the pond outside; the way he messed up Suzanne's make-up, leaving Imogen to get the blame. After all, it had to be her. What boy would play with make-up? What boy indeed. . . . It was constant battle. Tittle-tattle, untruths, whispered secrets all sought to undermine her and before long she realised that he had to go.

She grew to loathe her tall, rough-headed rival. Grew to despise his minor betrayals and his hypocrisy, and by the end of the second week, Imogen wanted blood. The only weak spot in the whole of Benny's careful armour was a crush he had developed on one of her girl friends. Mandy hadn't really liked Benny, but she did like the presents and had reluctantly agreed to go for a walk along the pier with him. Benny was in seventh heaven when he came home. He strutted around the house like a turkey cock and couldn't resist telling an astonished Imogen that Mandy had agreed to go to the cinema with him that Saturday afternoon.

'She adores me,' he said, grinning inanely. 'Not that she's my first girlfriend. I've had loads.' He paused, weighing her up. 'I bet you haven't got a boyfriend. I don't suppose anyone would look twice at you.'

The insult went deep. This was the first boy in Imogen's life and she felt suddenly awkward. Was she *ugly*? She stood in the middle of the room, her confidence sliding off her second by second. I hate you, she thought bitterly, I hate you.

'I'm meeting Mandy outside the Odeon,' he crowed,

delighted by her silence and by the hurt look on her face. 'I bet you wish you were coming.'

It was true, Imogen *did* wish she was going. In fact, she had even arranged for her and Mandy to go the cinema together – before Benny had put his oar in. He wasn't content with taking over her family, she thought miserably; now he had to take over her friends.

'Mandy said she was sorry, but she was sure you'd understand,' he went on. 'Aunt Suzanne's given me the money to pay for the film and for some chocolates.'

That was it. Imogen could have borne her friend's betrayal, even the implication that she was plain, but for Suzanne to give Benny money to enjoy himself – that was too much!

All afternoon Benny, outrageously confident in the flush of first love, whistled and sang his way around the house. The matinée was at two-thirty and by one he had already combed his hair seven times and changed twice. Sunning herself in the back garden Suzanne was blissfully unaware of the storm brewing and Elizabeth was out when Imogen walked to the bottom of the hall stairs. She listened carefully, hearing Benny's radio blaring and his reedy voice coming from the bathroom. He was trying to stick down his hair again, she thought, even though it would dry out minutes later and flirt up in tufts round his gormless face.

On and on went Benny's carolling. Imogen made her way into the back study and picked up the phone. She knew Mandy's number by heart and was fully prepared when she answered.

'Mandy?'

'Benny?'

It worked. Having practised mimicking Benny's voice for days, Imogen had it off to perfection.

'Mandy, I can't take you to the cinema,' she said.

There was a long lull. A silent, bone-crushing animosity coming over the line.

'Why not, Benny?'

Imogen's mimicry was so perfect that the girl was completely taken in.

'I'm taking another girl.'

55

There was a screech of fury.

'WHAT!!!!!!!!!!!'

'I knew you'd be disappointed.'

Mandy wasn't disappointed; she was apoplectic.

'How dare you!'

'Sorry . . .' Imogen said skilfully, then added as an afterthought. 'You see, I've got loads of girlfriends.'

The line went dead.

Upstairs Benny continued to fight with his hair for the next twenty minutes, then went out into the back garden and presented himself for Suzanne's approval. Through the dining-room window Imogen watched him preen himself and watched as he was given the money for his little outing. She didn't see the garden gate open at first. In fact, she didn't see Mandy until she had crossed the small lawn and faced Benny. The conversation was heated and brief, Benny's face a study as Mandy pushed him, fully clothed, into the garden pond.

Chapter Five

Benny had the grace to know when he had lost. He never knew what had happened, only that Imogen had beaten him at his own game. When he left two weeks later he had a grudging respect for her, and over the next few years he wrote to her on and off, telling her about his school and threatening further visits. They never came off. He might like to think he could take Imogen on again, but he daren't.

The fishpond episode delighted Suzanne. She repeated the story often to friends and described in gory detail the way Benny had surfaced with a koi carp slapping on his chest. And time continued to pass: but even at forty-five Suzanne was a copybook version of eternal youth. Her skin was firm from plastic surgery, her legs and backside free from cellulite, her hair altered as every style came and went. At forty-five she could pass for thirty, and took full advantage of the fact. Skirts yo-yoed and some of hers rose higher than most; make-up made erotic dolls of women; and hers was most spectacular. Her innate style and heady sexuality made up for the unconventional looks. So what if her nose might have looked better on a macaw? So what if her voice swooped from upper-class southerner to Yiddish frau? So what? She was Suzanne Jacobs, and bloody hell, that wasn't so bad.

And she was exactly what Imogen needed. The solution was obvious; Suzanne adopted the girl and took her charge around everywhere with her. Surrounded by cultured friends, admired by the avant-garde, doted on by the series of 'uncles' who still dipped their toes into Suzanne's water, Imogen grew from child into teenager. Her education was first-class, but limited. She had no desire for an academic career and was influenced by the Jewish ideal of woman-hood – the dream of marrying well. Even divorced, Suzanne could value the security of marriage, and she wanted that for Imogen.

Elizabeth was not so sure. Her granddaughter was clever, quick-witted – surely there was something more for her than marriage? Oh yes, she wanted to see Imogen emotionally happy, but she could remember only too well how she had struggled without an education, how she had grubbed to make a living. A man might leave a woman, but a career would always be there.

Yet Imogen had little interest in such things. She was happy in her life and indulged. What reason was there for her to study?

'She won't *need* to work with her looks,' Suzanne said to Elizabeth one day.

The older woman paused. Elizabeth was ageing, and a daily was coming in to do the heavy work. She wouldn't admit that she was tired, but she was. She had set out to secure her granddaughter's future and had succeeded. There was only old age left – and slowly and certainly her thoughts began to move back to the North.

'I've made a will, Lizzie,' Suzanne said suddenly, throwing half a cup of tea down the sink and turning to look at her employee. They had been together for nearly fifteen years. Fifteen good years, with arguments, fights and threatened dismissals. But after those fifteen years they were still together. Two dissimilar women who admired each other. '. . . and I've left most of my money to Imogen –' She held up her hands to prevent Elizabeth interrupting.

'Hang on, let me finish. You'll be provided for, you know that, and the house is hers. I'm not giving much to my relatives, they have enough. I just want to make sure that Imogen's secure. She'll be a wealthy woman one day.'

'I don't know what to say,' Elizabeth stammered honestly.

'I know,' Suzanne replied. 'But don't get too excited, I have to die first before she can inherit and I don't intend going young.' She smiled, a sudden warmth binding the two women. 'We've never really talked, have we?'

Elizabeth shook her head. Don't start now, she thought, please, don't ask me to be a friend. I work here, I don't want to have to start lying to you.

'We *should* have talked more,' Suzanne went on. 'You see, if I hadn't come across you that day on the pier, I don't know what I would have done. Everything looked so bloody hopeless. I did *so* want a child . . .' she glanced away suddenly. 'I still grieve for the things I never achieved. The man I never loved, the child I never gave birth to . . . Imogen isn't mine, I know that, but she's as near to mine as I'll ever get.' Her hand reached out to Elizabeth for the first time. Elizabeth hesitated, then took it. 'You can only judge a person's pain by what they have lost – and we've both lost more than most.'

Touched, Elizabeth wanted to confide. To sit down and tell her about Graham and Little Lever, and Julie, now coming into a dead middle age. Do you know what it feels like to travel on that train up to Manchester and stand by the day-room door, looking at your child and knowing, without doubt, that you can never reach her? No conversations to look forward to, no voice coming over the phone. No triumphs or confidences. You wanted to bear a child, Elizabeth thought; well, I *did* give birth, and I lived to see that child slip away from me. Not dead, nothing so kind, just lost.

'Are you all right?' Suzanne asked, suddenly alarmed by the broken look on Elizabeth's face.

No, she thought, I miss home, however hard it is. I miss the northern skies and the terraced streets, and Graham. Yes, I miss him now although I haven't seen him for two years. I'm getting older, I've done all I can. I want to go home.

'Mrs Jacobs –'

'Suzanne.'

She smiled, but couldn't say the name. 'I'm not as quick as I used to be. I know that. I feel . . . maybe I'm not pulling my weight.'

'Don't be silly,' Suzanne said, knowing there was more to this conversation than was immediately apparent. What was Elizabeth really trying to say? Her eyes studied the woman in front of her. She was older than she'd expected, tired. *I've been seeing you as I remembered you at first, not as you are now.* With shock, she realised suddenly that Elizabeth must be about seventy. Too old to keep working. Far too old.

'What is it? Tell me,' she asked.

But Elizabeth couldn't speak and her eyes closed. *I want to see the fireworks in the back yard again, and walk in the park with Graham. I want to remember old lady Forest and Julie. I want to go back, go home.*

'Lizzie, tell me what it is.'

But she couldn't get the words out. Too many years of working, too many years of keeping silent, of being careful. No one must know of Graham, or of Julie and Les. She had come down south with a trunk of secrets and carried them alone. No one had asked for her confidences, or offered to share her thoughts. All the years of lying and covering up suddenly and unexpectedly welled up in her, and she was bitterly tired.

'Lizzie, tell me how I can help . . . please, tell me.'

Imogen was safe, this was the time to go. She had done what she could. *Light the fire, Graham, I'm coming back.*

'Lizzie, tell me how I can help. What do you want?'

She turned and looked at her employer steadily. 'I want . . . I want to go home.'

Graham cleaned the house as well as he could. Got in some food, and some coal. The curtains and carpets were worn, the front room musty from lack of use, but he had kept his war letters in a box under the bed and had even read them the night before.

Twice-weekly trips to the hospital kept his condition controlled. Monthly calls to the clinic told him about his daughter's state, and the shed in the back yard was still full of paper and powder and all the paraphernalia of his fireworks. The bomb sites had long gone, but there were still some places where he lit the blue touchpaper and retired into his other world. Sometimes he had even dreamed that the light from one of his fireworks might travel miles; might even be seen by his wife, wherever she was. And in November – on the 5th – he lit the rocket he had named after her and wondered if – one November – she might see it and follow it home.

And now she was coming home. After so many years, Elizabeth was coming home. He moved to the window for the third time, looking out. The dark street looked back, empty. There were no people about, no dogs, no children. It was raining and only a solitary car crept past, its headlights dimmed. Would she come? he wondered. Would she *really* come? His thoughts turned back to the war, to the time before the war. To old lady Forest in the bedroom upstairs. Be quiet, she'll hear us, Elizabeth used to say when they made love. Be quiet. But she had still clung on to him and tucked her dark head against his neck in the old bed.

He watched the street. The time for her arrival had come and gone. There was no sign of her. Maybe he had imagined it. Dreamed it. Maybe this was to be the last of all the disappointments of his life. She had said she was coming. But the street was empty.

At the head of Mulberry Street Elizabeth paused. The rain had dampened her coat and her hat and made her feet numb. Nothing had changed here. Other areas had new blocks of flats, netted windows, babies crying on the balconies in their prams. But not here. Here the same terraces stood under the same sky, and the same old chimneys poked out into the misty cold.

Perhaps she had been wrong to leave Brighton. But there was no choice. She had set out to do what she had done, and now there was only one alternative open to her. Imogen had been heartbroken, begging her to stay, but she had insisted. I'll write, I'll visit, she had said. This is your home now, be happy. . . . Her granddaughter had begged her to stay, gone to plead her cause with Suzanne, and finally, she had decided to go with her grandmother.

No, Elizabeth had said. No, this is where your future is. This is your home, and all I want from you is to know that you're happy. . . . Give me an address, Imogen said. . . . No, I'll be in touch. Believe me, I know what I'm doing. Would I just get up and leave you? I'll always be there. I promise. Always and always. . . . Elizabeth turned into her old street and paused again. A car passed her, a dim light coming from the window of number 12. Do you want me back, Graham? she wondered. *Do you?*

Her feet slowed on the pavement, her eyes fixed on the dark-painted door. Cold seeped into her, and weariness, and a terrible fear of rejection left her standing outside long after she should have put the key in the lock. This is my house, she told herself, my house. But she couldn't move.

Graham hadn't seen his wife. He had only seen a stout woman with a suitcase walking despondently down the street, looking as though she had nowhere to go. He pitied her, in the rain, and then looked away searching for Elizabeth before glancing back. Then he paused, his eyes fixed on the stranger.

She looked back. The rain pattered on her, it marked the case she carried and it puddled down her face as he hurried to the door and opened it.

Chapter Six

Five years passed, taking Imogen to twenty-one. Her progress was a social triumph, but her life lacked direction. No career ever held her attention for long. She did flirt with the theatre, but the seduction was brief and incomplete. Mike told her she had talent, told her in one fumbling instant that he had always been crazy about her, becoming quickly that most notorious of creatures, a thing with one mouth and eight hands. Imogen laughed it off, kindly. She did most things kindly. She even drifted kindly.

Thre was no reason to burn with ambition. Her life with Suzanne was perfect. They rowed now and then, both of them too spirited to live in ideal harmony, but there was a safeness about Imogen's existence which made her feel guilty if she was discontented. How many other girls had her chances? Her opportunities? She never had to work for money, even though Elizabeth had insisted that she contribute something.

'Get a job. Anything. Just make sure you give something back to Mrs Jacobs.'

'I don't want any money,' Suzanne said, irritated when Imogen began working for a small boutique in the Lanes. 'Why the hell do you have this peasant mentality, Imogen? You don't need to work.'

She bridled at the word peasant. 'I think I should contribute –'

Suzanne's long-nailed hand extended, covered hers. 'You're here. That's all I ask.'

But was it enough?

Enough for Suzanne, surely. But for Imogen, no. Her twenty-first birthday had been welcomed, her coming of age seen as a precursor to all the platinum glory of her future. Having spent days preparing for a party, Suzanne invited all her acquaintances, old and new, to attend, and some of Imogen's friends were let in on the secret. She knew what was going on, of course; Suzanne's attempt at keeping a secret was laughable, and yet when she was ushered into the drawing room and the cry of 'Happy Birthday' echoed round her she acted surprised, throwing up her hands in mock embarrassment.

Suzanne had watched Imogen that night, watched how she moved easily between the sexes and the ages, saw how she handled every person with a skill which would have been surprising in a diplomat. Not that she was dull; far from it, her quick tongue and mimicry marked her out, but she *was* cautious, cat-footed, careful. Men watched her. Suzanne expected that. Imogen was twenty-one years old, five foot seven, full breasted and very much the female. What man wouldn't watch such a creature? Her face too had changed from her unremarkable childhood appearance. The blonde hair remained, but the pure bloody life inside made her grey eyes alert, her smile transforming.

She conned them all into thinking she was a beauty. Such was her personality. Asleep, her face had the blank look of the merely attractive, but alert, cracking jokes, listening, then she drew on some inner spirit – and no one was immune. Her laugh drew them too. A belt of a laugh, too loud really for good manners, but who cared about good manners? Across a restaurant, across a park, you could pick out Imogen's laugh, and remember it. No one else laughed like that, not from the throat or the gut, but from every cell. It warmed, it absorbed, it made a person want to get to know her. It dazzled.

She had been on top form that night, but when everyone went home – after four in the morning – Imogen sat in the garden outside and sighed listlessly. Surprised, Suzanne sat down next to her. The first birds were beginning to wake, the sound of the tide coming over the Regency terrace, a pipistrelle dipping amongst the rooftops.

'Are you okay?'

Imogen turned, looked at Suzanne and nodded. 'It was a great party.'

'That wasn't what I asked.'

She pulled a face.

'I'm fine.'

'You're a liar,' Suzanne said briskly, lighting a cigarette. The smell of tobacco mingled with the salt breeze, the heat of the August dawn promising a scorching day to come.

'I was thinking about Gran,' she said finally. 'Wondering, you know. . . .'

'She's not ill, is she?'

Imogen glanced over to Suzanne. 'No, of course not. You read her last letter. She's fine.'

'So why worry?'

'She's old.'

'Seventy-five.'

'That's old.'

'Not really, Aunt Lyla's about three hundred, and rising.'

Imogen laid her head back against the seat, mimicking the old woman's voice. ' "My dear, I can't eat a whole peanut. I have a small stomach. It's a sign of breeding." '

Suzanne laughed. 'Wicked. But accurate.'

The night was ending, the birthday sliding away. Something was in the air. Not just dawn, or the sea wrack, something deeper.

'What is it really, Imogen?'

'Don't you ever wonder why Gran left us?' Imogen said at last.

Suzanne had expected this conversation for years. Had prepared for it.

'She wanted to go home.'

'But where is home? I mean, I know it's up north, but why doesn't she let me know where? I've never questioned it before, never thought it was my business, in a way. She did so much for me, it seemed like ingratitude to pry.' Imogen paused. 'But it matters suddenly.'

'Perhaps she was embarrassed.'

'About what?' Imogen snapped. 'Her home? She should know that I could never be ashamed of her.' Her temper rose sharply. 'Couldn't she trust me, Suzanne? Couldn't she believe in me that much?'

'She has her reasons, darling, leave it for what it is.'

But Imogen wasn't about to stop there. 'I've been thinking back lately. I can't remember much because I was so little, but I remember old lady Forest and the way she talked about the mills and the town. She never said where it was, though. . . .'

It was Little Lever, Suzanne thought. Little Lever, up in Lancashire. And in Little Lever there is Elizabeth's husband, Graham, and on the outskirts of Manchester a woman called Julie takes her medication three times a day and never gets better. She's your mother, Imogen, and she's a secret. Suzanne inhaled deeply. She had known about the family for years, had had the money to find out, and the sense to keep quiet. Without realising it, Elizabeth had had a powerful ally in Suzanne Jacobs, both women hiding the truth to protect the one thing they loved above all.

'I could find out, perhaps.'

Suzanne's eyes narrowed. Oh shit. 'Don't do that, Imogen, it would only upset your grandmother.'

'Why?'

'Because she wants it this way, that's why!' she retorted hotly.

She didn't want Imogen to poke into the old hiding places. If she did, tragedy would follow. If she found out about Julie's condition, what would that do to her, wondering if, some day, she might follow the same route? And worse, if she knew her mother was alive, then what role was there for Suzanne? She was a mother to Imogen in all but name, a better mother than Julie could ever have been. Elizabeth had wanted it this way; Suzanne had wanted it this way; nothing was going to spoil it now.

Imogen needed to be protected, Suzanne thought fiercely. Her life had to be easy, untroubled. No traumas. No threat which might unbalance her. No one knew if the unstable genes in her mother might pass down to her; even the doctor Suzanne had questioned could give no firm opinion one way or the other. He just said that shock 'did things to people'. They had to make sure that Imogen's life was free of shocks. That was all.

'I was wondering about my parents too. . . .'

Oh God.

'. . . thinking about them. Gran never said much.'

'She never said a lot about anything,' Suzanne said calmly, although her chest was tight with anxiety. 'It was her way. I think it upset her to talk about it.'

'But shouldn't I know more?' Imogen asked frantically, staring Suzanne full in the face.

She glanced away, unsettled. Imogen saw the response and was immediately alerted. What did she know? What was she hiding?

'Do you know about them, Jaco?'

The morning mist was lifting, warm dawn nudging its way in. Leave it alone, Imogen. The truth can only harm you.

'No. I don't know anything.'

The lie was enormous, both of them knew it. It hung sadly in the honeysuckled air; it soured the sweet sea smell and it skimmed and then drowned under the dark wash of the fishpond.

And still Imogen persisted: 'Do you know anything I should know?'

No, nothing you *should* know, Imogen.

'No.'

No one slept that night.

Imogen kept her job in the boutique throughout that summer, and in the next year she went to work for one of Brighton's foremost milliners. The work was undemanding, mostly chit-chat, social small talk with the clients, and it never bothered her. Outside work she continued pretty much as she always 'had, seeing friends, going out with various boyfriends and writing home to the Post Office box number Elizabeth had sent her.

She had little reason to be discontented, and there were always so many people coming to and from the house that she was never lonely. But she was uneasy with men. Having been brought up surrounded by women, Imogen found herself a little ill at ease when alone with a man. In a group, she was fine, but in a one-to-one situation she was unsettled, and resorted to her wit to disguise her true feelings. Most men were intimidated. They could seldom think as fast as Imogen and felt inferior in her company. Suzanne was no help at all. She liked men, but was exasperated by them, and took no pains to cover her irritation. As a role model she was impossible, and so Imogen unconsciously decided to make friends with the men she knew. Friends, not lovers. Not yet.

Then one day during that summer she was sitting outside one of the cafés on the seafront, sketching caricatures of the passers-by, when suddenly a voice cut into her thoughts.

'That's good. Bloody good.'

She looked up, squinting against the sun. 'Oh, hi, Lorrie.'

The man slid into the seat next to hers. A fat man with a bald head, one of the fleeting uncles who had slid in and out of Suzanne's past. Lorrie Brent, who published a society magazine in London. It was an incestuous little tome, glossy pages, glossy pictures of the London scene, everyone crawling to Lorrie in order to get their photograph included. Suzanne and Imogen were the only ones who had declined, so naturally Lorrie invited them to every opening, every first night and every presentation.

'I want to borrow Imogen,' he'd said once to Suzanne. 'I'd like her to present the Chef of the Year award to the chef at the Hilton.'

Suzanne looked at him evenly: 'What for?'

'It would be good publicity.'

'For who?' Imogen countered. 'The chef or me?'

'For you,' Lorrie replied, aghast. 'Most girls in London want to do it.'

She shrugged. 'So let them. Anyway, what's the award? A wooden spoon? Or a year's supply of kitchen roll?'

'Don't be tart, Imogen,' Lorrie said, wounded. 'It's a plaque –'

'Like the stuff you get on your teeth?'

'– in silver, with his name engraved on it.'

'Oh, boy.'

'And the date and the name of the person who presented it.'

'Why me?'

He blinked, wrong-footed. 'It would be a feather in your cap.'

'Oh, Lorrie.' Imogen said, touching the back of his bloated hand gently. 'Thanks, but it's not really something that I want to do.'

He never stopped asking her, though. Can you present this or that? No, thanks, was always her reply. . . . So when he saw her on the seafront he was delighted and when he saw what she was doing, he was beside himself.

'Let me look!' he said, taking the sketchpad from her. 'Very clever, my lovely girl. Very clever indeed. I had no idea you could be so evilly funny.'

Imogen tried to take the pad back, but he held on to it, turning the pages and chuckling softly.

'These are wonderful. Savage, tender, amusing – Oh God, isn't that Colin Martin? And Mimi van Sough? Wonderful, wonderful, she would be *so* crushed.'

'Lorrie, give it back,' Imogen said quietly.

But he continued to flip over the pages and then stopped dead. His large, puffy eyes studied the caricature and then a low bubble of laughter began to shake him.

'It's me!' he said in astonishment. 'It's cruel, but sweet at the same time. I forgive you . . .' his gaze fixed on Imogen. 'What a little jewel we have, tucked away in geriatric Brighton. I always knew you were special, but I didn't know how.' Lorrie's hands rustled the pages excitedly. 'Imogen, dear heart, would you like to work for your old Uncle Lorrie?'

She smiled sweetly: 'I'd rather be boiled alive.'

'Naughty, naughty!' he admonished her, waggling a stubby finger. 'You might fight against it, but you know you're tempted. You could do three caricatures a week for the magazine. I'll pay you. Not much at first, but I *will* pay you, of course.'

'Of course.'

'You'd have to pop up to London to deliver every Friday –'

'Every Friday.'

'– and you must be on time.'

'On time.'

Lorrie stopped talking. 'Why are you repeating everything I say?'

Imogen shrugged. 'I thought I was taking orders and I wanted to commit them to memory.'

Taking a deep breath, Lorrie leaned across the table towards her, his shadow blanking out the light. 'Oh, come on, Imogen, do say you'll do it. It would be fun, and it's not as though you're doing anything else. Think of it,' he said, slapping the pad with the back of his hand. 'You've got ability, so why not capitalise on it? Why waste your life sitting around here, when you could be doing something with your time? Suzanne's life is fine – for Suzanne – but we both know that you want more.'

Imogen frowned. She was suddenly aware that this fat buffoon of a man was exactly articulating her thoughts. She was, if she allowed herself to admit it, bored.

'Listen, Lorrie,' she said tentatively, 'could I just try it for a month or so, see how it works out?'

He put his head on one side. A rim of white, untanned flesh showed suddenly above the collar.

'Three months' trial.'

'What happens if I'm proved guilty?' she asked smiling.

'Life imprisonment.'

Suzanne laughed at the idea, then shouted, then in a fit of pique, turned over the dish of pot-pourri next to her. She was dressed in yellow trousers and top, her black hair clipped back from her face, her eyes fierce with indignation. Bloody Lorrie Brent! Who the hell was he to tempt Imogen way? And for what? A dumb magazine stuffed full of collagened heiresses and exiled princesses in Hampstead? Do me a favour.

'*Why* do you want to do it?'

'It would be a change.'

'Hospitalisation would be a change. That isn't enough of a reason,' Suzanne retorted. 'You don't even like Lorrie, the fat poof.'

'I'm working for him, not marrying him,' Imogen countered smartly.

'He lives with Archie Nelland, you know,' Suzanne went on blindly.

Imogen clicked her fingers. 'Another chance lost.'

'. . . and Archie Nelland's mother was involved in that health clinic scandal in Zurich.'

Imogen's face was impassive. She knew better than to retort; Suzanne's temper would burn out if she didn't add fuel to the flames. Besides, why was she so upset? Most of her friends had picaresque pasts. Scandals, divorces, drugs, illnesses. Lorrie Brent wasn't any different from most of them.

'And his brother, Monty, works with that Italian designer. Oh, you know the one, his sister was body-painted by Salvador Dali and then she committed suicide in some town up north, Cleethorpes, or somewhere. . . .'

'*Cleethorpes!*' Imogen said, laughing.

'Cleethorpes, or Scarborough – listen, that doesn't bloody matter, what matters is that you want to work for Lorrie Brent.'

'I don't particularly want to work for him. But it would be a chance to see if I can do anything with my life –'

'Get your hair done, go out on the town. Get married. Believe me, *that* would be "doing something with your life".'

'Jaco, you *can't* believe that!' Imogen replied hotly. 'You just want me to get married – is that it? I can't believe it.' Her eyes rolled upwards. 'I'm just taking a job, not going into a flaming nunnery.'

'It's the same thing. Men *hate* intelligent women. You get a career and you might as well have SPINSTER tattooed on your forehead.'

'Oh, for God's sake –'

'No, not for God's sake, for yours!' Suzanne screamed. 'You'll have all this one day. You don't need to work. Set your sights on a man, not a job. See the world as it is. You're lucky, in demand, a good catch. You don't need to dirty your hands like other girls. You don't need all . . . all this . . . it's working class.'

She had gone too far, and knew it. White-faced, Imogen stared at her and then walked out, leaving the door open. They could have argued all night, that was natural for them, but a sudden and yawning gap had opened between them the very instant Suzanne had said 'it's working class'.

Imogen ran down to the front then turned, passing Roedean and moving on towards Rottingdean. After nearly an hour's walking she stopped by the stony beach, the wind blowing her hair over her eyes.

Impatiently she pushed it away. Working class. Yes, I think working class because I *am* working class, Imogen thought. I came from a working-class background and working-class family. My Gran was working class, and she kept us all going, and when I was settled she left. She didn't want to embarrass me with her *working-class* ways. Imogen took in a deep breath, seagulls crying overhead. Elizabeth had had no education, no style and yet she managed to secure her grandchild's future. How many upper-class women could have done the same, Imogen thought, without money and without connections? A violent pride rose up in her. Who had the right to look down on them as working class? Who cared what her Gran was and where she came from? She had provided for Imogen and had walked away when she thought she could do nothing more. She had wanted to save her granddaughter embarrassment. Had wanted to hide her working-class roots.

The insult wedged in Imogen's chest. You can't change where you come from, she thought, you can't hide it – but you *can* be proud of it.

She came back when the light was fading. Suzanne was waiting on the doorstep.

'Sorry. . . .'

Imogen paused then wrapped her arms around her. 'Jaco, I love you,' she said softly, then stood back and looked into her face. 'But I swear to God, if you ever say anything like that again, I'll leave.'

Chapter Seven

Lorrie's offices were at the back of Sussex Gardens in Bayswater. They were hot, without air conditioning; the only room with any space was his office. But there the furniture was curiously scaled down, his desk too small for him, his ashtray diminutive, his telephone undersized. All around, the walls crowded with photographs of Lorrie with Prince Charles, Lady and Lord so and so, Earl God knows what. The air smelled strongly of Eau Sauvage and the window opened inwards by the desk so that Lorrie had to squeeze past it every time he passed.

'Welcome,' he said half-heartedly, dropping his voice to a whisper. 'What do you think of this?' He scooted some papers across the desk to Imogen. A photograph of a man in a clown's outfit looked up at her.

'I'd stick to your usual tailor, Lorrie.'

He rolled his eyes. 'Very funny. It's Arnold Bockler. Can you believe it? He was caught coming out of a mews in Battersea the other night and now his wife's threatening to divorce him.'

She ignored the gossip and reached into her bag, bringing out several caricatures and passing them to him timidly. Two were of well-known figures, the third of three 'ladies who lunch' discussing a near-death experience. The caption read: '*Apparently when people in Hamptead die, their furniture flashes before their eyes.*'

Lorrie read it and bellowed with laughter, signalling for the printer to come into the office. 'Well done, Imogen,' he said, then passing the man the drawings, 'Get these in the next issue. There'll be more next week.'

Imogen glanced round. She was pleased with his

response and excited by the atmosphere and the rush of activity. That morning she had taken the train up to London and had spent an hour nervously marking time in Green Park, her hands fidgeting with her case. What if Lorrie didn't like her work? What if he didn't think it was funny? It was one thing to be asked to give a presentation, quite another to expect to make a career from her talent. Her confidence dipped suddenly. Maybe Suzanne was right, maybe she ought to just get married. Maybe, but maybe not.

She had to give it a try. That much she knew. The London traffic drummed behind her. If she made a success of this, she might make a name . . . her ambition surprised her, crept up on her. Why was it important now? Why? The answer was easy. The first issue that appeared she would send to her Gran. It would surprise her, she knew. It would please her to see her granddaughter doing well. If she knew where she was she could even take the magazine up to her, Imogen thought. But she didn't know where she lived; so she would have to send it.

A sudden cloud blocked out the boiling sun. What if anything happened to Elizabeth? What if she was taken ill, or worse, if she died? Who would tell her? Contact her? The thought terrified Imogen. How could she repay her grandmother for all she had done if she didn't know where to reach her? The cloudy sky darkened ominously. Maybe Elizabeth would slip away, die one day without Imogen knowing, her letters returned to her, unopened.

She stood up quickly, turning her steps towards Sussex Gardens. There had to be a way to find out where her grandmother was. She would write tomorrow, sending the magazine and asking her for an address. Surely she would tell her if she asked. Begged her. Surely. There was nothing to hide. She must know that her granddaughter could never be ashamed of her.

'Hey, wake up!'

Imogen's thoughts came back to the present. 'Sorry, I was miles away.'

Lorrie pointed to the space behind her. 'I've got someone I'd like you to meet . . . Ira Mazan.'

Imogen turned, a smile fixed politely on her lips.

74

He wasn't very tall, this Ira Mazan, and was dressed in white. White suit, white shirt unbuttoned at the neck, white shoes. But black hair, black eyes, a long nose. He looked, she thought incredulously, like an Aubrey Beardsley picture come to life.

'Hello, Imogen. We haven't met before, but my uncle knows Suzanne, and I've met her a few times myself.'

Imogen racked her brains, but no one called Mazan came back to her.

'I believe Lorrie's got you working for him. Watch it, he's a terrible employer.'

She studied Ira, noted the heavy accent, the pale nails against the dark-skinned hands. Jewish, like Suzanne.

'Ira's in publishing too,' Lorrie said, struggling past the open window. 'But more into . . . glamour . . . publishing.'

The visitor nodded, leaning against the desk and looking at Imogen's caricatures. He frowned, laughed, then looked at them again. He was about thirty, the heavy-lidded eyes darkly shadowed. Not handsome; fascinating.

'You're good,' he said at last, rising to go. 'When you go home, give my love to Suzanne and see if she remembers me.'

She did. Suzanne heard the name and responded with a long low whistle and a pantomime look of shock horror. 'Ira Mazan. Wow!'

Imogen buttered some French bread and passed a piece to Suzanne. 'He said you knew his uncle.'

'I did.'

Imogen looked at her quizzically. 'I don't remember him.'

'It was just before you came here. My husband – the son of a bitch – had left for one of his oversleeze trips, and I met Mazan.'

'And?'

'It didn't work out.'

Imogen stopped chewing. 'Why?'

'He was a little . . . too colourful.'

'Dear God, I didn't think anyone could be too colourful for you.'

Suzanne frowned. 'Well, he was. I remember Ira very well too. He made something of an indelible impression. He was wearing a white suit –'

'He was wearing white today!'

'Apparently he always does in the summer. White in the summer, black in the winter. The first time I met him his dress sense was so bad I thought he was blind.'

Imogen laughed shortly. 'He's in publishing.'

'I know, tits and bums –'

'Oh no!'

' 'Fraid so. He liked to call it glamour, but it's porn really. Soft porn, I grant you, but porn nevertheless.' She studied Imogen urgently. 'He didn't suggest anything, did he?'

'Like what, stripping off in Lorrie's office?'

'Seriously, Imogen, watch out for him. He's very dangerous. He sort of creeps up on you. The effect's cumulative – like lead poisoning.'

'But he seems nice.'

'I know. Loads of people adore him. MPs, actors, writers. He's sympathetic, caring, helpful, attentive. He says exactly what they want to hear and then, as soon as the door closes behind them, he wipes them from his mind. No one gets close to Ira. No one. He's the original cat that walked alone.'

'What about girlfriends?'

'Dolly birds. Nothing serious. He beds them and moves on. Rumour has it that he has shares in Interflora.' She looked at Imogen hard. 'Don't even think it.'

'What?'

'You won't change him. Don't fall for him. Stay away from that one.'

But it was difficult to stay away from Ira. He kept coming into the office and chatting when Imogen was there, Lorrie hustling them out on to the London streets. So what else was there to do, except go for a coffee? And then lunch? And then dinner – no, not dinner. Imogen had more sense than that.

'Come on, what's the harm in it?'

She stopped and looked at him. The sun shimmered on his white suit and the dark black of his hair. Exotic.

'I have to go home.'

'I'll drive you.'

'To Brighton!'

'Why not?'

The journey passed quickly, Ira making her laugh and telling her gossip. Just like Suzanne. Only he wasn't really like Suzanne. . . . And all the time Imogen kept remembering what she had said – he listens, then dismisses everyone from his thoughts. No one gets close. Forget it. Besides, he was the publisher of a soft porn magazine – oh, no, Imogen, you can do better than that.

Finally he stopped the car outside the house and turned off the engine.

'Can I come in?'

His door was opened as if by magic. 'Well, well, well. Ira Mazan,' Suzanne said, her hair blowing around her face in the wind. 'What brings you to breezy Brighton?'

'I've come for the cure.'

'You're ill?' she asked lightly. 'Nothing minor, I trust.'

He slid out of the car easily, Imogen following, hot with embarrassment. 'You don't change, Suzanne.'

'No,' she said coolly. 'I still *bite*.'

'I brought your charge home,' he said, then added, 'Intact.'

'God help you if you hadn't,' Suzanne replied, walking away.

He called out after her, 'Can't I come in?'

'No,' she shouted back, taking Imogen's arm. 'And stay away from her.'

He moved over to them quickly. Very quickly, his eyes narrowed against the wind. 'I won't harm Imogen,' he said. 'Believe me. I just like her, that's all.'

Suzanne shook her head. 'Listen, Ira. You're a great guy, but you're not welcome here –'

Imogen was hot with fury: 'Suzanne!'

'You're not welcome,' she repeated. 'Stick to your own turf, Ira. I can't put it more plainly.'

He paused, his expression altering unexpectedly – from anger to acceptance. In a sudden and remarkable gesture, he took Suzanne's hand and shook it. 'You're right,' he said, and an instant later, drove away.

Imogen was livid. 'What did you do that for?'

'Your own good,' Suzanne retorted bluntly.

'He was only a friend.'

'No,' she said, turning away. 'Ira Mazan doesn't know how to be that.'

The letter from Elizabeth came a day later, full of astonished pride at Imogen's achievement.

> *My dear,*
> *Well, what a lovely surprise. I could hardly believe my*
> *eyes when I opened the magazine and saw your cartoon.*
> *You are clever. Well done. I'm well, thank you for asking,*
> *and I can see from the photograph you sent that you are as*
> *bonny as ever.*
>
> *I can't send you an address, love. Sorry to disappoint,*
> *but I have my reasons. It's lovely to think that you miss*
> *me. Goodness, I certainly miss you. But it wouldn't be*
> *right for you to come here. I'd like to have a chat though,*
> *so I'll phone on Wednesday – if that's fine with Mrs*
> *Jacobs.*
> *All my love,*
> *Your Gran*

She had spent a long time writing the note, not wanting to refuse Imogen anything. But this was the one thing she could not grant – her address. If Imogen came up to her, if she met Graham, if she heard about her mother, if she found out that her Gran had been lying to her all these years . . . no, she must be kept away for her own good.

Elizabeth glanced over to her husband. He was asleep, his glasses in his hand, a Zane Grey book resting on his chest. He had improved, but not enough. His temperament was still too morose, and his memory was failing. Elizabeth might tell him repeatedly about Imogen, but he muddled her up with Julie and kept asking constantly why she had recovered and gone to Brighton without seeing him. After a while, Elizabeth referred to neither child, and he soon forgot both.

He watched television instead. Placid, without response,

except when a war film came on and he would begin to shake. Turning it off, Elizabeth held him, listening to the babble of confused memory and fear, and then, when he was quiet, she gave him a tablet. Medicating him back into calm. They existed on their pensions and on the monthly small sum sent by Suzanne, living frugally, quietly, away from the neighbours – most of whom were newcomers – the old ones never asked questions about the past.

Only Elizabeth remembered Julie, and prayed that her daughter would die before she did. She didn't like the idea of her child carrying on alone, because Graham wouldn't visit any more, and there was no one else. Oh yes, if Imogen had known she would have helped. Elizabeth knew that for a certainty. But she didn't want her granddaughter dragged back up north to care for her sick mother. What would be the point? Julie wouldn't understand or appreciate the sacrifice, and all Imogen's future would disappear overnight. It would be a waste, a blind, futile waste of life.

So Elizabeth kept silent, and visited her daughter alone. She kept watch over her child and their secret, and she prayed that Imogen would never know.

He was sitting at the table next to hers inside the Grand Hotel. Seemingly bored, he toyed nervously with his scone and glanced round, obviously looking for someone. Sketching the passers-by in the lounge, Imogen had been aware of him for some time and had even done a thumbnail sketch, but when he got to his feet and then sat down again, she was curious and stared at him. He couldn't see her, but she had ample time to study him: the long, awkward limbs, the wheat-coloured hair grown on to his collar, the narrow, alert face. A public school boy, she thought to herself at first – then realised he was older than she had thought.

Twenty-four, twenty-five, she decided. His face wasn't that young looking, but his mannerisms, the excruciating embarrassment apparent in all his gestures, made him seem woefully immature. He toyed with the scone again, chased it round the plate, then flushed darkly as it flirted on to the tablecloth. Imogen smiled in sympathy then leaned forward when she saw a middle-aged woman approach the table.

The young man rose, backed into a fig tree and then sat down again, straightening his hair and looking round to see if anyone had noticed his clumsiness.

Tactfully, Imogen glanced away, then after another moment looked back. He was listening avidly to his companion, and Imogen realised that she knew her. That she was, in fact, the milliner for whom she had worked several summers ago. Mrs Winner, the stalwart of the Conservative Association, the wealthy owner of a shop in the Lanes and one in South Molton Street, W1. Mrs Winner, face salmon pink from hurrying, a straw hat perched on her head like a half-opened can. Mrs Winner, signalling for the waitress and then flicking the crumbs off the table with her glove. Oh, poor young man to be waiting for Mrs Winner. . . .

Fascinated, Imogen watched them, remembering how she had been regaled with stories of Wonder Son, as they had nicknamed her son in the shop. No child was ever smarter, ever more handsome, ever more destined to do good. Wonder Son could do no wrong, and had, apparently from birth, assumed in his mother's eyes some point well above sainthood. Imogen stared disbelievingly. So this was Wonder Son? This poor, embarrassed and mortified wretch, now half obliterated by the fig tree since his mother's bulk had forced the table back.

Imogen sketched Mrs Winner furtively, covering the paper with her hand when the subject swept past *en route* to the Ladies. Unfortunately Imogen was so engrossed that she failed to pull in her legs as Wonder Son passed a moment later, and with a sickening crash, he fell at her feet.

'Oh God . . .' he groaned, scrambling to get up.

'Are you all right?'

He blinked, glanced away, and then nodded. 'Fine.'

Imogen found his embarrassment contagious. 'Are you . . . are you having tea here?'

'Tea,' he repeated stupidly, his colour still high.

'Yes, the stuff that comes in pots,' Imogen replied, smiling.

'Yes, tea,' he agreed finally. 'With my mother.'

'Oh, that *is* your mother,' Imogen said lightly. 'I thought I recognised her. I used to work in the shop in the Lanes.' He said nothing. He was still paralysed with embarrassment. 'I'm Imogen Forest,' she added.

'I'm Giles, Giles Winner.' He extended his hand, withdrew it, and then extended it again, smiling.

He smiles well, Imogen thought, there's a warmth there.

'What are you doing?' he asked. 'I mean, I don't want to pry, to be curious. It was just that. . . .'

Imogen passed him the pad and he looked at the drawing of his mother, another smile crossing his face. You're not quite the dope you appear, Mr Winner, Imogen thought. I bet you're good fun away from your mother. I bet you'd like Suzanne too. . . .

'Whatever are you doing?' Mrs Winner snapped.

Giles slammed the book closed and handed it back to Imogen. 'Talking . . . we were talking,' he blurted out. 'This lady used to work for you. Imogen, Imogen Forest.'

Mrs Winner's recall was absolute. 'Oh yes . . .' She managed to crush into the two words a whole mass of disapproval. 'You're Suzanne Jacobs's ward, aren't you? You worked in the Brighton shop.' She turned back to her son. 'Come on, dear.'

'But I was talking –'

'I know how you love to talk, dear, but we have to get back to our table –'

'Mother,' he said coolly. 'I'd like Imogen to join us.'

Mrs Winner's eyes fixed on her son, and then slowly, very slowly, beamed down on Imogen. She breathed in through her nose like a horse and then smiled her lighthouse smile. On, off.

'Of course, my dear, of course, you *must* join us.'

It turned out that Giles was a designer, ran the hat shop in London, and that his degree in art had served him well. He eulogised the paintings of El Greco, the lines of Giacometti, and was delighted when Imogen came back with her own ideas. Soon Mrs Winner was edged out of the conversation – and didn't like it.

'. . . we doubled our profits last year,' she said suddenly, breaking into the flow.

Imogen smiled; Giles blinked.

'You can say all you like about art and line, but I know what the customers want. A hat! A hat is what they want!' she said emphatically.

Imogen glanced at the tablecloth, biting her lip. Giles stared out to sea and thought about drowning.

'You could give me anyone's head and I could make a hat to fit it – in the dark. No one understands a cranium like me.'

It was too much. Imogen, clenching her teeth, glanced over at Giles. He had the look of a man about to pass out.

'. . . Not that everyone can wear a hat. Only a real lady can carry off some of my styles.' She touched her straw brim. 'You have to have the bone structure. A hat, you see, tells you the character of a person.'

'God . . .' Giles groaned.

'*What?*' His mother's eyes flashed.

'Sorry, Giles,' Imogen said quickly, turning to Mrs Winner. 'I just kicked him accidentally,' she shrugged. 'I thought it was the table leg.'

Giles shot her a look of grateful understanding.

They walked down to the funfair afterwards, Mrs Winner excusing herself and hurrying off to the shop and the waiting craniums. Giles walked quickly, his long-legged stride looping amongst the day trippers. Imogen hurried alongside. He talked quickly, away from his mother; he apologised too, although there was no need. But his embarrassment took time to heal, and in his uncertainty Imogen found herself drawn to him, caring suddenly and unexpectedly for a stranger.

He wasn't keen on the idea of the ferris wheel, but went along with it, anxious not to disappoint Imogen. His hands, clutching the metal bar across his stomach, clenched as they rose up in the cool summer air, the screams of the children around them making him wince, his eyes closing as the wheel turned over. Imogen laughed, her hair blown back, her mouth drying in the rushing air, and soon Giles found himself relaxing, his own spirit lifting with hers.

The wheel came back to earth too soon, and as it stopped, he changed. He was diffident again, and Imogen had the impression of a man suddenly drawn away from her. Now you see him, now you don't. She tried to make

conversation, to encourage him to talk, but some block had
arisen between them, and he was only half there. The
distance between them was puzzling, even disturbing. She
had liked him, and thought he liked her, but now he was
acting as a stranger would, and when, inadvertently, she
touched his arm to draw his attention to something, he
froze.

He saw her home, walking along the seafront with his
hands clasped behind his back. Intuitively, Imogen kept the
conversation light, waiting to see if the other Giles would
come out to play again. But he didn't, he remained kindly,
bashful and reserved, and yet when he arrived outside her
door, he paused. Imogen wondered if he wanted to see her
again, waited for the invitation. But it didn't come. Instead,
she breathed in deeply and said, 'Suzanne's having a party
on Saturday. Would you like to come?'

His acceptance was immediate: 'I'd love to.'

She smiled, relieved.

Suzanne was delighted. She knew Mrs Winner and was
well aware that the invitation would get up her nose.
Cautiously she glanced over to Imogen sitting by the
window, her head bent over one of Elizabeth's letters. So it's
finally happened, she thought, she's fallen in love. It was
obvious to her, even though Imogen tried to play it cool. She
mentioned Giles once too often to be indifferent and she
kept changing her mind about what to wear for the party – a
sure sign. She even asked Suzanne if she minded if she went
up to London to 'look for something special'.

'Course not, you go and have a day out,' she said gently.
'I just hope Giles appreciates it, that's all.'

Imogen glanced away. 'Oh, it's not for him. . . . I just
need a new dress.'

'Like I need root canal filling,' Suzanne teased her. 'Oh,
go on, get something that will knock him dead.'

She did. She bought a dress which was short and flirty
and made her feel confident, and she had her hair done and
spent several hours doing and re-doing her make up. The
day wore on fitfully, the caterers coming in to prepare the
buffet, the waiters polishing the glasses, the florist arriving
with bowls of blooms. The house, freshly tidied and

prepared, waited for all its guests, and when the phone rang around six, Suzanne answered it hurriedly.

''Lo?'

'Oh . . . is Imogen there?'

'Who is it?'

'Giles . . . Giles Winner.'

Suzanne took in her breath. Oh no, don't let this be what I think it is.

'*Imogen!*'

She hurried down the stairs, smiling. Her skin glowed, her whole body shimmered with excitement.

'It's Giles.'

Imogen took the phone eagerly.

'Hi.'

'Hello, Imogen. . . . Listen, I've got a problem. . . . I can't . . . I mean, I'm still in London, I can't get to Brighton tonight.' Her heart juddered. 'I can't tell you how disappointed I am . . . Imogen . . . sorry. I really am terribly sorry. . . .'

'It's okay,' she said, forcing herself to sound light-hearted, nonchalant. 'Maybe we could. . . .'

'Yes . . . maybe we could. . . .'

Her hands were damp.

'Well, anyway. . . .'

She waited for him to say he would call her. But he didn't. 'I really am sorry,' was all he said.

Silently she put down the phone.

Suzanne materialised with a glass of wine. She said nothing, just pushed it into Imogen's hand.

'He cried off.'

'Why?'

Imogen shrugged. 'He said he was in London still.'

'Like London's Abu bloody Dhabi! It's only fifty miles away. He could have made it.'

'I wonder why he did that,' Imogen said quietly. 'We got on so well. I know he liked me. Why did he do that, Jaco?'

'His mother, probably,' she replied. 'Mrs Winner doesn't think her son should mix with the likes of us.'

'No . . .' Imogen said softly, remembering how Giles had changed so suddenly the afternoon they were together. 'No, there's something else.'

84

'Well, either way, a man crying off at the last minute's inconsiderate, heartless and worse, bloody hurtful.'

'But I like him, Jaco,' Imogen said softly. 'I really like him.'

'Then more fool you.'

Imogen didn't see Giles for nearly four weeks, then suddenly, one afternoon in early October, she bumped into him after delivering her caricatures to Lorrie. He seemed at first pleased, and then sheepish.

'I was hoping we'd meet again,' he said.

I'm on the phone, she wanted to say. But didn't.

'It's good to see you, Imogen. D'you want a coffee?'

She hesitated, and then followed him to a table outside a small café.

The conversation was strange, oddly intense. Within minutes Giles was telling her about his family and she was telling him about her background, about Elizabeth and the way they had come to Brighton. He confided in her and she confided in him; they drew closer to each other as the minutes passed. They seemed to need each other, to hurry their conversation along, to know everything and share everything, and express everything. Except some things – like Giles's past relationships. Nothing was mentioned about those. Off limits. Imogen might admit that she had never been in love, but he drew back, uneasy. Admitting nothing.

What stopped him, she wondered? What the hell was it? Fear of rejection? of being laughed at? What? . . . He leaned towards her, talking, telling her about his work, forcing the pace and then stopped suddenly. Drawing back. And Imogen kept listening, trying to read between the lines, trying to interpret not what he said, but what he didn't say.

The day slumped past them, the lights coming on in Covent Garden, the first theatre people crossing the webbing of streets. And still they talked, Giles ordering sandwiches and further coffees, the waiter smiling indulgently. Then a sudden unwelcome rain shower forced them in, hurrying them out of their safe nook, pushing them amongst the noisy crowd inside the restaurant.

Giles was obviously embarrassed, discomforted, nervous. The close companionship they had shared was shattered. The comfortable intimacy, gone. With something close to panic, Imogen tried to restart the conversation. It was useless.

The noise disturbed him. The people around him made him uneasy and he kept glancing round, his fingers drumming on the table. 'Well,' he said finally, 'I've kept you long enough . . . I'll see you to the station.'

Imogen rose to her feet obediently. She had no understanding of his mood changes and felt drained, empty, longing to be gone. They caught a taxi at the end of the street and Giles opened the door for her when they reached Victoria station. She got out without smiling. Remote. Moody for once. In silence, they walked down the platform. In silence, they stood back for the arriving passengers to get off.

I don't understand you, Imogen thought miserably. I care for you but I don't understand you, and I can't cope with this.

He stood beside her, awkward, glancing round. 'Will you be okay?' he asked.

'Fine,' she said, stepping forwards.

He knew he had disappointed her. Worse, that he had inadvertently hurt her. But he couldn't, didn't know how to make it right again.

'Take care of yourself. . . .'

'Yes,' she said. 'You too.'

Then she turned and stepped on to the train. He caught her jacket, gently drawing her back.

'Listen, Imogen, I'd like to see you again.'

She waited. Don't push him, he'll run off. You'll lose him. Wait.

'. . . I care about you. I mean, I like you. I'm fond of you.'

She lifted her hand to touch his arm, then hesitated. Waited.

'When are you back in London?' he asked.

'Next week. Tuesday,' she said.

'Can we meet at the same place, around five?'

'Fine,' she said quietly.

'We could talk. I like talking to you.'

'I like talking to you too,' Imogen replied. Yes, I like you,

86

Giles. No, wrong, I love you, damn and blast it. Why? Why you?

'Until next week then,' he said, turning away without touching her.

She watched him go, watched him dodge the other passengers, weaving his way between them without making any contact. She waited until he was out of sight, wondering if he would look back.

He didn't.

Chapter Eight

Imogen felt sorry for Giles Winner. Above all he stirred her protective instinct. Mrs Winner didn't like her. Some surprise. Thought she was flashy, uncertain of her background. But Giles leaned on Imogen, turning away from his mother and turning to her instead. She took on the role meant for an older woman, offered comfort, a listening ear. Security. Continuity. And her reward was a soft blooming of friendship, then something more.

Love? She wasn't sure. Maybe it was too strong a word, too soon. But although Giles didn't express himself directly, his looks, his pleasure on seeing her spoke for him. Love, well, who knew? But that it was the beginning of love was obvious. Imogen waited. There was no rush. There was no one else. And time was on her side. After all the confident, aggressively sexual men who had skirted her life, he was different. He asked nothing physically – no Ira Mazan, no Mike – he asked only her companionship, and that she gave willingly.

'So, has he made a pass yet?' Suzanne asked several weeks into the relationship.

'He isn't like that,' Imogen replied, on the defensive.

Suzanne raised her eyebrows. 'Why not? It's natural.'

'Not to him.'

'Oh.'

That was it. 'Oh.' Amazing how much criticism could be implied in one syllable. 'Oh.'

'He's shy.'

'He's slow.'

'I don't want him to jump on me.'

Suzanne turned to look at her. 'Well, that's good, because

I don't think he knows how. His mother's to blame,' she went on. 'All that cosseting's bad for a man.'

'Giles needs time, that's all.'

'Listen, darling,' she said quietly, 'I don't say drop him, I just think you should see other people. You know, play the field a bit. He seems a little . . . a little too intense for you.'

'He's just different, that's all. You'll see, he'll surprise us.'

'That's what worries me.'

The winter came with a suddenness which caught everyone off balance. The trains between Brighton and London were delayed, cancelled, but Imogen still had to go up to town twice weekly to deliver her caricatures to Lorrie. Her world narrowed down to the space between the tracks. The South-East line taking her to London and back. Click, clack went the train on the tracks; click, clack; to London and back.

She never stayed in town, even though Giles had a flat over the milliner's in South Molton Street. Instead she stayed talking to him until the last minute, carefully working out the latest time she could leave to catch the last train home. His workroom was orderly, everything on shelves, designs pinned on a cork board, materials held fast in several metal clips, or rolled up and deposited in the store room behind. His work absorbed him, his clever eye for detail and design bringing him customers, his gentle courtesy keeping them.

'I like this,' Imogen said one evening, picking up a wide-brimmed hat and trying it on then turning to grimace at him.

He studied her then rose to his feet quickly, pulling the brim down over her left eye. 'Better.'

She looked into the mirror. Yes, better.

'Here,' he said, suddenly excited, 'put this one on.'

Obediently she did so. Her face, shaded by the brim, looked older, the hat giving her a mystery she did not possess in reality. She saw it, and he did.

'Good, now try this.'

One by one she tried on the hats, turning her head, pulling back the brim, pushing the crowns forward, assuming characters with every different style. Giles was absorbed, and because she wanted to please him, Imogen kept modelling, smiling when he smiled, frowning when he frowned, arguing now and then when he dismissed a style.

'No, it's good, Giles,' she said, taking it from him and trying it on again, 'Look, if you just lifted the crown it would be great.'

He studied the change, nodded, and then drew the alteration on the sketch he had previously made. They worked together for several hours, absorbed, intent on what they were doing, Imogen feeling the thrill of his enthusiasm and a physicality he did not usually express. He touched her, moved her shoulders, lifted the line of her chin, and rested his hands against her throat as he studied the mirror.

Is he looking at me? she wondered. Or the hat? Does he see me, or the effect he is producing? But she said nothing, a compliant, accomplice to his obsessive demands.

He changed before her, became confident, even demanding.

'No, this way. No, let me. Imogen, sit still. Good, good. . . .'

Good. Good, Imogen.

She sat, she posed, she felt his hands on her and the warmth of his closeness, and when finally he achieved the effect he wanted she smiled at his reflection in the mirror. He smiled back, then hesitated. His smile cooled, faltered, and in that instant, she turned and stood up. She was several inches shorter than him, and instinctively tilted up her face to his. Every inch of his skin seemed magnified, his eyes, grey flecked with black, luminous. The light behind him outlined his head, the hair drawn back from the narrow face. He was close, only inches away, and yet as she waited for him to kiss her, he pulled back.

Imogen tore off the hat and angrily threw it across the showroom. Giles turned, stunned. 'What the hell –'

'What's the matter with you, Giles?' she snapped, 'Don't you like me?'

He crossed the floor, picked up the hat and then turned back to her.

'You know I do –'

'So why don't you ever touch me?' she asked. Embarrassment made her skin colour, but anger made her refuse to back down.

'I . . . I . . . .'

'*What?*' she demanded. 'Tell me. You don't have to be afraid of me.' She moved towards him, well aware that she might be rejected again and yet determined to force the matter. Slowly she reached up and touched his cheek. 'I care for you,' she whispered. 'Will you kiss me . . . please.'

He looked at her without replying, without moving, or responding.

'Giles . . . please.'

He kissed her timidly, his lips cool. She responded gently, reaching up and taking him in her arms. He sighed, moved his lips against her neck. Tender, rather than passionate. He sighed, drawn to her warmth, yet nervous of it, cautious. And she continued to hold him, to talk to him softly, to express emotions she had never felt before, holding him under the showroom's clinical light and drawing him into the unlimited depth of her own pity.

'How the hell do I know!' Suzanne snapped. 'I've been calling the bloody station for hours. The trains are off. Cancelled. Leaves on the line, or some other barmy excuse. Bloody leaves!'

Lorrie was impatient. 'She said she'd bring the drawings by six. She's never been late before. Never.'

'Listen, I don't give a damn about the drawings, I'm more worried about her. She always rings if she's delayed. You know Imogen, Lorrie, she'll deliver, she always does.' Suzanne glanced at her watch anxiously. 'I can't think where she might be.'

'I need those caricatures –'

'Yes, yes!' she replied hotly. 'I'll tell her when she rings. She's probably stuck at Haywards Heath or something. Everyone gets stuck at Haywards Heath, it's written into the small print on every ticket – *Thou shalt spend time in the wilderness.*' Her tone hardened. 'Stop panicking, Lorrie, I'll get her to phone you when she gets in.'

'It's unprofessional –'

'Oh, dry up!' Suzanne replied hotly. 'You know Imogen,

since when has she ever let anyone down? If she's late, it's for a very good reason, believe me.'

It was a good reason. The best. While Lorrie fretted for his deadline and Suzanne tried to get through to British Rail, Imogen was losing her virginity in a showroom over a hat shop in South Molton Street. All thought of drawings had gone; all thought of Brighton had gone. All that mattered was that she was with Giles. Their lovemaking was tentative, and even to Imogen it was immediately obvious that Giles was inexperienced too. Gently, achingly carefully, they touched and explored each other, coming together finally not with urgency but with the quiet coupling of two souls who had found an unexpected and moving communication. They lay on the old couch used for the machinists' tea breaks, their bodies denting the springs, their heads resting against each other.

He said nothing, just held on to her fiercely, almost desperately, but when Imogen finally moved and looked into his face she found him silent, uncommunicative.

'Giles . . . what is it?'

The sigh came unchecked, almost painful.

'Giles . . .' she repeated, knowing in that instant that he would never explain.

Her heart shifted, uncertainty lodging inside her. She had expected something different. Joy perhaps, contentment certainly, but there was only a dark and silent expanse come to swallow both of them. She knew there was no going back. No return. She had asked for commitment and he had given it. To expect more now would be to destroy him. So she laid her head on his chest and listened to his heartbeat and heard in her heart the tears falling.

'Next time bloody ring me!' Suzanne hissed, following Imogen as she walked up to her room. 'I don't care if you want to stay in London, just let me know.'

Imogen turned at the top of the stairs, next to the Rodin sculpture of The Lovers.

'I did phone –'

92

'At one in the morning!' Suzanne retorted fiercely. 'What the hell good was that? Lorrie's been going mad.'

'Oh, God, the drawings!' Imogen said, leaning against the statue. They were still in her bag. Forgotten until then.

'You didn't take them to him?' Suzanne asked incredulously. 'What were you doing?' Realisation was not slow in coming. 'Oh . . . I see. So how was it?'

Imogen could feel herself blushing, unwelcome colour giving her away.

'What?'

Suzanne raised her eyes heavenwards. 'You know what I'm talking about! You've been with Giles, and unless I miss my guess, you weren't playing baccarat.'

'Jaco!'

'Don't "Jaco" me!' she replied. 'Just tell me – how was it?'

Imogen hesitated. 'Sad.'

'*Sad?*' Suzanne repeated, bewildered. 'What does that mean?'

'Just that. It was . . . sad.'

Slowly Suzanne walked up the stairs, then stopped a couple of steps below Imogen. Her hair was untidy, the odd grey patch showing through at the roots. Tomorrow she was going to the hairdresser's; tomorrow she was going to look thirty-nine again. But tonight she looked her years.

'Are you okay?'

Imogen sat down wearily, drawing her knees up under her chin.

'I love him, you know.'

'I gathered that.'

'But he's very . . . very lost.'

Suzanne touched her shoulder then sat down next to her, pulling her dressing gown around her shoulders. Outside a bird began singing and a ship's horn sounded eerily over the dark water.

'Be careful –'

'Of what?'

'Pity,' Suzanne said simply, kindly.

'Oh, Suzanne –'

'Yes, I know . . .' she said evenly, 'but remember the old

saying: "Never sleep with a man whose problems are worse than your own." '

'Actually the quote is, "Never sleep with a *woman* who's problems are worse than your own." '

'Same thing.'

'Not quite,' Imogen said firmly. 'Besides, I want to help him.'

'You're only young, darling. Love is supposed to be happy. You need to be someone's partner, not someone's therapist.'

Imogen studied her for a long, thoughtful moment. 'I want to help him, Jaco. He needs me.'

For an instant Suzanne could only think of a woman in a mental ward in Manchester. Imogen's mother. A woman who had needed help all her life. A woman who was beyond help. Then she thought of Graham Forest, and of Elizabeth. . . . How strange that Imogen should ally herself with a man who was troubled; should, by instinct, seek out someone who was needy. Like grandmother, like grand-daughter, she thought. It was in their blood, she realised. The need to help, to comfort, to succour.

'I don't want you to be hurt, Imogen.'

'I won't be.'

She was stubborn. Knew it all. Like every other person in love, seeing what she wanted to see – and she wanted to see herself as this man's saviour.

'Don't get too involved –'

'*I love him!*' Imogen said vigorously.

'Does he love you?'

The ship's horn sounded again; floated over the deep water towards the Brighton shore; called out in the night to be heard.

'I think so.'

'You think so. . . .'

'All right, I *know* he loves me,' Imogen said, her face flushed with colour again. Indignant, hurting.

'I'm not saying he doesn't,' Suzanne said gently. 'I'm just warning you to be careful, that's all.'

'He's unhappy . . . just unhappy. It'll all work out, you'll see,' Imogen insisted. 'It will. You'll see.'

*

Elizabeth was tired, but content. She had gone with Graham to see Julie, they had even walked hand in hand up to the hospital entrance, and although she had dreaded the visit she was heartened by her husband's tenderness. Five months had passed, five months in which she had read Imogen's letter and followed the cautious blossoming of her granddaughter's love affair.

The letters brought back memories for Elizabeth of other letters from the war years. Letters written from Germany, from Graham. Letters tied in furtive strings and hidden under the bed – where they still were, old and yellow, the words committed to memory. But these missives were new, freshly minted; Imogen was happy, eager to pass on her good fortune.

She loved this man, Elizabeth realised. Loved him with a completeness and an understanding unusual in a girl of her age. There was no reference to sex, but Elizabeth knew they were lovers and felt no disapproval. No envy either. In some strange way Imogen's life, as always, affected the people she knew nothing about. Her joy seeped into Graham by proxy, her sheer ebullience pulling him back from the edge and leading him home in the heart.

He opened up little by little. Not completely. There was no trace of the young Graham Forest left; but there was a lift in the melancholia, a will to try for whatever time was left, to grasp happiness. Past seventy, he somehow regained part of the tenderness of his youth, and expressed it hurriedly, urgently. Elizabeth, always quick to respond, took the hand offered, the kiss bestowed, the smile returned. The stranger who had so cruelly usurped her husband's place was not gone, but now he only visited, leaving periods in between when Graham reverted to the man she had first loved.

The snatches of intimacy were all the more valued for their fleeting and uncertain quality. Neither of them knew how Graham would be on a given day. He awoke either dim with depression or calm, his eyes opening gradually, gauging the measure of his mood. Elizabeth often watched this process of waking. Clenching her fists, she followed her husband's cautious entry into the day, and if he smiled at

95

her she relaxed; but if he turned away silent, she knew that the twenty-four hours to follow would torment both of them.

She no longer blamed him for his condition, knowing that it was beyond him to control himself; and when she saw how he tried to escape the vacuum of his own misery, she learned to admire the bravery in the man. He fought for his happiness daily, and she fought with him. But neither of them could change Julie. She was too weak to fight; too psychologically flawed to recover, and besides, she didn't *want* to be a part of the world.

They both accepted the fact late. After years of hope, they finally realised that all hope had gone.

'Julie, love, it's me. I've brought your Dad along.'

She was middle-aged, slow in a print dress.

' 'Lo, love,' Graham said, sitting down next to his daughter, his feet flat on the floor. 'You're looking nice.'

She could have been blind for all her eyes expressed.

'I've brought some beef tea and some of your favourite biscuits,' Elizabeth went on, a little breathless after climbing three flights of stairs to the ward. 'Look, love, they're the ones you like.' She laid them on Julie's knee. Nothing. No response. She could have laid a lighted match there and still had no response.

'Did you like the concert?' Elizabeth asked, her eyes moving towards the window. The blind had gone and a pair of lemon curtains had taken their place. In a few years they would have faded, she thought. Yellow was a bad choice for a place like this.

'The matron said that the music was lovely. . . .'

The conversation jumped and lurched on, Graham sitting on one side of his daughter, Elizabeth on the other, Julie unmoving, uncomprehending. Blank. Thank God Imogen isn't here, Elizabeth thought. Thank God she never needed to know about her mother.

'We'll come back soon,' Elizabeth said after another half an hour, touching Graham's shoulder and standing up.

Julie never moved, even when the door closed behind them, she never moved.

They walked across the hospital yard, standing back as a

doctor passed and smiling, even though they didn't know him. Well, you never knew, did you? He might be Julie's doctor and it didn't do to look ungrateful. . . . They were slow, because Elizabeth was stout and Graham was rheumatic, and besides, there was no rush. The February day was chill, but a few good-tempered daffodils broke up the banks of blank grass on the road outside. Look Graham, she said, daffodils. It's spring. . . . He turned, stared at the flowers, absorbing the wash of colour and thinking of the curtains in Julie's room.

He couldn't move fast, but he slowly struggled up the bank and picked one daffodil, glancing round like a child to see if anyone had noticed. Shyly he came back to Elizabeth, and shyly he slid the flower through a buttonhole in her coat. Oh, love, she said, that's nice. . . . The dead fall of the day shuddered around the couple, the hospital holding their child rising grimly behind them. I never sent you flowers, did I? . . . Once, she said, a long time ago. . . . He frowned; I should have sent more. She pinched his cheek, the daffodil bright against the old coat. He hung his head. I always loved you though. . . . I know, love, I know.

A week later he was dead.

Chapter Nine

'Oh, Gran, he's marvellous,' Imogen enthused over the phone.

Elizabeth had come back from the funeral alone and now listened alone on the telephone in the empty front room. Her grief was vast, but lessened by the last few months of happiness. Graham, it wasn't long, but it was good while it lasted. Thank you for that, love.

'Your young man looks very handsome. Thanks for the photograph,' Elizabeth said, glancing at the picture on the fireplace. 'I hope he's good to you.'

'He's great,' Imogen replied eagerly.

It was the truth. Giles was gentle and tender, and loving. Not passionate, that wasn't his nature, but he was kind and needy and Imogen responded to that.

'Gran, I want you to meet him,' she said quietly.

Elizabeth was touched. 'Oh, love –'

'Now don't say you can't come down,' Imogen went on. 'You know you're always welcome here. Jaco was saying that it's been too long since we saw you. Please, Gran, please come.'

She was tempted. Wanted to escape the little house and the ghost of Graham. There was always time to mourn, but not now, now it was time to celebrate. Imogen was in love. Her granddaughter was in love. Time to forget, to move on.

'I'll come down soon –'

'When?'

'Next week.'

'*This* week.'

Elizabeth smiled. Yes, the trip would do her good. Brighton air, Doctor Brighton taking away the pain.

'Yes, I'll come on Friday.'

Imogen was waiting at the barrier at Brighton station. She turned, waved, walked towards her grandmother with her arms open, a man following her. A young man, dark blond with a shyness about him.

'Oh, Gran,' Imogen said, squeezing her and turning to her companion. 'Look Giles, this is my grandmother.'

She said the words with such pride that Elizabeth was too moved to answer and merely smiled. The young man returned the gesture. He was expensively, if casually, dressed, and had the unforced air of someone well educated and wealthy. Yes, Imogen was right, he *was* shy, but it was an upper-class shyness, not awkwardness. You've done well to pick him, Elizabeth thought suddenly, turning back to her granddaughter.

Then she paused.

Imogen saw her hesitation and smiled nervously.

She's pregnant. Elizabeth knew at once. She's carrying. God. . . .

'How are you, love?' she said, slipping her arm through Imogen's. The gesture took her granddaughter back years to the time they had linked arms on the pier, hurrying to meet Jaco.

'I'm well.'

And pregnant.

'And happy?' Elizabeth asked, scrutinising Giles's face. They don't know yet, she thought incredulously, they don't know.

'Yes, I'm happy,' Imogen said hurriedly, quick with joy. 'Really happy.'

The sunlight hit them as they moved out of the station. It fell on Imogen's blonde hair and the fine down on her cheeks. She has an aura about her, Elizabeth thought. This is something beyond beauty. Love has made an angel of her. If only Julie could see her daughter now.

'We thought we could go out for lunch.'

Elizabeth hesitated. Her coat was old, her shoes polished but shabby. She wasn't ready for lunch in Brighton with this spectacular pair. I should have bought something new, she thought angrily. I had enough money for that, why didn't I think of it? Because I was thinking of Graham, that's why. . . . But the excuse wasn't good enough; she should have smartened herself up, made herself look good for her granddaughter.

Imogen did not read her thoughts, but saw her hesitation.

'If you'd rather not, we could eat at home.'

Elizabeth relaxed visibly.

'Yes, I'd like that.'

Suzanne was in the drawing room talking to someone when they came in. She turned, rolled her eyes heaven-wards and then smiled at Elizabeth, noticing the purplish shadows under her eyes – a sure sign of uncertain sleep. She knew of Graham's death, just as she knew everything about Elizabeth Forest, and had been more than eager to agree to Imogen's suggestion that her grandmother visit. Grief carried alone was too much to ask of anyone, she thought, remembering how Elizabeth had helped her years before.

'I asked for *peach* curtains,' she said bitingly, jerking her head towards her unlucky visitor, 'and they sent me their John West special.'

'Madam, we sent exactly what you –'

'– didn't want,' she finished for the hapless man. 'Just take them away and bring back the others Monday,' she said, ushering him to the door. 'I expect them at nine.'

The door clunked closed behind him.

'So, how was the journey?' she asked Elizabeth, guiding her out into the back garden where a table was set for four. Uncomfortably, Elizabeth sat down. She should have laid this out, she was the housekeeper here. It wasn't right that she was eating with Mrs Jacobs.

Her discomfort was noted immediately by Imogen. 'It's just something simple. Jaco can't cook.'

Elizabeth jumped in hurriedly: 'I could make some-thing –'

'No. You're the guest,' Suzanne said brightly, pulling on a pair of Dior sunglasses and beginning to eat.

The conversation flowed surprisingly well, Imogen eager to talk to her grandmother, Suzanne as unaffected as ever, her shoes slipped off on a sudden whim, her toes flicking at the water in the pond. The sunlight warmed them; only Giles remained quiet, his wine untouched.

'So, what do you think of him?' Suzanne asked finally when the couple left for a walk.

Elizabeth hesitated. She was uncertain of her status, unwilling to offend, or to seem over-familiar.

'Well, Mrs Jacobs –'

'Suzanne,' she corrected softly. 'You don't work for me now, Lizzie, and I'd like to think of you as a friend.'

The hesitation was embarrassing to both of them; Elizabeth hot in her coat, Suzanne wary behind her sunglasses.

'Imogen is very happy,' Elizabeth offered finally. And pregnant, she wanted to say. But what if Mrs Jacobs didn't know? What if she too was oblivious to the obvious?

'I think it's serious.'

You can say that again, Elizabeth thought.

'I think Imogen might want to marry him. . . .'

'She's pregnant.'

Suzanne sat rigidly in her seat. The sun bored down on the top of her black hair and was reflected in the black lenses of her sunglasses.

'What?'

Elizabeth faltered. 'I might be wrong –'

'Lizzie, you're *never* wrong about people,' Suzanne replied, throwing her cigarette end into the pond. It hissed beside her left foot. 'I never thought – did Imogen tell you?'

'No – I'm probably wrong,' Elizabeth blustered, wondering why she had said it. Why had she been so indiscreet? If Imogen was pregnant, how would Mrs Jacobs respond? Would she be pleased, or angry? Damn her big mouth, why hadn't she stayed silent?

'Pregnant,' Suzanne said wistfully. Her head turned to profile, her eyes unfathomable. A plane passed overhead and the greedy mouth of a fish sucked at the air on the pond's surface. 'Pregnant. . . .'

'I shouldn't have said anything.'

Suzanne turned, her voice suddenly low, without its usual vitality. 'Imogen having a baby. . . .' She seemed bemused, bewildered. 'How time passes.' Her hand fidgeted on her lap, toyed with the edge of her silk shorts, then suddenly she reached out. The long arch of her hand glowed under the sun, the manicured nails dark coral, the veins shadows of blue under the skin.

Automatically Elizabeth took Suzanne's hand. Squeezed it, then glanced over to her. She was crying. Without a sound, the tears coming quickly under the black lenses.

'Who'd have thunk it, hey?' The joke fell to earth heavily. 'Oh, Lizzie, what a life.'

'Do you mind? – I mean, if it's true?'

She shook her head. 'No, I don't mind.' Her hand was hot and heavy in Elizabeth's. 'I don't mind at all, I'm just surprised to realise that she's adult. But then people grow up, have their children, and die. It's the way of things.' She said the words cautiously, then placed her other hand sympathetically over Elizabeth's. 'I'm sorry about Graham.'

Elizabeth jumped as though she had been punched, her hand jerking away from Suzanne's, her face white. 'I don't know what you mean.'

'Lizzie,' Suzanne said softly, startled by the fierce reaction. 'It's all right, I haven't said anything to Imogen.'

The older woman struggled to her feet, awkwardly rising out of the ornate garden chair.

'I don't know what you're talking about –'

'I'm talking about Graham,' Suzanne said shortly. 'Sit down, Lizzie – and calm down.'

She hesitated, but old habits die hard, and she obeyed.

'Now, listen to me,' Suzanne said quietly, her voice dropping in the still garden air. 'I know everything about you. I know about Graham and Julie. . . .' There was no reaction from Elizabeth, so she carried on. 'I wasn't prying, I just wanted to know what was going on. You've coped marvellously all these years. I understand why you didn't want Imogen to know. I just wanted to help. . . . Oh Lizzie, don't go quiet on me. I wasn't ever going to interfere –'

'Does Imogen know anything?'

'No,' Suzanne said, eager to reassure her. 'She knows nothing – even about her mother.'

As she said the words Elizabeth turned her head and looked into Suzanne's face, her reflection coming back to her from the blank lenses of the sunglasses.

'You had no right to pry.'

Stunned, Suzanne took in her breath.

'It was my business. *Mine!* I never asked you for help, Mrs Jacobs. I worked for you, I was your employee, no more. You love Imogen and you've been good to her, don't think I don't thank you for that, but my life is my own. You have no business poking around in my affairs.'

'Oh, shit,' Suzanne said simply, taking off her glasses and looking hard at the woman next to her. 'I didn't want us to fall out –'

'*What did you expect?*' Elizabeth snapped. 'How would you feel, knowing that someone had been spying on you? What did you find out, Mrs Jacobs? About my background, the grim little town I come from? My husband, and my daughter?' Her voice was thick with outrage. 'Julie's sick, mentally ill. She won't recover. She dribbles –'

'Lizzie –'

She cut her off. 'No, let me finish! And don't call me Lizzie, I hate it. I've *always* hated it. "Busy Lizzie", the loyal employee. Well, I've been loyal to you, kept your secrets for years, so now you can do the same for me. I don't want my granddaughter to know any of this. She *mustn't* ever know about her mother.'

Suzanne's temper flared. 'Don't talk to me like that!'

'I can talk to you any way I like!' Elizabeth replied hotly. 'And I won't be patronised by you.'

'I wasn't patronising you!'

'You were! Probably without realising it, but you were, Mrs Jacobs.' She paused, suddenly calm. 'I didn't want to lie to you or to Imogen, but the truth would damage her. I don't want her to worry about her mother, to feel she has to look after her, and worse, to wonder if she might. . . .'

'Be like her?' Suzanne finished the sentence.

The words stamped heavily on both of them, Elizabeth realising then that Suzanne must already have considered the possibility – and yet she still loved and supported Imogen, just as she had always done. They looked at each other for a long moment, understanding finally that they were allies, not enemies.

'Let's be frank,' Suzanne said coolly. 'I don't want Imogen to know about her mother for two reasons. One, she might worry about any mental problems she might have inherited; and two, she would cease to think of me as her parent.' The truth was blunt. 'The bottom line, Elizabeth, is this. I want Imogen to look on me as her mother, not Julie. For that reason I am quite prepared to keep your secret. It's not a noble reason, but I never was someone who went a bundle on morals. I just want to keep her, and I'm afraid that if she found out about Julie, I would lose her.' Her voice rose with nerves. '*If* you're right and Imogen *is* having a baby, then that's all the more reason for silence. I'll give her all the financial support I can, and both of us can give her all the love she needs.' Her hand reached out again. 'But there is to be *no* talk of Julie, no mention of anything in the past. Ever. We have to work together on this. . . . Well, is it a deal?'

Elizabeth hesitated, thinking back to the day she had stood on the pier and despaired. She had wanted a safe house for her granddaughter and a good future; under Suzanne's care Imogen had had both. She was now happy with her own man, and carrying her own child. She would never be short of money or, apparently, of love. Elizabeth had set out to do what she had intended – and yet for an instant, she couldn't take Suzanne's hand.

Be quiet, Elizabeth, a voice said. Be quiet as you have for so many years. Graham is dead, Julie is locked away, if you stay silent Imogen will bring her own baby into the world without any dark shadows to fall over its crib. Oh Imogen, it's not as though I am taking anything away from you, Elizabeth thought helplessly, you never even knew your mother.

But still she hesitated.

'If she ever found out, you know she would never forgive us?'

Suzanne nodded slowly. The shadow of her outstretched hand fell over the patio, the sun glinting on the heavy gold bracelet.

'We could both lose her. Imogen would never forgive us for lying to her,' Elizabeth said quietly.

Suzanne was calmly assured. Determined. 'She'll never find out. Believe me, she will never find out.'

Under the sun their hands met, clasped, and then shook in agreement.

Chapter Ten

Elizabeth was right, Imogen was carrying a child. Only weeks into her pregnancy, only one missed period. Nothing more. Yet the news came as no surprise to Imogen; the first time she and Giles had made love there had been no contraception, only afterwards did they think about that. But afterwards was too late. Imogen was already pregnant. The news she greeted with tremendous and immediate delight, Giles shyly, proudly happy. Until he told his mother.

Mrs Winner's face contracted, her lips thinned with temper. 'Well, tell her to get rid of it.'

'What!' he replied, shocked. 'I love Imogen –'

'She's not the girl for you,' his mother replied, turning away from him and reaching for some feathers in a box over the workbench. Haphazardly she rummaged through the stock. 'You could have anyone, a man like you. Any girl you liked.' Her eyes were narrow with spite. 'I thought you were shy around women. Shy, hah!'

'I love Imogen,' he repeated evenly. 'I want to marry her.'

'No!' The word was a command. 'Not her. Listen, Giles,' she said softly, enticingly, 'we have a business, you and I. A client list anyone would envy. There's money here, more money than you imagine. Don't think I let your father off lightly when I divorced him.' Her head ducked downwards, wattles loose under her chin. 'You're making a name for yourself, look how that magazine article talked about you. Giles, I didn't pay for all your education just so you could marry the first bitch who got herself pregnant to catch you.'

He coloured, turned away. Since his parents had

divorced when he was ten, Giles had relied solely on his mother; had looked to her for his emotional succour, his financial support and his future security. She had encouraged him to do just that, applauded him when he did well at Eton, encouraged him when he went to university, then sucked him into the business. There was to be no lone career for Giles Winner, no singular status. The exclusive business which had educated him now shackled him; the woman who had loved him now smothered him; the money which had smoothed his life was now demanded back. Recompense. You owe me, she said. *You owe me*.

His life was full of women. The women at the shops, the milliners, the designers, the machinists – they all teased him, made fake passes at him, flirted with him. A man more sure of himself would have responded in kind. Flirted, become a mock gallant. But Giles had neither the inclination nor the skill, and saw them as a threat, not a pleasurable diversion. Females terrified him, swamped him, suffocated him. All women were his mother. Thin women, young women, clever women, stupid women – all of them reflected something of her and all gave him the familiar sensation of panic.

Until Imogen. Imogen didn't threaten him. Oh, she had at first. Her sex saw to that, but gradually, slowly, carefully, she built up a friendship and then a trust, and then – ah, then, a love. He *did* love her. Giles Winner, who had turned away from every pair of feminine eyes, gradually found that after a while he could look evenly into hers without wanting to run. The sense of safety she provoked was as profound as the sense of fear had been before. There was no colouring of his mother in this girl, no hint of the overbearing guilt every other woman had provoked. She was his coming home – and he had longed to come home.

The passion was more important on Imogen's part. For Giles, sex was not important, closeness was. But to lose her – no, that was unthinkable. Cowed by his mother, by the succession of 'aunts', staff and the unending female social circle which had gathered round him from the cradle, Giles was suddenly defiant, goaded into protecting this unlikely and beloved redeemer.

'No, Mother,' he said quietly. 'I want Imogen and I want to marry her.'

She thought, stupidly, that she still ruled him.

'If you choose her, Giles, I can't approve.'

His eyes flickered; a moment between submission and rebellion. 'I can't help that,' he said finally.

She knew she had lost, that somehow Imogen had wedged herself between them, and in that instant, she hated her.

'Giles, darling. . . .'

He turned away, conversation over.

'Giles. . . .'

Nothing. The decision, the first emotional decision of his life, was made.

He told Imogen that night that he wanted to marry her. She stared at him, transfixed, amazed by the alteration in him, his voice steady, firm. He was standing in the garden at Suzanne's, looking down into the fishpond, where a koi carp was coming up to feed. His hair fell across his forehead and rested against the collar of his shirt; his eyes narrowed against a late sun. For a moment it was she that was nervous; this Giles was urgent, different, hurrying things along as though by considering his decision longer he would change his mind. She recognised the reasons for his attitude and, loving him, gave him the option to reconsider.

'Giles, I don't want you to fall out with your mother over me.'

He stared down into the water. Suzanne had erected a stone putto over the pond; the water trickled over his grey limbs. Cold.

'My mother has ruled me for far too long,' he said calmly. 'I don't love her, Imogen, I don't even like her. She nearly killed my father, you know. Rode him, harangued him, nagged him. "The money," she used to say, "think of the money".' His head went back, his eyes for a second raking the closed sky. 'She built up that business to punish him, to prove what a failure he was, to point out that she could achieve more than he could, even without his education. "Look what I've done," she'd say. "All your bloody university degrees couldn't make a man out of you." He was limited . . .'

Giles paused, his eyes turning back to the pond. The koi carp still suckled at the water's edge. '. . . not overly bright, a nice man with a good family background and contacts, a GP on Wimpole Street with an upper-class patient list – she hated that; hated all the rich women who came to see him with their minor ailments. He had little going for him as a doctor – a good voice, a sympathetic approach, but not much else. He never wanted anything else. He just wanted to be comfortable and enjoy his life. She got pregnant to catch him,' Giles said bitterly, icily. 'That's why she reacted so badly when she heard about us. She knew my father wasn't in love with her, but she chased him, and chased him, and they finally had an affair. She would never admit that being pregnant forced his hand. She lied about my birth, saying I was a premature baby.' He smiled without humour. 'Premature by two months. So many lies to keep things respectable.'

Imogen's hand stretched out, touched his arm. He seemed not to notice her. All the hidden confidences, the whispered secrets, boiled out of him.

'She thought the family would accept her when she was married, but my grandparents thought she was an upstart, a gold-digger, a woman on the make. They were right, and they despised her. They were hopelessly mismatched, my parents. When I was a child I used to wake up and hear them arguing; my mother screaming at my father, demanding that she be introduced to his friends. He gave in sometimes, but she couldn't behave properly. She bragged, made people uncomfortable, embarrassed all his professional acquaintances, cost him friends, peace of mind. She belittled him, emasculated him. . . .'

'Giles,' Imogen said softly, 'don't get upset.'

He continued without even indicating that he had heard her. The years of silence were over; at last he had someone to listen to him.

'He walked out several times, and then came back. That was the worst, the returns. There would be weeks of calm and then it would all begin again. She started to change when I was about ten. Suddenly she decided that if she couldn't get what she wanted from my father, she would punish him. You see, the money wasn't enough, she had wanted the social status too, and when that wasn't forth-coming, she became dangerous.' He breathed in, held the breath for a long instant, took strength from it. 'It was then she began a business.

'Her clientele was impressive because she was so damned good. Well-known people came to her, and she thought that that proved she was socially acceptable. She didn't realise that they laughed at her behind her back. Mrs Winner could make hats, but not friends. Her ingratiating ways with the customers made everyone wince – everyone except her. She didn't see it,' his voice dropped, suddenly flat. 'I stopped hating her then, I felt such humiliation for her instead.'

Imogen's hand tightened on his arm. She knew he was close to tears.

'She seemed so helpless in a way, so *silly*. . . .' He stopped, pressed his lips together. Imogen could imagine how his pity had shackled him to his mother. Beware of pity, Suzanne had said.

'She divorced my father and got everything she could out of him financially to pay for my education. He wanted me to go into medicine, like him, but I wasn't interested. I think that was what finally separated us; my father saw it as a betrayal. I had chosen my mother over him.'

Giles turned and looked into Imogen's face. 'But what could I do? How could I have left her? I might not like her, but I was all that was left, and I owed her so much. . . . She knew how I felt when I made the decision, she even held me for once, loved me . . . but she soon forgot and somehow decided that I had stayed with her because I wanted the business. It was too late to argue, too late to go . . . too late.'

Frowning, Imogen listened, understanding at last how his mother had manipulated him. No wonder he mis-trusted women, no wonder he kept his distance. His own mother had cheated him, and he had grown up believing that every other woman would do the same.

'Giles, it's over. Forget the past.'

He looked at her for a long time without speaking, only touched her face and her hair gently.

'The past is what we are, Imogen,' he said at last. 'The past is the truth of us.'

They married quietly, with little fuss. Giles had few friends and Suzanne's circle was narrowed down to a select few. Elizabeth came to Brighton for the ceremony, and even the appalling Benny turned up, now fully grown and bearing an offering of cut-glass brandy goblets. People were generous with their gifts, Lorrie sending linen and chivvying Imogen to get back to work; several of Suzanne's old flames turning up with bizarre offerings. Suzanne herself presented Imogen with a copy of her will.

'Dear God,' she said when she read it, 'I can't accept –'

'Don't bugger about,' Suzanne said impatiently. 'You're like a daughter to me, Imogen, you know that. I just wanted to make that clear at your wedding.' Her head tipped to one side. 'Besides, I want to provide for the baby too.'

'I can't thank you enough –'

Suzanne put her hand over Imogen's mouth: 'Make this marriage work, darling. That's all the thanks I want.'

The most surprising gift came from Ira Mazan. On the morning of the wedding a car drew up and a driver rang the bell, passing Imogen a box. She opened it hurriedly, knowing who the sender was, and whooped with amazement when she found two ivory statuettes lying on a bed of red velvet. Fascinated, Suzanne peered over her shoulder.

'Well,' she said tartly, peering at the figures, 'I suppose we should be grateful that they're fully clothed. What does the card say?'

Imogen read it and passed it to her. In black ink he had written, *I can be a good friend. Remember that always. Ira.*

'Perhaps you misjudged him,' Imogen said quietly.

'Words are cheap,' Suzanne responded. 'Time will tell just how good a friend he is.'

The service was short, hurried, unromantic. The newly-weds left for a honeymoon in France, Elizabeth and Suzanne watching them leave from the front door of the

Brighton house. The two women, so dissimilar, so closely bound, waited until the car was out of sight and then, in unison, turned and walked back into the house. For Elizabeth it should have been the culmination of her dreams; for Suzanne, it should have been the realisation of her hopes. On that day, they were each only partially grateful to the other, and neither needed to say a word.

'She wore pale violet, and she had her hair piled high on her head. Mrs Jacobs had bought her some pearls and her ring was lovely, a ruby dark red, set in gold.' Elizabeth paused; Julie was unmoving. 'You would have been so proud, love, if you'd seen her. She was all lit up, happy, young, all her life before her. If I had died in that moment I would have been pleased to go.'

She lifted her daughter's hand. Julie's nails were short, thickened and yellowed.

'I remember when you got married, how you looked.' Suddenly, tenderly, she lifted Julie's hand and laid it against her cheek. 'I won't ever leave you, you know. I'll keep coming and visiting and one day, maybe, you'll say something.' She stared into her daughter's face. 'When you're ready, Julie, only when you're ready. . . . 'Til then I'll just keep talking and you'll keep listening. Because you *do* listen, don't you?' she urged, 'I'm sure you do. I'm not a clever woman, love, not like your doctors, but I know you, and I know you're pleased about Imogen, just like I know you're proud of her.'

Julie sat still unmoving, her hand held against her mother's cheek.

'She's having a baby soon,' Elizabeth went on. 'Your baby's having a baby of her own. I know you can hear me, and I know that you're pleased. Think of it, Julie, your child is going to give birth. It's the start of another life, a new life with all that means. Hope, dreams. . . . Julie? Julie, can you hear me? Tell me, love, just once, that you can hear me.'

It could have been her imagination, but she doubted it. Almost imperceptibly, Julie's hand moved and fluttered for an instant against her mother's face. The action was so tiny, so strained, that it could have been missed. But it *was* there, and for years afterwards Elizabeth would think of it and know that her daughter had heard her.

PART TWO

The flower that smiles to-day
    To-morrow dies;
All that we wish to stay
    Tempts and then flies.

('Mutability', Percy Bysshe Shelley)

Chapter Eleven

Two and a half years later,
Winter, London

Ira was sitting with his legs crossed, a copy of *The Times* on his lap. He had read the first page and then lost interest, his gaze shifting to the street outside the restaurant. Waiting. The day was morose, November sullen, a wind coming peevishly down the narrow confines of the city. A taxi stopped, then moved on, a woman pausing to open her umbrella. Nothing smiled. Not the day or the passers-by. An alien world, without heart.

He coughed twice, surprised that the gesture did little to clear his throat. He coughed again. Weather like this stuck in his craw, and he longed for sun. He had the money, could be in Italy now, wearing white, not black, under a London sky. But he had stayed behind to sort out the magazine, fighting a lawsuit, winning but having to pay the costs. Bloody London, bloody small-minded, penny-pinching, nitpickers. The last issue of the magazine had been a sell-out, the publicity ensuring a fleeting rise in circulation. Fleeting, Ira knew, because everything was fleeting.

Except friendship.

'Who died?'

He looked up at the sound of her voice and smiled. 'Imogen,' he said, kissing her on both cheeks. 'You look fabulous.'

She made a face. Never liked to be complimented and suspected flattery, even though she knew his judgement was valid.

'Well done, I heard about the case,' she said, sitting down. 'I heard about the costs too. Ooch!'

It was Ira's turn to grimace. 'I can afford it.'

'I know. "Where there's muck, there's brass," as my grandmother always says,' she smiled wickedly, 'and there's plenty of muck in your magazine.'

'Oh, Imogen, don't preach, it'll make you old before your time,' he replied easily, passing her a menu and watching as she read down the list of courses. Her head was inclined downwards, her long, straight nose elegant, her clothes understated sex appeal. Imogen Forest, now Winner, was there ever a name more apt?

'Stop staring, Ira,' she said, without looking up.

'I can't help it. You look better every time I see you,' he said simply. 'Happiness is good for women.'

She closed the menu and leaned back in her chair.

'*Marriage* is good for women.'

'But not men.'

'Not all men, that's true,' she replied flirtatiously.

Their relationship had surprised everyone; their friendship, at first so tentative, growing stronger as time passed. Giles had no competitor in Ira and knew he could trust his wife, but Imogen adored Ira Mazan, drawn to his raddled glamour and steady, unexpected admiration. They were two handsome people, who appreciated each other's looks and sex appeal without needing to consummate it. In Ira, Imogen lived vicariously, some of his tinselled existence seasoning her own happy but limited life.

For Ira, it was different. In Imogen, he saw beauty which was not for sale, or for spoiling. She was his ideal, his safely married fantasy, his imaginary, off-limits, harlot. He admired her wit as much as her figure, and liked her cheek as much as her bloody-minded honesty. It came as a refreshing contrast to the limpid-eyed devotion of his girlfriends. Imogen was perfect and perfectly unobtainable. She was, to Ira Mazan, the woman he wanted in his magazine and in his bed – and the knowledge that she would never be in either cemented their friendship.

Imogen thought about Ira too. Wondered about him, was

curious about him, but cautious – even in her fantasies. Giles was her husband, tender and unemotional in bed, loving in life. Ira was the unknown quantity; to allow even light-hearted thoughts about his sexuality would be to invite disaster.

She had it under control.

He had it under control.

But both of their hands shook when they lifted their glasses in a toast.

'Here's to my godson, the handsome Rowan.'

'To Rowan,' she agreed, taking a sip of the champagne Ira had ordered. 'I'm having a little birthday party for him later, just a few of his friends, and Giles.'

'How is he?'

'Doing well, we had a good season.'

'I meant Rowan,' Ira said.

'Oh, fine. Thriving,' Imogen replied, glancing outside at the rain. 'Lorrie wants me to go back to work for him. He says the magazine needs some bite, and some apt social comment. He wants me to draw some more caricatures for him.'

'D'you want to do it?'

She thought for a long moment. 'I'm not sure. I mean, I've been happy at home with Rowan, but it's limited, being at home all day with a baby. I don't think Giles would approve though, if I did go back to work.'

Ira drained his glass. 'You're not housewife material.'

'Maybe, maybe not,' she replied lightly, but there was an edge in her voice which Ira picked up immediately.

'You're bored, aren't you?'

'I have no right to be bored,' she responded sharply, 'I have a husband and a child, a nice flat –'

'Over the shop.'

'Yeah, but the shop happens to be in South Molton Street, Ira, so don't get sniffy.'

He raised his hands in mock surrender. 'Okay, it was just a throwaway comment.'

'Like hell; your comments are never throwaway. You said it to provoke me.'

'Imogen, aren't you happy?'

'Sure.'

He raised his eyes, then flicked at some imaginary speck on his black jacket, waiting for her to continue.

'You see, I feel guilty, Ira. I've got everything I ever wanted. Everything my grandmother ever wanted for me – and worked so hard to get. I've got money, a lovely home, a baby, and a great husband –'

'So how come he came last?'

'What?'

'If Giles is so great, how come he came last?' Ira repeated.

Imogen's eyes narrowed. She adored Ira, but at times she found him taxing; too clever by half.

'I love Giles.'

'I know.'

'We have a good marriage.'

'I'll take a dozen.'

She frowned. 'What?'

'Sorry, I just got carried away with the sales pitch.'

Piqued, Imogen glanced away.

'I could work from home,' she said idly. 'If I do go back to work for Lorrie, I could do the drawings at home.'

'Giles at one end of the studio with his hats, and you at the other with your cartoons. What a happy state of affairs.'

'It could work,' she said defensively. 'I did well before I married. People liked my work.'

'That was before Rowan came along.'

'Listen, Ira, I had a baby, not a stroke. Women do work after having children, you know.'

'I'm all for it,' he said smiling. 'You were the one who seemed uncertain.'

'It would be a change.'

'Yes.'

'A different outlook.'

'True.'

She pressed the point. 'I don't want to undermine him, Ira. I don't want Giles to think that I'm in competition with him. His mother was his rival, not me.'

Ira leaned forwards. So this was the real reason for her hesitation. Giles. Imogen was prepared to play the eternal Dr Watson to his Sherlock Holmes just to avoid antagonising him.

120

'You wouldn't be his rival –'

'He might see it that way,' she said softly, then continued, suddenly desperate to confide. 'I would hate to threaten him. Emasculate him.'

'How, for God's sake?' Ira asked incredulously, his mind hingeing on the word 'emasculate'.

'He would think I was being disloyal,' she said, her voice dropping so low that he had to strain to hear it.

What kind of marriage was it, he wondered? And what kind of man was Giles Winner to limit his wife's talents in order to feel safe? An old rumour surfaced at the back of Ira's mind; a bad rumour, a jealous one, from a long time back. He had dismissed it at the time, put it down to bile – but now he wondered. And he listened.

'. . . Giles loves me. He would interpret my working as a betrayal.'

'I don't understand.'

'He soon feels threatened,' she said, then paused, wondering if she was being disloyal. Giles had been a good husband, an affectionate father, but the friendship between them was oddly stilted. After a time, Imogen had found herself watching her words, walking on soap bubbles to avoid friction. Not that Giles was bad-tempered, he simply withdrew from her if he felt in any way uncomfortable – and many things made him uncomfortable. Her old friends for instance, and Suzanne, and even Elizabeth. He had wanted a confidante, but now he wanted to ensure that Imogen's sole attention focused on him.

The girl who began as his wife soon altered in his eyes to a surrogate parent. What he despised, he also yearned for. He believed what he said – 'The past is what we are; the past is the truth of us' – and he wanted to escape. But it wasn't enough; he also wanted to be safe, to keep himself within the confines of the known.

And when Rowan was born Imogen truly became the mother figure. To two children – him and the child. He relied more and more on her advice, on her sense of style, listening to her judgements and often acting on her criticism. At first she had wondered if her husband would resent it, but Giles *needed* it; longed for her absorption in his work and, by extension, him. The partnership which had promised to be so fulfilling slowly shifted into an uneven division of labour, Imogen taking on the role of the absent Mrs Winner – a role she was too young and too reluctant to shoulder.

The sex life, never truly passionate, dwindled. He was the one who used the baby as an excuse; he was the one who told her she must be tired; he was the one who treated her as an Earth Mother when she was barely twenty-four. Yet she felt unable to complain. Giles was neither difficult nor unattentive. He was gentle, courteous and respectful – he displayed, in fact, all the qualities of a dutiful son.

The situation, once accepted by her, became the norm. She saw her mistake too late. Having been amenable and agreeable, she had good-naturedly relegated herself to a pseudo Mrs Winner senior and realised what she had done too late. I am not the wife of this man, she thought chillingly after their second anniversary, I am his protector.

'Imogen?'

She turned back to Ira, surprised to find that her thoughts had wandered. Her natural caution reasserted itself suddenly. How could she really confide in anyone? Not Ira, or Suzanne. After all, hadn't the latter warned her? And later, hadn't she made her promise to make a success of the marriage? It was all Jaco had ever asked of her; for all her years of emotional and financial support it was the only repayment required. I *must* make this marriage work, Imogen told herself impatiently, I *must* make it work.

'I was just thinking,' she said slowly, picking up the menu again. 'Perhaps we should order?'

She said the words to give herself time to think, to regain her composure. It was a risk if she did take Lorrie up on his offer, but then again, it might be the making of her. If she was not solely involved with Giles, he might come to see her in a different light. If she was busy, not constantly in the flat or at his beck and call, he might remember her as she was, not as he had made her. A life of her own called, a little peck of status, and, Imogen realised guiltily, a chance to extend her domestic lease.

Ira watched her steadily: 'Well, have you decided?'

'I'm going back to work for Lorrie.'

He smiled sardonically. 'Actually, I meant had you decided what to eat?'

'Steak,' she said, smiling when she realised that she had given herself away.

'Bloody?'

Giles took the news in silence. He was playing with Rowan that night and was sitting with the child on his lap, his face expressionless. Imogen had decorated the flat in South Molton Street simply: the walls were stippled, the windows blinded with drapes, and a couple of heavy Italian settees flanked a glass table. Her taste, learned from Suzanne, was immaculate, although it had little of her mentor's florid opulence.

'Well, what do you think?'

Giles stared at his son. 'I think that Rowan's teeth are bothering him.'

She shook her head disbelievingly. 'They aren't – and that wasn't the question. I asked you what you thought about my working part time for Lorrie. It would only take a little of my time –'

'You have a son.'

'I know that!' she snapped impatiently. 'I'm not about to put Rowan into care! I'd be working at home, after all.' Her tone softened. Don't antagonise him, go easy. 'It would make a change for me, Giles. You used to love the caricatures, you know you did.'

'You weren't married then.'

Her temper flared. 'What the hell has that got to do with it? I could work in the studio with you – or up here, if you prefer.'

'We don't need the money,' he said quietly, stubbornly. 'You know what a good season we had. That spread in *Harper's* helped enormously.'

Imogen bit her lip, watching her husband. his head was bent towards his son, his long hair falling over the cheekbones. A tall, angular man; an attractive, diffident man – and a quietly demanding one. Demanding by nature, demanding by choice.

'Listen, Giles, I just want to do something for myself. It would give me a break. Besides, I miss the work, I didn't admit to myself how *much* until Lorrie got in touch –'

'I suppose Suzanne put you up to this,' he said, avoiding her eyes.

'Jesus!' Imogen snapped, getting to her feet and walking out.

She took the stairs two at a time, running into South Molton Street and turning at the corner into Oxford Street. The cold day had lifted, the night almost benign as she hurried along, her hands deep in her pockets. From a nearby pizza parlour came the sound of laughter and she stopped suddenly, glancing in. A group of students – obviously foreign – sat around a middle table, deep in conversation, their faces animated, the girls leaning towards the boys in spontaneous and flattering attention.

We never go out, Imogen thought suddenly. We live in a flat and we talk to each other and to Rowan, but nothing more. Our lives are so protected, so safe, that the world passes by us. In our twenties we are as detached as pensioners. She watched the group longingly, her thoughts turning back to Brighton. The smells of memory returned sharply: Suzanne's kosher food, the burning of incense, the dark scent of expensive leather and books sneaking seductively from the library – the room Suzanne hardly ever visited.

'Books, who needs them?' she used to say, tapping her ears. 'Learn to use these, darling, that's the way to learn about life.'

Old faces came back too. Mike, the actor, Pendle Gates, the antiquarian, even Benny, hopelessly foul Benny who had stayed with them all those summers ago. And the sound of laughter, always laughter, even after all the door-banging and the hysterics – always laughter.

We don't laugh, Imogen thought suddenly. We love each other so *seriously*. She turned away from the pizza parlour window and moved on, her temper flopping like a limp flag. How could she argue with him? He would never shout at her, never hit her, never be violent, physically or emotionally. He was spent, over; at twenty-seven Giles was already

124

exhausted by life. But not me, Imogen thought des-
pairingly, not me. I was brought up to fight – first by
Elizabeth, and then by Suzanne. I was encouraged to be
smart, funny, and I used to laugh more.

She remembered mimicking people, her talent amusing
Suzanne's friends. I had such confidence then, Imogen
thought incredulously, just as I used to have such a sharp
eye. Another thought followed on immediately. Maybe I
couldn't even *do* the caricatures any more, maybe I've lost
the knack. . . . A bus horn startled her and she stepped
back from the edge of the pavement, her heart banging. Get
a grip, girl, just calm down.

But I don't *want* to be calm, she thought defiantly. I don't
want to be old before my years and content with my lot. God
forgive me, I want to be myself, and that's not just Giles's
wife and Rowan's mother. There is more than this, there *has*
to be. . . . Her steps quickened, her thoughts beating in
rhythm. Was this the end? Just marriage, just motherhood?
No, Imogen thought angrily, there has to be more, there *has*
to be.

She thought of Ira suddenly. Did she envy him? Did she
want some of his glamour, however sordid? Was that it? She
shook her head; no, she liked Ira, but she wasn't envious of
him, she knew too much about his kind of life – it was too
similar to all the other superficially glamorous lives of
Suzanne's friends. Suzanne. . . . Imogen stopped walking;
a man with a bow tie bumped into her and apologised before
moving on. Suzanne had wanted a child all her life; she had
longed for motherhood, but had been cheated. Her pleasure
in Imogen's happiness and at the birth of Rowan had been
genuine, but tinged with regret. . . . How could she not be
happy with her lot, when others envied her? Imogen
wondered sharply. How could she be so dissatisfied? It was
wrong, terribly wrong, something would happen if she
didn't stop looking for trouble. Something terrible, something bad.

Like what? A thought came into her head, but she
dismissed it. Giles was a good man, a good provider and
husband, a good father – but cold. God, how cold he was.
Cold in bed, cold to the touch, cold in the middle of the night

when she woke and turned towards him. His skin was always cool against hers, his hand always out of reach. Maybe he didn't find her attractive, maybe that was it? No, it was just his way, Imogen told herself. It was just his way. He was preoccupied, concerned with business, ambitious.

And cold. Cold after two and a half years of marriage – and after ten, twenty, thirty, how cold then? How chilled would that little space between them in bed become? Her eyes closed, blocking out the thoughts, although her brain ran on. He had said he found the heat unsettling in the summer, so that was why he was sleeping in the spare room. Nothing serious, he had assured her, just a way of getting some sleep in the middle of a hot London night.

Just a way of getting some sleep. That was all. She knew that. It wasn't important, was it? So after a while, if Imogen woke and found Giles gone, she picked up the baby and took Rowan back to bed. He never felt too hot, or never seemed to. In fact, he could lie next to her and never move. Happy. Close. Natural.

Imogen never challenged Giles about his occasional nocturnal wanderings, but when summer was over and the autumn set in the bedroom was no longer airless, the air no longer humid – and he still spent some nights in the other room. Then she *did* question him about it. He hesitated, muttered something about bad dreams. She told him that that was when he needed someone with him. For comfort.

Safe in the old role, Imogen seduced her husband back, and she did as she promised; when he had nightmares she held him and soothed him and mothered him. For several months he had stayed in their bed, but now suddenly he had started sleeping away from her again. . . . This time she was out of temper and falling rapidly out of love. There was no explanation given and none asked for; the question mark hung between them and embarrassed their silences, so when Lorrie's offer suddenly materialised, it came as a massive relief to Imogen; a way of taking her mind off her anxieties.

And now Giles was playing up about her work. Being unreasonable, being unfair. Imogen stopped walking again and moved into a call box, punching out a number and listening to it ring at the other end. Only eighteen months before, she had finally convinced Elizabeth to have a phone installed.

But the phone kept ringing, unanswered, Imogen pressing her warm forehead against the cool glass of the call box. Then slowly, reluctantly, she put down the phone. Maybe it was as well; maybe it would be too much to ask of her grandmother.

So Imogen dialled another number, and this time the phone was picked up on the third ring.

'Hello?'

'Lorrie, it's Imogen.'

'Well, well, well. So have we made our mind up?'

She winced. 'Well I don't know about yours, but mine's made up. Yes, I'd like to work part time for you again.'

'Wonderful –'

'Just part time.'

His voice was steely. 'I can't afford any more, dear, the magazine's not doing that well.'

'Don't try and snow me, Lorrie, we both know you're thriving,' she replied evenly. 'I could start next week.'

'What about tomorrow? I want some caricatures for next week.'

He was pushing her and she knew it. But Imogen wanted to be pushed, wanted to have her hand forced.

'Okay, Lorrie, you're on.'

Chapter Twelve

Suzanne had a winter cold. Flu, she called it. Flu, she insisted to the doctor who was on his third visit that week. I have flu, she said, sneezing and gesturing towards the thermometer on the bedside table. Read the bloody thing, if you don't believe me. He was patient, chattered on fast, very fast, as he always did when embarrassed. As he always was. The sea wrack nuzzled against the bedroom window and the doctor kept talking, telling Suzanne something incomprehensible about his childhood music teacher, his medical bag on his lap, his arms folded over it protectively.

She watched him, her expression wiped clean as a sheet of paper. Blank with exasperation.

'Suzanne – oh, sorry, I thought the doctor had gone,' Imogen said, backing out of the doorway.

'Darling, come in,' Suzanne said hurriedly. 'Dr Warner is just leaving.'

He muttered something inaudible, grinned sheepishly, and walked out. When she heard the front door close, Imogen turned back to Suzanne.

'Whatever he's on, I want some.'

'Jesus, I don't understand a word that man says. Do you really think he's a doctor?' Suzanne asked, her eyebrows raised. 'I mean, perhaps for years he's been trying to tell us he's come to do the drains.'

'In that case, he should sort out your sinus trouble,' Imogen said drily, before changing the subject. 'Rowan's asleep.'

Suzanne blew her nose noisily. 'I wonder if it's a good idea for you two to be with me at the moment, Imogen, I mean with this flu.'

'The doctor said it was only a cold, and also said you were past being contagious,' Imogen replied lightly, sitting down on the side of the bed and staring hard at Suzanne. 'Your hair looks different, Jaco.'

'It's called the bedroom bouffant,' she replied tartly. 'You lie down for so long that when you get up you look like Napoleon in a bloody tricorn.'

Imogen burst out laughing, then slowly, wistfully, stopped.

'So, what is it?' Suzanne asked. 'Trouble?'

'Not really.'

'Potential trouble?'

'I don't know.'

'How many guesses do I get?'

Imogen smiled faintly. 'I've agreed to work part time for Lorrie again. Well, actually I started last week. The new cartoons are in the latest issue.'

Suzanne sneezed twice.

'. . . Giles has been a bit – well, difficult – about the whole thing. He didn't want me to do it, and because I've gone ahead he's hardly speaking to me. Do you think I was wrong to go back to work?'

Suzanne sneezed again.

'Is it one for no, and two for yes?' Imogen asked.

'Don't be chippy, darling,' Suzanne replied, dabbing at her eyes. 'So Giles is really pissed off, is he?'

'Well and truly.'

'Didn't you discuss it with him?'

'You can't discuss things with Giles, he goes deaf when he doesn't want to hear things.'

'Pardon?'

Imogen shook her head. 'Very funny, Jaco.'

Gently, Suzanne tapped the back of Imogen's hand. 'Listen, he's just sulking, that's all. Doing his me Tarzan, you Jane role. He'll come round, give it time.' Her eyes narrowed slowly. 'Incidentally, why *did* you go back to work?'

'Because I wanted to,' Imogen said baldly. 'I adore Rowan, but just sitting around all day and going in and out of the showroom when Giles asked me for my opinion wasn't enough. I felt cooped up. . . . So when Lorrie asked me back, I suppose I jumped at it.'

'Well, at least Giles can't worry about Lorrie being after you. That is one advantage of working for a homosexual – no sexual tension.'

'Except amongst the boys,' Imogen countered, changing the subject. 'I saw Ira the other day.'

'I know. My spies reported many sightings.'

'Not many, Suzanne,' Imogen said seriously. 'Only a few.'

'You're not in love with him, are you?' Suzanne asked suddenly.

'No.'

'Sure?'

'Positive.'

'Because he's not –'

'Jaco, I'm *not* in love with Ira.'

She nodded. 'Good.'

'We're friends, that's all.'

'Aaaaargh.'

'What does that mean?'

Suzanne toyed with the end of her sheet. 'It's just that I remember how friendly you were with Giles, and look what happened there.'

'Giles is my husband.'

'I know. I remember the wedding.' She leaned forwards, stared into Imogen's face. 'Aren't you happy? You can tell me, darling. Honestly, you can tell me if you're unhappy.'

Imogen wanted to; in fact, she was desperate to confide, but she resisted. Her malaise was her own fault; Giles's behaviour was due to her – it must be. If he was unhappy, she had failed him. And if she had failed him, she was the only person who could make things right again. Out of the corner of her eye, Imogen saw Suzanne watch her. If she told her her problems she would help; she would want to; she would feel she had to. She would, as always, act as her mother and be protective. But it was too much to ask of Suzanne – just as it had been too much to ask of her grandmother. Imogen wasn't a child any more; she had her own son now and she had to learn when to stop leaning.

'I'm okay, it's just the job that's caused a problem,' she said evenly. 'You wait, things will sort themselves out.'

But the winter was a savage one, and as the weather chilled, the atmosphere between Giles and Imogen worsened. Her work for Lorrie was well received; readers even began to write in, praising the caricatures, and a couple of celebrities bought the originals. At first Imogen had kept her work hidden in her portfolio, aware that it irritated Giles to see the drawings, but after a while she framed some and hung them defiantly in the flat. He passed no comment and stopped asking her to advise him on his work. Tit for tat. Withdrawal, as ever his most effective punishment.

And it *did* punish her, Imogen finding his retreat baffling then frightening, and when she overheard him talking to his mother on the phone late one night, her worst fears were realised.

She listened by the door, knowing she shouldn't. Eavesdroppers only hear bad of themselves, the old adage went, and it was true.

'. . . Rowan's fine, you should see how big he's grown now. . . . Listen, Mother, Imogen and I are having some difficulties. . . . I'm sorry about what happened. I was thinking that perhaps we should meet up and have lunch. . . .'

The betrayal was immense. Ever since their marriage Giles had continued to run the South Molton Street shop and studio, but his communication with his mother had been by fax or letter, any closeness suspended. For over two and a half years he had stood by his decision to choose Imogen, and now, at the first sign of trouble, he had changed his allegiance and run home. It was more the action of a boy than a man.

'. . . she's busy, working again. . . . Yes, I know, I don't like the idea either. But she won't listen. . . .'

Imogen could imagine Mrs Winner's face, fresh with triumph, her mind already thinking up ways to drag her son home. Giles, you fool, you bloody, unthinking fool.

'. . . lunch, then. Fine, I'll phone you tomorrow and check the time with you.'

He put the phone down just as Imogen entered the room. She knew from the way he jumped guiltily that he realised she had overheard – and yet he said nothing, just watched her. Her thoughts lunged backwards without warning – to a young man in the tearoom in the Grand at Brighton; an embarrassed young man uneasy in his mother's company. Aware of the imminent crisis, Imogen wanted to take hold of him, to make him laugh and break the months of debilitating animosity – but she couldn't, something prevented her, and instead she reacted flippantly, walking in and standing in front of her husband, her hands on her hips.

'Oh dear, Giles,' she said in a perfect imitation of Mrs Winner's voice. 'You have been a naughty boy, haven't you?'

He flushed darkly and turned away.

Her hand snatched at his arm, her voice back to normal. 'Running home to mother, Giles?' she said, hating herself, hating the hard words and the bitter tone. 'Well, I hope you know what you're doing.'

'Imogen,' he said flatly, shaking her off and moving away. 'I have to work.'

She moved after him, suddenly desperate. 'Giles, don't. Listen to me, please.' Her eyes fixed on his when he turned. Come back, come back. 'We have to talk this out. It's stupid, behaving like this. We love each other –'

'Imogen, I told you, I have to work.'

His expression was blank; gone. Just as he had the day he left her to catch her train. I should have listened to Suzanne, she thought helplessly. I should have listened.

'I love you.'

She waited for him to respond, but the moment ticked past and another began.

'Giles, don't you love me any more?'

He seemed to hesitate, to want to respond, but then he drew back. Old habits, dying hard. He was injured and his only way to avoid further pain was to retreat. It would have been impossible to guess from his expression how much he was feeling, how much he ached inside. All his life he had learned to suppress his thoughts, his weaknesses, his emotions, and now, when he most wanted to, he was no longer *able* to express himself. It was not that he wanted to hurt his wife; it was not that he wanted to side with his mother; but the safety marriage had offered had been ephemeral. The *past* is what we are, he thought grimly, and whether we like it or not, it *is* the truth of us.

In his eyes, she had gone. Without meaning to, without wanting to, Imogen had changed. It was not her fault, it was his. He knew and accepted that. The last two and a half years had been an attempt at normality; but they had failed. He felt suddenly guilty, suddenly ashamed, and in an uncharacteristic gesture he caught hold of her and held her tightly against him. Her body moved urgently against his, her head turned upwards, her eyes pleading.

He kissed her without feeling anything, and without any sensation he undressed her and lay on top of her on the settee in the showroom. Hungrily Imogen clung to him, whispered to him, tugged at his clothes, undressed him, aroused him; and he responded automatically, a sexual function performed without emotion, without heart. Finally, when he climaxed she breathed out, slowly, and smiling, stroked his back.

His silence did not worry her. Neither did his immobility, but for years afterwards she would remember the first hoarse sob which came so unexpectedly from him, the sound so terrifying that she flinched. For many minutes he cried steadily, without words; cried darkly and drily after the tears had finished; cried until the light faded in the showroom and he fell asleep, Imogen silent beneath him.

She did not cry; *could* not. She only knew that under the tears there was something other than unhappiness. Not even misery, nothing so simple; nothing that could be cured. Her husband had told her something beyond words – and she had heard it. She didn't want to hear it, or to recognise, or understand it. She only wanted to be rid of the sound – and knew she never would be. The tears were not a release, but a confession. She knew it, and in knowing it, lost every last ounce of hope.

Chapter Thirteen

'No wonder the bloody circulation's rising, you never write a bad word about anyone.'

'Being envious won't alter a thing, Ira,' Lorrie replied phlegmatically. 'Besides, you can't complain, you're doing all right, even if none of your readers can actually be seen reading your magazine.'

'This is the eighties, Lorrie, people see as much on page three of the *Sun* every morning with their Bran Flakes.'

Lorrie winced. 'What a disabling thought, Ira,' he said coolly. 'Anyway, at least I have the sense not to mix business with pleasure – I heard you're having a fling with Miss December. Or should I say "The Glorious Twelfth"?'

Ira paused at the other end of the line. He disliked Lorrie Brent, always had done, and yet they rubbed along in business quite amicably, swapping contacts. Their worlds were not as dissimilar as at first appeared, Ira's magazine, *S'expression* achieving the rare distinction of being soft porn combined with truly clever writing. After a while, the articles seduced other people into contributing, and writers who would never have written a syllable for *Penthouse* found themselves willing to express their thoughts on Ira's pages. The fact that such thoughts came pressed between the breasts and loins of various nubile women added a certain piquancy to the layout, and sent circulation soaring.

Lorrie's magazine, by contrast, had not one whit of journalistic ability, but had made a fortune simply by being so 'nice' to everyone. Women who would never rate a second glance on the street were transformed by Lord Lichfield into beauties; and men who had inherited vast wealth without even breaking into a sweat suddenly became tycoons. The layouts were sumptuous, celebrities lounging in their homes – in exquisite taste, of course – or leaning against handy, enobling pillars. Everyone wanted to be in *Exclusive*, and everyone who wanted to see everyone appearing in *Exclusive*, bought it. The result was a marketing triumph.

'I saw your coverage on that duchess in the last issue,' Ira said pleasantly. 'The photographs were good. What did you use, a filter or a mosquito net?'

Lorrie winced. 'Very humorous. I suppose you're going to tell me that you never touch up your subjects – if you'll pardon the expression.'

'I pick my girls for their looks, not their social connections.'

'Well, you couldn't, could you? I mean, Tracy from Deptford would hardly rate a mention in the Diary pages, would she?'

'Lorrie, don't preach to me about moral ethics. If you could, you'd have a whole photo spread on bloody Hitler. I can see the title – Adolf At Home – and the questions. "Well, Mr Hitler, I know you get bored talking about politics, perhaps you could tell us what type of food you and Eva enjoy? And your holidays? And what about a cute little picture of you with the dog? Oh, and a Jacuzzi, how lovely." '

'Have you finished?' Lorrie asked coldly, fighting to suppress the image of Hitler in a Jacuzzi.

'Just don't preach to me,' Ira replied. 'You and I make a lot of money by mass-marketed pap – but we should at least have the balls to be honest about it.'

Unable to think up a crushing rejoinder, Lorrie changed the subject.

'Imogen's just been in. I heard you two are very thick.'

'We have been for years, Lorrie. It's called friendship – you know, that thing you keep quoting about your pal, Daniel.'

He flushed hotly. 'Daniel and I are friends.'

'Sure, I believe you. Just like Imogen and I are friends.' Ira paused for a beat. 'I saw those last caricatures. She's really coming on, those were bloody clever. Especially the ones of the MPs.'

Lorrie relaxed, on safe ground again.

'She's got more of an edge now,' he said, thinking. 'You know, I've noticed a big difference in her over the last year or so. She was always good, always punchy, to the point, but now there's something else. Sometimes there's even a little savagery in Imogen's work.'

Ira caught the word and frowned. Savagery. Lorrie wasn't as stupid as he looked. He had noticed the difference, underlying dark notes. Ira had seen them too; the hardness of line, the occasional acid undertone. They made excellent caricatures, but they surprised him. Imogen had always been clever, witty – but cruel? Seldom.

Being a perceptive man, he wondered what had caused the change. Certainly, to talk to, Imogen was the same as she had always been. Her vitriol was restricted to work. But what had caused it? A critical observance of the foibles of humanity, or a bitterness within her? Or around her. That was more like it. There was no darkness in Imogen; there never had been; that was why he admired her so much. But something had shifted her perception, and unless Ira was very much mistaken, that something was Giles.

He had never taken to Giles Winner. Had thought him too cold, too reserved for Imogen's warmth. And he had been right. As the years passed, her vivacity did not draw her husband out; instead his reserve limited her. The quick wit was no longer quite so spontaneous, the laugh was not so ready. If they met for lunch it took her several minutes to relax, to revert to the Imogen of the Brighton years. Her beauty had altered too; the pungent sexuality toned down, cooled.

Cooled – Ira mused on the word, uncomfortable with its connotations. Why had she cooled? Because she lived with a dry, controlled, cold man? Because Giles had sapped away the hugeness of spirit and chilled the sparkiness of her temperament? And how much more of her liveliness would he dampen? And for how long? . . . Ira didn't like the idea, it needled him, and he had, suddenly, a premonition of Imogen's future.

He could see her older, careful with her speech, tight. Her appearance would change too, that lushness of skin and body tightening. The image unsettled him, but he couldn't shake it. He had thought Giles was a weak man, but now he wasn't so sure.

'Ira?'

His thoughts came back to the present. 'Yes?'

'I was wondering about Imogen. Just an idea. . . .'

'Go on.'

'Do you think she might take on some more work? I mean, you know her better than I do, and I don't want to put forward the idea if you don't think it would go down well. But you see, she's getting quite a following and there might be room for a few more caricatures.'

Ira hesitated. He knew Giles had been against Imogen's return to work, but for several months she had said nothing. No hint of disharmony, discord. Maybe he had adjusted to the idea. Maybe.

'Ask her.'

Lorrie nodded. 'Yes, I think I will. I mean, talent like hers should be utilised.'

'Especially if it puts more money in your pocket,' Ira countered smoothly. 'I just hope that you'll make her a good offer, Lorrie. Something worth while.'

'I wouldn't cheat her!'

'Of course not,' Ira replied. 'Because if you did, you'd have me to contend with.'

Elizabeth had fallen asleep in front of the fire in the kitchen, her head lolling to one side until she suddenly jerked awake. The room had cooled down, the fire only a bare smoulder, the dark night blackening the windows. With difficulty, she got to her feet and drew the curtains, turning on the light and padding over to the kettle. The silence pressed down on her, Graham's photograph on the mantelpiece fading yellow in a brass frame. She could turn on the radio, or the television, but she didn't feel like it. She could go to bed, but she was no longer tired. Sleep had come and caught her by surprise as it did so often these days. Caught her in that one instant when she sat down with the local paper on her lap.

Funny how old age slows everything, she thought.

Everything, that is, except memory. The brain, so ponderous in its everyday function, seemed to quicken when she looked back. It was no problem to recall Julie as a baby, or the fireworks in the back yard, the smell of burnt paper and the match stubs lying on the flagstones. But Elizabeth couldn't remember what she ate for tea. Funny that, she mused. Funny how she felt so idle. So useless.

She'd got used to looking after people. Old lady Forest, Graham, Imogen, Julie. And now there was only Julie left. The old lady had gone, Graham was dead, and Imogen had a husband to look after her. There was only Julie left, and she needed far more nursing than Elizabeth could ever give her.

The thought depressed Elizabeth. The house was empty and quiet, the walls still thin. From one side of her she could hear voices raised in argument, from the other side, a baby cried to be fed. But no one cried for her, no one needed her any more. She was sandwiched between other lives, living out the remnants of her own.

There was no self-pity in the thought. Elizabeth had done what she had set out to do; the only thing that still worried her was Julie. And even that had been taken care of; Suzanne had promised to make sure that if Elizabeth died Julie would receive proper medical care until the end of her days. It was the final pact between them. After all the other pledges, this was to be the last one. Their secret was well tended and should remain hidden for ever. After Elizabeth was dead, Suzanne would maintain the deception, and when Julie died, the last secret would be laid to rest with her.

I have done my best, Graham. Elizabeth thought suddenly, looking at his photograph. I can honestly say that I have done my best. For as long as I have left to live, I can enjoy Imogen's happiness and her family, knowing that the past is safe.

The thought comforted her, and, against all logic, she felt suddenly tired again. Her eyes closed, the lids crêpey, her skin slack around the jowls. An old lady alone in a cold kitchen, rocking herself back into sleep.

*

While Elizabeth slept, Giles stirred in bed, turned over and looked into his wife's face. Her eyes were closed, her breathing even. Carefully he rose and silently pulled on his dressing gown, walked down to the studio and flicked on the light. The showroom sprang into life, the drawings brilliantly simple and effective, staring out from the numerous cork boards.

Thoughtfully Giles walked around the studio, then moved on into the back workshop, passing the machinists' tables and the huge cardboard rubbish boxes, placed at the end of every row. The machines were silent, turned off for the night, the hats in their various stages of development lying haphazardly on the wooden bench. He touched the net on one, and the bleached straw of another, picking up one more and staring critically at the brim. His eyes narrowed as he turned the hat round, judging it from every angle, and then, confidently, he wrenched off the brim and wrote an instruction note to the machinist for her to find in the morning.

His hats had been seen at Ascot, at Glyndebourne, and at numerous society weddings. They had been tipped at Claridges, shown off at Harry's Bar and on many occasions photographed for *Exclusive*. He was made. The predictions Mrs Winner had made for Wonder Son had come true. Giles was a success. Money was his; status was his; prestige was his. His natural aloofness, so different from his mother's ingratiating familiarity, achieved what she could not. Respect. No one tried to make a friend of Giles – but all his customers listened to his advice.

He flattered the women by making them look their best. They paid him for that service and came to him repeatedly. But after a number of invitations had been refused, they stopped extending others. Giles Winner was obviously a family man, devoted father. He was interested in his home life and his work. No more.

A family man. . . . Giles mused, frowning at the words, his eyes turning upwards almost as though he expected to be able to look up into the flat above. His wife was asleep, his son also asleep in the nursery next to their bedroom. His family was safely ensconced, away from the world.

Separated, segregated, removed from everyone. He liked the idea, it felt familiar. After all, he had lived *his* life apart from others. Except his mother. . . . Giles walked over to the phone and thought about calling her. Pictured her waking up and pulling off her eyeshade. Irritable, hot-breathed, sour from sleep.

But he didn't make the call. The temptation was almost irresistible, but he managed to move away at the last moment. Of course his mother had been delighted at their reunion; she had even resisted the desire to overly criticise Imogen. Oh, she made the odd prickly comment, but they were few and far between; she wanted to test the water before jumping in and possibly drowning.

He needed her. Finally Giles admitted it. He needed his mother as others needed a partner. In fact, she *was* his partner. His first and, if he wasn't careful, his last. She forgave him everything, never taxed him, never argued with him, never pushed him – at the moment. Because, at the moment, she was working herself into the gluey space between her son and his wife. Giles had enough sense to realise that if she succeeded the shrew would return, the ridiculous, haranguing, demanding cow would rematerial-ise. But he *knew* her, knew her ways, knew she wanted the best for him. After all, hadn't she devoted her life to him, and to their business?

Which was more than Imogen had done. Giles picked up another hat, a velvet fedora with a satin trim. He tried to stop the uncertainty creeping up in him; his face remained impassive, his eyes steady. But his stomach was suddenly nauseated and for an instant he wanted the woman and child upstairs to be gone. He wanted his rooms back, his flat returned to him, his clothes in the wardrobes alone, his own food in the fridge. They were choking him, turning him into a hobbled, pestered man.

They demanded so much from him; so much affection. His son wanted him to play, to join in his games, to take him to the park on Sundays. And Giles did. He bought the toy boats and pushed them away from the mud edges of the lake and fed the Canada geese and did every other normal thing that every other normal family man could be expected to do. But it felt so strange, so uncomfortable. He would look round furtively at the other fathers, wondering how they could laugh so easily, and pick up their children with such confidence.

He couldn't do that. Didn't know how to at first, then decided he would learn – and then he realised that he didn't *want* to. Rowan loved his father, and Giles loved his son – from a distance. If he could have placed his child in a bubble, removed from his contact, then he could have coped. But this clinging, affectionate, warm little person was terrifying. Still only a toddler his own son frightened him.

Imogen saw his reserve, but never mentioned it. She seldom commented on anything any more, except his work – and she only did that to please him. Her advice was good, he admitted that, but limited. She knew Mrs Winner was back on the scene and judged accurately that the mother's opinion had precedence over the wife's. Yet they stayed together, both believing that it was a bad patch. They stayed together without talking in the shaky belief that silence might serve better than speech. If they talked, what little bond that remained between them might be broken for ever. And both loved each other too much to risk that.

Their marriage existed only for the infinitesimal flickers of tenderness which caught both of them unawares. They might be eating and suddenly Imogen would look up and catch her husband's eye; and his look would have all the longing and gentleness she first remembered, and so she would smile and glance away, holding the gesture as another woman would hold a bouquet of flowers. At other times, Giles would be working and turn to catch Imogen's reflection in one of the mirrors in the showroom – and see her working, and see in her then all the sweetness of her kindness. Both of them would wait in that instant for some communication to reawaken them both; sometimes even touch hands; then both would turn away and continue with what they had been doing before.

Love *is*, then love *was*, then love became fractured; the disjointed flashes of pure feeling recharging both of them, forcing both of them to stay, and keeping any real wretchedness at bay. How can we be unhappy and still feel like this?

Imogen would wonder. How long can we keep this afloat on such little dribbles of affection? Giles wondered. . . . But neither asked the other what they thought, and after sex, or after food, or after dawn, they lived together and yet always apart.

Giles turned back to the mirror and laid his hands against the glass, staring into his reflection. Then, rhythmically, he began to pound the glass, his hands now fists, as he repeated over and over, *I don't want to be this man . . . I don't want to be this man. . . .*

Chapter Fourteen

Three further years passed. Rowan grew into a child more like his mother than his father, although Imogen was careful not to cosset him; she had seen what such behaviour could do and wanted to avoid a repetition of the past. She brought him up tough, and spirited, her own will injecting into her child some of the vivacity she now found hard to express herself.

Many times they visited Brighton, and Suzanne always welcomed them, drawing Rowan into the picaresque circle of friends she had always cultivated. Imogen watched her son enjoy what she had enjoyed and was grateful to see that he flourished as she did. But not in London; not in South Molton Street. There both of them were curtailed. Rowan more subdued, Imogen less animated. Both careful. Controlled.

Over the years she and Giles had talked of moving. They should get a house, with a garden for Rowan. It would be healthy. Nice, to get out into the country. Or even Kensington, somewhere leafy, with trees. The capital was no place to bring up a child. . . . But they never left the flat over the studio; instead they redecorated it and made it opulent and fashionable, and fabulous. But few ever saw it. Only Ira came a couple of times, and Suzanne visited when she came to town to shop.

'Bloody taxi!' she moaned, throwing down her bags and falling heavily on to one of the divans. 'Hi, darling!' she shouted, grabbing hold of Rowan and kissing him noisily. He grinned, hair floppy, like Giles's.

'Hi, Jaco.'

She laughed, then her eyes narrowed as she studied

Imogen. Oh, the boy was fine, more than fine. She had said as much to Elizabeth over the phone the other day. Rowan's great – but *Imogen*? Okay, she'd lied. Okay, no more. What else *could* she say? She seems all right, she never moans, never says anything's wrong. But they don't go out enough for a young couple, and they seem so serious. . . . Suzanne sighed; maybe marriage did that to everyone, maybe it was just the way things went after the first few years. Besides, Giles had never been the lively type, more's the pity.

The thought caught her unawares. Why was it a pity? Imogen had married the man she loved and had a splendid, confident, healthy son, even a thriving sideline career. She had what Suzanne had wanted for her; what Elizabeth had wanted for her. Security, love. But. . . . A picture of Ira Mazan flashed into Suzanne's head and she frowned.

'What is it?' Imogen said, poised with a bottle of wine in one hand and a glass in the other.

'I was thinking about that nebbish Mazan,' Suzanne replied lightly.

'I'll give him your regards,' Imogen responded. 'I'm seeing him next week.'

The picture lodged in Suzanne's head and wouldn't shift. Ira Mazan. Come summer he'd be in his white suit again, his hair dark and well shaped, his eyes shadowed. He would be laughing somewhere, cutting someone down to size, flicking imaginary bloody flecks off his jacket. Mr Smoothy, Mr Slick, Mr Bad Guy – and yet, and yet. Another picture joined the first: two handsome, glamorous people together – Imogen, blonde and full-busted, Ira hard and flash, loving her. Not a bad picture really, even for all his faults, even despite his toe-rag of a magazine. Not a bad picture, Ira and Imogen. . . .

God, what *am* I thinking? Suzanne wondered, but the thoughts still persisted as she looked at Imogen. I've never seen you laugh with Giles, she realised, suddenly startled. Jesus, I've seen you laugh with everyone *but* him.

'Well, what is it?' Imogen persisted, curious.

Suzanne took the bull by the horns: 'Is everything all right between you and Giles?'

'Fine,' she said quickly; too quickly.

'No problems?'

'None.'

'I just thought that you might have moved out of this place – and bought more of a home by now.'

Imogen poured out two glasses of wine. Her hands didn't shake. She had composure, control – she had learned that much from her husband.

'We'll move when the time is right, but Giles likes it here. It would be a drag to have to travel from home to the showroom every day.'

'I was thinking of Holland Park, not bloody Bengal,' Suzanne said drily. 'You've been here for years, don't you get bored?'

'You've lived in Brighton for decades, don't you?'

The strike came unexpectedly. It hurt.

'Hey, Imogen, this is me, remember? I'm the one who doesn't criticise. I was just making a suggestion, that's all.'

She thought Imogen would respond as she always used to; that her hand would come out and touch hers to signify an apology, and to offer affection. But Imogen's hand remained around the glass. Removed. At a distance. Just as she was.

'Sorry, Suzanne. I didn't mean to snap.'

The chill was colder than the wine. It slid over both of them; it crept up the walls and round the windows. Each piece of furniture said don't touch; each book repelled; each surface was shiny with disuse. The flat was wiped clean of warmth, Suzanne realised with real anxiety. The effect was terrifying, unexpected, and the alteration had come within the last eighteen months. What *is* happening here, she thought helplessly, what the hell is happening? And what is happening to my child? The girl I love above everything, the daughter who is more mine than my own could ever have been. Where is the girl I took in? The sassy, feisty, funny blonde who made me laugh – who the bloody hell crushed her spirit and turned her into this tight and brittle hex?

But she said nothing. There was nothing Suzanne could say at that moment; she merely sipped her wine and as soon as she could, she left. Only out on South Molton Street did Suzanne relax and feel warmed by the sun, reluctantly glancing back when she reached the end of the street. But there was no one looking out from the window, no one trying for an instant to escape from the tomb of the flat. The atmosphere of the place had alarmed her, and told Suzanne something. Imogen was bitterly unhappy, but she would never admit it. Only something terrible would force her to leave; and only something more terrible would force her to stay.

The following month Imogen visited Brighton and for a while she seemed to regain something of her old spirit. But only days after leaving she began to be restless, to long to return, while at the same time she dreaded going home. Something called her, something irresistible and enticing begged her back.

And back she went, the train pulling into Victoria station earlier than expected. Her hands shook as she hailed a taxi and got out at South Molton Street. She had decided to face her husband, to force a confrontation and a discussion about their marriage. All was not lost, she told herself, it could still be worked out. But as Imogen approached the shop her spirit failed and she hesitated, the key in her hand. She had not told Giles she was coming back; she had not wanted him to prepare himself, or worse, make an excuse to be out. So she was going to surprise him instead, return unexpectedly, and maybe, just maybe, she might succeed in surprising him into a response.

Her hands continued to shake as she turned the key in the lock and pushed the door open, walking in quietly. There was a light under the showroom door, as there always was when Giles was working. Nervously Imogen took a deep breath and then walked in.

There was no one there – but there *was* a light on in the far workroom and she walked towards that, mentally rehearsing what she wanted to say. We are still fond of each other, still care for each other. You know that. We have a beautiful child, we can make it work, Giles. There's no real reason why we can't make our marriage work. No real reason at all.

The walk seemed to take minutes, although it was only seconds until Imogen reached the door of the workroom –

and then stopped. Giles was in there, and he *was* working. In a way. He was talking to someone sitting on a stool, the figure's long back facing Imogen, a large panama hat perched on a narrow head above a slim white neck.

And Giles was talking.

'Beautiful, you look wonderful, darling. . . .' His tone was soft, far softer than any tone he had ever used with her, even years ago, when she had sat on the same stool and modelled for him. Even then.

'. . . the colour suits you.' His hands slid down the long back tenderly. So tenderly that Imogen felt her throat constrict, bile entering her mouth, sticking to her gums and making her gag.

He crooned on. Not like Giles at all. Not like any voice he had ever used with her. Gentle, kind, a warm voice.

Who brought it out of you? Imogen thought blindly, savagely, dangerously jealous. *Who* managed to make you talk and look like that? Who? Who? . . . She walked towards them, rigid with hatred, both of them so engrossed that she was virtually upon them before Giles finally glanced into the mirror and saw her. He paled, rocked on his feet, and then looked at his companion.

Imogen looked too. Looked at the face of the person who owned the long back and the slim neck; looked, and looked, and looked, until she could see nothing else but the wide white face of the boy staring back in the mirror, and the bowed and guilty face of her husband standing behind.

147

Chapter Fifteen

Within forty-eight hours Imogen had moved out of the apartment, taking a second-floor self-contained flat in Maida Vale, with two bedrooms and a small lounge. Rowan stayed on at Suzanne's; Imogen had phoned and asked if he could stay in Brighton for a while longer. She said nothing about what had happened; she couldn't articulate the shock, couldn't admit to herself the enormity of the event, and merely said that they were having some redecorating done at South Molton Street. Suzanne suspected nothing, never realised that Imogen had moved out alone, and would stay alone; simply agreed to keep Rowan for a while longer.

The request was not that surprising. Imogen had never been a possessive mother and had always encouraged her son to be independent, wanting him to enjoy a circle of friends which extended beyond his school chums. She always knew that Suzanne would look after Rowan, just as she had looked after her. There would be outings, fun, a mixing of clever brains which could only stimulate a growing child. She said as much over the phone: 'It will be good for him, Jaco, if you don't mind.'

Suzanne glanced over to the fair-haired child sitting on the carpet in front of the television. He was watching one of the many videos Imogen had bought for him, his eyes fixed on the screen, his elbows resting on his bony knees.

'He's fine with me,' Suzanne agreed, glad of the company. 'We're off out tomorrow. A surprise trip, God help him.'

Imogen smiled, keeping her voice light. No one would have known there was anything wrong. 'Where are you taking him?'

'France,' Suzanne whispered.

Imogen's mind went back to the numerous trips Suzanne had taken her on. The jaunts over the Channel, the thrill of watching the coastline disappear – if only for a few hours. She would hire a car and take Rowan to lunch somewhere vastly expensive, buy him outrageous presents, and force him to speak French.

'I know they're all bloody foreigners, darling, but it's chic to be able to speak the language,' she would say, as she had said so many times to Imogen when she was a child.

She would push Rowan without his realising it; making life fun; making him progress sturdily into the outside world; giving him all the ammunition he needed to succeed in life. Just as she had done for Imogen. Only Imogen had failed, not succeeded, and now she felt the full impact of that failure with such despair that she could hardly continue the conversation.

Of only one thing was she sure: Rowan had to be protected. She wanted him out of the flat, away from his father, away from the corrupting chill of betrayal. For a while – however much she loved him – Imogen had to keep him away from her trauma. When she had regained her composure, then she would bring her son home – to their new home, the flat she would *make* home. But not yet, it was too soon, too much for him to understand. Too much to explain, and besides, how *could* she explain? She didn't understand it herself.

Another woman would have shattered her. But the idea that she had been rejected in favour of a *man* – the thought made Imogen close her eyes, her lips bloodless. But the image was there under her lids, as it always was: the boy in the mirror, the wide white face under the ludicrous hat. No, not a boy, not a *boy*. Not Giles, not Giles. It couldn't be, it couldn't. He was married to *her*, for God's sake! He was a married man, a father. . . . And yet, and yet . . . her mind shunted. There had been signs, but she hadn't seen them. Hadn't wanted to. His physical timidity, the lack of interest in her. Other men had wanted her, Imogen knew that; could recognise all too easily the looks Ira or Mike had given her; the look Giles never once showed. All her life men had brushed up to her, touched her, warmed to her. But not him. Not her husband.

Was that why she had wanted him? Wanted the person who held back? Wanted the challenge? No, she thought violently, she had wanted him because she loved him, and much as she felt betrayed, much as she felt bitter and injured, she couldn't deny that. Why hadn't she seen it? Why hadn't someone else? Why hadn't she been warned? . . . But she had, and she knew it. No man, on making love, should be as bereft as he had been. No man, with his wife, should weep after having sex with her. No man in love felt only misery after consummating that love.

Unless he was trapped; unless he was uncertain. She should have confided in Suzanne, even Ira; should have spoken out, articulated her doubts . . . but she had believed that she could compensate for any loss; could repair the injury; nourish an ego deflated and confused.

'The past is what we are. The past is the truth of us.' She remembered his saying the words so many times. But she hadn't wanted to know about his past, hadn't pressed him. She had been full of the future, and now the future was gone. There *was* no future. It had closed, excluded her, shut her out. The rejection left her winded. All her life Imogen had been loved; and had loved in return. Elizabeth had lived for her, Jaco had lived for her, her son lived for her. But the one man she had loved had made his choice – and it wasn't her.

Hurriedly, hardly able to avoid breaking down, Imogen finished the conversation with Jaco and put down the phone, turning around and looking at her new home. The place was rented, furniture used by others, the smell unfamiliar, the walls hung with unknown pictures. From having everything, almost overnight she had nothing. Her home had gone, her marriage ended, her hopes usurped by the wide-faced boy in the mirror.

Her hatred was vast, unlimited, all-consuming. Slowly she paced the flat, measuring out the distance, room to room, wall to wall. She had to come to terms with what had happened, for Rowan's sake, if not her own. There was a future; she had a son, that was her future. . . . But she couldn't stop seeing Giles in the tea-room at the Grand years before; couldn't stop wanting him, waiting to hear his voice, and the muffled sounds from the showroom below. You didn't want me, she thought, the realisation screaming inside her head. You didn't want me.

I can beat this, she told herself, walking into the bathroom and washing off her make-up. I can, and I will . . . but when she dried her face and looked into her reflection, all she could ask was why? Why? Why? Why? . . . And when no answer came she threw a towel over the mirror and lay down on the bed, dry-eyed, blind.

Another night passed. Dreams came in and out, unbidden. Surreal dreams of Imogen opening a glass of wine for her and Giles. But when she pulled the cork a young man's head appeared, squeezed itself out of the glass funnel, the panama hat jaunty on the broad white face. In her dream she tried to push the boy back into the bottle, strained to force him down, and when she finally did, she hid it. But the boy kept knocking on the glass side of the vessel, knocking, knocking, until Giles heard it and he let the boy out. . . .

She woke crying. Throwing back the covers she paced the floor, her back wet with sweat. The strange bedroom, with its used furniture, frightened her. This is not my home, this is not my home . . . Imogen thought hysterically, slumping down on the side of the bed and staring at the phone. I could ring Giles, I could try to . . . to do *what*? she asked herself. *What* could she do? The choice had been made – and it wasn't her. Imogen Winner. Imogen Loser. Imogen Over.

Ira found out first. He called round to the showroom and ran into Giles coming out into South Molton Street. He stopped short, glanced round guiltily.

'Hello, Ira.'

'Hi,' he responded, moving towards the side door which led up to the flat. 'I was just going to say hello to Imogen –'

'She's not here.'

He wasn't alarmed. Thought she was out shopping, or taking Rowan to school.

'So when's she back?'

Giles glanced round, dropped his voice, leaned towards Ira. 'She . . . um, she won't be back.' His tone was cool, remote. He looked, under the summer sun, like a schoolboy, unnervingly young for his thirty-one years.

'What d'you mean, she won't be back?'

'She's gone –'

Ira was irritated, alarmed. 'Gone where, for God's sake?'

'Moved out,' Giles said, still glancing round, still trying to keep his voice down. 'She's in Maida Vale.'

'Maida Vale!' Ira repeated hotly. 'What the hell is she doing there?' His eyes narrowed. 'And where's Rowan?'

'With Suzanne in Brighton.'

The full seriousness of the situation was apparent at once. This was no argument. Imogen had left, gone. And she meant it, otherwise she would never have pulled her son out of the last week of the school term and send him home to Suzanne. Something devastating must have happened to make her behave so rashly – and so hurriedly.

'What did you do to her?'

Giles looked evenly at Ira. He had the advantage of height and yet he felt belittled by the contempt in the older man's voice. He had never liked this man, this exotic Jewish hybrid, with his gaudy magazine and his gaudy lifestyle.

'You're so pally with her, you should know what happened. She left, Mazan, upped and left, with our son –'

'*Why?*' Ira countered, his voice low. But the threat in his tone carried and a couple of passers-by glanced at the ill-matched men with open curiosity.

'Because she wanted to –'

'Why?' Ira repeated, his eyes fixed on Giles.

Giles shifted his feet, his hair flopping over his forehead. Nervously he rolled up the sleeves of his silk shirt.

'We had an argument – it's over.'

'What's over? The marriage?'

'Why don't you ask her?' Giles said, turning away.

Ira caught his arm and pulled him back. 'I'm asking *you*. What happened?'

Giles tugged his arm away, his expression calm, although he felt clumsy with embarrassment. 'Listen . . . just let it drop, okay?'

'No,' Ira countered, 'it's not okay, I want to know what happened. Imogen thinks the world of you, she wouldn't up and leave unless something major had happened.'

Giles moved away, bumping into a black dustbin in his hurry to escape. For an instant Ira nearly followed him, then he called out, 'Where is she?'

'145, Carnwell Road,' Giles called back, then disappeared into the crowd.

Suzanne had been alive long enough to realise when someone was lying. And Imogen was certainly lying to her. The thought she found sobering, surprising, and then worrying. She had phoned the number at Carnwell Road several times and the answering machine had taken her messages; but Imogen hadn't called back, and now the second day without news had dawned.

It was more than worrying. Imogen wasn't the type to worry anyone. And she wasn't the type to forget her responsibilities. Rowan was fine, happy, at that moment making a model robot, but Imogen didn't know that. . . . Suzanne's thoughts ground on relentlessly, a suspicion taking hold, her hand extending hurriedly for the phone. But there was no reply from Giles's showroom either, just another blasted answering machine.

They had split up. Suzanne knew it, even though she hadn't been told. They were apart, and that was why Imogen had left Rowan with her. But why hadn't she confided in her? Why?

Thoughtfully Suzanne glanced at the preoccupied boy. So like his father, same hair, same narrow face, same way of dipping his head when he was thinking. But the eyes were Imogen's. Intelligent eyes which looked at you and held the look. Fearless.

Imogen had made her son that way, refusing to cosset him, forcing him to make friends and express his own personality – just as Suzanne had done with her. It was a good grounding for life, a way of making sure that the character was strong enough to take the knocks which were sure to come later. Oh yes, Imogen was a good mother . . .

so where the hell was she now? And why hadn't she called for two days?

The fall came unexpectedly. Imogen had been preoccupied and had gone downstairs hurriedly, missing her footing and falling down the last ten stairs. She fell awkwardly, pain searing through her right foot, her breath jerked out of her. Agonisingly slowly she tried to rise and then dropped down again, crawling back upstairs, her right foot dragging behind her.

At first she thought the pain would die down, settle, but as the hours wore on Imogen realised that she had injured herself badly. Without asking anyone for help, she called a taxi and took herself to Outpatients at St Mary's. They discovered that she had broken a bone in her foot; then set it in plaster and told her to rest it for six weeks. They asked if she had anyone to look after her. Yes, she had friends. Rest it, keep it up, they said. Yes, she agreed, taking the painkillers and getting a cab back to Carnwell Road.

It was only a broken bone, an unconvenience. That was all, Imogen told herself, phoning Suzanne as soon as she got in.

'. . . it'll be all right, I just have to rest it.'

'For how long?' Suzanne replied, aghast. 'Jesus, darling, come home, I've got a new housekeeper. Filipino, wonderful woman – even if her cooking's a culinary tribute to the canning industry. Come home, Imogen, I'll look after you.'

She backed off immediately: 'I'm okay, Jaco, honestly. . . . But I wonder if you could look after Rowan for a little while longer – until I get back on my feet.'

Suzanne's patience snapped. 'Imogen, you know that I'll look after him, but only on one condition – stop lying to me. I hate people underestimating my intelligence, and you've been doing that for the last three days.' Her voice was needle sharp. 'Have you left Giles?'

Imogen replied flatly: 'He was unfaithful.'

The words came out before she could think, or consider the impact they would have. They were true, after all.

'Giles, unfaithful?' Suzanne repeated dumbly. 'Giles doesn't know *how* to be unfaithful.'

'He does, and he has been.'

At the other end of the line Suzanne frowned, drumming her foot irritably on the carpet.

'I can't believe it.'

'I saw them,' Imogen said evenly. Be careful, she thought to herself, be careful, don't tell everything. . . . But why not? Jaco would sympathise, would commiserate . . . but I don't want commiseration, Imogen thought bitterly, I don't want her to know that I was rejected for a man. It would be too much to bear. Too humiliating, too shaming.

'You *saw* them?'

'Yes, Jaco, I saw them. And it's over. I can't go back to him now. It wouldn't be right, and it wouldn't be right for Rowan –'

'Did he admit they were having an affair?' Suzanne pressed her. 'I mean, perhaps it looked worse than it was. It could have been innocent . . . after all, Giles is hardly the womanising type.'

Imogen winced. Oh yes, she had confronted her husband when the boy had gone. She had stood up to him and watched as he began to explain, to bluster, to tell her he had tried to change . . . to *change*. She had screamed at him, incoherent with grief and confusion; accused him of marrying her under false pretences, of lying to her, of cheating her. And he had nodded and agreed, and asked her to forgive him – which was the last thing she could do. Because alone, she might have simply walked away, hidden the facts, lied, but there was Rowan to consider, and Rowan to answer to, and all the hideous truths would one day have to come out. He loved his father, he would want to know about his father, he would want to see his father, and he would, in the end, have to judge his father's behaviour.

Was he his father's child? He had his genes, his blood . . . Imogen couldn't think clearly, and had turned away from her husband as they stood in the showroom, sitting down amongst the net and the feathers. Dream hats, dream lives. . . . All their hopes were suddenly exposed for what they were – shabby and sordid, wide and wicked – reflected in the showroom mirror where the boy had been. Was he homosexual? Imogen finally asked. Yes. . . . Ah. . . . The confession didn't help. Were he and the boy . . . were they *lovers*? . . . Yes.

Perhaps he had been thinking of the boy when he had left her bed at night, Imogen thought then, bleary with shock. All the times they had been making love, had her husband been thinking of his body and his face, while looking at hers?

'Are you sure?' Suzanne repeated.

Imogen stared at the phone, fighting to remember what she had said.

'Yes, Jaco, I'm sure. . . . I need some time to think. That's why I want you to keep Rowan for a while. I've spoken to them at the school, the summer holidays begin next week, so he won't be missing anything.'

'Except you.'

'I know,' she said honestly. 'But I'm not fit to be around at the moment. Let me just settle down a bit, please.'

'Take as long as you like,' Suzanne replied, her own heart chilling as she listened to Imogen. 'But I'm worried about you. How can you cope on your own?'

'I'll be fine. Honestly. I'll work here, keep myself busy. Do Lorrie's drawings until the foot heals. I want to be alone for a time . . . please Jaco, don't press it.'

'But who'll look after you?'

'Friends . . . and there are shops nearby. I can cope.'

'But –'

'Drop it, Jaco!' she snapped. 'Just let me be on my own. Please.'

Suzanne knew better than to pursue the matter. 'Do you want to talk to Rowan?' she asked, her tone altered. Cautious.

'Yes, put him on.'

Keeping her voice light, Imogen explained to her son that she had had an accident but that she would be fine in a little while. She told him to be good, and that she would come down to Brighton and visit just as soon as she could. She said nothing about his father and, oddly enough, he did not ask about Giles. Apparently Rowan was more than happy to be with Suzanne and after another few minutes, rang off.

Slowly putting down the phone, Imogen moved to the

window painfully. The medication was wearing off. She was glad of that; glad to feel the pain, punishing herself, letting herself slide into the raw red world of her own agony. All her emotions fixed upon her foot, concentrated on the ever-present reminder of her incapacitation. She was temporarily crippled, hobbled in the heart and in the body, locked into her own distress. Clumsily she reached for the crutches and moved towards the door, wincing every time her foot hit the floor, inflicting more damage on herself than was necessary, punishing herself for what she had done, or what she had failed to do. Her husband did not love her, she had failed him as a wife, and worse, she had failed as a woman.

In the rented flat her confidence soured. She could not work, could not think clearly, and throughout the long days to come, kept the blinds drawn and the answerphone on.

'She's late with the drawings,' Lorrie said meanly, squeezing past the open window and passing Ira a glass of white wine. 'I can't reach her by phone either, even at the new number she gave me.'

Ira sipped the wine and grimaced. 'Have you ever thought of chilling it?'

'The fridge is broken,' Lorrie said dismissively. His meanness was legendary. The fridge, to Ira's certain knowledge, had been down for four summers. 'I can't rely on her any more.'

'Listen, her marriage has failed and she's broken her bloody foot, what do you expect?'

'Professionalism.'

'Aw, nuts, Lorrie,' Ira replied, laying down the glass and leaning over the desk. 'Give Imogen a break, she's in trouble.'

'I'm not here as an advice service, I need results.'

'You've *had* results for years from her,' Ira countered. 'Just back off for a while, she'll come round.'

'It's been three weeks,' Lorrie replied, fanning himself with his fat hand. 'I can't *afford* to indulge her.'

Ira's mind shifted quickly. 'You still want that spread on Mannard Blake, don't you?' Lorrie was not slow to take the hint. '. . . because if you do, then go easy on Imogen.'

'That's blackmail, Mr Mazan.'

'No, it's business,' he replied, his temper warming as quickly as the wine. 'I've done you plenty of favours over the years, you owe me one now.'

Lorrie was hot with indignation. 'Well, go and talk to her then. I can't be buggered about.'

Ira raised his eyebrows.

'Besides, that Blake character is dodgy, and he has a face like an obscene phone call,' Lorrie went on. 'He'd be perfect for a caricature. Go and see Imogen, Ira, please. Get her back to work. If anyone can, you can.'

The flattery left Ira cold; other reasons pushed him to Imogen's address, his many calls having been ignored. He thought of ringing once again, but decided against it, and instead arrived on her doorstep, where he jabbed the bell twice. There was no response. He waited, wondering what to do, and only when he was about to walk away did he catch sight of Imogen coming down the road. She walked slowly, using a pair of steel crutches, her eyes screened by sunglasses. Laboriously she made her way towards the flat, her head bent down, her attention elsewhere.

'Well, hello stranger.'

She started, leaned against the wall.

'Ira.'

Her face was without make-up, her foot still in plaster. She seemed detached; not pathetic, merely remote.

'You look bloody.'

She smiled: 'You look very *white* – it must be summer again.'

He took the plastic bag of shopping out of her hand, then the key, opening the door and standing back for her to walk in. 'How's the foot?' he asked.

'Bad. I'm afraid it'll put an end to my ballroom dancing.'

The joke never got off the ground.

Slowly she took the stairs one at the time, Ira following.

'You didn't return my calls, or Lorrie's. What's going on? He says you're not delivering on time.'

Without replying, Imogen took the keys from his hand and opened the door of the flat. It was stuffy, the blinds drawn, several newspapers left scattered. By the window the remnants of last night's supper lay drying on a plate, and a bouquet of flowers had wilted from lack of water.

He looked round, astonished: 'This is *gemütlich*.'

'I didn't know you were coming, or I'd have dusted,' she replied sarcastically, falling heavily into a chair. The room sang with despair.

'Imogen, listen, why don't you let me help?'

'I don't need help,' she said, taking off her sunglasses. Her eyes were dull.

'You should go home. Go to Brighton, stay with Suzanne for a while. She'd get you back on your feet in no time.'

'I don't want to go to Brighton,' she said woodenly, without feeling.

'I know it's difficult for you, but giving in is not the answer.'

Silently she reached down to her foot and lifted it on to a stool in front of her. Ira moved forward to help.

'I can manage,' she said warningly.

He stopped in his tracks. This was not the Imogen he knew; this was someone altogether different. A cold woman, a hard woman. Even her appearance had changed; the glamour had gone, the sexuality repressed. Even on crutches the old Imogen could have turned heads, but this one was locked in on herself. Asexual, swamped in an overlarge shirt, aggressively distant.

'You need help.'

'I need peace and quiet,' she replied, her eyes flickering.

'I'm sorry about you and Giles.'

'Thank you.'

'Oh, shit, Imogen!' he snapped. 'Snap out of it, for God's sake. You have friends, people who care about you, a son. I know it's been hard –'

She closed her eyes, effectively blocking him out. Ira saw the gesture and slumped into a chair beside her. The room was chokingly hot, and smelt of paint. Suffocating, full of sour air.

'Get yourself tidied up, we'll go out for lunch.'

'I don't want to go out,' she said simply.

He studied her profile, thinking of the time he had driven

her back to Brighton so many years before. The life which had emanated from her then had been like a fire, a warmth which drew people. Brave and confident, she had always made him laugh, and stayed the one constant in a tired and dirty world. He knew her qualities and could count them in his sleep, and he realised then that he dreaded the loss of her more than he dreaded anything on earth.

'Let me help. I've always told you that you can count on me as a friend. Talk to me, Imogen, please.'

She laid her head back against the chair, and opening her eyes, turned to look at him. He expected her to speak, but there was such hopelessness in her that she seemed diminished, cowed by the room itself, and stayed silent.

'I saw Giles. He said you'd broken up.'

'Everyone knows, I suppose.'

He nodded. 'Yes, but no one knows the reason *why* you broke up.'

She stared at him, held his gaze. It seemed as though the real Imogen wanted to communicate, but another part of her prevented it.

'It doesn't matter anyway.'

'Of course it does!' he said fiercely. 'You have to talk things out.'

'Why?'

He was momentarily wrongfooted. 'Because it helps.'

'Why?'

'Imogen, don't keep saying why!' he replied angrily. Ashamed, he dropped his voice. 'I think you should go home.'

She closed her eyes again, cutting him off.

'Go home, please. Recover. Get back to yourself.'

Her mouth opened, then closed. Words balled up in her throat. She had wanted to talk, longed for Ira or someone to come to the door. But when the bell rang she hadn't answered it, just as she hadn't returned the calls on the answerphone. After a while, neighbours left shopping outside, with a note; necessities were delivered, the shops dropping off milk and papers. Her injury provided her with the perfect reason to withdraw; she couldn't get about, and before long, she didn't want to.

Instead she withdrew. The medication made her hazy, at times unsteady on her feet. Once she had even fallen, breaking a plate. After that, she had weaned herself off the painkillers, preferring to feel everything instead. But the shock of Giles's betrayal had unbalanced her and, unable to function normally, physically or mentally, she began a slow and unstoppable slide into despair.

And the image replayed and replayed inside her head. The boy in the mirror, the reflection of her husband's face, and the confession afterwards. . . . She dreamed that the furniture in the flat was growing, towering over her, the cream walls building higher and higher, the door handle rising above the ground so that she could never reach it to turn it and escape. Then in her dreams, someone took away her crutches, hid them, so she had to crawl around the floor. . . .

She woke up only when a door banged, or a dog barked. Woke to the realisation of the rented flat and the full horror of her situation; woke dizzy with fatigue and thick with depression, the whole of the future blacked out. Non-existent.

'Go home to Brighton,' Ira said again, watching her and seeing her slip away instant by instant.

'No,' Imogen said simply.

Brighton was another world, a good world, a world closed to her. In Brighton, Rowan was safe. She had been safe there too. . . . Her mind wandered in the hot, airless, stale room. . . . After another moment, she even forgot that Ira was there.

161

Chapter Sixteen

'I don't like it, I don't like it at all,' Suzanne said over the phone to Elizabeth. 'Imogen's depressed. Very depressed.'

The word panicked both of them. They both knew too well what it meant. Depression. Imogen. Julie. How bad was it? How bad could they let it become?

'I thought she was coming round,' Elizabeth said, thinking of the last phone call. Imogen had sounded strained, but she had managed to convince her grandmother that she was better. She had lied to protect her. How they all lied to protect each other.

'How bad is she?'

'Bad,' Suzanne said flatly. They had no secrets, these women, only a complete and unabridged trust. 'If it had only been the marriage breaking up, I think she could have coped, but when she injured herself as well she seemed to go downhill fast.' Suzanne paused. Rowan was out with a friend of hers, gone to the Aquarium. It was safe to talk. 'She thinks she's failed. She thinks that she's let us down –'

Elizabeth snorted: 'Rubbish!'

'I know that, and you know that, but she doesn't. She thinks she should have made a success of the marriage, and now she's ashamed.'

'But you said that it was Giles who had been unfaithful to her, not the other way about.'

'That makes no difference!' Suzanne said sharply. 'Imogen doesn't see it as his fault. More like hers. *She* should have known, *she* should have done something. *She's* to blame.'

'It's ridiculous,' Elizabeth said flatly, her protective instinct raised, her old fight coming to the fore. 'If anyone is to blame for this, it's Giles.'

'But it doesn't matter who's to blame really, does it? All that matters is that we pull her out of this depression. She thinks she's protecting us by not confiding, but she's giving up and she can't even think clearly any more . . . I'm going to London tomorrow,' Suzanne said suddenly. 'I spoke to Ira and he saw her the other day. He's worried about her, and much as I distrust the creep, I know how much he cares about Imogen.'

'No, don't go to London,' Elizabeth said sternly, her thoughts running on as she looked out of the window beside her.

It was hot in London, but in Little Lever the day was overcast, threatening rain. Northern weather, bringing the children home from the streets, and the birds into the shelter of the window ledges.

'No, you mustn't go,' she said again. 'There's another way.'

Carefully she spelt out her plan. Suzanne listened, horrified, her voice rising.

'*No, never!*'

'Trust me, Mrs Jacobs, I know this child. I knew her before you did. She is stronger than you think.'

'It's too dangerous,' Suzanne said, for once in her life nervous. 'It's too risky.'

'I know my granddaughter. She can take it.'

'No,' Suzanne insisted.

'Yes,' said Elizabeth, forcing the younger woman, driving her to agree. 'We have to do it, the time is right now.'

'I can't –'

Elizabeth's courage was formidable: 'Do you love her?'

'You know I do.'

'And do you trust me?'

Suzanne did not hesitate. 'Implicitly.'

'Then we do it.'

The pact was made in that instant.

The following morning Elizabeth travelled down to London by train, Suzanne meeting her at Victoria station and driving both of them over to Imogen's flat. The blinds were down at the windows, and the bell went unanswered.

Fiercely Suzanne jammed at it, five, six times, until finally a voice answered.

'Yes?'

'Imogen,' she said firmly. 'Open the door, it's Suzanne.'

The door buzzed, the two women striding in and moving up to the second floor. Imogen was dressed in a soiled T-shirt and jeans, her hair greasy, flat to her head and she was supporting herself on crutches. She seemed indifferent, not even surprised to see Suzanne, but when she spotted Elizabeth she tried to straighten up and smiled half-heartedly. 'Gran.'

Elizabeth moved over to her and hugged her quickly. 'Well, love, you look a proper mess, and no mistake,' she said, firmly ushering her back into the flat.

The shaded, soiled atmosphere swamped Elizabeth, the bowl of rotten fruit and the sink full of dishes catching her eye. She sensed the depression in every inch of the walls, knew it, recognised it from her own past. In that instant she expected to see Graham or Julie, and tasted the sour bile of fear in her mouth. Oh no, she thought, not my baby. Not Imogen.

'Get yourself cleaned up,' she said, watching Suzanne's face as she glanced, shellshocked, at the flat. 'I'll tidy this mess away.'

Imogen was clumsy, muzzy-headed. 'Why? Where are we going?'

'We're going for a drive,' Elizabeth said shortly. 'Get ready, Imogen. Go on!'

Obediently she struggled to the bedroom, the door closing behind her. Suzanne glanced round, then looked at Elizabeth. 'Dear God,' she said, aghast. 'I had no idea.' Her long nose sniffed at the air. 'It smells odd in here.'

'That's despair you're smelling,' Elizabeth said unemotionally. 'I could recognise it anywhere.' Quickly she rolled up her sleeves and filled the sink with soapy water, then she lifted the blinds and threw open the windows. 'No one can describe that smell until they experience it. It's not unpleasant, not sour, just hopeless. At its worst, people die with that smell about them.'

The warm London air swelled in the flat, birdsong coming

valiantly over the sound of traffic. Hurriedly Elizabeth washed the dishes, Suzanne folding the newspapers and pushing them into the bin, then throwing away the dead plants. Both women worked on in silence, too shocked to speak further, too concentrated on what was to come.

Half an hour wore past slowly, then Imogen came back fully dressed, her hair newly brushed, even a little lip gloss on the otherwise dowdy face. She seemed ashamed, clumsy, unable to apologise or explain, but when she saw her grandmother drying the dishes, she stumbled over to her.

'No, Gran.'

Elizabeth shook her head. 'It needed doing. Now,' she said, drying her hands, 'are you ready?'

Imogen knew better than to argue. The two women she loved above everything had come for her. The rest she would wait to find out. Only one thing bothered her.

'Where's Rowan?'

'With Tita,' Suzanne said reassuringly. 'She's very competent, don't worry. He even likes her cooking. Brave boy.'

They moved down the stairs, Suzanne helping Imogen, Elizabeth following. Outside, Suzanne's dark grey Mercedes waited, a ticket on the windscreen.

'Oh, shit!' she said, screwing the paper and throwing it into the gutter. 'Come on, Imogen, get in.'

She slid into the front passenger seat, Elizabeth into the back; Suzanne turned on the ignition and then pulled out into the traffic.

She drove as she had always done. Fast. Weaving and dodging in the London traffic she soon cleared the capital and made for the motorway, her hand stretching forward to turn on the stereo. To the sounds of Mozart the three travelled on, hour after hour passing, Imogen shifting her position frequently to get comfortable.

Suzanne glanced over: 'How's the foot?'

'Painful.'

'You want some tablets?'

'No,' Imogen said, adding softly, 'No, thanks.'

In the back, Elizabeth sat straight-backed, her handbag on her lap. She had been travelling for most of the day and yet she wasn't tired; she had had all the rest she needed for a while. The speed didn't worry her; neither did Suzanne's driving, although she closed her eyes sometimes when she overtook, and the noise of the music irritated her on the high notes. Otherwise she was fine. Fine. Ready and willing to do what had to be done.

She watched the back of Imogen's head and when her granddaughter drifted off to sleep she touched her shoulder for an instant to adjust her blouse. Imogen didn't stir; too tired to wake, or to think. Too tired to do anything any more. Elizabeth did not worry about what was to come; she had made up her mind, and knew with instinctive confidence that she was right. But Suzanne had been reluctant, indeed once or twice Elizabeth had caught her eye in the mirror and given her the thumbs-up sign to reassure her.

I know what I'm doing, the gesture said. Trust me, I know this child – have I ever done anything to harm her? Have I? . . . Suzanne's eyes returned to the road, turning at the sign pointing to the North. We're going home, Elizabeth thought, suddenly exhilarated as she reached into her bag. The photograph was old, the frame brass, cheap. But it was still Graham's photograph and it calmed Elizabeth for the instant she looked at it. Then, having regained her composure, she wrapped it in a handkerchief and pushed it back into her bag.

The morning passed, the afternoon coming in and still Suzanne drove, only calling in for petrol once. Elizabeth asked her if she needed a break, but she was running on adrenalin and didn't want to stop.

'No, I'm fine, let's get on with it.'

They both looked at Imogen. Darkly asleep. 'Are you sure about this?' Suzanne asked for the twelfth time.

Elizabeth nodded.

'Okay,' Suzanne said, starting up the Mercedes again. 'Off we go.'

The weather darkened around the Midlands, and faded as they reached Lancashire, finally arriving in Manchester in a downpour. Frowning, Suzanne looked at the map her dark eyebrows drawn together, the windscreen wipers whooshing against the wet windows.

'Where are we?' Imogen said, waking.

'Just wait a little longer,' Elizabeth said, touching her arm. 'Just trust me.' She glanced at Suzanne. 'Do you know the way?'

'No one could possibly know the way up here.' She turned the map round, screwing up her eyes. 'Even Ranulph Fiennes would have his work cut out for him.'

'Are we on the right road?'

'Listen, we could be in bloody Belgrade for all I know. Don't they have signs up north?'

'What's that?' Elizabeth said, pointing through the rain.

'Oh,' Suzanne said simply, pulling out from the kerb.

It took another thirty minutes for them to find the place. Elizabeth's knowledge of the roads was not good; she had always come by train and bus before, but she recognised the roads and began to help, telling Suzanne where to turn. Imogen was silent, unresponsive. She asked no questions, just waited. Trusted.

This place used to be deserted, Elizabeth wanted to say. When I first came here, the bus only stopped at the end of the road and you had to walk the rest of the way. It was all right in the summer, but in the winter the wind could needle its way into your bones. Look, she wanted to tell Imogen, there used to be grass banks there, and once your grandfather picked me a daffodil. Your *grandad*, love. You never knew about him, did you? Time you did, love, time you did. . . . Her hand rested on her bag, feeling for the photograph underneath. Consoling herself, taking comfort from touching his image.

The entrance drive was short, the hospital huge and flat-fronted. Unwelcoming, dour, under a leaden sky. Imogen watched without recognition, Suzanne depressing a shiver as she turned up the heating in the car. The front doors were closed, bolted, the car park empty apart from an ambulance and a consultant's Rover outside the Catering doors. Slowly Suzanne eased the car into a space and then turned off the engine.

Her eyes caught Elizabeth's in the mirror again. Well, what now? . . . Trust me, the look came back. Believe me, I know what I'm doing. . . . They had planned it all, until this last moment, and now Suzanne didn't know what to do. She seemed older, oddly out of place in these surroundings. Too dark, too foreign, too nervous.

'Come on,' Elizabeth said to Imogen.

She turned, her eyes wide with uncertainty.

'Come on,' Elizabeth repeated, heaving herself out of the car and opening the door on her granddaughter's side. Clumsily, Imogen got to her feet, struggling with the crutches. She shivered once in the unfamiliar cold air.

'Well, are you coming too?' Elizabeth asked, bending down and looking at Suzanne.

'No.'

'Are you sure?'

Suzanne looked into the older woman's eyes, then glanced at Imogen who had moved several feet away.

'If you're wrong –'

Elizabeth cut her off. 'I'm not.'

'But if you are –'

She moved away suddenly, taking her granddaughter's arm and steering her towards the side entrance.

Obediently Imogen went where she was guided. The place rang hollowly with the sounds of bells and phones ringing; a nurse rushing past fixing on her cap as she went. She asked no questions even then, only felt the pressure of her grandmother's hand on her elbow as they moved further into the building.

Having been housebound, Imogen was unsteady, almost dizzy, her progress slow. The place frightened her, unsettled her, the faces of the patients vacant, without expression. The smell was clinical, unfeeling, the walls bare except for the markings of directions. Ward One, Ward Two, Day Room. At the end of the first passage she stopped, suddenly alarmed.

'Where are we?'

'A hospital.'

She looked at her grandmother, frightened. 'I'm *not* ill. I'm *not*!'

Elizabeth soothed her at once. 'I know. We're visiting someone, love. That's all.'

Imogen wanted to go, to leave, to be back in her flat. To be safe, cocooned. She didn't want to be here. Why had they brought her here? To see whom? She didn't know anyone in hospital; especially not a hospital like this one. Her panic scratched at her and made her stop again, suddenly defiant.

'No.'

Elizabeth had been prepared for this and kept her tone even. 'Come on, nothing will hurt you. I promise. Don't you trust me?'

Imogen looked into the plump face, at the blue eyes, even and steady. She saw a dumpy woman, old and yet strong as a lion. She saw the woman who had looked after her all her life – and she saw the woman she trusted above anyone.

'Come on,' Elizabeth said, guiding Imogen onwards.

They turned into the Day Room in time to see two others leave. The room was suddenly theirs; only one other person remained, and she wasn't even looking at them. She was looking out of the window, as she always was. A middle-aged woman in a print dress and short white socks, a book on her lap. A woman with a moon face and the heavy-lidded eyes of someone on permanent medication.

Elizabeth guided Imogen over to her, helping her grand-daughter into a seat.

Alarmed, Imogen edged away from the woman, glancing at Elizabeth. But her grandmother wasn't looking at her, she was rummaging in her bag. Finally she brought out a brush and then, smiling, she began to comb her daughter's hair. The action was rhythmic, gentle, the brush making the thin hair fan out, giving it a momentary vigour and life.

'I've brought you a visitor,' she said, smiling at Imogen.

She was rigid in her seat, not understanding.

'. . . a new face. Someone different to see you. . . .'

Imogen said nothing, just stared at the immobile woman who stared, in turn, stared at the blank window. Her eyes never blinked, never moved, her hands lifeless.

'. . . and I brought some chocolate for you too,' Elizabeth went on. 'Dark chocolate, your favourite.'

Imogen could take no more and struggled to get up.

'Sit down!' Elizabeth ordered.

Startled, Imogen slumped back into her seat, studying the woman in front of her. There was no one there, she realised, no one to fear or even pity. The woman was a shell, a skin, an empty case from which some personality had walked. But who was she? *Why* had her grandmother brought her here?

'The sister said you'd been watching television,' Elizabeth went on to her daughter. 'That's nice. I used to have a black and white set, but now I've got colour. So much better. Mrs Jacobs got it for me.'

Still no response.

There never was, but Imogen wasn't to know that. Wasn't to know that for twenty-seven years Julie Forest hadn't responded to anything or anyone.

'Who is she?' Imogen asked suddenly, fiercely.

Taking in her breath, Elizabeth glanced over to her, her hand poised in the action of brushing her daughter's hair.

'Don't you know, Imogen?'

'No!' she snapped. '*I don't*! Who is she?'

'Look at her,' Elizabeth said gently, taking her daughter's head in her hands and turning her face towards Imogen. 'Look at her.'

Frightened, Imogen studied the woman's face. The blank eyes, the lifeless skin, the flat, unfeeling, uncaring expression. She stared and stared, and suddenly she thought she saw something, or *somebody*, else. Then she panicked and frantically heaved herself to her feet, struggling with her crutches, half falling as she staggered to the door. No, she thought, no, it couldn't be . . . it *couldn't* be. . . .

But she was slow, too slow, to outrun Elizabeth. Stout she might be, and old, but she was quicker than Imogen and caught up with her as she made her way down the passage to the Exit doors. Fiercely she caught hold of her granddaughter's arms and turned her round.

'Let me go!' Imogen hissed.

'You know, don't you?' Elizabeth said, her grip tightening. 'You know she's your mother, don't you?'

Imogen tried to shake her off: 'My mother is dead. Dead! You told me so, you told me that for years.' Her glance moved down the corridor. 'If that's my mother, why did you lie to me. *Why?*'

'To protect you!' Elizabeth shouted back. 'Because I loved you and never wanted you to know what had happened to her. Because I wanted you to grow up without worries, without problems, without responsibility. I didn't tell you because I loved you.'

'So why tell me now?' Imogen shouted hoarsely. 'Why now, after everything that's happened to me? Why bring me here now and show me my mother now. *Why now?*'

Elizabeth stared into her granddaughter's eyes – and then answered her. 'I wanted to show you what you could become.'

The words made Imogen gasp.

'I brought you to show you what you could lose. For God's sake, Imogen, don't get like her. Don't –'

Frantically Imogen shook her off and began to hobble away. Elizabeth's heart shuddered. Maybe she *had* been wrong, maybe it was too much; maybe it would push Imogen over the edge, not save her.

But the thought rested in her head for only an instant. She *was* right, she knew she was. . . . Quickly Elizabeth hurried up the passageway, catching up with her granddaughter and pushing her against the hospital wall, all kindness suspended.

'You want to give up? Then give up! Give up your child, give up your son. Just like she gave you up. She rejected you and now you want to reject your child too. I thought you were better than her. *Stronger* than her. I thought you had more guts.' She pushed her granddaughter, poked her finger into her shoulder, goaded her. 'I brought you up tough. I brought you up to be a fighter. *So now fight!* You want to give up, you want to give in?' Elizabeth pointed down the corridor. 'You want to be like her? *That's* giving up, *that's* giving in. That's your mother, and if you're like her I was wrong about you. Think about her, Imogen, think about how she looks, what she is. How she spends her life. Think about this place and that room, and tell me –' she jerked Imogen's face towards her. – 'tell me, look into my eyes and tell me you want to give up.'

Imogen stared at her grandmother's face, at the woman who had loved her and protected her, and suddenly, helplessly, she began to cry.

But Elizabeth wasn't about to let her off. 'Tell me, are you going to give up?'

'No,' Imogen said between sobs.

'What did you say?'

'I said no.'

'I can't hear you, Imogen,' she shouted. *'Tell me again.'*

'No! No! No!!!!!!'

Elizabeth nodded, then took hold of her granddaughter, and rocked her for a long minute.

'It's time to go home now, love. It's time to go home.'

PART THREE

Look in my face: my name is
Might-have-been

('A Subscription', Dante Gabriel Rossetti)

Chapter Seventeen

'Welcome back,' Ira said simply, passing Imogen a bunch of white lilies.

She smiled hugely. 'Oh, lilies, how lovely,' she said. 'Who died?'

'Don't overdo the gratitude,' he responded, walking into the flat. 'You know how emotional excess embarrasses me.' His glance settled on the boy sitting by the window. 'Hi, Rowan.'

Rowan turned, grinned, and passed Ira an instruction book. 'I've got a new computer. Mum bought it for me this morning.'

'It can do everything apart from iron,' Imogen said wryly.

Ira turned, caught her eye. Held it. 'You okay?'

She nodded. 'I'm fine. More than fine. I'm back.'

'You look good,' he said approvingly. 'Those crutches did nothing for you.'

She laughed, walking into the kitchen and making some coffee for them.

Two months had passed. No one would ever know what they had cost Imogen, no one would ever be allowed to know. After seeing her mother she had gone back to Brighton with Suzanne and slowly, over the weeks, had crawled back into herself. She only realised later how close she had come to shedding her personality; how her life and spirit had teetered on the borderline of sanity. Her grandmother had saved her. With Suzanne's help. She owed them her life, and knew it, and took it upon herself to reward them.

I will be happy, she told herself. And I will make my child

happy. It never occurred to her to include a man in her future plans. She was still too raw from her marriage collapse to consider any other relationship. Time would tell, but for now she had to think of the present, and besides, her confidence was too shaky to risk any further rejection.

Which was why she treasured Ira so much. He made no demands, although he was attracted to her, and when she returned to London he was the first to visit.

'Will you divorce Giles?' he asked bluntly.

She nodded. The decision had been made down in Rottingdean village, by the pond, on a day spiked with rain. Summer rain, coming from over the Channel. There was no other feasible outcome apart from divorce; the marriage was over, ended. What point was there in carrying on? There could be no reconciliation; best to finish it once and for all. So when she returned to Suzanne's she asked to speak to her lawyer – and Tony Rosenstein did the rest.

'We'll get a divorce on the grounds of adultery,' she told Ira.

'His, of course.'

She glanced at him steadily. 'Yes, his.'

'He must be mad.'

'No,' Imogen said calmly. 'Homosexual.'

Ira whistled softly under his breath. The old rumour came back suddenly. So it hadn't been jealousy, a petty-minded comment made by someone who was envious of Giles Winner's success. It had been true all along. He felt a quick nudge of guilt. Maybe he should have hinted something, suggested something to Imogen, warned her? But how could he have done? Half the men in London were accused of being gay at some time or other, and most of the rumours turned out to be false. But not this time . . . and not for Imogen.

He watched her out of the corner of his eye, musing, wondering how she felt. How the knowledge must have hurt her, humiliated her. The irony was incredible. Here she was, lusted after by most men, and the one she married turned out to be gay. Oh God, Imogen, what a bloody mess.

'It must have been a hell of a shock.'

She nodded, then asked him, 'D'you know the story about the twins?'

He shook his head.

'Well, there were twins and it was their birthday. So the father takes the first twin to a stable and says "Happy Birthday" and opens the stable door. The stable is *full* of manure. Naturally, the kid cries and runs off. Then the father gets the second child and repeats the process, only this time the boy shrugs, walks into the stable, and closes the door.' Imogen paused for effect. 'A few hours later, the father comes back and looks in, to find his son digging away, shifting the manure. "What are you doing?" he asked. The kid turns, smiles, and says, "Well, with all this shit there must be a pony somewhere." '

Ira burst out laughing.

Imogen raised her eyebrows; 'That's my motto from now on, Ira. After all this shit, there must be a pony somewhere.'

'The worst is over.'

'God, I hope so,' she said wearily. 'I should have known about Giles.'

'How could you? You were very young when you married.'

Imogen frowned, pushing away the coffee. 'I *should* have known.'

'You don't,' Ira said briskly. 'I was the last to know about my wife.'

Startled, Imogen looked at Ira.

'I never knew you were married.'

'Not many people do,' he responded, leaning back in his seat and picking imagined flecks off his trouser leg. A nervous habit, giving him away. 'We weren't married long. She was a dancer.' He laughed outright. 'Seriously she *was* a dancer, not one of the pin-ups. I met her in Rome when I was just starting the magazine. She was beautiful in that full-throated, full-bodied way Italian women are, and she was older than I was and very *athletic*. We married in a frenzy and had a child in a frenzy, and only after I heard about two other men she was seeing, only then did I divorce her in a frenzy.'

'You have a child?' Imogen asked, turning her body to face him, her curiosity alerted. This wasn't like Ira, he never confided anything personal.

'I have a daughter of eighteen, called Tusha. Tusha

177

Mazan. The word is supposed to mean "wellborn", but I think that was another of my wife's many fabrications. Tusha has always lived with her mother; astonishingly, she was a good parent.' He stroked the length of his nose with his forefinger. 'Now I'm not too sure.'

'So where's your daughter now?'

'In Italy still,' he replied, 'until September. I've persuaded my ex-wife to send her to finishing school in Switzerland. It's a conventional thing to do, I know, but it might help her to settle down.' His eyes narrowed, under the shadowed lids. He seemed older, suddenly serious, with no trace of the flamboyant showman for once. 'She's very headstrong. Stubborn. Too much like her mother for comfort.'

Imogen listened carefully. 'Does she look like you?'

He laughed suddenly. 'No! She has her own special attraction, and she uses it. She could, to be frank, become a real whore.'

The word pumped into the air, its savagery apparent.

'You think finishing school will calm her down?' Imogen asked.

'I don't think a frontal lobotomy would calm her down,' Ira said coldly. 'She isn't the type to be controlled. . . . I should have been more involved with her upbringing. I blame myself for that. So many mistakes, Imogen. We all make them in life, but we can't go on blaming ourselves for ever.' He drained his cup. 'I envy the way you've brought up Rowan. I admire that. How will you cope on your own?'

She shrugged: 'I was pretty much on my own when I was married, Ira. Giles never took much interest in his son. We'll cope.' Her voice hardened, took on an edge. 'I'm going to go out to work –'

'What for? You have enough money not to work.'

She put up her hands to stop him. 'No, hear me out. I *want* to do this. Suzanne has supported me for years, then I was married. For the first time in my life I want to look after myself. I can do it, I *have* to do it.' She studied him for a long instant, trying to make him understand. 'My grandmother worked like a dog for her family, I want to prove that I can stand on my own two feet.'

'I doubt if Lorrie will have enough work for you to bring in a full-time wage.'

'Then I'll get something else.'

He frowned, cautiously critical. 'Imogen, you aren't trained for anything. You can't just go out there and get a job.'

'Why not?' she countered. 'My grandmother did it.'

'But you're not her. She worked –'

'As a housekeeper?' Imogen finished for him. Gently she punched his arm. 'What a snob you are, Mr Mazan.'

'But be reasonable, you have a position to keep up.'

'As what?' Imogen replied, astonished. 'I'll soon be a divorced woman with a child. A single parent, living in rented accommodation.'

'The difference is,' he said coolly, 'that you have a choice. You have money. You could ask Suzanne for help; buy a place of your own, or even go back to Brighton –'

'That would defeat the purpose, and you know it,' she retorted hotly. 'I want to make my own money, in my own way. I can do it. I know I can.'

'Listen, I've got more experience than you, and I'm telling you, it will be harder than you think.'

'Everything on earth is harder than you think,' she replied bluntly. 'Marriage was harder than you think. . . . Don't patronise me, Ira, I know it won't be easy. You see, I've been spoilt. I took everything for granted. I was loved, protected, cosseted all my life. I was told I was pretty, clever, amusing. I wanted Giles and I got him. Why not? Everyone else had loved me, so why shouldn't he?' She shook her head; a slow fall of hair shifted then settled on her shoulders. 'I didn't think for one minute that it could go wrong. That's the curse of confidence, Ira. To be blind to the possibility of failure. I thought I had it all mapped out, and then it began to fall apart, seam by seam. Slowly, but very surely, I lost my status. I no longer held the premier position in my husband's life; his mother snaked back in, then his lover. From having been always number one I became number three – at the back of the line. Rejected, demoted. And I couldn't cope with it.'

'No woman could have done.'

She frowned. 'I don't know. Perhaps some could have coped better than others. I didn't. I'm ashamed of that.' Her face brightened. 'But I'm going to change, Ira. I'm going to prove that I can make a life for myself and Rowan – on my own.'

'If you need help –'

She smiled: 'Yeah, I know.'

It wasn't as easy as she had thought. Ira was right, she had no qualifications, and so, naturally, her value on the job market was limited. Having worked out her finances, Imogen realised that she needed a part-time job to supplement the wage she received from Lorrie. It was a good sum, but not enough to cover all the expenses incurred by her and her son. Luckily, Rowan's school fees were met by Suzanne, and although Imogen could have applied to Giles for maintenance, she asked nothing from him.

And he offered nothing. He only requested time to see his son. Affection at a distance. One weekend a month, please. Fine, she said. One weekend a month it is. Are you okay? Sure, how are you? Fine. . . . They never said they missed each other, never lied that much. Imogen never asked after his work, and Giles never asked how she was coping. He presumed, as did everyone else, that she would be supported by Suzanne. He was wrong.

'You're working in a part-time job? You must be bloody crazy,' Lorrie said to Imogen on the Friday morning she delivered her latest caricatures. 'What the hell are you trying to prove?'

She was wearing white trousers and a long white jacket with a black shirt. Stunning at ten paces.

'That I can cope.'

'So who cares?' Lorrie said, pushing the intercom buzzer and waving the drawings at the printer when he walked in. 'You know that I can't give you any more work.'

'I never asked,' she replied evenly.

Lorrie liked to gossip; liked to gather information to pass round.

'So where are you working?'

'In Vigo Street.'

'Doing what?'

'As a telephonist in Fillibert and Royal's.'

Lorrie slapped his hands flat on the desk. 'Jesus! You're *mad!*'

She had expected the response; was prepared for it. It was the same response she had had from Suzanne. But not from Elizabeth. Her grandmother had approved. Welcomed the news.

'You don't know how to work a switchboard,' he said dismissively. 'The nearest thing you ever got to that was ringing Directory Enquiries.'

'I've been trained,' she said doggedly, refusing to be baited even though she was getting steadily more uncomfortable.

She had been hired as a telephonist, and had presumed that she would be accepted quite readily in the small advertising company. She was wrong. Having told no one of her background, or her husband, she was amazed at the way she was treated: as a menial, no more. Her voice was mimicked, and when she used the paging system – a means by which she could call out a message through speakers all over the building – her words came back, echoed by the listeners. Flushed with embarrassment, Imogen struggled on, trying valiantly to master the lists of names and corresponding intercom numbers. But there was little encouragement to do the job well. If she made a mistake, people slammed down their phones and others sighed extravagantly in exasperation.

Their rudeness baffled Imogen, as much as their over-inflated egos; their habit of ringing in on car phones when they were just round the corner struck her as absurd. She had grown up with much sharper minds, and found their pretensions laughable. She also found out about their weaknesses – the way they held meetings three times a week in the boardroom, which only a few select cients attended, the 'pitch' being a limited viewing of some skinflicks hot off the Soho press. She told Ira, knowing it would make him laugh, but her employers had no sense of humour. The men were irritating, making frequent sexual comments; the women patronising and condescending.

Apparently the latter regarded Imogen as a loser, a poor little rich girl who had fallen on hard times. And oh, how they loved to rub it in.

At first Imogen found the situation baffling, then threatening, and then finally she responded with her deadliest weapon. Her tongue.

'So, sweetheart, what are you doing this weekend?' one of the designers asked, ogling her over the desk.

'Avoiding you,' Imogen said deftly.

Another tried a different tack.

'Come out for a drink. We could have fun.'

She looked the man up and down, then replied, in cut-glass tones, 'I'm sorry, I don't think I could go for a man who looks like he's been dressed with a shovel.'

She thought that once bitten, they would shy off. She was wrong again. Her responses, designed to fend off attention, provoked it instead.

'Listen, you can't be doing this for real,' one director, Harvey Preston, said to her. 'What are you *really* up to?'

'I'm earning my living, that's all,' Imogen replied evenly.

He was suddenly nasty with irritation. 'Do you know you're full of shit?'

'I'm sure you're right, Mr Preston. You do seem to be an authority on that subject.'

But she knew that she couldn't keep it up for ever. The job covered her expenses, but she dreaded any of her old acquaintances finding out exactly what she did. The fall from grace would have been too much to bear, following a marriage and health breakdown. Tentatively, at first, she had hoped to make friends at Fillibert and Royal's, but there was an unmarked division between the ranks, and she was low in the pecking order. The directors did not mix with the menials; the secretaries did not mix with the telephonist; and the account executives only mixed with God.

Having been socially in demand all her life, she found the decline in status winding. Imogen was no longer in demand – if anything she was ostracised, seen as a woman down on her luck having to make ends meet as best she could. The truth rankled.

'So get a better job,' Ira said when she phoned him one night.

Imogen had just had a bath and was wrapped up in a towelling robe and sitting on the edge of the bed. Next door she could hear the sound of a televised football match, and Rowan cheering on his side.

'I *can't* leave the bloody job. As you so rightly said, Ira, I'm not qualified.' Imogen chewed her lip thoughtfully. 'If only I could get more work doing the caricatures.'

'It's a limited market –'

'Tell me about it,' she replied acidly. 'You know, the thing that really gets to me is I'm smarter than those idiot directors at Fillibert and Royal, and they treat me like a rubbing rag.'

'You threaten them.'

'How?' Imogen wailed.

'Because they can't work you out,' Ira responded. 'They know you've got class and they're not stupid enough to believe that your career prospects are limited to working as a telephonist for them.' He paused. 'Think about it – they know you're out of their league, but they can't work out *why* you're there. It must be driving them mad.'

'I'm doing it for the money. Why else?'

Ira was thoughtful for a moment. 'Do they know about the caricatures?'

She pulled a face. 'No, I've kept my mouth shut about those. Not that I haven't been tempted to tell them. You know, the other day I saw a design they were doing for a new health drink and one of the directors asked me what I thought. So naturally I told him –'

'Oh God.'

'I *was* polite about it, Ira. I just made a couple of suggestions and when I'd finished he gave me such a bloody foul look and stormed off. Later I heard one of the secretaries talking about "critics being people without talent". Stupid bitch.'

He laughed, but knew how such slights must rankle with her.

'So how long are you going to keep it up?'

'I don't know, Ira, I honestly don't,' she said quietly. 'I'm glad of the wage and for the moment I feel pretty good about things. I'm looking after myself and Rowan, and that's what I said I would do. As for the future, who knows? Lorrie might want more work from me – although I doubt that – or someone else might. . . . I'll tell you one thing though, if those creeps at work don't stop provoking me, they'll live to regret it.'

Ira smiled, relishing the idea of a showdown. It appealed to the malicious streak in his nature. 'That sounds dangerous,' he said.

'I mean it. If they don't back off, one day I'll really let rip.' She paused. 'Just let's hope something turns up before then.'

Ira frowned. 'Listen, much as I'd like to, Imogen, you know I can't use your work in my magazine. . . .'

She grinned mischievously. 'That's a shame, I'm good at nudes.'

'. . . but I could ask around for you, see if anyone else is looking for talent. And you *do* have talent, Imogen, always remember that. You have a quick eye and a quicker brain. Those last cartoons you did for Lorrie in the March issue – now those were *funny*.'

'Yes,' she agreed, 'but I had a gift with that man Mannard Blake. I've seen better looking Photofits.'

'He speaks well of you too,' Ira said wryly, changing the subject. 'What about Rowan? How's he coping?'

Imogen shifted the phone to her other ear. 'He's fine, talks about his father a lot. He loves Giles, so I encourage it. I don't want them to be enemies, that wouldn't be fair.'

'And you're always that,' he said gently.

'Thanks.'

'Don't mention it,' Ira replied, waiting a beat. 'Are you free for lunch tomorrow?'

'Are you paying?'

'Are you kidding? Who else?'

Chapter Eighteen

Six months later,
Paris

Simone Duchamp was coughing, her eyes running, a handkerchief pressed against her mouth. Above her head a pigeon cooed listlessly in the moist morning air, coming in to land on the window ledge over her head. Impatiently she flapped it away. Determinedly, the bird held its place. She watched it, studied its bleak red eyes, then coughed again. This time, the bird flew off.

It was always the same. Every time Simone was upset, she coughed. The 'Camille syndrome', she called it. A broken heart, a busted bronchus. C'est la vie. It was Ira's fault, the bastard. His fault, his phone call, his blasted peace offering coming before breakfast, coming in *his* place. What good was a present? You couldn't hold a conversation with a bottle of perfume, you couldn't make love to a scent.

He shouldn't have phoned. That was the first mistake. And she shouldn't have taken the call. That was the second. Simone coughed again, walking over to the phone and jerking it off the handset. In staccato French she demanded her breakfast; her maid hurried in and ran to organise her clothes for the day. The mistress was up with the sun, she said when she went back into the kitchen. God help us all.

Fitfully Simone regarded the perfume, then calmly and coldly she poured it down the toilet. At once, she began coughing again, and walked into the bedroom. Money and gut-wrenching work had made her wealthy; more work had made her respectable – at least outwardly. Casinos were never *that* respectable to anyone. But money was. Money bought politicians power, prestige. Money bought men. Most of them, except Ira.

She could open casinos in Paris, London and New York; could be photographed in Lorrie's *Exclusive* and for the *New York Times*; could be listed as one of the best-dressed women in Europe. Could be envied; could be lonely. . . . Throwing away the handkerchief Simone looked into the mirror and then picked up a lipstick. Slowly she outlined her face, her eyes, her nose, her lips, and then she backed away, standing beside the bizarre red image of herself.

Thirty-nine years old. In public. In private a forty-six-year-old. Broad shoulders, flat hipped, long from the thigh. Bone classy; with ivory skin. Her mouth was never without lipstick, her eyes always outlined with grey pencil. Not black, that was expected, common. Grey was class. Her hair had class too, tied back. Tightly. In a chignon at the base of her narrow, unlined neck.

She coughed again, once. Then swung away from the mirror and began, fitfully, to glance through the photographs she had had taken the day before. But her mind wandered, and for once, business could not absorb her. She had heard about Imogen from one of Ira's friends. A malicious little bottle-opener of a man, hurrying to pass on the scalding news. They see a lot of each other. She's stunning. And young. . . .

Oh yes, Simone knew all about Imogen Winner. Just as she knew about Suzanne Jacobs. The worlds of money and eccentricity were too closely intermingled not to cross over. They were all part of the European set; not the British class system, too cosmopolitan for that; too risqué, too exotic, too foreign. Simone sighed. She had seen her competitors come and go for years, but had outlasted them all. True, she'd been worried about Justine, Ira's wife. But she'd finally gone too, moved on. Off on to another husband. Lost her looks too, in the end. Simone smiled to herself, another one gone. And in the end, Ira still coming back to her.

Until now. Now there was one woman who seemed to be holding on to him. Seemed to *matter* to him. She coughed, dry-throated, thinking of her rival. Imogen Winner. Had been married to Giles Winner. A homosexual. Oh yes,

Simone knew all about Giles. She had known for a while, and never thought fit to mention it – until she heard about Ira and Imogen. Then she mentioned to anyone who would listen. Especially when she was at the London casino. . . . Not that it mattered, she said with mock sympathy. People were broad-minded these days. But still, what a shock for the poor girl. What a humiliation. And how could she *not* know? What real woman couldn't have known?

Idly, Simone looked at the empty perfume bottle and then picked it up and smashed it on the marble floor, the few remaining drops of scent splashing over the toes of her pink Charles Jourdan shoes.

At that moment in London Ira was phoning his daughter, all thought of Simone gone. His head was bent down, his immaculate appearance for once ruffled, his hair uncombed. All the previous night he had been phoning Switzerland, talking to the headmistress of the finishing school, demanding an explanation.

'Mr Mazan, I can't tell you any more. Your daughter has run away.'

'Run away! What the hell are you talking about? Can't you look after her?'

'We aren't warders,' the woman replied frostily. 'And your daughter is not a girl who is easy to handle.'

'What is that supposed to mean?'

The woman was firm. 'Tusha is very determined. In fact, I wanted to have a word with you last week, but I thought I would give her a second chance. She doesn't want to learn anything, Mr Mazan. She spends the whole time on the phone or missing lectures –'

'Listen, we can talk about her behaviour another time; now I want to know where she is.'

'I don't know.'

His voice was shuttered, soft with fury. 'Do you want me to come out there and find her?'

'I don't think that will be necessary, Mr Mazan, I'm sure Tusha will come back of her own accord.'

She didn't. She came to London instead, arriving hot and

sullen in the foyer of Ira's magazine offices, a soft leather bag at her feet. Dressed in jeans, with her long dark hair loose, she had the insolent composure of a person used to money, and the body movements of someone used to sex. She was, in short, trouble.

'I want my father,' she said to the receptionist.

'Who is . . . ?'

'Ira Mazan.'

The middle-aged woman hesitated, studying the girl. Well she'd never heard that her boss had a daughter, but there *were* similarities. The same way of holding herself, the same darkly shaded eyes − but there the resemblance ended. Ira had humour, charm; this girl had neither.

'I'll just buzz him. Your name?'

'Tusha,' she said sulkily. 'But he'll know, he only has one daughter. Well, only one he owns up to anyway.'

Ira came downstairs immediately, taking hold of Tusha and hugging her. Her expression remained vacant, bored, her arms by her side. It was obvious, said the receptionist later, that he adored her. The fool.

'Tusha, God it's good to see you,' he said, standing back to look at her. 'You look tired, I was worried about you. Madame Gilibert phoned me, she said you'd run away.'

'I'm hungry, Dad, can't we go and eat?'

He was only too willing to please her. 'Sure, sure, sweetheart, just let me finish upstairs and I'll be with you.'

'I'll come with you,' she said.

He paused, embarrassed. Embarrassed, the receptionist recalled later, Ira Mazan *embarrassed*.

'No, I think you should stay here.'

'I want to go with you −'

He didn't want to argue. He wanted to please her because she had come to him, after all these years, and not her mother. Tusha had run away to *London*. He was her father, it was right she should come to him. He took her arm, smiling proprietorially. This is my girl, his look said. See, this is my daughter. Good-looking, isn't she?

She was, she turned heads, fascinated with her dark surliness and yet when Ira reached his office he paused again.

'Wait outside, darling. Please.'

She shot him a heavy-lidded look. 'Please let me come in, Daddy. Please.'

The office was cool. Air conditioned. Double glazed. White, with black furniture and several glass vases of Arum lilies. Black leather Italian settees were pushed against the walls, and a white marble and glass table in the centre faced Ira's desk – on the top of which was a selection of his magazines, *S'expression*. Indolently Tusha picked one up.

'No!' Ira snapped, taking it out of her hand.

She smiled slowly. 'Oh, come on, Daddy, don't you think I've seen dirty pictures before?'

Her words made him pause, suddenly on the defensive. 'They aren't pornography, Tusha.'

'Not far off,' she replied, sitting down and flicking through one.

He was violently embarrassed and didn't know what to say, watching his daughter look at the nudes and turn the magazine round to study the centre pages.

'Good God,' she said simply, throwing the magazine back on to the table and looking round. 'Mama said you were doing well. She *didn't* send her love, by the way.'

'You mother and I have very little in common,' Ira said quietly, sliding behind his desk and watching his daughter.

'She said you owed her money.'

'I don't.'

'She said she was putting the lawyers on to you.'

Ira frowned, leaning back in his chair. 'Fine. I'll be happy to talk to them.'

Tusha turned suddenly, glancing over the back of her seat with a flirtatious expression on her face. 'Did you miss me, Daddy?'

Ira stared at her for a long moment, trying to remember her as a child. *Had* she ever been a child? he wondered suddenly.

'Yes, I missed you.'

'Good,' she said, turning off the charm and getting to her feet. 'Because I'm coming to live in London with you.'

'What about finishing school?'

'I'm finished with finishing school,' she said dismissively.

189

'I want to spend some time with my father now. Get to know you.'

Ira felt a sudden jolt of anxiety. He liked his life the way it was. Private, with no one poking their noses into it. He could go where he liked, when he liked, with whom he liked. He was popular and known around town. To have his daughter living with him didn't gel. He knew nothing about her, and unless he missed his guess, Tusha was only coming to him to avoid her mother. . . . But he loved her, and he was proud of her, and like many a father before him, she was his blind spot. So Ira looked at his daughter and saw someone he could show off, spoil, treat like a pretty doll.

And Tusha looked at her father and saw a man who published a soft porn magazine. A Jew with connections all over the world, with the rich and the powerful, and with the *demi-monde*. The thought excited her. Her mother had become a bore, a drag, a whiner. She had wanted to escape, to turn the numerous telephone calls with her father into a real relationship. He was lonely and he would be easy to handle, Tusha thought. Oh, and he was rich. Very rich.

Imogen looked up at one of the directors of Fillibert and Royal. 'There's a message from a Mr Collins.'

'Christ!'

'No, Mr Collins,' she said smoothly, passing him the paper and answering the next call.

The afternoon had been murderous, far too much work for one person, the switchboard literally jammed with calls. Calmly Imogen tried to cope with them, one at a time, but all too often the secretaries wouldn't answer their phones, or take messages – by the time her break had come, Imogen was snappy with irritation.

Finally relieved, she walked to the end of Cork Street and phoned her neighbour, knowing that Rowan would be there until she returned. It was an arrangement that suited them both. Marylin Finn had an adopted son about Rowan's age, and was glad of the small wage Imogen paid her.

'Hi, Marylin, is Rowan there?'

'Hang on, I'll get him.'

There was a short lull on the line, then: 'Hi, Mum, what's wrong?'

'Nothing. I just missed you,' she said lightly, leaning against the glass door of the call box. 'What's new?'

'There was a message on the answerphone,' Rowan said, careful to remember and repeat it exactly. 'It was from Ira – he said could he come round tonight, he had someone he wanted you to meet.'

Imogen frowned and rubbed her forehead. 'Okay, I'll phone him. What d'you want for dinner?'

'Chips.'

'Yeah, I know,' she smiled, 'what else?'

'More chips?'

'God, I love a smart mouth,' she said, laughing. 'See you later, kiddo.'

Ira arrived soon after nine, Tusha in tow. Rowan had opened the door to let them in, and stood in fascinated awe, as the girl walked past him. Imogen smiled and came forwards.

'Hello, so who's this?' she said.

Ira beamed. Ever the proud father. 'This is Tusha, my daughter.'

'God,' Rowan murmured from the settee.

Imogen ignored him and offered the girl a seat. 'So, you're Tusha. Your father's talked a lot about you.'

'And you,' she replied.

This is a tough one, Imogen thought. This is trouble. Her expression remained welcoming, but her eyes missed nothing; not the slight downturn of the sullen mouth, or the slow, blinking glance Tusha gave her father when she looked at him. She's flirting with him! Imogen thought incredulously. Dear God, the girl's making up to her own father.

Ira seemed blissfully immune; he was too delighted to have his daughter with him to notice anything wrong. In his eyes, Tusha was still the little girl he used to buy toys for, and talk to over the phone. Still the little princess who could do no wrong. So who cared if her teachers had said she was troublesome? And what if she had been caught in her dormitory with a boy when she was at school? She had just gone off the rails for a while. Now she was at home with him she would be different.

'So you're going to stay with your father?' Imogen asked.

Again the slow blink before answering. She reminds me of a glorious lizard, Imogen thought suddenly.

'Yeah, I'll stay with Daddy.'

'I might buy a bigger flat,' Ira said, turning back to Imogen. 'It would give us more room.'

For what? Imogen thought wryly. Orgies? Watch out, Ira, don't be fooled by her.

'I might start looking tomorrow. Get somewhere with two entrances. Then Tusha can have her privacy.'

And you can have yours, Imogen thought, pressing her lips together to prevent herself laughing. This is *never* going to work, not in a million years.

'Tusha could get a job.'

Tusha turned to look at her father, her face hardening.

'A job?'

'Sure, something to keep you occupied.'

'I don't want a job, Daddy,' she said, her tone sugared.

Here it comes, Imogen thought, the first hiccup.

'But sweetheart, everyone works. You'd get bored otherwise. I mean, what would you do with your time?'

Don't ask, Imogen said to herself.

'I don't want to work,' Tusha insisted. 'I want to spend time with you.' She looked down thoughtfully. 'But if you really want me to get a job – I could work on the magazine.'

Imogen had never seen Ira drop anything before, but as the words left his daughter's lips he tipped the contents of his wineglass down the front of his trousers. 'Jesus Christ!' he bellowed.

On her feet at once, Imogen rushed for a cloth, dampening it and passing it to the distracted Ira.

'It's red wine!' he snapped furiously. 'It'll never come out. People will think I've wet myself.'

'Never,' Imogen said lightly. 'They'll just think you've haemorrhaged.'

'Oh, very funny,' Ira snapped, casting a quick look at a laughing Rowan. 'This suit cost a fortune.'

192

'If you take your trousers off,' Imogen said calmly, 'I'll try and get the stain out.'

Ira's eyes were black with indignation. 'My daughter is here. How could I take my trousers off in front of her?'

Oh, but I imagine that many others have, Imogen thought to herself.

'You don't have to take them off in front of her. Go in the bedroom.'

'It's a good idea, Daddy,' Tusha said as her father walked out, adding softly, 'I'm sure you know the way.'

Ira didn't hear her, but Imogen did and turned slowly on the balls of her feet. Towering over the seated Tusha she smiled and then leaned towards the girl.

'Tusha, just a word of advice,' she said sweetly. 'I'm on to you. Your father isn't – yet – but I am. So don't push your luck. Do we understand each other?'

Tusha narrowed her shadowed eyes, her mouth surly with anger.

'You don't own him.'

'Neither do you,' she replied.

'Oh, but I will,' Tusha said with certainty. 'You just watch me. Within weeks, I'll have him eating out of my hand.'

Chapter Nineteen

Apparently, apart from her other talents, Tusha had second sight and her prediction became truth. Fascinated, Imogen watched as the girl wheedled her way into her father's affections, going to view new houses, buying furniture and clothes, and generally running through his money with the skill of a seasoned shopper. Nothing was denied to her, nothing held back. What Tusha wanted, Tusha got.

It was pointless to even try talking to Ira. For years he had felt guilty about neglecting his daughter and now he was eager to make amends. The magazine was doing well, so why shouldn't Tusha have the money? Besides the clothes made her look good, and he liked to show her off. So the skirts were too tight and too short, but she was a kid, and kids dress that way. Don't they?

'Well, what *do* you think?'

Imogen glanced out of the window in time to see Tusha getting into an open-topped car.

'Ira. . . .'

'Go on, tell me, what do you really think about the outfit?'

'Honestly?'

He nodded.

'She looks like a tupenny-ha'penny tart.'

He let go of the blind and sat down in his office chair. 'She's like her mother,' he said wearily. 'I thought, you know . . . maybe I was being old-fashioned. How do I know what kids wear these days?' he shrugged. 'But I know how the men look at her – and I don't like that.'

'So tell her to tone it down.'

He raised his eyes heavenwards.

'What are you – crazy or something? D'you think she'd listen to me?'

'You're her father, *make* her listen.'

He frowned. 'Does your son listen to you?'

Imogen nodded. 'Most of the time, yes. If he doesn't I just beat him.'

Ira grinned. 'Tusha's too big for that.'

'She certainly is.'

'You know, Imogen, I've found out that she's been sending her mother money. *My* money . . .' Ira paused; he felt a chump, a forty-carat mug. And it hurt. 'I asked her about it and she said, why not? Did I mind?' His voice rose. 'That woman took me to the cleaners once, I'll be buggered if she'll do it again.'

'Then give Tusha an allowance, and take your credit cards back.'

He shook his head. 'It would be mean.'

'It would be sense,' Imogen countered.

'She's my kid.'

'So what?'

'*So what!*' Ira repeated sharply. 'So she's my flesh and blood. What's mine, is hers. That's the way it is in families. You know that. It's the way it is in yours.'

Imogen steadied her voice. 'I'm not saying cut her off without a penny, Ira, I'm saying control her spending. I never abused Suzanne's money, she gave me an allowance while I was growing up. I understood that. Tusha should too, unless. . . .'

'Unless what?'

'Nothing.'

'Oh, shit!' Ira said furiously. 'Finish what you were going to say, Imogen.'

'Your daughter will understand unless . . . unless she's on the make.'

'She's my daughter! How can you say that about her?'

'She's not the Virgin Mary, Ira –'

'*I'm a Jew!*' he howled. 'So what's with the Virgin Mary?'

'All right, all right,' Imogen conceded. 'But she's not your mother either. . . . Tusha has her faults, and you should face up to them.'

'I want you to talk to her.'

'No.'

'Imogen. . . .'

'Don't try and wheedle your way round me, Ira, it won't wash. *You* talk to Tusha.'

He did, to no avail. Tusha spent money the way other people breathed – constantly. He had the sense to see that she was using him, but he genuinely loved her and refused to admit her failings. On one thing only was he adamant: she had to stay away from the office and anything to do with the magazine. He didn't want her around the printers, talking to the girls, or worse, seeing the photograph layouts. He thought it would corrupt her. For a worldly man, he was *that* naive.

'He's completely taken in by her,' Imogen said to Suzanne over the phone.

Suzanne was plucking her eyebrows, short yelps of agony punctuating the conversation.

'Well, she is his daughter. Ooch!'

'And family ties go deep,' Imogen said, her thoughts running on. 'I talked to Gran yesterday, she said she'd been to visit my mother last week.'

Suzanne stopped tweezing. 'How are you feeling about all of that?'

'The same,' Imogen replied honestly. 'I can't feel anything much for her. I know I should, I know she's my mother, but there's nothing there. You're far more a mother than she ever was.'

Suzanne breathed out slowly, releasing the tension. For weeks she had waited for the shift in their relationship; for the dreaded alteration which would make Imogen turn from her to her real mother. She had been unaccustomedly nervous, ill at ease, knowing that at any time the girl she had loved for so long could relegate her to second place. After all, Julie Mallinson was her real mother, and she wasn't dead; she was alive. When Imogen thought of her family now her view would be altered. She would first think of the woman up in Manchester, and then of Suzanne.

The fear had dogged her sleep; after so long to lose Imogen would be like losing a part of her own body.

'Jaco?'

'Yes?'

'I don't think of her as my mother. You brought me up, you and Elizabeth. You taught me everything. She is my mother by blood, not by heart.'

Suzanne found it hard to speak.

'I love you.'

'Sure,' Suzanne said finally. 'What's not to love?'

They changed the subject quickly, causing as little embarrassment as possible.

'I'm going to an opening next week with Ira.'

'Are things getting serious between you?' Suzanne asked, her curiosity on the rise.

'No, we were friends before and we're friends now. Nothing changes. He's my companion for the night, that's all.'

'Some companion. What a glossy, seedy fellow to spend an evening with,' Suzanne said, smiling. 'Your reputation will be ruined.'

'It already is,' Imogen replied seriously. 'People have found out about Giles. I don't know how, Jaco, I never said anything, but they *did* find out. Lorrie knows, and Ira said that he overheard someone else gossiping about it.'

'That's awkward,' Suzanne said, the words a pounding understatement. Oh God, to have to face people, to have to listen to the whispers and the idle chit-chat. To have them look at you, and point. . . . No wonder you feel safe with Ira, Suzanne thought drily; next to him you look almost respectable.

'Where's the opening?'

'A new gallery in Sloane Street.'

'Have a good time,' Suzanne said genuinely. 'You deserve it. You should get out and about, Imogen, you were locked away far too long with Giles.'

'Has he? . . . I mean, well, has Giles? . . .'

'What?'

'Has he ever contacted you?'

'No,' Suzanne said sharply, 'and if he ever does, God help him.'

'It doesn't pay to be bitter.'

'Oh, I'm not bitter,' Suzanne said evenly. 'I'd just like to cut off his balls and use them as doorstops.'

'I wanted to go with you!' Tusha screamed from the top of the stairs. *'You promised me!'*

Ira was beside himself. 'I never said I'd take you, sweetheart.'

'You did! You did!' she howled, sitting down on the steps and crying bitterly, her hair falling over her hands. 'I wanted to go so much. I was looking forward to it – and now you're taking *her*.'

At the bottom of the stairs Imogen stood impassively watching the performance. Because she knew that was what it was – a performance. Tusha wasn't really upset; she didn't really want to go. She just didn't want her father to go with Imogen. Oh yes, unless I miss my guess, Imogen thought, you want me out of the picture so you can get your mother back in. Well, hard luck, kiddo.

'Come on, Tusha, stop crying, please . . .' Ira glanced balefully over his shoulder. 'Help me. Suggest something.'

'Poison.'

Tusha stopped crying immediately and glared at Imogen, her eyes red-rimmed with petulance.

'I hate you!'

'Tusha!'

'Forget it, Ira, let it go,' Imogen said quietly. 'Your daughter will come round in her own good time.'

'She hates me, Daddy,' Tusha said plaintively.

'No, darling, Imogen doesn't hate anyone.'

Don't be too sure.

'She does . . . she does . . .' Tusha wailed, suddenly recovering and looking into her father's face brightly. 'Couldn't we *all* go? I mean, I could be ready in a minute, and we could all go together.'

Ira looked pleadingly at Imogen.

'What do you think?'

'Are you serious?'

198

'Please, Imogen. It would mean a lot to her.'

'No doubt it would mean a lot to my child too,' Imogen said coldly. 'If she goes, he goes.'

Which was how Ira Mazan and Imogen Winner arrived at the opening on Sloane Street with two children in tow. The gossips had a field day. Who was the mother of the sulky girl in the green dress? Imogen Winner? And who was the boy? Wasn't it Giles Winner's son? But wasn't Giles Winner gay? . . . The gallery hummed with curiosity at the mismatched foursome, Imogen glancing imperiously around as Ira whispered slyly in her ear. 'I think we've just caused a stir.'

'Good.'

'People will talk about us.'

'Good.'

'They will say that we are sleeping together,' Ira said, smiling darkly.

'Not so good.'

'Do you mind?'

Imogen shrugged. 'Do you?'

'No, not me.'

'Me neither.'

He stared at her: 'I think you look wonderful tonight.'

She turned, smoothed down the front of his jacket. 'You don't look so bad yourself – for a porn king, that is.'

He pulled a face: 'I'm a respectable publisher.'

'Sure, and I'm the Virgin Mary.'

'I'm a Jew,' he said, laughing. 'So what's with the Virgin Mary?'

Simone Duchamp had had enough. More than enough. Ira hadn't returned her calls, or even contacted her, even though she knew he had visited Paris. So this Imogen Winner really had a hold on him, Simone thought furiously. This little cartoon scribbler thought she had it made. Well, she was wrong, she hadn't taken her rival into account; and her rival wasn't about to step out of the picture so easily.

Imogen had no idea she even had a rival. Let alone an angry one. But the rumour mill which had begun in London had spread its poison to Paris and to Simone, the inaccuracy of the reports growing daily. Ira Mazan was in love with Imogen Winner. They were inseparable; they even went out together with their respective children. An affair was obvious; even marriage might be on the cards.

The idea would have made Imogen and Ira laugh. They hadn't even held hands, let alone shared a bed. Their relationship was based on friendship, that powerful, consuming affection others found impossible to understand or emulate. To outsiders, they *had* to be having an affair, otherwise what was the point?

The point was obvious to them. They needed each other for company. They needed each other for companionship, and they both needed someone to trust. The fact that they were both good-looking and glamorous helped. They matched, just as their humour did. Their past lifestyles might be widely divergent, but the similarities outweighed the differences. Ira might run a soft porn magazine, but he was fast becoming a hard disciplinarian with his daughter; just as Imogen was with her son. As the months passed, Tusha found that her father's previous indulgence was wearing thin, and his anger at her way of dressing and behaving came as a shock to her. She had expected a freewheeling, rich, indulgent parent, and had found that Ira was not quite the pushover she had expected.

He reined her in slowly, but very firmly. No, she couldn't go out, and yes, he wanted her back before dawn. Who was this boy she was seeing? And why hadn't she been looking for a job? All Tusha's pleading was to no avail, Ira was adamant. He might live a certain way, and enjoy the company of a certain kind of woman, but the ones he cared about had to behave differently.

'You should act like a lady,' he snapped, staring at the low-fronted T-shirt and the torn jeans. 'Stop dressing like a slut.'

'Your magazine's full of sluts –'

'That's business!' he roared. 'You're my daughter. And my daughter doesn't behave like a tramp.'

Tusha fell into a sulk and stayed in one for days, Ira bemoaning his lot to Imogen.

'I can't control her. She's impossible.'

Imogen could have told him that months earlier.

'I'm sending her back to her mother if she doesn't improve,' he said, exasperated. 'She has everything, you'd think she would want to do something with her life.'

Imogen shrugged, leaning back in the chair in Ira's office: 'She's spoilt.'

'So what can I do about that?'

'Nothing, the damage is done,' Imogen said simply. 'All you can hope for is that she'll find something she wants to do.'

The intercom buzzed beside Ira. Irritated, he picked it up. 'Yes?'

'Simone Duchamp is on the line again,' his secretary said. Ira frowned, then apologised to Imogen and took the call.

'Simone. How are you?'

There was a rumble of noise over the line. From where she was sitting Imogen couldn't hear what was said, but she could see Ira's face darken and watched with amusement as he began to pick at the knee of his trousers. His fingers tweaked at the silk, his anger condensed into the one gesture of sublime annoyance.

'. . . Yes, I know I said I would call. I've been busy. I'm not able to take time off just like that. . . . Simone, I never said we were going away. . . .'

Imogen's eyebrows rose. She pointed to the door to suggest that she should leave, but Ira shook his head.

'. . . I don't want to fight with you! Listen, either calm down or get off the bloody phone. . . .'

Again, the outburst from the other end.

'. . . .You're reading it wrong. Don't listen to what people say . . . Simone, oh, do me a favour. Just grow up.'

The line went dead.

He replaced the receiver and then took off his jacket, hanging it carefully over the back of his chair before he sat down again.

'That was an old friend.'

Imogen's eyes widened. 'A *friend*?'

'Well, we had a thing going . . . once . . . she just can't let go.'

'What happened?'

'She got pushy.'

Imogen smiled. 'I meant what happened between you?'

'We had an affair, years ago. It's been one of those on, off things. You know how it goes.'

'No.'

'No, no, you wouldn't. Of course not,' he said awkwardly, fiddling with the inkstand on top of his desk. 'Why did I buy this? I mean, who the hell uses ink any more?' He buzzed for his secretary then passed it to her, his voice rising. 'Get rid of this. Give it to some struggling writer, someone who deserves it. Just get it out of my sight.'

The woman beat a hasty retreat.

'What a nebbish,' he said with disgust.

'Who is?'

'I am! I am!' he said angrily. 'That bloody inkstand sums me up, doesn't it? I publish soft porn and yet I have a desk set straight out of Dickens. Who the hell am I kidding, Imogen?'

'She really got to you, didn't she?'

'It's not her,' he said furiously. 'It's Tusha – and you.'

'Me?'

'Yes,' he said simply. 'I look at you and you're what I want my daughter to be, and yet how can I expect it of her? What kind of example do I set her? . . . Some father, hey?'

'You're a good father.'

'In my business? Such a father she should have.'

Imogen frowned, leaning forwards. 'Ira, you're a good father.'

'I want her to go away. Live with her mother, anyone. But not with me. She sees my life and she *likes* it . . . well, I don't, not any more.' He stopped, aware that he had said too much. 'You made me feel like that. Embarrassed about what I do.'

'Ira, you love your work,' Imogen said, smiling and trying to defuse the situation. 'Any man would.'

'It's not respectable.'

'No, that's true. But you *are* good at it.'

He stared at her. 'It would never work, would it?'

'What?' she asked, although she already knew.

'Us . . . I mean, I've thought about it.'

'Me to.'

'. . . fantasised . . . but it's not on, is it?'

'We're friends, Ira.'

'Yeah. Good friends.'

The silence slid in between them.

'I want you in my world, Imogen. But not part of it. Not the sordid bit.'

'There's another part?'

He laughed, the tension lifting.

'People are talking about us.'

'I know.'

'I suppose Suzanne's pissed off.'

'No. Just apoplectic.'

'Well, that's something,' he said, smiling gently. 'You're the best thing in my life, you know,' he went on, his honesty catching her off guard. 'That's why I don't make a pass at you. I don't want to mess it up,' he rushed on, hugely, hopelessly, embarrassed. 'Not that I haven't thought about it. Not that I'm not attracted to you. I'm human, you know. I'm not gay. . . .'

Clang.

'Tactless, huh?'

She had the grace to laugh. 'It wasn't your best line, and that's a fact.'

He smoothed his hair, patently mortified. 'So we'll just keep things as they are?'

'It would be best,' she agreed.

'Friends?'

'Always.'

'Not lovers.'

'No.'

'And we're never going to even think about it.'

'No,' she said definitely. 'Never.'

'Good,' he replied, smiling with relief. 'So how about coming to a first night with me, Saturday?'

They didn't think about it – for about a week. But then they started to muse about having an affair, and then dream about it, and then both of them pulled themselves up short again, Imogen looking at Rowan, and thinking, no way. There is no way I'm going to jeopardise his future . . . and Ira looking at his lifestyle and thinking, back off, it would be a disaster and then you'd lose the only real friend you've got.

But the electricity between them remained, and it was patently obvious to everyone who saw them together. Exchanged looks, furtive snatches of conversation, that easy understanding that comes between people spontaneously, excluding all others. Locked into their own promise, they both resisted the temptation of touch, and restricted their movements to asexual pats on the back, or quick, uncomplicated kisses on the cheek. They had it mastered; oh, *how* they had it mastered. It was under control. No problem. . . . No way.

For nearly another year they continued in this fashion, Imogen recovering gradually from her broken marriage and hurried divorce, Ira providing the ear at the end of the phone, or the companion she needed to get out and about. Without the money to socialise, Imogen relied on Ira's invitations and as many of his contacts were known to her, their worlds began gradually to merge more and more.

Unfortunately her work as a cartoonist was limited, only dribs and drabs coming in, Lorrie providing the only secure income – apart from the part-time job. But Fillibert and Royal were taking their toll on Imogen, her temper bubbling dangerously under the surface as she was persistently patronised.

'I can't read your bloody message!' Tony Royal said imperiously one morning, after a particularly frenetic session on the switchboard.

'It's perfectly clear,' Imogen said calmly, looking at the paper. 'The name is "Bold".'

'It doesn't look like that,' he replied meanly. 'Can't you write properly?'

'It's more your reading ability that's in question,' she answered, acid in her voice. 'After all, it's only one syllable, even an account executive should be able to manage that.'

He stared at her, open-mouthed.

'What makes you think you can talk to me like that? I pay your wages.'

'Oh, and don't I know it!' she snapped. 'Ever since I first came here you've held that over my head like the sword of Damocles.'

The phone rang, interrupting them. White-faced, Imogen answered it.

'It's for you.'

The man was sharp with fury: 'Do you have a name?'

'Imogen,' she said, deliberately provoking him.

'Not *your* name – the client's.'

'Mr Littlebridge,' she replied, passing him the phone with a sour look.

She expected to be fired that day, and then realised that they would probably have to find a replacement before they got rid of her. The partners, always rude, walked past without comment; the secretaries were their normal, patronising selves. Smouldering with annoyance, Imogen sat in front of the eternally ringing board, the lights flashing, her voice calling out over the paging system to the usual taunting echo. Who needs this? she thought with dangerous fury, who needs to take this kind of punishment? Oh yes, she needed the job and the money, but this treatment no one needed. Imogen's eyes fixed on the board, her head down. It seemed for an instant that every line was ringing, the sound of the bells drilling into her head, the buzzing intercoms scratching at her nerve ends. One more call, she thought, just one more call, and that'll be it. One more rude client, one more ignorant remark, one more sexual innuendo. . . .

Then it happened. She was answering an incoming line when a hand materialised over her shoulder, waving a copy of the *Evening Standard*.

'Well, well, well,' Paul Stein said unpleasantly. 'What do you think about this?'

Her tone was lemon-bitter. 'You can read. Congratulations.'

'So who was out on the town last night?' he continued, ignoring her and reading out the caption, ' "Mr Ira Mazan, publisher of *S'expression* with his companion, Miss Imogen

Winner, the caricaturist for *Exclusive"*.' His voice was low with jealousy. 'It seems we have a celebrity in our midst. I suppose you should charge us an appearance fee just for clocking in.'

Her expression was steady: 'What I do in my own time –'

'– and *who* you do it with,' he countered, giving her an insolent look, his eyes resting for a long instant on her bust. 'We can only hazard a guess at the part-time work you do for Mr Mazan.'

Imogen rose to her feet slowly. Deathly slowly, Paul Stein backing off. With steady hands she picked up her bag and her jacket, then, with considerable aplomb, she walked to the door without looking back, the phones ringing furiously behind her.

'You can't just walk out!' Paul Stein howled. 'You have a job to do.'

'You do it,' she said coldly. 'As you've said so often to me, "Any bloody fool can do this job." So you're eminently qualified, I'd say.'

The twenty incoming lines were immediately boiling with calls, the intercoms buzzing. Paul Stein sat down and tried frantically to answer them, his hands fumbling with the switches. He looked shellshocked, white around the gills, as Imogen walked out. Still smouldering, she rounded the corner – then paused beside the nearest call box. Her mouth lifted in a smile, a low giggle starting in her throat as she lifted the receiver and put in the money. Carefully she composed herself, then dialled Fillibert and Royal.

Finally a stricken male voice answered.

'What on earth is going on there?' Imogen asked, her voice perfectly mimicking one of their biggest, and wealthiest, clients. 'I've been calling for over five minutes.'

'Mrs Levinson,' Paul Stein replied frantically, completely taken in. 'Please let me explain –'

'I don't want to hear it! Your whole company is totally unprofessional. Amateur!' Imogen paused momentarily, allowing him to blather out some more banal excuses. 'It's no good!' she interrupted, her tone outraged. 'Frankly, I've not been too happy with your work for some time, Mr Stein – in fact, this is the last in a long line of irritations.' Imogen paused, ready to deliver the final blow. 'In short, I am going to take my account elsewhere.'

Outside Imogen put down the phone with a flourish. Inside Fillibert and Royal, Paul Stein fainted.

Chapter Twenty

Suzanne could hardly speak for laughing. 'Go on, tell me again. Tell me what you said.'

Imogen duly repeated the conversation.

'Well, it had to happen,' Suzanne said, when she could speak normally again. 'You proved your point about working, but that job was the pits.'

'The money was all right,' Imogen said, suddenly regretting her hot-headedness. 'I'm not making enough with Lorrie –'

'. . . which is where Dickie Bedlington comes in.'

'Dickie who?'

'B-e-d-l-i-n-g-t-o-n,' Suzanne repeated slowly. 'He's an old friend of Michael's –'

'Are you still seeing him?' Imogen asked, surprised.

Suzanne glanced into the mirror over the fireplace. 'Beggars can't be choosers, darling.'

'Michael is an old poseur.'

'True, but he serves his purpose.'

'Is that enough?'

'How's Ira?' Suzanne asked deftly.

'Point taken,' Imogen replied, reverting to the previous conversation: 'So who's Dickie Bedlington?'

'Your saviour. He's just starting up a new magazine and he saw your caricatures in *Exclusive* – and now he wants to meet you.'

'That simple?'

'Well . . . I made him dinner.'

'*You made him dinner?*' Imogen repeated, aghast. 'And he *still* wants to meet me?'

'Don't be sarcastic, sweetheart. You'd be surprised what a

bit of home cooking can do,' Suzanne said thoughtfully. 'I knew immediately how to get round him – he had the look of a man raised on dairy produce.'

An image of Dickie Bedlington swam dizzily in front of Imogen's eyes.

'What's the magazine like?'

'Respectable – but don't let that put you off.'

Imogen ignored the remark. 'So when am I meeting him?'

'I thought we could arrange it for the weekend. You could come down with Rowan. He's very big in the Tory party.'

'Who, Rowan?'

'Dickie Bedlington!' retorted Suzanne, exasperated. 'Wear something nice, Imogen, something virginal.'

'Oh God. . . .'

'I'm just tipping you off. I know his wife and she always looks like she's just fallen out of a stained-glass window. He likes that type. Nothing scary.'

'Anything else?'

'Yes,' Suzanne said smoothly. 'Don't bring Ira.'

Dickie Bedlington had a face like an over-ripe cheese. Round, smooth and bland. He had a body like that too, squeezed into a brave little pinstripe, his shirt buttoned high under his chin, his neck coming to grief under several inches of starched cotton.

'Mrs Winner,' he said happily, extending his hand.

Imogen took it. 'It's lovely to meet you.'

'And you, and you,' he said, beaming. 'I've seen your work and I admire you a great deal. You have a *sharpness* –' he savoured the word, rolled it on his tongue. 'I think you and I could work well together.' He wheezed into a chair and crossed his ankles, his hands resting on his knees. 'I'm launching a new magazine. Nothing like Lorrie's, not at all. Something a little more . . . political. *Sharp.*' He obviously liked the word. 'We could do well, in this climate.'

'And you want caricatures?' Imogen asked.

'We want cartoons – no, as you say, *caricatures*. Something incisive –'

'Sharp,' Suzanne echoed.

'Yes,' he agreed happily. 'Something *sharp*.'

Imogen carefully avoided Suzanne's eye. 'Well, I've brought some with me for you to look at –'

'Good,' he said, leaning forwards, his hand extended. 'I was hoping you would.' His eyes ranged over the sheets of drawings, his brow unlined. 'Yes, this is the kind of thing we want. Incisive. To the point. *Sharp*.'

Imogen warmed to the compliments. 'How many would you want? And how often?'

'A couple of caricatures per issue,' Dickie Bedlington said, suddenly businesslike. 'I thought the sum of. . . .'

Imogen blinked, the amount was generous, far more than Lorrie paid, and enough to avoid taking any further part-time jobs. Mr Bedlington had arrived just in the nick of time.

'I'd want a contract.'

'Of course,' he agreed readily.

'When would you want me to start?'

'I want delivery on the sixteenth. Is that all right with you?'

Imogen tried hard to appear nonchalant. 'No problem. Are there any particular topics or people you want covering?'

He had his answer well prepared. 'I want a political angle, as I said. So MPs obviously should feature – along with the relevant contemporary themes of the month. Make the drawings as hard as you like, but not hatchet jobs. We like a little refinement too.' He paused, weighing up his new employee. 'Perhaps it would be a good idea for you to start moving in political circles. Attend the odd do, you know the kind of thing.' He rose to his feet, the business concluded. 'There is a fundraising dinner at Grosvenor House next week, I'll get you tickets.'

The speed at which things were moving was impressive.

'How many would you like?'

'Two, please,' Imogen said automatically.

'Two it is,' Dickie agreed, extending his hand again. 'I'll show you around, introduce you to various people. You should enjoy yourself. Mix work with pleasure.' He paused again. 'I'm very pleased we'll be working together.'

They walked him to the door and then watched as he

drove off. Only then did Imogen let out a whoop of delight and grab hold of Suzanne.

'No more bloody part-time work!'

Her face was a study: 'Who is the *second* ticket for?'

'Ira,' Imogen said simply.

'Ira!' Suzanne repeated, horrorstruck. 'What the hell are you thinking of, taking him to a dinner like that?'

Imogen was suddenly cool. 'Listen, Jaco, that man has stood by me and helped me for a long time. He took me out when I couldn't afford to go out, and he was always there for me – I'm not dropping him now my luck's changed. It wouldn't be fair.' Her tone lightened. 'Besides, you know that there are quite a few respectable people writing pieces for his magazine.'

'They write for him as a *publisher*, they don't choose him as a dinner companion.'

Imogen was genuinely surprised by her attitude. 'Jaco, you brought me up surrounded by oddballs. None of your friends were conservative – and you've never been a snob. So why change now?'

Suzanne glanced away, fiddling with the heavy gold bracelet on her arm.

'I never wanted to be socially acceptable. It would have been a bore. But you're different, Imogen. You wouldn't want my kind of life. I've always been out of the usual run of things, never looked the part, never really wanted to belong. But you need to find yourself a husband with the right kind of social contacts. You don't want to commit social suicide by mixing with the wrong types.'

'I can't believe you're saying this!' Imogen replied, sitting down. 'I don't give a damn what anyone does. If I like them, that's enough. I'm not going to change myself to catch a husband – I've already done that, and it didn't work.'

Suzanne waved her hands imperiously. 'Forget Giles, that was a mistake. He was hopeless – but he was one step up from Ira.'

'You *are* a snob,' Imogen said coldly, getting to her feet. 'You talk about being open-minded, but you're more bigoted than anyone when it comes down to it. This job has come at just the right time – don't think I'm not grateful for that. But I'm not going to pretend to be someone I'm not, just to fit in. I've never done that before.'

'All right, all right!' Suzanne said hurriedly. 'But there is enough talk about you and Ira already –'

'Unfounded.'

'Be that as it may, people believe that you're having an affair, and it can only count against you. I can find you a better escort, Imogen, honestly I can.'

But Imogen's mind was made up and she dug in her heels. Ira had been good to her, and this was a way of thanking him for his help. Publicly, openly. Oh yes, the fact that it was bound to cause talk also appealed to her. She had been cowed for too long by circumstances and was suddenly defiant and gloriously reckless; she wanted to rejoin the fight, to tell everyone she was back in the spotlight. And what better way to make sure that everyone noticed her? Besides, who cared what people thought? They had already had their share of gossip about Giles, she might as well give them something else to talk about. Imogen felt good, confident and alive – after all the shit, there *was* a pony there after all.

Suzanne was full of it. 'Imogen's rising faster than a helium balloon,' she said to Elizabeth over the phone. 'You'd be delighted to see the change in her, and in Rowan. He's coming on. Very funny, more like his mother than his father, thank God.'

'Making friends at school?'

'Horribly sociable, with that kind of easy confidence that makes grown men weep,' Suzanne said, laughing. 'I adore him, and I can't tell you how long I've waited for something to break for Imogen. She deserves some luck.'

Elizabeth could only agree with that.

The news cheered her, lifted her spirits. Age was tackling her at last; she knew she should lose weight, take exercise, go out more. But she didn't; her time was over and she was content to live vicariously through her granddaughter and Rowan. I came home when I should, and I'll stay here until I die. The thought was not a depressing one; it was comforting.

'Imogen phoned me yesterday to ask after her mother. She sends stuff for her too. She's a good girl.'

Suzanne asked the usual question, expecting the usual answer.

'How's Julie?'

'No different.'

They both paused; Elizabeth changed tack: 'So who is Imogen going to the dinner with?'

Suzanne paused. 'Ira Mazan.'

There was a low chuckle at the other end of the line. 'I bet she's doing that deliberately.'

'As a career move, it stinks.'

'Oh, leave her to it,' Elizabeth said affectionately. 'Imogen will live her life her own way, whatever anyone says.'

Ira resplendent in a dinner jacket, Imogen glowing in a long-skirted silk suit, they arrived at Grosvenor House. He knew what it meant for her to choose to go with him and he felt a rush of extraordinary gratitude for the gesture. How like her, how typically generous, and how typically provocative. They walked into a sea of curious glances, Ira spotting several acquaintances almost at once, Imogen buttonholed immediately by Dickie.

'I want you to meet Arnold Miles,' he said nervously. 'He's the MP for Kensington. Very important.'

Imogen allowed herself to be led over to a stocky, badly suited man, standing next to his wife.

'This is Imogen Winner,' Dickie said deferentially. 'She'll be working on the magazine, doing our caricatures. You might have seen some of her work in *Exclusive*.'

Arnold Miles studied her thoughtfully. 'I know your work. Very clever, Miss Winner.'

'Thank you,' Imogen replied evenly, 'and it's *Mrs* Winner.'

'Of course,' he agreed stiffly, turning to the woman beside him. 'This is my wife, Claudine.'

Imogen smiled, but the stranger took an instant to respond; a slight, flat-chested woman in black, her pale hair drawn back in a crude French pleat. Nervous, drawn, overshadowed by her husband.

'You did a lovely cartoon of Arnold the other month,' she said quietly. 'I was wondering if . . . well, do people ever buy the originals? I would like to buy . . . if it's possible. . . . If it isn't, I understand, but if it is –'

Her husband cut her off. 'Of course it's possible, Claudine!' he said impatiently. 'You just have to ask, that's all.' He turned to Imogen. 'How much would it be?'

His tone jangled on her, his arrogance, coupled with his rudeness to his wife, making Imogen wince. She stared at him coolly.

'That one's not for sale.'

He knew she was being difficult, and hesitated, then smiled briefly before moving away. Obviously embarrassed, Claudine hovered, unsure whether she should follow him. Gently Imogen touched her arm.

'I don't want you to buy it. You can have it.'

'*Have it?*' Claudine repeated softly. 'But . . . I can't do that.'

'Why not?' Imogen countered. 'You wanted it, didn't you?'

'Yes . . . but I didn't mean to imply that you should give it to me.'

'You didn't,' Imogen responded evenly. 'I just want you to have it.'

She smiled, touched. Then nodded and walked off to join her husband.

'Why did you do that?' Ira asked, materialising by her elbow.

'I felt sorry for her.'

'You should have stung that bloated carcass of a husband for a couple of hundred.'

'Oh, Ira!' Imogen said playfully. 'You've no soul.'

'He has a fortune, he can afford it.'

'That,' she said calmly, 'is not the point.'

There was no time to discuss the matter further, Dickie reappearing and tapping Imogen on the shoulder. 'This is Tom, Tom Wrigley,' he said, smiling broadly. 'He's the MP for Manchester South.'

Imogen glanced up at the bearded man who stood next to him.

214

'I saw that cartoon you did of me,' he said at once. 'I should give you a piece of my mind.'

'Oh,' Imogen replied calmly. 'Can you spare it?'

He paused, taken aback, and then burst out laughing. Well over six feet in height, he was dark and bearded, his eyes grey. He was not handsome in any conventional sense, but he did have a loose-limbed ease of movement which gave him a solid charm. He was also a northerner. Which helped.

'I believe your family come from up north?' he said, when he'd stopped laughing.

'They do. But my grandmother always votes Labour.'

His eyes flickered with amusement.

'What about your mother?'

'Present, but not voting,' she said quietly.

He didn't understand and let the comment pass.

'So you've come to watch us all so you can go away later and draw blood with your pen?'

It was Imogen's turn to smile. 'I think you can all defend yourselves against my little assaults.'

'Any man assaulted by you would have to count himself lucky.'

Behind her, Ira groaned.

'I think, Mr Wrigley,' Imogen said wryly, 'that you're sending me up.'

'Only gently,' he agreed, smiling, 'and only with respect. After all, you're the one with the last word. A person can take a pretty revenge in print.'

'I don't write, I draw.'

'They say a picture is worth a thousand words.'

Imogen smiled. 'Only if it happens to be by Leonardo.'

'I look forward to seeing the results of this evening,' Tom Wrigley said, 'but for now, I have to go. Goodbye for now, Mrs Winner.'

'And good riddance,' Ira mumbled as he walked off. 'God, what a schmuck.'

'I liked him,' Imogen said defensively. 'He was just playing a game, that's all.'

A sudden unaccustomed sensation jolted Ira. It was a peculiar feeling, not unlike a bad hangover. With incredulous horror, he realised he was jealous.

'He's not your type.'

She turned to look at him. 'Oh, and what *is* my type, Mr Mazan?'

'I don't know,' he said spiritedly, 'but *not* him.'

'Oh, Ira, come on,' she said, laughing and drawing him away.

The evening was a success, Imogen making an impression, favourable in some quarters, distinctly unfavourable in others. Her personality was too strong to be met by indifference in anyone, and her looks guaranteed attention. Effortlessly she drifted around the company, coming back to Ira to exchange views or gossip, her eyes taking in details of the MPs' appearances, her ears picking up on the wives' conversation.

The women did not know what to make of her, and were puzzled by her generosity to Claudine Miles.

'I suppose she only did it to get in with Arnold,' Sarah Bentley said sourly. 'Showing off like that, flirting.'

'Oh, drop the feminist bit,' Penny Fairbane replied sharply. 'You're becoming a bore.'

Sarah turned on her, her wide face flared with colour. 'Not half as boring as you are about your little hobby.'

'I didn't know you had a hobby,' Claudine said timidly, sipping a warm glass of sherry.

'She stuffs things,' Sarah replied flatly.

There was a snort of laughter from Penny. 'I bet you wish you could say the same.'

'I don't call having my hand up the backside of a dead animal an enriching experience. Besides, it's macabre, trying to make them look as though they're still living. No one can bring the dead back to life.'

Caught in the crossfire, Claudine peered anxiously over her glass.

'Oh, I don't know,' Penny said, smiling broadly. 'You managed it with your husband.'

'Now just wait a minute! My husband –'

'Ladies, I'd like you to meet Mrs Imogen Winner,' Dickie said suddenly, interrupting the imminent fight. 'She will be doing her clever caricatures for my new magazine.'

Sarah studied Imogen minutely, Penny immediately extending her hand.

'I'm Penny. I'm Douglas Fairbane's wife – and I stuff things.'

Imogen laughed, liking the ebullient woman in front of her. She looked like fun, and had a kind of spiky charm, her dark hair cut short to the chin, her eyes heavily made up and oddly mesmeric.

'Do you charge by the hour or the inch?'

Penny guffawed and linked arms with Imogen, leading her away. 'I think that you and I might well be friends,' she said, pointing to a woman across the room. 'That is the unbelievable Maxie Penn – everyone's little pen pal – and why not? She's quite fantastically beautiful.' Penny stared at the ivory blonde. 'I wonder what will happen to her after she dies. I mean, if ever a carcass needed stuffing, that one does.'

Imogen studied the woman, deciding that she was quite the most spectacular creature she had ever seen. This girl was not beautiful, she was unearthly.

'We all hate her, of course. That's because we're jealous – mind you,' Penny said sincerely, 'you could give her a run for her money.'

Imogen smiled, her eyes still fixed on the girl. Maxie Penn was about thirty, slim to the point of frailty, and yet powerfully sexual, her movements taking little space, her voice low, to invite people to move towards her. She compelled attention, and deserved it.

'She's thick, of course,' Penny said with delight. 'Can't hold a real conversation, but who cares? With a face and figure like that, who needs conversation?'

'What does she do?'

Penny turned back to Imogen. 'Maxie's a professional girlfriend. She used to be with Tom Wrigley, but now she lives with the MP, Harry Taylor.' She lowered her voice. 'Rumour has it that he pays her to go out with him. Who knows? It might be true, I can't imagine what else she would see in him.'

Imogen looked round. 'Where's he?'

'The short guy by the window,' Penny said, 'talking to that delectable piece in the silk dinner suit.'

217

'That delectable piece,' Imogen said, smiling, 'is my escort.'

'No!'

'Yes,' she said, adding calmly. 'Ira Mazan.'

'The porn guy?' Penny asked delightedly. 'Oh, how wonderful. Is he good in bed?'

'What!'

Her amazing eyes turned on Imogen: 'Well, *is* he?'

'I don't think –'

'Oh, you're shocked, what a bore! I forget how prudish the English are. You see, my family are Italian and I was brought up to think of sex as a reward. You know, you work all day and then you get your reward at night. Simple, healthy. Besides, if you don't use it, you lose it.' She studied Imogen, waiting for her to confide, but when she said nothing more, Penny continued. 'The other notable girl-friend is Danielle Ferryman. She's with Trevor Rowe-Thorne. Not as gorgeous as Maxie, but *smart*. Has her own interior decorating business and could buy and sell him.' Penny narrowed her eyes suddenly, scanning the room before glancing back to Imogen. 'The one you have to look out for is Sarah Bentley. *What* a bitch, and a feminist to boot.'

'I'll never remember everyone.'

Penny shook her head. 'Oh yes, you will. You're clever enough.' Her voice lightened. 'I love your caricatures. My old man went ape when he saw that one of Tom Wrigley. He loves all your stuff in *Exclusive*. He's only sorry that you haven't done one of him.'

'I don't specialise in MPs,' Imogen said, glancing round. 'I do whatever, and whoever, is in the news.'

'Poor Douglas, he's never likely to get picked then. He never does anything exciting.'

'What about Claudine?' Imogen asked curiously.

'Married to that ego-crusher Arnold. A leading *member* of the Tory party.' She laughed loudly. 'And *how* he puts his member about. She knows, but she can't do anything because she loves him and because she has three little kids.'

'Have you got children?'

Penny shrugged: 'No, can't. I went and had all the tests, even dragged Douglas along, but it's no go. Apparently he's short of something and I'm missing something and so – no go.' Her voice shook for an instant, then righted itself. 'It used to hurt a lot, but you get used to things. *Anything*. So I got a hobby instead of a family. Taxidermist to royalty, I am.'

Imogen grinned. 'The Royal Family have things stuffed?'

'Only the lesser members,' Penny replied, laughing. 'No, I don't stuff things at the Palace, I stuff animals for the Saudi lot. Big cats, et cetera. They pay very well, and I've just got a new machine from the States which sucks all the moisture out of the carcass.' She drew up her hands towards her and then grimaced. 'It makes it easier to stuff things. Only thing is, the first time I used it, I got the timing wrong and someone's greyhound was in too long. Came out like a flaming playing card.'

'What's so funny?' Ira asked, drawn over to them by the gales of laughter.

'This is Penny, Douglas Fairbane's wife,' Imogen said.

'And you are Ira Mazan,' Penny said, her fabulous eyes fixing on Ira's. 'You are the most fascinating man here tonight.'

'And you are a woman of rare taste,' he countered, immediately at ease. 'So, Imogen, have you got the low-down on everyone yet?'

'Penny's been invaluable,' she replied, spotting Maxie Penn crossing in front of the window. 'Look, Ira, doesn't she make your heart beat faster?'

He smiled, watching the girl pass, but Penny caught him looking quickly back at Imogen, and smiled to herself. Well, well, well, she thought, so that's the story, is it?

'How about asking her for a photo session, Mr Mazan?'

Ruefully, he shook his head. 'I don't think she would be open to suggestion.'

'She might be, but her boyfriend wouldn't,' Penny said, suddenly spotting someone else she knew. 'Oh, look, Simone,' she said, waving the woman over.

Slowly the Frenchwoman walked towards them, taking plenty of time, allowing everyone to take in her height and the beauty of her clothes. Impressed, Imogen watched her, then frowned when she saw the look on Ira's face.

'Ira?'

He seemed ill at ease, suddenly rigid, his lips tightly compressed.

'Hello, Simone.'

'*Bonsoir*, Ira,' she replied evenly. Her hair, as ever sleeked back into its chignon, shone with good health, her long neck circled with three strands of black pearls. '*Comment ça va?*'

'I'm well,' he replied coldly, 'How are you?'

'Still waiting for the phone call you promised me three weeks ago.'

Imogen glanced down; Penny was riveted.

'This is not the time.'

Simone was glacial: 'When would be?'

'I don't want to argue,' he said sharply, turning to Imogen. 'This is –'

'– Imogen,' Simone finished for him. 'So *you* are the compelling Mrs Winner. How do you do?'

Imogen took her hand reluctantly. 'And you are?'

'Madame Simone Duchamp,' she replied, releasing her grip. 'Ira and I are old friends.'

'I bet,' Penny murmured under her breath.

'Who did you come with?' Ira asked, his voice tight, unfamiliar.

'I came alone,' Simone replied. 'After all, this is an event I wouldn't want to miss. A fundraising evening for the Conservative Party.'

'But you're French, aren't you?' Penny asked, her tone innocent. 'So how come you're interested in an English political party?'

Simone turned to her, her eyes steady. 'You're Italian, so how come you're married to an English MP?'

Round one, France.

'I'll get some more drinks,' Ira said hurriedly.

'No more for me,' Imogen said.

'Had enough?' Simone asked, her tone acid.

'No, it's just that I know when to stop.'

Round two, England.

Suppressing a smile, Ira turned and disappeared into the crowd.

*

As luck would have it – or as Simone had organised it – Imogen ended up sitting well away from Ira, next to Tom Wrigley, with Ira placed next to Simone. He saw the place settings and looked angrily at the Frenchwoman, who affected an air of nonchalant indifference. Bemused by the sudden turn in events, Imogen sat down, throwing a puzzled glance at Ira. He shrugged, mouthed something incomprehensible, and was repeating it when someone touched Imogen on the arm.

'What a pleasant surprise.'

She turned and smiled automatically at Tom Wrigley.

'Oh, hello again.'

'I was hoping that we might have a chance to talk,' he said easily. 'What happened to your escort?'

'He met his Waterloo,' Imogen said, smiling and turning her attention to Tom Wrigley for the rest of the meal.

They left around twelve, Ira driving Imogen home and accepting her offer of a coffee. Quietly they walked up the stairs, Ira keeping his voice low as Imogen unlocked the door. The flat smelt strongly of roses – red roses, the ones he had sent her that morning. She flicked on the light, then went into the kitchen to turn on the kettle. Softly, mesmerisingly, it began to hum.

'Is Rowan asleep?'

'I don't know,' Imogen replied, 'but I hope so. He's in Brighton with Suzanne. He wanted to go down for the weekend – apparently it's the London to Brighton race tomorrow. You know how he loves old cars.' She paused. 'Giles will be there.'

'How does that make you feel?'

She shrugged. 'He's Rowan's father. I can't stop them seeing each other.'

'Will he be alone?'

'No,' she said softly. 'Giles is still with Terry.'

Ira raised his eyebrows, leaning against the door as she made the coffee. 'He must be *meshuga*.'

She frowned. 'You've lost me. What does that mean?'

'Mad,' Ira translated. 'How could he prefer a man to you?'

'Drop it, Ira,' she snapped, then softened her tone. 'I'm sorry, but I'll never get used to it – and talking about it doesn't help.'

She lifted the cups and carried them into the lounge, Ira following. Placing them on a side table, Imogen passed him a sheaf of drawings and then settled herself on the settee next to him. He felt dizzy having her so close. Oh, God, he thought, pull yourself together. Get a grip.

Her head was bent down, her hair falling out of the carefully arranged pleat and curling in strands down her neck. Keep your eyes on the bloody papers, Ira, he willed himself. Yet when Imogen passed him one of her latest caricatures, his hand was shaking when he took it, and when she leaned her arm along the settee, only inches from his thigh, his temperature rose dramatically.

'They're good . . .' he said, keeping his eyes on the page, the drawings blurring before him. Get out now, he thought. Go on, get out.

'Maybe,' Imogen went on, musing, apparently immune to his discomfort. 'But I thought something punchier might be best – for the first ones at least.'

He nodded as though he had heard what she said. But all he could really hear was the unhealthy rushing of blood in his ears and an unwelcome sensation of long-suppressed excitement.

'Look at this, Ira.'

He *was* looking – but not at the drawing; at the line of her cheek and the slope of her shoulders in the thin dress. God, Ira thought helplessly, I want you. . . .

She turned, stared at him expectantly. He blinked, caught out.

'Are you okay?' she asked, puzzled by the expression on his face.

'Fine,' he croaked.

'You look odd.'

'Odd' wasn't what he wanted to hear.

'I'm fine. Just had a bit too much wine, that's all.'

Imogen frowned, then leaned over and laid her hand on his forehead. He thought for an instant that he might pass out.

'You *feel* cool enough,' she said, mystified. 'Perhaps you should go to bed.'

Ira lost the ability to speak, and sat, stupefied, his eyes fixed on her upturned face.

'Imogen . . .' he said finally, his left hand extending and stroking back a stray hair from her forehead. 'Imogen, I. . . .'

His technique failed him. For years he had seduced women with ease, but now, confronted with the reality of Imogen, the potent, warm, breathing, loving reality of her, he couldn't articulate his feelings and leaned forwards instead, his lips moving over hers.

She hadn't expected it, and for an instant didn't know how to respond. This was Ira, the man she had adored for over ten years, her adviser, confidant, friend. She thought at first that she should pull away, but the soft pressure on her mouth continued and she felt suddenly hungry for him. Lazily her eyes closed, his arms moving round her as he slid to his knees and pulled her down on the carpet beside him. They moved together, Imogen greedily touching his hair, his face; Ira fondling her breasts under the thin silk, his hands reaching for the zipper on the back of her dress.

She moaned, rolled over on to her side to help him, feeling the heat of his hands on her back as he began to slide the zipper down. His mouth pressed against hers, his tongue moving avidly against hers, his breathing fast. Hurriedly he tugged at the zipper, Imogen unfastening his shirt, her hands moving against his chest.

Suddenly he let out a curse.

'Bloody hell! The thing's stuck!'

'What?'

'The zip! The sodding thing's jammed,' he said fiercely, staring at the back of her dress and frowning.

Imogen sat up. 'It can't be,' she said, reaching behind her, her hands fumbling with the zipper.

'Just hang on a minute,' he said, trying to control his impatience as he pulled at the offending article.

Softly, Imogen began to laugh.

'. . . it'll be fine,' he said, kissing her hurriedly, trying to keep the excitement going. 'Just relax.'

'I *am* relaxed,' she said. 'It's the zipper that's seized up.'

Breathing in sharply, Ira tried to keep his patience. 'Can't you get the damned dress off any other way?'

'Only by cutting it off,' Imogen replied. 'And as it cost me a fortune, Ira, don't even think it.'

'I'll buy you another dress!' he said frantically. 'The most expensive dress you want. Any amount of dresses. . . .'

He realised his mistake as soon as the words left his lips. This wasn't an ordinary woman to be bought, this was Imogen. His fantasy, his perfect dream female. This was no easy conquest to be treated cheaply.

He stopped fumbling with the zipper, looked deep into her eyes, and then zipped the dress up and turned away.

Imogen frowned: 'Ira?'

'No . . .' he said gently, getting to his feet, turning off the lamps and throwing several cushions on to the floor. Then he kneeled down and pulled Imogen to him, lying with her on the carpet, their bodies pressed against each other. The dim evening light came through the windows, the high summer trees outside waving patterns against the indigo sky. In a far street a car alarm started up, and then died away, leaving only an echo.

'I love you . . .' he said simply, 'but I won't *make* love to you.'

She nestled against him, laying her head against his.

'Why? . . . Don't you want me?'

He sighed. 'I want you more than anything, or anybody. That's why I won't make love to you.'

'I don't understand,' she said softly. 'Why not?'

'It wouldn't be right,' he said, touching her closed eyelids gently with his fingers. The right eyelid, then the left. 'Which finger?' he said.

She touched his forefinger and he smiled. 'That's for luck.'

'You made that up, Mr Mazan,' she said, smiling.

'No, I didn't!' he said, with mock horror. 'It's an old Yiddish custom.'

'Like hell.'

He held her tightly and stroked her hair. 'I love you,' he repeated.

'I love you too.'

'You're the best thing in my life.'

Tenderly, Imogen touched his face: 'And whatever anyone says – you're a gentleman.'

'From your lips to God's ear,' he replied, smiling. 'From your lips to God's ear.'

Chapter Twenty-One

Tom Wrigley looked at the caricature in Dickie's new magazine and laughed outright. The likeness to the ego-inflated Arnold Miles was bitingly accurate, the expression on his moon face captured perfectly. He glanced at the foot of the drawing to find the simple 'I.W.' signature – Imogen Winner – and then sat back in his seat and mused about her. She was clever, and he liked that; he had enough confidence to be able to hold his own with a bright woman; but she was obviously involved with Ira Mazan.

Tom scratched his beard, then stood up, stretching his long arms. Ira Mazan – what an unlikely partner for a woman like Imogen Winner, what a socially *dangerous* partner. . . . Ah, but Imogen had little to lose, had she? her own reputation being knocked sideways by an unlucky marriage. Tom thought of what he'd heard about Giles Winner. A hat-maker! And a homosexual hat-maker at that. Whatever possessed her to marry someone like him? Tom wondered, leaning against the windowframe and lighting up a cigarette. But then, whatever possessed her to get involved with Ira Mazan? She had an unusual taste in men, he had to give her that, he thought smiling. Still, he liked a woman with a mind of her own. A clever woman.

Maxie hadn't been clever. Beautiful, yes, and sexually desirable, certainly. But not clever. Never said anything to make him laugh – and Tom Wrigley liked to laugh. Not many women could make him laugh, he thought suddenly, and that was a shame. You got to know a lot about a person by their sense of humour. . . . He inhaled deeply, staring over the Thames towards the far bank. Apparently she came from the north too. That was another point in her favour; a woman like Imogen would know instinctively how to treat his constituents, it was in the blood. And they would automatically take to her too. One of their own kind.

He shook his head suddenly. What was he thinking of? Imogen Winner was involved with someone else, she obviously wasn't available. Tom smiled to himself. She wasn't available *now*, he thought, but in time . . . oh yes, in time, if he played his cards right, he could stake a claim. He was only up against the likes of Ira Mazan, after all. An MP against a porn publisher – no contest.

Penny Fairbane called Imogen the next week, suggesting lunch. They met at a small French restaurant on the Brompton Road, Penny waving frantically as Imogen walked in. She smiled and sat down, staring at Penny. Her hair had been newly cut and was startlingly short, her long, darkly made-up eyes sparky with good humour.

'I like your hair.'

Penny touched her head self-consciously. 'Douglas doesn't, he says I look like I've just been deloused.'

'Charming.'

Quickly she leaned across the table. 'Tom Wrigley was asking me about you. I think he's interested.'

Imogen raised her eyebrows. She liked Tom, but she hadn't thought of him since the night they met. The night she and Ira had attempted to have sex; the night she found out what real love meant. Oh Ira, Imogen thought tenderly, I miss you, and although I know you're right about us, no other man comes close. Damn it. Why do I love the men who can't love me properly in return? The ones, either by inclination or a misguided sense of honour, who won't have a physical relationship with me? Her confidence dipped suddenly. Wasn't she desirable? She had thought she was, but now, at over thirty, she felt horribly cornered. It had been fun pretending to be involved with Ira; it had served them both well. He hadn't wanted any complications with his daughter around, and she was still recovering from Giles.

But now she *had* recovered fully, and now she wanted someone who wanted her, who was attracted to her. The need for a physical relationship struck her unexpectedly and sharply, the lack of a man in her bed felt as a loss, a disappointment in her life. Idly, Imogen glanced round the restaurant. It was full of couples. She turned to the window: the street was suddenly choked with men and women walking hand in hand, or with arms linked. It was natural, after all, she was young, healthy. She *should* have a man – and Rowan should have a father.

Ira had been good to her; that was fact. He had been a constant and amusing friend, a gentleman, against all the odds. But Tusha had gone back to her mother and before long he was bound to revert to his old ways. It was in his blood; it was in *her* blood, Imogen realised suddenly. I want to hold someone, to turn in the night and know there is someone there. I want, she thought with real surprise, to come *first* with someone.

'Oh, yes, he looked *really* interested,' Penny went on, 'and he's not short of a bob or two.'

'Who?'

'Tom Wrigley,' Penny replied impatiently. 'Aren't you listening? I was just saying that he was doing well. All the women like him. He might not be *that* good-looking, but he's all man.'

All man.

'Oh, I know he's not funny like your Mr Mazan,' she continued, breaking off a piece of her bread roll, 'but he's big and rather lusty. Maxie said that he always made her feel great.'

'He seems nice enough,' Imogen said thoughtfully.

' "Nice enough"!' Penny said, pooh-poohing her. 'Some interest! You should be a bit more enthusiastic. Word has it that if there's another reshuffle he could be invited to join the Cabinet. That speech he made in Brussels really got the big boys' attention.' She chewed thoughtfully before continuing. 'Tom's on the lookout, I know that. He was fond of Maxie, but she isn't wife material – *you* are.'

Imogen stared at her in blank astonishment. 'Pardon?'

But Penny refused to be abashed. 'Think about it from his point of view, Imogen. You're good-looking, clever, and you've got a child. You could be the answer to all his prayers. An enviable wife and a ready-made family.'

Imogen laid down her glass, her tone cold. 'Penny, has it ever occurred to you that people are supposed to fall in love spontaneously? Not plan their relationships?'

She nodded. 'Oh yeah. I used to believe that too, but all the men I fell in love with gave me nothing but grief. Then I met Douglas and decided I was going to marry him for a variety of reasons, none of which had anything to do with hormones.' Her eyes were dark with sincerity. 'And do you know, this relationship actually *works*.'

'You were lucky.'

'I was cautious,' she responded. 'I didn't want any more trauma, so I picked someone who wouldn't give me punishment. So what if Douglas isn't great in the sack? So what if he checks all the bills? He loves me and he won't leave me, and after a while I grew to love him. It works, honestly.'

Imogen glanced away.

'Well, he can't have been that interested in me, or he would have invited me out.'

Penny had waited for this. Her face beaming, she leaned across the table. 'Well, actually, Tom is coming to a party at our house next week, and I want you to come too.' She carried on quickly, 'Some of the other MPs and their wives are also coming, so you'd know plenty of people. Oh come on, Imogen, what have you got to lose? I mean, you don't have to get involved if you don't want to, but you could at least think about it.'

'I don't know. . . .'

'Are you *that* much in love?' Penny asked, thinking of Ira.

Imogen looked steadily at the woman opposite her: 'No, not *that* much.'

He stood at the entrance, his back to the car. The soft sound of the radio crept over him, the summer evening sounds making lazy inroads into the quiet. Nervously, Giles pressed the buzzer again, waiting for Imogen to answer. She had said come at two, and it was now two-thirty – where was she? She knew he was due to take Rowan out today. . . . Again he pressed the bell, and her voice sounded suddenly over the intercom.

'Giles, is that you?'

'Yes.'

She came down without opening the door for him. Rowan ran ahead of her, shouted a hurried greeting to his father as he raced to the car.

'New car,' Imogen said evenly. 'You must be doing well.'

'The last season was good,' he replied, his eyes averted.

Imogen glanced away from her husband. They could never look each other in the face. They could be polite, dignified, especially when Rowan was around, but the love had long gone.

'So, where are you taking him –' she began, then stopped suddenly, seeing the person sitting in the front seat. 'How's Terry?'

Giles scuffed the toe of his shoe on the pavement, his embarrassment obvious. It was a child's gesture; God, you never really grew up, did you? Imogen thought. Maybe it even explains your homosexuality, a longing to return to the past, to schooldays.

'He's fine.'

She struggled to keep her voice calm. This was her rival, the white-faced boy in the mirror, grown fatter now, glossy, like a sweet-eater.

'You've been together a long time.'

'Yes.'

The air was heavy with unease.

'Almost like a marriage.'

He turned his eyes screwed up against the sunlight. 'Sorry,' he said.

She was surprised by the unexpected apology, and oddly touched. I should still hate you; should still despise the boy you chose instead of me. So why can't I? You cost me so much, and gave me so little. I remember that summer, that horrible summer when I first came to this flat, long before I bought it, long before I had the money to be *able* to buy it. I remember being ill, waiting for the phone to ring – and it never did. You cut me off, Imogen thought, you made your choice and never looked back. You damaged me.

She was suddenly chilled with unease. 'Will you have Rowan back by nine?' she asked, already turning to go.

Giles nodded, but she didn't see the gesture, only heard the car start up and the quick call of 'Goodbye' from her son.

Alone in the flat, Imogen thought about phoning Suzanne, but decided against it and instead poured herself some wine and sat down by the window, her bare feet propped up on a chair in front of her. Rowan had been awkward that morning, difficult, unlike himself. Apparently his schoolwork, usually good, was falling off, his concentration fading. Surprised, Imogen had phoned his teacher, but had been told little, only that her son could be disruptive at times. Good company, popular, but wilful. He needed more discipline, the woman implied, without actually using the word. More discipline and more control. They both knew he needed a father.

Rowan was growing up: already nine years old, tall, quick-witted, amusing. There was little of his father in him, except when he was confronted with unpleasantness; then he drew back, folded inwards. Cut off. Imogen had noticed the tendency for years, had tried to draw him out of it, had reasoned with him that people only solved problems by facing up to them. But in this, he was his father's child.

His moods always accelerated after visiting Giles, and that worried her. She didn't want to separate them, to punish her son for her own bigotry, but she was anxious about the future and suddenly aware of Giles's limitations as a father. But who else was there? Ira had been no kind of father figure for her son. He was too glamorous, too impossibly glitzy to emulate. Since Rowan's birth, he had been a fixture in Imogen's life, but he had little real influence on the boy. There was no paternal feeling between them; affection, yes; good humour, plenty; but Ira had never once tried to discipline Rowan, leaving that to Imogen, not wanting to interfere – even if he had known how to.

Imogen had done a good job bringing up Rowan; she knew that, but now, suddenly, it wasn't enough. Rowan was a boy, and therefore needed the example of a man to follow. It was bad for him to be surrounded by women, even the best kind of women. He was growing up, his personality developing; before long sexuality would be developing too. . . . Imogen shifted uncomfortably in her seat, draining her glass. She had to face up to the fact that she was worried every time she saw her son go out with Giles and Terry. What did he see? Nothing corrupting, she knew that for a fact. Giles was too careful to expose any of his feelings publicly; that had always been a problem for him, with men or women. But did her son pick up on the undertone of their relationship? Did he watch them and wonder? Especially now that he was old enough to wonder.

She had waited for his questions, but they never came. She had even prepared an explanation, but it was never asked for. Time had passed without Rowan expressing any interest in his father's life, without him asking one question. At least, not of her.

'Well, *has* he?'

Suzanne was blurry from sleep. She had had her legs waxed and then dozed off during her facial, the phone call an unwelcome interruption to her dreams. Idly she rolled on her stomach, the beautician beginning to pummel the back of her legs.

'What *are* you talking about, Imogen?'

'Rowan!' she said hotly. 'I want to know if he has ever asked you about Giles, you know, if he . . . if he is. . . .'

'A ponce?'

'I *hate* that word,' Imogen snapped. 'Can't you think of any other way of putting it?'

'A man of alternative affections?' she queried. 'Will that do?'

Imogen sighed with irritation. 'I'm worried about it. I was just thinking about it and I realised that Rowan has very limited male company.'

'A ponce and a porn king,' Suzanne said wryly. 'Yes, I see what you mean.'

'Don't get clever,' Imogen said warningly. 'I'm not in the mood.'

Hearing the edge in her voice, Suzanne waved away the beautician and sat up on the bed, a towel wrapped round her.

'Go on, tell me what's bothering you.'

'Rowan . . . he needs a father.'

'So what can I do about it? I can't even find a husband.'

'Seriously, Jaco, he should be with a man who acts normally, someone who can take him fishing –'

'In London?'

'There's a canal round the bloody corner, isn't there?' Imogen shouted. 'Don't split hairs, you know what I mean. He needs a man who can take him to football, to the cinema. A man who can talk about whatever it is that males talk about –'

Suzanne's eyes widened. 'Are you *sure* that's what you want?'

Imogen nodded. 'Rowan's growing up fast. He's developing so quickly, and I want him to develop as he should. He can only judge the world on what he sees, and if he sees an . . . odd . . . relationship, then he might think that's normal. I'm not criticising Giles, but I don't want my son thinking that that is the *only* way to live.'

Suzanne rubbed some oil off her nose, thinking carefully. 'Is he interested in girls yet?'

'I don't know, I haven't noticed,' Imogen said, suddenly alarmed. 'What age *do* boys get interested in girls?'

'Around puberty, I suppose. Unless you're Ira – and then it's around eighteen months.'

'Maybe I should talk to Rowan.'

'About what?' Suzanne countered. 'Not the birds and the bees. . . . Oh God, spare the poor little bastard that.'

Impatiently, Imogen stood up, holding the phone to her ear: 'I want my son to know about women.'

'He does, he lives with one.'

'Yes,' Imogen said calmly. 'Giles was very close to *his* mother too.'

'You are *not* like Polly Winner.'

'No.'

'No!' Suzanne insisted.

'But she was divorced and she brought Giles up on her own,' Imogen replied. 'Just like I'm bringing Rowan up. Think about it, Jaco, just think about it for a minute. Rowan is his father's child. There have to be similarities between them. I *have* to give my son the best chance in life. I don't care how he chooses to live later on – that's for him to decide – but I *do* care about the way he's growing up now. I want

233

him to realise that love can be between men and women; what a woman can offer a man, and what a man can offer a woman.' She shook her head. 'I know he's only nine. I know he's a child, but Giles once told me that "the past is what we are" – and now I believe that. I want my child to see love now, to feel it and understand it, so later he can go out and find it for himself.' She felt suddenly drained. 'I want him to have a father, Jaco, someone to show him another way of living; of loving.'

'Giles is his father.'

She nodded. 'Yes, and Julie is my mother. But just think what would have happened if I had been left with her. Elizabeth had the sense to take me away and I was lucky enough to get you as a surrogate mother.'

'I was lucky too, sweetheart,' Suzanne said gratefully.

Imogen paused, savouring the warmth between them. 'Funny how things repeat themselves, isn't it?'

'Like how?'

'Elizabeth wanted another mother for me, and now I want another father for Rowan. . . . I just hope he gets as lucky as I did.'

Simone phoned Ira from New York, then again from London, then finally from Paris. He returned none of her calls, just screwed up the messages and dropped them into the bin, giving his secretary instructions that she was to tell Madame Duchamp that he was abroad. Where? Anywhere, just abroad. She'll want more details. So say I'm ill. Say anything, just get her off my back.

Simone didn't believe the secretary, of course. But she stopped calling, her pride preventing her. Enough is enough – for now. Or so she told herself. Just wait, he always comes back. When he misses me, then he'll call. . . . Breathing in deeply, Simone walked down the steps into the Paris casino, her hand resting lightly on the banister rail. The scene invigorated her, filled her lungs and her heart. Oh, the money, she thought, the money, as, walking round, she nodded briefly to various croupiers.

It had been a good year, many losses for them, many winnings for her. Many players. Many nights ending in many mornings, doors closed, clocks rewound, the takings passed over to the inspectors, the girls leaving drowsily for home. Except the other girls, waiting in the other rooms, the rooms behind the backgammon tables. The night girls. Simone leaned against the banister rail, smiled quickly at a well-known player, and thought of the other side of her business.

She had no moral qualms about the agencies. None at all. To Simone, they merely represented more business. Men wanted girls to sleep with, and girls wanted easy money. That was the basic premise, no more. She understood the reasoning; had she been a different type of woman she might even have been attracted to the life itself. But Simone wasn't sensual, she was avaricious and worldly. She wanted money not sexual gratification, and if that meant working for it then she would rather toil vertically than horizontally.

The girls were hired for their looks, but also for their temperaments. Discretion was the byword, the agencies so discreet that many people thought them only a rumour. The casinos provided the perfect foil; rich men could visit a casino more easily than they could a brothel, and many of the guests had too much to lose to want to be seen anywhere compromising. They trusted Simone Duchamp, reassured by her classic appearance and her quiet manner. They trusted that she would understand their every whim, and keep such information a secret.

She was good at keeping secrets, this woman. Very adept, very skilful, very quiet. No one doubted her integrity for an instant; no one had to, there had never been a breath of scandal regarding her clubs. To all intents and purposes, Simone Duchamp ran casinos in Paris, London and New York, no more. Unless you were one of the select few who had been privately introduced to her; and one of the select few who had met up with *her* select few women, who would treat you to anything you wanted. For a price.

So in safety many men visited the rooms off the casinos, and had done for many years, some even bringing their sons when they came of age. Twenty years of experience had brought Simone to the top; and twenty years of experience had kept her there. She treated everyone as though they were house guests. She remembered to ask about their wives – or not, depending on the visitor's preference – and she behaved with absolute and complete refinement.

For twenty years she kept it up. For twenty years from country to country, girl to girl, client to client. Her memory, always sharp, never failed her, and if occasionally it did, there were always the files on which to fall back. Small files, like leather-bound books. Not hidden – Simone was too clever for that – just placed in amongst the expensive first editions in her home. People never looked for the obvious, she knew that. She understood people, this woman.

She understood *men* perfectly. Fell in love once or twice and then fixed all her hopes on Ira Mazan. He was the one she wanted, and the one for whom she was prepared to wait. Let his women come and go; let his daughter come and go; let his youth and even his health come and go – in the end he would come to her, and stay with her. They would make a fine couple, she with her business, he with his. She had built the agencies up over the years carefully resisting the impulse to tell him, impress him, show off for him. Look, Ira, look at what I've achieved. He was fascinated by the casinos, how could he fail to be mesmerised by the agencies? Oh yes, Simone assured herself, when the time was absolutely perfect, she would tell him – and then he would be hers.

That was the plan, and to that end Simone had worked. Yet even Ira was not to be included in one aspect of her business. The file side, the secret side, the records side, the side which was going to provide Simone with a healthy and extremely affluent old age. He wouldn't approve of the idea, she knew that, he had *some* scruples. She hadn't, but that didn't matter; Ira was a man and only a woman could understand blackmail. So she kept the forward planning of her pension fund a secret from everyone, and then, finally last month, she told Ira about her agencies.

She told him with consummate pride. Waited for his response, for the admiring laughter which was sure to come. But didn't. He sat, stony-faced, unable to understand what she was talking about. Agencies, call girls. Jesus, whores! . . . She hadn't expected that. Thought she knew everything about men. Especially this one. It's a front, no one knows, Ira. You run brothels? he'd said. He looked shocked. Ira Mazan, *shocked*. Who'd have thought it? Not her.

It left the saliva bitter in her mouth. Left her blood cooled, her mind clicking over. He was shocked, but he'd recover. He'd get used to the idea. Thank God she hadn't told him about her plans for retirement. . . . She sat in a white satin gown like a winter rose, black with anger underneath. And he looked at her and then at the casino around him, and seemed to want to leave. But he didn't. Instead his eyes closed for an instant. . . . He was thinking, she knew that, thinking of who he was and what right he had to criticise her. Thinking that he was in the glossy, sticky nest of his own making, and thinking that he belonged there.

So who cared if he didn't call. Who cared? He knew his place. Oh, he might fight it for a while, but a dog comes home to its own kennel at night. He might think he wanted to be respectable; might long for Imogen Winner; but she wasn't home to him, no matter how much he wanted her to be. . . . Simone laced her fingers and leaned forward on the desk. You'll think it over and before long it won't seem so bad. You'll look at Imogen Winner and you'll know that she's off limits. You'll know, because in the end you'll face up to the reality of who you are. . . . Simone smiled behind her hands. I know men, Ira, and I know you.

He knew it too. And that's why he didn't call her.

Chapter Twenty-Two

'Tom's going to be late,' Penny said, her voice dropping as she scanned the room. 'But he'll turn up, I told him you were coming.' Idly she touched her cropped head. 'Come and have a word with Danielle –'

'I can't remember who she's with,' Imogen said quickly.

'Trevor Rowe-Thorne,' Penny reminded her. 'He's the lawyer who advises the Tories. He spends a lot of time *advising* them, and he charges well for the service.'

'Is he any good?'

'Who knows?' Penny answered, shrugging. 'A lawyer is a lawyer, is a lawyer. I'll tell you one thing though, he'll never marry Danielle – whatever she thinks. He's not into marriage, he's too ambitious to settle with anyone.' She pointed to a burly man across the room, holding court in front of the fireplace. 'And that's Jimmy Bentley, married to Sarah – the ball-breaker.'

Carefully, Imogen scrutinised the Tory PR man. He was thickset, bushy-eyebrowed, with clumsy hands and a habit of finishing people's sentences. In fact, at that very moment he was completing Harry Taylor's joke.

'God help him if he tries that with Arnold,' Penny said, watching him. 'He just can't let anyone have the last word. It comes from being in PR, I suppose,' she went on nonchalantly. 'He has to let everyone know he's hanging on every flaming word that comes out of their mouths.'

Imogen glanced round. Penny's house in Barnes was a tribute to little money and a great imagination. The room in which they stood was obviously in need of decorating, but the pictures covered most of the damp spots and the numerous stuffed animals on shelves, or under glass, gave a wild, faintly primeval air. Everywhere Imogen turned, glass eyes watched her, foxes creeping out of long-dried vegetation, a squirrel caught, forever perched on a broken branch.

'Douglas lets Jimmy finish his sentences too,' Penny continued. 'Even Tom.'

'Who once lived with Maxie.'

Penny grinned. 'You catch on fast,' she said approvingly. 'I told you, it's not that complicated, once you get to know everyone – and their little foibles.'

'Such as?'

She leaned towards Imogen, her voice lowered: 'Harry's fine, unless you mention height. He is *very* touchy about that. And don't let on that you know he wears built-up shoes.'

Imogen glanced over, her gaze resting momentarily on Harry's feet.

Penny nodded. 'Apparently they add about an inch and a half to his height – and the other inch and a half is supplied by his hair. Never did a man put a blow-drier to such good use,' she giggled mischievously. 'Maxie says that when he comes out of the shower without shoes, and with wet hair, he's hardly more than a dwarf.'

'Oh come on!' Imogen said laughing. 'He's not that short.'

'No, unless he happens to be standing next to Tom, and then, you watch, Harry will find some excuse to sit down, or lean against something – anything, rather than be seen talking to Tom's top shirt button.'

They were suddenly interrupted. Sarah Bentley cutting into their conversation, her powerful voice sharp with irritation.

'Did you hear about the Paris trip?' she snapped. 'I thought your husband was supposed to be going on that with Jimmy.'

Penny frowned. 'He was – what changed?'

'Apparently the Prime Minister doesn't think that our husbands are needed there.'

'So what?' Penny countered. 'That means I've got Douglas at home for the weekend –'

Sarah's wide, high-cheekboned face was rigid. 'You really

have no ambition, have you?' she said coldly. 'It was an important trip –'

'Oh, dry up,' Penny said evenly. 'We all know the reason you wanted Jimmy out of the way, Sarah. You had that little feminist rally all set up, didn't you? And now he's home, you'll have to call it off.'

Imogen looked at Sarah, noticed the shift in her expression, her pale grey eyes fixing on Penny with real dislike. This one is deadly, she thought to herself.

'It's got nothing to do with that.'

'Whatever you say,' Penny responded carefully, watching Sarah as she moved away. 'Stupid cow, she'll ruin his career with all her bloody crazy feminism. She can't resist a cause – especially one that puts down men. I can't think why she ever married, she obviously detests men. it was fate that she had a son –'

'Sarah has a *son*?'

Penny nodded. 'Yeah, and the poor little bugger's already henpecked. That woman,' she said darkly, 'is a real harpie.'

Imogen's attention was suddenly taken by a small woman in a long voile dress, her head dipped downwards, a heavy fringe covering most of her eyes. 'Isn't that Claudine?' she asked.

Penny stared. 'Good, she said she'd come, but I wondered. Whatever she does depends on Arnold, and he, as usual, wouldn't commit himself in case anything better came along.' She gestured for Claudine to come across to them. Shyly, she waved, looked around and then timidly moved through the guests.

'Hello,' she said to Penny, then smiled at Imogen. 'Thank you for arranging for me to have that caricature of Arnold. It's wonderful.' She spoke hurriedly, as though anxious to finish what she was saying before boring anyone. Her voice was quiet, quick, her breathing shallow. 'Arnold wasn't sure he could make it. But I'm glad we did.' She smiled, glanced up at both of them suddenly. The gesture was anxious, expecting rejection.

Imogen found her touching, oddly poignant. 'How are your children?'

Claudine smiled again, flattered to be asked. 'Oh, fine,

thank you. Freddie's walking now.' A pause. 'How is your son?'

'Oh, Rowan's been walking for years,' Imogen teased her. 'He's nearly ten, and getting difficult.'

Penny was losing interest. She had no children and, having nothing to contribute, was mentally itchy.

'Hey, look who's arrived,' she said, gesturing to the tall figure who had just walked in. 'Tom Wrigley.' She winked at Imogen. 'I told you he'd come, didn't I?'

He spotted her at once and moved across, pausing only to look at a pair of ferrets in a glass case.

'Newly stuffed?' he asked Penny, kissing her on both cheeks. 'They remind me of a couple I know.'

She grinned broadly. 'Don't be unpleasant about Sarah and Jimmy,' she said wickedly, turning his attention to Imogen. 'Look who's here.'

'I'm glad to see you,' he said genuinely, shaking her hand for an instant. 'I was hoping we would meet up again.' He was wearing a sports jacket and open-necked shirt, his dark beard newly trimmed, his hair thick, curling at the collar. He didn't look like an MP – even a Tory MP – he looked like someone from the media, someone smooth, a good talker, a good listener. Good with words, good with women. Good for nothing.

Surprised by her sudden feeling of animosity, Imogen tried hard to cover it.

'I was hearing all the gossip,' she said lightly.

'All of which is true,' he replied, taking a glass of wine from Penny. 'Perhaps we could go for a drive afterwards?'

She imagined his car – a BMW or a Mercedes? Not a Rover, too sound. Not an Audi, too middle-aged. A sports car, no, too Ira. . . . Oh, Ira, she thought suddenly, what would you make of all of this? White wine in Barnes, Tory MPs, Freddie beginning to walk! . . . this isn't you. This isn't me.

'. . . well, *would* you?'

Startled, Imogen blinked, and looked up at Tom as he stood waiting for an answer.

'Pardon?'

'I said, would you like to come for a drive?'

'What for?'

He blinked.

'Just a drive,' he replied, puzzled. 'You know, we could talk.'

'About what?'

The wine in his glass was warming. He felt relieved that Penny had moved off and that only the gentle Claudine remained.

'Life.'

'Oh, life . . .' Imogen said thoughtfully. 'Where would we go?'

He was baffled. 'Anywhere. Is there anywhere particular you *want* to go?'

Home, she thought.

'No . . .' Imogen said quietly.

He was too mystified to back off, and pressed the point. 'So we'll go?'

'Fine. Why not?'

They left shortly afterwards, Penny raising her eyebrows and giving Imogen a furtive thumbs-up sign from the doorway. Behind her Arnold Miles was holding forth about the German economy, and Harry Taylor was fondling Maxie's leg as she lounged on a windowseat. Only Douglas, Penny's long-winded husband, looked out of place, his mournful face below his thin red hair taking on an expression of exquisite unease. Captured by the gregarious Jimmy, he watched Imogen and Tom leave and thought about what his wife had said the previous evening. She was matchmaking again, he realised. God help Tom Wrigley, may he rest in peace.

But at that moment Tom was perfectly content. He drove along happily – in a black BMW – and chatted about anything that came to mind. *His* mind. Not Imogen's. She listened politely, asked questions, looked out of the window. And longed to be home. He had a wide range of interests. *His* interests. And a vast knowledge about work. *His* work. Any reference he made to her career was brief and superficial, although he complimented her frequently on her looks. That was what women liked, after all.

And Imogen smiled. A lot. She kept asking questions too,

long after she wanted to know the answers, and she made mental notes, ready to pass on every detail to Ira. What a bore, she'd say later. What a forty-carat windbag. . . . She felt suddenly ill at ease, disturbed. I don't like you very much, Mr Wrigley. I don't really like your friends either. It's not you, she thought to herself; any other woman would probably be glad to be in my place, but we've nothing in common. Nothing at all.

Tom thought it was going really well. Imogen was asking about his work and his life and she seemed interested. Didn't she? . . . He drove on. Mind you, perhaps he *was* talking about himself a little too much. Perhaps . . . he shrugged mentally. No, women like a man who knows his own mind, who's confident. He was doing fine, after all, she was listening, wasn't she?

She was virtually catatonic.

'Of course, I travel a lot. . . .'

Please God, get me out of here.

'. . . and I have a lot of time for my constituents.'

Lucky Manchester.

'. . . it's not a job everyone would want to do.'

But a man's gotta do what a man's gotta do.

'. . . but someone has to do it.'

Imogen bit her lip. Hard.

'It's gruelling work. People don't realise just how much work an MP does. They have no real understanding of the life. The demands, the hours. . . .'

Time, gentlemen, please.

'. . . there's so little time to make relationships, and an MP needs a steady home life.'

He finally stopped for breath at some traffic lights and glanced over at Imogen. She looked out of the window fixedly.

'You have a son, don't you?'

Slowly she turned her head and looked at him. She saw a just man who was doing his best. An attractive man. It wasn't his fault that he didn't know how to talk to women. Only Ira knew the questions to ask, and Ira, oh, Ira, well, he was off bounds. The right man, in the wrong life.

'Yes,' she said finally, 'I have a son called Rowan.'

'How old?'

'Nearly ten.'

Tom nodded. 'It must be difficult bringing up a child alone. You're divorced, aren't you?'

She nodded.

'You were married to Giles Winner, weren't you?'

Her eyes narrowed; suddenly she felt cornered.

He didn't see the reaction. Ira would have; finely tuned to every nuance of a woman's feelings, he would have picked up on it in an instant. But not Tom Wrigley. The lights changed, and he drove on, pursuing the point.

'Wasn't it Giles Winner you were married to?'

'Why do you want to know?'

He shot her a quick glance. 'Sorry, did I say something wrong?'

It was her turn to feel uncomfortable. She had over-reacted and knew it. She had given herself away, let it show just how much it still mattered. What did he know? Imogen wondered. Did he know *everything* about Giles? Had he heard the rumours? Of course he had, she realised, vulnerable and embarrassed . . . everyone knew.

The heat in the car became suffocating, the smell of leather sickening as she fumbled for the window switch, Tom frowning and pressing the button for her. The air fell into the car, slapped at her skin, sobered her. Get a grip, it was a long time ago. Forget it. Everyone does, everyone has to, in the end. . . . Oh, but you can't, she thought bitterly. When you've been rejected and hurt that much you cover it, but you never bury it. . . . Her hands were damp, a sudden and overwhelming desire to cry welling up in her. What am I doing? I don't want to be here. I don't want to be with this man and have to make small talk and pretend an interest I don't feel . . . I want to be home, or with Ira. I want to be safe.

'Did I upset you?' Tom asked, pulling into a layby and turning off the engine.

The traffic pounded on their right. The night was coming in early, taking the day away. On the windscreen, a bug crawled.

'Please, take me home,' Imogen said simply.

'I don't understand,' he replied, turning in his seat to look at her.

She kept her head down.

'Did I say something?'

'No. I don't feel well, I just want to go home,' Imogen replied gently. It wasn't his fault, don't punish him.

'What, is it because I asked about your husband?'

She got out of the car fast, slamming the door. He followed, amazed, running after her as she made her way down the side of the road.

'Imogen! *Imogen!*'

She stopped walking.

'I want to go home, Tom. I'm sorry if you think I'm making a scene, I probably am, but I have to go home.'

He was much taller than her and could hardly hear for the traffic; he bent down towards her to catch her words.

'Okay, okay Imogen, just come on back to the car and I'll take you home.'

She turned. An open-topped sports car passed, blaring music.

'Sorry. . . .'

He said nothing in response, merely slid into the driver's seat and turned the car back to London. The silence was punishing. Nothing to lighten the mood, no conversation, no jokes. No understanding; none at all.

'She gave him the brush-off,' Penny said, peering at the stuffed fox on her workbench. Frowning, she looked over at her husband, his narrow head bent down over some papers, his shock of flat red hair almost lurid under the overhead lamp. Slowly Penny glanced at the fox again and then back to Douglas, a smile lifting the corner of her mouth. It had never occurred to her before, but there was a similarity between them. Foxes and Douglas; all those stuffed animals looking like a set of stuffed Douglases. A new species, Giganticus Foxicus Governmenticus. . . .

He looked up, knowing she was watching. Immediately Penny glanced away, picking up two hazel glass eyes from the box on the shelf behind her.

'What did you say?'

'I said that Imogen gave Tom the . . .' she paused, then playfully flirted the tail of the fox. '. . . the "brush-off".'

He didn't get the pun, and laid down his papers wearily. She liked the fact that he came down to the basement to work even though it was crowded, her table taking up much of the room. Apparently her husband didn't seem to think it was odd for him to be reading Conservative party papers in amongst the carcasses of dead animals, stuffing, and wire frames. He didn't even seem to notice the heavy chemical smell, and never criticised Penny for the fact that her new dehydrating machine took up all the space in the garage, forcing his Rover outside.

He liked company, so he was prepared to follow his wife wherever she was. And that was usually the basement. It was a small area, flag floored, low-ceilinged, damp in winter – but they'd made many decisions down there, about their lack of a family and about Douglas's work. He hid down there too. When persistent constituents harassed him, or when he was trying to concentrate on some difficult issue. It was quiet usually, peaceful, Penny fully absorbed.

But not now; now she wanted to talk.

'I said that Imogen isn't interested in Tom Wrigley.'

'Why should she be?'

Penny rummaged in the cardboard box for another pair of artificial eyes.

'Are these too dark?'

Ruefully Douglas looked at the eyes and then at the fox. 'They're okay.'

'I'm not sure,' Penny said half-heartedly.

'Darling . . .' Douglas began, glancing at the shelves and at the accumulated rabbits, birds and ferrets amassed on them. '. . . don't you think you should try selling some of these? I mean, we could do with the money.'

'I *do* sell, Douglas,' she replied hotly, holding the eyes up to the fox's empty sockets and trying to gauge the effect. 'It's just that business is a bit quiet at the moment.'

'So why keep stuffing more, if you can't sell these?'

Penny gave him a hard look. 'It's a hobby. You told me to get a hobby, and I did – so don't start complaining now.'

'Yes, but other wives play bridge.'

246

Her expression was incredulous. 'Only the older ones. Besides, some of the wives have more entertaining hobbies, Douglas – like Sarah and her feminism. . . .'

He shuddered. He didn't like a woman with a low voice and a heavy alcohol consumption.

'And now Maxie's sleeping around again. or you could look at Claudine's hobby. Motherhood. Maybe you'd like to listen to her babytalk day in, day out: "Freddie's learning to walk, Freddie's learning to talk, Freddie's learning to puke." '

'Maxie doesn't count,' Douglas said stiffly. 'She's not a wife.'

'The others are,' Penny countered. 'Anyway, I thought you were proud of my work.'

'I am, darling,' he said hurriedly, nudging away a detached tail and taking his wife's hand. 'It's just that we're so hard up, it would be good if you could sell some of your –' he struggled to find a word – 'creations.'

Penny assumed a wounded look. 'I'll try, honestly I will.' Then she changed the subject quickly. 'I thought that Imogen and Tom would hit it off. I really did.'

'Why? They have nothing in common,' Douglas replied, looking back at his notes. 'Tom's an MP and Imogen's a caricaturist – what's the link?'

'They're single.'

'Oh.'

'Don't go "oh", Douglas. It's a real point in their favour. After all, there aren't that many eligible men around forty, she *should* be interested. I mean, she's been having an affair with that Ira Mazan for ages, I would have thought that Tom was a few steps up from him.' She sighed, stroking the fox's brush thoughtfully. 'So many married people we know are having affairs, it seems crazy that two single people shouldn't hit it off. Besides,' she said emphatically, 'Tom's rich.'

'Maybe Imogen didn't fancy him,' Douglas offered gently.

Penny stared at the top of her husband's head in surprise. His hair was limp against his skull, his forehead elongated. He looked intelligent, she thought. So much for looks.

247

'What do you mean, "maybe she didn't fancy him"?'

Sighing, Douglas laid down his papers. 'Just that.'

'Douglas . . .' Penny began, leaning across the table and staring into his eyes with an appealing look. 'Do *you* ever fancy anyone? I mean, apart from me.' Her voice was soft, benign. 'You can tell me. . . . Do you?'

His expression defied description. He hadn't seen the cliff and had very nearly fallen over it without realising. Arranging his melancholic features into a smile, Douglas lifted his wife's chin.

'Darling, who else could I possibly want? I love you.'

Penny smiled, her marvellous black eyes tender.

'Well, if you *do* ever find yourself attracted to someone else, Douglas, and if you *do* ever sleep with someone else . . .' She paused, stroked his ginger hair. 'I'll maim you.'

'Penny!'

Her lips rested on his forehead for an instant, then nuzzled softly against his ear.

'Sshhhhh . . . ssshhhh. . . . I know you're the faithful type, Douglas,' she crooned, her voice mesmerising. 'I know that. But just remember, if you should stray. *If* you ever do, I will have you mounted, stuffed, and put in a glass case before you can get your trousers back on.'

Elizabeth had thought about phoning Imogen all day and then, finally, at ten, she did call. But the answerphone was on and only an automatic message came down the line. Intimidated, Elizabeth put down the phone, cursing herself for not leaving a message. Damn machines, she thought, how was anyone supposed to feel comfortable talking to a machine?

It was difficult to know what to do, and Suzanne for once had been unhelpful. . . . I don't know, honestly, I don't. Tell her, if you think it's right. . . . But what do you think? Elizabeth countered. We always make decisions together, do *you* think I should tell her? Or wait a bit? Maybe Julie will get better. . . .

Elizabeth looked at the phone for another moment and then slowly went upstairs, turning on the electric fire in the bedroom. She felt the cold now, even though she had a goodly padding of flesh. Her blood had thinned, that was it. Graham had always said that people's blood thinned when they got old. She walked flat-footed to the heavy mahogany dressing table, picking up a rubber doll she had given to Julie when she was a baby. It had had clothes once, but now it was mother naked and the rubber had darkened and gone stiff.

Sighing she laid down the doll and pulled off her clothes, unfastening her hair and coughing. The sound came back loudly in the silent house. Suddenly lonely, Elizabeth turned on the radio, listening to a late play. I wonder what old lady Forest would have made of all this, she thought. Imogen in London, divorced, with a boy. All on her own. But doing well in her work. Almost famous. . . . Elizabeth heaved her legs up on to the bed. I'll just catch a quick minute's kip, then I'll phone Imogen again.

Her eyes closed, but her memory played against the lids. Graham and his fireworks, Mrs Jacobs and that terrible kosher food, Imogen and Giles waiting at the barrier at Victoria station for her all those years ago. And Julie . . . aahhh. . . . Elizabeth's eyes opened, fixed on the Anaglypta ceiling. Julie, ill. But not the usual illness, this was something else. Ill in the body now. Pneumonia. Not that serious, they said; under control. Well, *was* it? Elizabeth wondered. And why had they bothered to get it under control?

She turned over heavily, staring at the dressing table again and the little worn crucifix a neighbour had given her years before. Elizabeth wasn't much for church, didn't really think there was a God. Too much bloody suffering for that. Think of Graham and the camps, think of Julie. . . . What kind of God made you sweat blood? . . . But she hadn't thrown the crucifix away, just in case there *was* a God and He happened to be watching.

I don't agree with what they say in the Bible either, Elizabeth thought, wiping her mouth with a handkerchief. All that about animals and Arks and Adam and Eve. Silliness, that was all. Only one thing she could agree with – 'God helps them that helps themselves' – well, that much was true. And if there was a God, and if He did suddenly materialise in front of her now, there was no one better qualified to say that she'd helped herself.

Worked hard, I have, Elizabeth thought. Got on with it. Not much time to think about anything; too worried about work, and money, and family. She reached out her left hand, taking warmth from the electric fire. Well, God, I've never asked you for much. I asked you to help me find a home for Imogen and you did that, so now I'll ask you one more favour. It'll be the last, I promise.

Let Julie go, God, please. I don't want my daughter to outlive me. I don't want Imogen saddled with her. Worrying, wondering what to do for the best. She'd ruin her chances, I know she would. She'd come up here, look after her mother. Try to do the best for her. I bet she'd even bring her out of that hospital – and for what? Julie can't understand. She'd just stick to her daughter like a leech and then what would happen to Imogen?

She's had enough, God. What with that husband of hers, and the way she's struggled to bring up her son on her own. No, God, you can't ask it of her. I didn't mind, it was my job, but it's not Imogen's. . . . The heat in the bedroom was building, Elizabeth warming up and longing to drowse. But her mind ran on relentlessly. . . . I don't want to make that call, God, she said. I don't want to tell Imogen her mother's ill. I want . . . oh God, she thought, closing her eyes against tears. Forgive me, please. It's not unkindness, she's my child, after all, but I want Julie to die. To let go. . . . If that's wrong, God, you can punish *me* for it. After all, I never had much time for you, so I suppose I've got it coming. But I stand by what I believe, and I believe this would be right.

The room warmed, darkened, the electric fire giving a reddened glow to the faded walls. Across Manchester, Julie breathed in and out; in Little Lever, Elizabeth breathed in and out. Let me phone Imogen and tell her it's over. Do that for me God, please. Then it's neat, tidy, done with. Then I can go, without worrying. . . .

In and out they breathed, mother and daughter. In and out. In unison, miles apart. Julie and Elizabeth. In and out.

Living and dying in time. The night closed in, the fire burning on, the crucifix glowing hotly in the bloodied light.

Chapter Twenty-Three

Imogen was in Lorrie's office, showing him the new caricatures for the next issue. She was wearing a red dress, her hair loose around her shoulders, a tan giving her appearance a heady sensuality. Even Lorrie noticed.

'My goodness, you're looking luminous,' he said, lowering his bulk into his chair. 'What's the secret?'

'It's hard work,' she replied easily. 'You should try it.'

Lorrie ignored the remark. 'I hear that you're doing more for Dickie Bedlington's rag.'

'He asked me to, yes.'

'It will never keep going,' Lorrie said, in an attempt to cover his real concern. The Bedlington magazine was flourishing, giving Lorrie a run for its money now that it had adopted *Exclusive*'s viewpoint: hype the rich, powerful and successful and bugger hard news.

'Oh, I think it will,' Imogen replied evenly, 'and I also think that there's room for both of you.'

Lorrie's doughy face was sulky: 'I hate competition. Ira's the type that thrives on that. I loathe a struggle. We were doing so well on our own.' His eyes hovered above Imogen's head for an instant. 'I feel betrayed, with you going off and working for them.'

'Oh, Lorrie, don't be childish,' she rebuked him. 'You know damn well you couldn't give me enough work. I had to find work elsewhere to keep going –'

'Word is you're keeping going pretty well now,' he remarked meanly. 'What with my magazine and Bedlington's and now the freelance work.'

'Oh,' Imogen said easily. 'You heard.'

'Of course I did! I know everything that goes on in this

town,' he retorted, crossing his thick ankles. 'Apparently some very wealthy clients are coming to you to have their little portraits done –'

'Caricatures, Lorrie,' she corrected him. 'I'm not an artist, I just do caricatures.'

'I didn't think people *liked* to be laughed at.'

'No,' Imogen agreed, 'but they *do* like to be famous.'

'So you've succumbed to the lure of the celebrity, have you?'

She stood up, smiling. 'I never resisted it, Lorrie,' she said. 'When do you want the next lot?'

'Week on Thursday,' he said simply as she closed the door.

The phone rang only minutes later.

'Is Imogen still there?'

'Hello, Suzanne, how are you?' Lorrie asked, turning on the fan on his desk and causing a sheaf of papers suddenly to be propelled into mid-air. 'Shit!'

'No, I'm feeling better than that, Lorrie,' she replied coolly. 'Is Imogen there?'

'No!' he snapped, turning off the fan again. 'She's just left. Why?'

'I wanted to talk to her, that's why. People generally use phones for that purpose.' She paused. 'Do you know where she's gone?'

'Try Ira,' Lorrie said, knowing just how to provoke her.

'I did. She's not there either, and he's not meeting her for lunch.'

Lorrie lost interest. 'I don't know where she is. Sorry.'

'Well, if you see her, let her know I called. It's urgent.'

His curiosity came back, newly charged. 'How urgent?'

Oh, yes, Suzanne thought, how you would love to know. How you would love it if I confided; said, Lorrie, Imogen's mother is dead. Oh, you didn't know about her? No, well, we kept it a secret for years, she was hospitalised up in the North. She was ill, you see. Mentally ill. Keep it to yourself, though. We don't want everyone to know. . . .

'It's nothing really urgent, Lorrie,' she lied, 'just tell Imogen to call me if she comes back.'

*

But Imogen didn't go back to Lorrie and she didn't call in to see Ira either. Instead she met up for coffee with Penny Fairbane and Maxie Penn and then went to have her hair done. She was singing under her breath as she walked past the end of South Molton Street afterwards; she even considered calling in on Giles, but decided against it – a surprise like the last was enough for one lifetime.

Her good mood was due to a calmness in her. She hadn't wanted to go out with Tom Wrigley and had been relieved when he didn't call her after he had driven her home. No one would have expected him to. Least of all her. He was offended by her behaviour and had lost interest. A fact which didn't worry Imogen one jot. Maybe she *did* need a man, certainly Rowan needed a father, but not yet, not just yet. She wanted to remain aloof from the dating scene; apart from relationships, safe from injury. Better to be alone than humiliated or mistaken.

Her calmness soothed her. I am in control, she thought; for once in my life, things are calm. The work is going well, very well, she admitted to herself, and money was no longer a problem. Now she could afford to have the flat re-decorated, the carpets replaced, the plumbing made good. It was her home – hers and Rowan's – it had to be welcoming. She swung her bag as she walked, happy without effort. Even Rowan was settling down more, he was not so withdrawn, not so moody at times. Her worries had been for nothing; he had even mentioned the girl who lived next door, his face flushing scarlet.

'. . . he said she was pretty,' Imogen told Suzanne over the phone. 'It's a good sign, isn't it?'

'It depends. If it turns out that she has a face like a brick outhouse, we'll *really* have something to worry about.'

Oh, but Imogen knew it was fine. Just fine. Her son was going to be okay. He had noticed girls, thank God.

'Perhaps I should give him a couple of copies of *S'expression* too, just to make sure,' Ira offered when he called round.

Imogen paled.

'Only joking!' he said, bursting out laughing. 'It was a joke – God's honour.'

254

'You wouldn't, would you, Ira?'

He raised his hands in mock defence: 'No, no way. . . . Anyway, he's at that difficult stage.'

Her eyes narrowed, on the defensive. *'What* stage?'

'Too young for the pictures and too old for the editorial,' Ira said, laughing.

Imogen smiled to herself as she walked along. It was good to feel at peace. She had some new friends, and her life was busy; in time a man would come along, but there was no way she was going to force anything. Still humming under her breath, she turned the corner into her road, stopping dead when she saw Suzanne's car outside her door. Her feet stopped, her heart banging. No, not Rowan, don't let it be Rowan . . . or Elizabeth. . . .

Slowly she began to move again, the gate seeming to back away as she approached, the distance lengthening. The street was empty, apart from a dog scratching itself on the kerbside. Go on, get on with it, find out what's happened, she willed herself, turning into the path which led to the front door of number 145. Suzanne was standing there, her arms folded, her eyes staring off in the other direction. She was beautifully dressed in a navy suit, a wide-collared white blouse setting off her suspiciously black hair. Spotting Imogen, she straightened up and faced her.

'It's not Rowan.'

'Thank God –'

'It's your mother.'

Imogen rocked, Suzanne catching her left elbow and taking the key out of her hand. 'Come on,' she said, steering her up the stairs and making her sit down in the flat. 'Here, drink this.'

Obediently, Imogen drank the brandy, warmth coming back to her hands.

'What happened?'

'Pneumonia,' Suzanne answered softly. 'She died last night.'

Imogen nodded, felt the slide of tears and bowed her head.

'I want to go up there.'

'I know, I knew you'd say that,' Suzanne replied. 'D'you want me to stay here and look after Rowan?'

Imogen nodded, dumb with shock.

'How's Gran?'

'Calm. But then she always is, in a crisis.'

'Had my . . . had my mother been ill for long?'

Suzanne glanced away, remembering what Elizabeth had told her. 'No, it was very sudden.'

'She wasn't that old, was she?' Imogen said, turning to look at Suzanne, her eyes filled. 'Only fifty-one . . . and she didn't have much of a life, did she? No happiness, no success, nothing really. . . . I suppose they'll give us her things.' She thought of the hairbrush suddenly and the carved wood box Julie had always kept by her bed. Empty, without trinkets. She didn't know what to put in it; couldn't remember.

Imogen stared at Suzanne, her face blank, her eyes burning.

'Did she say anything? I mean, at the end . . . did she say? . . . you know, Jaco. You know what I mean.' Imogen hesitated, hardly able to speak. 'Did my mother ask for me? Did she? Did she?' Her voice fell to an echo. 'Did she *remember* me?'

'She was too sick.'

Imogen nodded, recognising the lie.

'I just wondered. . . .'

'I know, darling,' Suzanne said helplessly. 'I know. . . .'

They sat in silence for nearly an hour, the phone finally breaking into the quiet. Frowning, Imogen got up to answer it, her voice shaky.

'Yes?'

'Imogen, it's Tom Wrigley.'

She said nothing.

'Are you all right?'

'We've had a bereavement,' she said, trying to think clearly. 'I have to go up north.'

'I'll take you, I have to go up tonight myself. Let me give you a lift.'

She couldn't think clearly; answered automatically.

'Yes, thanks.'

'I'll be round in about half an hour,' he said, checking the address. 'I'm sorry, Imogen . . . was it someone close?'

She shook her head. 'No . . . not really. But they should have been.'

It was only seconds after she put down the phone that it rang again. Ira on the line.

'Sorry, Imogen. I've just got the message Suzanne left at the office. Are you okay?'

Slowly, she rubbed her forehead: 'I'm going up north tonight, Ira –'

'I'll take you.'

'I've got a lift,' she answered.

'Suzanne taking you?'

'No . . . Tom Wrigley.'

He was thrown. 'Tom Wrigley! Why? He doesn't even know about your mother, does he?'

Imogen struggled to focus her thoughts. It was unlike Ira to be angry, especially at a time like this.

'Look, he was going up and he just offered me a lift, Ira,' she said, her tone edgy. 'If you'd phoned first, I would have gone with you.'

'Yes, sure,' he said bitterly, then brought himself up short. 'Sorry, Imogen . . . I wasn't thinking. You go with him and phone me if you need me, okay?' His heart was quick with temper and frustration. 'Just ask and I'll be there.'

'I know, you always are.'

It was the truth and both of them knew it. For years Ira had been the man to whom Imogen turned for comfort, advice and companionship. No other man had been allowed to enter her life; no other woman had entered his and stayed. He was her first and last port of call, her sheet anchor, the man upon whom she relied. The man she put first. Until now. Now suddenly there was someone else – Tom Wrigley. At a time when Imogen would naturally and instinctively look to Ira for help, British Telecom had worked it on him.

He tried to smile, to console himself with the idea that it was only a lift, a drive up north, a kindness extended to someone in trouble. But he knew better. This was the beginning of something he had seen months earlier, when Imogen had first met Tom Wrigley at Grosvenor House. She might not have recognised it, or admitted it to herself, but Ira knew at once. Tom Wrigley was right for her; just as he was wrong. He could try and cling on, try and use an old friendship to bribe his way back into the forefront of her affections – but it was no good, and he knew it.

One day you *had* to stand aside, Ira thought, surprised how much it hurt. One day some man *had* to come along, it was inevitable. I knew it, so why wasn't I better prepared? Because I love her, he thought, and there's no way on earth of preparing to receive love, or preparing to lose it. You had your day, Ira, every dog does – and yours was a long and sunny one. . . . He tipped back his head suddenly, embarrassed by the unexpected tears. I don't want you to go, Imogen, he thought. I don't want to stop hearing your voice on the phone, or stop laughing at your jokes. I don't want to hand you over to another man.

But I will, he thought. Oh, yes, I will. . . . Step aside, Mr Mazan, and let the lady pass.

After the funeral, Elizabeth and Imogen sat in the kitchen in Mulberry Street, Little Lever. The same clock ticked on the same tiled fireplace; the same divan was under the window. Nothing had changed since Imogen's last visit; nothing had changed since Graham's death; nothing ever changed here. Only the weather, and now, for once, the sun was shining, drawing the children out on to the narrow street.

Imogen glanced over to her grandmother. She had lost her child, but seemed calm, resigned. Almost at peace. What goes through your mind, Gran? Imogen wondered. All those years you kept your secrets, all those years you looked after us, what was it all for? What did you get from life? A small terraced house with a damp problem. You were so brave, so full of courage. And I admire you so much.

'What was he like?' Imogen asked suddenly.

'Who, love?'

'My grandfather . . . your husband.'

She smiled from the heart, slowly.

'He took me to the market once, when we were young.

Bought me a cushion. I kept it for years. And in the war, he wrote home. Lots of letters, like you couldn't imagine. I fell in love with him, then I hated him when he came back. . . .' She paused, fiddled with the old chain round her neck. 'Then I loved him again – when he tried. And he *did* try. You know, when I was pregnant with Julie I was scared of telling him, we had so little money and he was never one to get on. I waited for months, until I was so far gone that I couldn't hide it any longer, and then I told him.' She stopped again, weighed the words. 'He said he wanted a little girl. To look like me.' She hesitated. 'I was older than he was, and so worried I'd lose him. You know how it is, women lose their looks, men wander . . . but not Graham. He never wandered.'

'What happened?'

Elizabeth backtracked the years.

'He was ill, like your mother, but not so bad. He recovered, in a way. Knew all about you. Was proud of you. . . . D'you know, love, the night I came back I couldn't face him? I stood on that street outside and I hadn't the nerve to knock. My own home, my own husband! And I couldn't face him. . . .'

Imogen glanced at the photograph on the mantelpiece. Old, yellowed.

'Do you miss him?'

She took a moment to answer, then nodded. 'Every day . . . it's like that. Love. You can't seem to find a piece of yourself once they've gone. They take it with them, I think. Oh, I don't mean they break your heart, nothing fanciful. But there's a little bit of your soul that goes with them. Perhaps it's supposed to. Perhaps they hold it for you, until it's your turn.' She paused, smiled deeply. 'Wait until you find a man who'll do that for you. It's the way of things; the right way. No rhyme or reason to it, just a rightness about it.'

Imogen tried, but couldn't fully understand what her grandmother was saying.

'Just wait, Imogen, there's someone out there for you too. There always is, we just stop looking, or stop hoping. . . . Don't do that, no one lives properly when they're alone.'

'But what happens if you don't find someone?'

'You always do,' Elizabeth said emphatically. 'The trick's not finding them – but recognising them.'

Outside Tom Wrigley sat in this BMW and waited for Imogen. He was patient, working on some parliamentary papers, his head bent down. The sun glinted on the windscreen and made the car hot, his window letting in the unaccustomed sun. He didn't understand what was going on; his mind was partly with Imogen and partly with work. Preoccupied. But he didn't leave, even when he should have been on his way back to London. He waited instead, knowing that she would come out eventually.

Patiently he ate the chocolate melting in his glove compartment, smoked three cigarettes and then watched a boy doing wheelies on his bike. But he didn't go in, even though he had been invited into the little house. It was too soon, too quick, he knew that. Knew that if he wanted to keep Imogen he had to allow her to come to him in her own time. Not his. So he kept waiting, even managing to prepare a boring speech in the car before finally stretching his legs and walking down the street.

She had told him about her background and about her mother. Told him everything – even about Giles. She talked in the way people do when their defences are down: offering everything in trust; totally vulnerable. He listened, for once. Found that he *wanted* to listen, and that, after a while, he could see past the lovely face and the image, could see Imogen as she was, and as few had ever imagined her.

This was no ordinary girl. This was someone remarkable, out of his class, out of *anyone's* class. Not by upbringing, or breeding, not by intelligence, wit or beauty; Imogen was set apart by goodness – and there was so little of that. Tom had had only limited experience of it himself; he had even grown to mistrust it. But now it had come to him, been offered to him; come complete and untainted in a woman who had crossed his life – and could so easily leave it.

If he let her go, he let himself go. Tom recognised that fact immediately, feeling something from the gut as well as the heart. There would be other women, there always were; but they wouldn't be Imogen, and they wouldn't touch him, move him, as she did. . . . He was momentarily scared by the force of his feelings, the intensity of his affection. *If I accept her into my life, if she accepts* me, *nothing will be the same. There will be no place for superficiality, dishonour. . . . But you always wanted an honest relationship,* Tom told himself, *this is what you've always looked for. Something solid, something real, something* good.

The boy on the bike passed him, riding through an earlier puddle, the spokes of the wheel shining suddenly in the northern sun. And still Imogen and Elizabeth talked; and still Tom waited. Around him, the dirty bricks were banked up in regimented rows, terraces of houses, coming one after the other, a window cleaner whistling at the end of the street. The air was cold with coming rain, the sun suddenly striking a billboard on the side of the corner shop. Tom blinked, then read the sign.

It was for a car, but he could never remember later which car. He could only remember the slogan: THE BEST IS NOW.

He wasn't a superstitious man, but the sign seemed to glow large and luminous out of the dark brickwork. THE BEST IS NOW, he read again, then turned and slowly walked back towards his car. Imogen came out at that moment, nodding to the window cleaner, her hair white gold under the slackening sun. She paused for an instant and looked round at the street, exhausted and pale, then finally she glanced over to Tom.

He never knew why he said the next words, only that they came into his head and were spoken spontaneously from the heart.

'It's time to go home.'

'I know,' was all she said.

PART FOUR

Boys and girls come out to play,
The moon doth shine as bright as
day.
(*Nursery rhyme*)

toujours gai, archy, toujours gai
it's cheerio, my deario, that pulls a
lady through

(*archys life of mehitabel*, Don Marquis)

Chapter Twenty-Four

He stroked the inside of her thigh slowly, Imogen arching her back. They had made love for hours, Tom at first finding a gentle and willing partner, then as time progressed, a woman who was deeply sexual. Greedy. Hungry. He responded to her completely, fascinated by the dark and uninhibited pleasure she took from lovemaking, knowing instinctively that the years of self-imposed celibacy had enhanced, not muted, her desires.

She took pleasure from him and gave pleasure, and then fell asleep, her body against his body, her legs lying over his thighs, her head against his. Deeply content, she slept without moving, then stirred, suddenly wakened in the early hours. The room was unfamiliar to her and for an instant Imogen could not remember where she was and her mind moved back to the time of her injury – and Giles's betrayal. She turned, caught her breath.

'Are you all right?'

She nodded, but remained motionless. He touched the skin on the back of her neck. Damp from fear.

'Imogen . . . are you okay?'

He turned her, took hold of her. Said nothing else. The hotel room smelt of mimosa and sun, the night coming in semi-dark, a slow moon rising.

'I love you,' he said, kissing her, resting his hand against her back, then letting it slide over her breasts. 'I love you more than I have ever loved anyone else.'

She said nothing, merely turned towards him, held him, took his hand and guided it down her stomach, moaning.

'I don't want you to worry about anything any more,' Tom went on gently. 'I want you to be happy. . . .'

She sighed, rolled over on top of him, her hair falling over his face.

'Imogen . . . I want you to be happy,' he repeated, excitement making his voice dark, disembodied. 'I want you to forget. . . .'

Her mouth nuzzled the hair on his chest, her tongue lingering over his nipples.

'Mr Wrigley,' she said softly, mischievously, 'why don't you shut up?'

'I knew it!' Penny said to Claudine. 'I just knew they'd get married.'

Claudine sipped at her water. Tiny sips, as a small child might drink.

'It was very quick, wasn't it?'

'That's the way it goes sometimes.' Penny glanced at the wan little figure across the table. 'How long did you and Arnold go out before you married?'

'Five years.'

'Five years! That wasn't a courtship, that was a sentence.'

Claudine looked down into her glass. 'I loved him . . . I still do, even now.'

Penny was all ears. '*Still do?*'

'He's having an affair,' Claudine said simply, as though it didn't matter. 'I found out yesterday. He told me – oh, not in so many words – but it was obvious.' Her hands went up to her fringe, toyed with the straight hair. 'I suppose he's disappointed in me.'

Penny's voice was hard. 'Disappointed in you. Hah! He's no right to be disappointed in anyone but himself.'

But he wasn't about to question his actions, Penny realised. Arnold Miles had had many affairs. God knows why, he wasn't an oil painting, but the women seemed to be attracted to his status, panting after the glamour of his position, rather than the man himself. For years Penny had watched Claudine suffer from her husband's infidelities; had listened; had sat through many lunches and long nights letting Claudine talk. In the end it was always the same: Arnold came back, Arnold stayed. Why? she wondered. He didn't particularly like his wife, and he obviously had no respect for her. Perhaps it was the children, Penny thought ruefully. Three little Mileses velcroing the marriage together.

'Can't you talk to him? Let him see how much this matters to you?'

Claudine flushed. 'He always comes home –'

'You always *let* him come home,' Penny countered. 'Maybe if he wasn't so certain of you, he would think twice about screwing around.'

Claudine's head rose, her eyes blank with injury. 'I don't want to lose him,' she said hopelessly, without realising that she already had. 'I love him too much.'

Penny changed the subject quickly, avoiding a scene. They were in a crowded restaurant; tears would be noted, commented upon, the event gossiped about. No, not here, Claudine, she thought protectively, the bastard's not worth public humiliation.

'I thought Danielle might join us,' she said lightly, glancing round, praying that the hurrying compact figure might suddenly emerge, bustle into their hot little conversation, tell them about her business. Do anything to take away the sour smell of imminent disaster. 'She said she'd try to get here.'

On cue, Danielle Ferryman walked over to their table, slammed down her handbag, sat down and crossed her legs. She was wearing a tailored green suit, her hair held back with a velvet band. Over made-up, as usual.

'Hi, what's been happening?' she asked, her voice slightly high-pitched, strained. As it always was, her nervousness showing.

Penny shrugged: 'Nothing much –'

'Arnold's having an affair,' Claudine said softly, drawing the newcomer into her misery.

'Oh,' Danielle said noncommittally, taking out a packet of cigarettes and lighting one.

'I don't think you're supposed to smoke here,' Claudine said timidly. 'There aren't any ashtrays.'

Danielle looked round, then flirted some ash into a small vase in front of her.

'So what are you going to do about it?'

'What? Well, I suppose the head waiter will tell you –'

'Not about my smoking!' Danielle snapped impatiently. 'I meant, what are you going to do about Arnold?'

She blushed, as she always did with Danielle. She might admire her friend's business acumen, the amount of money she made and her independence; but she couldn't get used to Danielle's brusqueness and found herself uneasy in her company.

'What *can* she do about it?' Penny cut in, annoyed by Danielle's ill-humour.

'She could divorce him.'

Claudine shot Penny a hunted look.

'They have three children, Danielle, that is not the brightest suggestion you've ever come up with. The children have to be considered, you should know that.'

'I never thought of that, sorry. It didn't occur to me. I don't have children, and neither do you.'

The jibe struck out, and for an instant Penny flinched. Danielle didn't want children, but she knew how much Penny had longed to have a family of her own. The remark was spiteful – even for Danielle.

'Why the bitchy mood?' Penny asked her. 'Trevor not being as attentive as he could be? Or is Tom's marriage getting up your nose?'

It was Danielle's turn to look discomforted. She had longed for Tom Wrigley to show some interest in her, but he never had, and when she went to live with Trevor Rowe-Thorne afterwards she had expected him to propose. But the years had passed and the proposal never came. Her business flourished, and they stayed together, but she had never managed to turn herself into Mrs Rowe-Thorne, and now, approaching forty, her anxiety made her acid.

'What the hell has that got to do with anything?' she asked Penny sharply.

'You know as well as I do. You wanted Tom –'

'Oh, hi, everyone. . . .'

All three of them looked up; Maxie slid into the seat next to Penny, smiling. Several heads immediately swivelled towards the table, Maxie blithely unaware of the commotion she was creating. As if by magic, a waiter appeared and

268

took their order, Maxie gazing around her with all the animation of the Sphinx.

'I've just bought a new dress,' she said, pulling it out of the carrier and holding it against her breasts. 'What do you think?'

It was a strappy little number and left several male diners gasping for breath.

'You don't think it's too much for the dinner next week, do you?'

'Arnold's having another affair,' Danielle said impatiently, irritated with the attention Maxie was provoking.

'Oh, sorry,' she said absent mindedly, reaching across the table and taking Claudine's hand. The gesture was well meant, kind.

'I think she should divorce him.'

Maxie turned to look at Danielle; her eyes, always heavy-lidded, gave the heady impression of someone newly awoken from sleep.

'Oh, no! Claudine has children.'

'But what good is Arnold as a father?'

'I'd like children,' Maxie said listlessly, pushing the dress back into the bag. 'But I'm not sure that Harry would make a good father.'

Danielle was sharp with irritation. 'You're not even married to him!'

'Oh, but I could be,' Maxie countered.

She hadn't been boasting, merely stating a fact. She could have got Harry to take her up the aisle. What was so difficult for Danielle was easy for Maxie.

'. . . but he's so short.'

Penny laughed outright. 'You don't marry them by the inch, Maxie,' she said, adding slyly, 'At least, not in height.'

Maxie missed the point entirely. 'But I'm not that tall, and if I married Harry we'd probably have short children. . . .'

Danielle stared at her, stunned.

'And if I had boys, they'd be short and have to wear those things on their shoes. Oh, what *are* they called?'

'Ladders?' Penny offered.

'No, Penny,' Maxie said gently, 'they're called . . . *lifts* . . . that's it, like the things that take you from floor to floor.'

269

Danielle ground out her cigarette, her eyes fixed on the silent Claudine opposite her.

'So what *are* you going to do?'

Claudine looked up from under her fringe.

'Nothing.'

Maxie nodded. 'That's right,' she said simply. 'You just sit it out.'

'I'm just glad that Sarah isn't here,' Danielle said hotly. 'With all her feminist views she'd have you packed up and moved out in a minute.'

Claudine looked appealingly at Penny.

'I don't want to leave Arnold. . . .'

'And you mustn't,' Penny said firmly, turning back to Danielle. 'You should put a lock on that tongue of yours, it'll get you into trouble one day.'

An uncomfortable silence descended, Maxie picking at her Caesar's salad, Claudine sipping at her water, her full plate untouched in front of her.

'Well, I'm glad Tom married Imogen,' Penny said finally. 'I like her. She's fun.'

Maxie glanced up, still chewing daintily. 'Where are they living now?'

'In Kensington, at Tom's old flat, and at the weekends they go up north, to his constituency, some place outside Manchester.'

Danielle pulled a face. 'Ugh.'

'What's wrong with the North?' Penny asked, 'You are *such* a snob.'

'I just like it here,' Danielle replied, refilling her glass, her lipstick leaving a jammy crescent on the side. 'Mind you, I suppose she'll feel at home up there. After all, she is a northerner.'

The malice was obvious in Penny's voice. 'Tom was lucky to find her,' she said evenly, knowing just how to provoke Danielle. 'He never had much luck with women before.'

Maxie opened her eyes wide. 'Oh, but *we* had a good time when we were together. Really, we did,' she said guilelessly.

Defeated, Danielle lasped into a sullen silence.

*

270

Imogen had no idea of the gossip that surrounded her second marriage. All that mattered to her was that she had found Tom, a man she loved, a man she respected. It had been unexpected, coming naturally, his support at the time of her mother's death allowing her to lean on him. The place so willingly occupied by Ira had been usurped, the tall heavy figure of Tom Wrigley taking the place of the exotic, and intriguing, Jew. The two men were totally dissimilar in appearance and temperament. Ira cared nothing for convention; Tom was anxious to be seen to be doing everything right. Ira had no social ambitions; Tom was socially ambitious. Ira had no real love of money, merely wanting to make it to spend it; Tom had come from a pedestrian background and was hugely aware of the prestige money bought.

His family had come from the North; middle class, his parents both teachers. Of four children, Tom had emerged physically larger and mentally smarter than the rest. By the age of fifteen he was head and shoulders above his peers, both intellectually and bodily, his natural competitive streak making him a formidable athlete. At first he had little charm, but over the years he developed an openness of nature which was beguiling. He was direct – and up north, that was charm of the first order.

In any profession he could have done well; in politics, his achievements could be major. Only one thing held him back – a slight, but persistent, inferiority complex. In amongst the public-school-educated MPs at Westminster he felt ill at ease, boorish at times. If he had chosen to be a Labour MP it would have been easier, but for a Conservative he was unusual: hard-working and clever, yes; polished, no.

He had needed a suitable consort, a wife to add gloss, a social patina. It was not the only reason Tom married Imogen; he loved her; but it was *part* of the reason, and he admitted as much to himself. He could have married other women, Sloane Ranger types, but they would have unnerved him. Belittled him, their background a constant reminder of his own beginnings. He needed class, but class on an equal footing – which was why Imogen was so perfect.

She was known to be intelligent, even respected in her own field. She was lovely, an enviable partner. But she was also a wild card, the joker in the pack. Her background, as the charge of Suzanne Jacobs, gave her a wealthy but unusual history; and her involvement with Ira Mazan was fascinating. Had Ira been poor, it would have counted against her; but he was rich, knew most people in politics and had often contributed to party funds. The MPs might not approve of him, might look down on his origins and his business empire, but they couldn't help admiring him.

Born in the North, brought up by Suzanne Jacobs, protected by Ira Mazan, Imogen had a glossy and fascinating past; and, having been raised with a foot in both camps, she could move between the North and the South with consummate ease. She was the perfect wife for Tom Wrigley – up-and-coming MP – and he knew it.

Imogen knew it too. Just as she realised that her husband was a fiercely ambitious man. Tom saw no reason why he couldn't become a minister, and she agreed with him. Her own career would carry on, her contacts would help – together they could achieve anything they set out to do. They were two people with dreams, and they were in the happy position of being ambitious for each other. Tom Wrigley's star had always been set to rise, but with Imogen's help it would rise faster, and glow with a brighter light.

Elizabeth had not expected so much for her granddaughter. This was even more than she could imagine. Imogen had married an MP – an MP! She glanced at Graham's photograph. Well, who'd have thought it? Little Imogen, married again, and to a man like that.

She liked his name. Tom Wrigley. Good name, northern name. No messing with a name like that. She watched him on the news, the name written underneath. Listened to every word he said; liked the trim, dark beard, the bigness of him. Big men don't have to be petty. You don't get a big man being peevish. Oh yes, she was proud of her granddaughter, and of him. She walked down the street straight-backed, knowing that people pointed her out. It was worth all the long years of sacrifice and work – worth it all now.

She thought of the day on the pier, Suzanne Jacobs coming like a sultry angel out of the sea wrack. You out of work? You need a job? . . . Elizabeth had been carrying Imogen, letting her work her own magic on the woman. Is she yours? What a name, Imogen. What a face. . . . Elizabeth smiled, sat down, took off her shoes and rubbed her swollen feet. If she hadn't gone down that pier that day. . . .

But she had. Her feet had taken her there. Luck had drawn her to the spot. No, bugger luck! she thought laughing. It was meant to happen. It was *right* that it should.

'So Imogen's married an MP,' Lorrie said, leaning against Suzanne's french windows in Brighton, the sun shining on his paunchy skin. 'You must be *thrilled*.'

Idly she rubbed some tanning lotion on to her skin. He watched her, intrigued. In good shape for a woman over sixty. Tight body, hair without any grey. Mind you, anyone could cheat that. It just took money, and Suzanne had plenty of that.

Yawning, Suzanne leaned back against the lounger. 'I told you Imogen was remarkable,' she said nonchalantly. 'I don't know what all the fuss is about.'

Lorrie moved out on to the patio, immediately regretting it as the heat boiled the top of his head.

'It was a close-run thing with Ira though, wasn't it?'

Lazily Suzanne opened one eye.

'In what way, Lorrie?'

He sat down, breathing noisily.

'I mean, she could have ruined her chances there.'

Suzanne had never liked Ira, but as the years had passed and he had proved himself a steady friend to Imogen, she had relented. Distant gratitude now replaced loathing.

'I like Ira.'

'*You can't stand him!*' Lorrie spluttered.

Calmly, Suzanne smoothed her left arm. 'Don't spit on me, Lorrie, this stuff isn't water-repellant.'

Embarrassed, he ignored the remark. 'I thought you were up in arms about her and Ira.'

Suzanne smiled behind her sunglasses. She knew the

reason for Lorrie's visit: he wanted to make sure that now Imogen was married she would continue to work for him. He had come to plead his cause with Suzanne, without realising that she had no intention of interfering.

She had what she wanted. Imogen had triumphed over her difficulties, come out winning. Ah, but it was Imogen Winner no more, Imogen Wrigley now. Suzanne jammed on the name. Wrigley was hardly the name of a romantic hero, but still, you couldn't have everything. The tag 'MP' which followed would make up for it. . . . Her skin was warm under the sun. If only toady Lorrie would leave, she could enjoy herself.

But what about Ira? she thought. What about him? He had behaved impeccably, even if he had turned up for the wedding in a white silk suit. 'Oh no,' she'd murmured to Imogen. 'For God's sake don't let him near the piano.'

Imogen had smiled, but soon after had walked over to Ira, laying her hand on his arm.

'Thanks for coming.'

He kissed her on the cheek. A little too long. They both knew that everyone was watching – and remembering what they had heard.

'You did that deliberately,' she said, when he drew back.

The dark-lidded eyes were steady: 'Always keep 'em guessing, kiddo. Always keep 'em guessing. . . .'

Suzanne turned her head, still thinking. Lorrie was hyperventilating in the sun lounger next to hers. *Had* they been lovers? she wondered, *had* they? Imogen had never told her, and she had never asked. The affection was obvious; too close perhaps for lovers. Not many people romantically involved could keep such affection intact for years. Lovers? . . . Oh shit, she thought, who cares? Who in the hell cares? Imogen was happy now, the past was over. Dead, buried.

Suddenly Suzanne thought of Elizabeth and frowned. Come back and live with me, she'd said. I'm alone, you're alone, why not? The house is too big for one. Come back. . . . Would you live with me? Elizabeth had countered. Would you come up to Little Lever and live here? I'm alone too. Why not? . . . Suzanne thought of the grim little house and shuddered. No, I'll stay down here, she thought, wondering why Elizabeth was being so stubborn about the bills. She had offered money many times, offered to put in central heating, a new bathroom, but Elizabeth always resisted, just accepted the monthly wage they had agreed on years before. I can manage, I can cope. . . . Like grandmother, like granddaughter, Suzanne thought wryly.

Another marriage. Well, who'd have thought it? she asked herself, smiling. It could have been me, *should* have been me. Once. But not now; now I like my freedom, like to do what the hell I want, when I want. Besides, there's always Mike, even if he isn't so hot in the sack any more. Suzanne was blithely content: she had the house, the money, the cellulite treatment. . . .

'Do you think Imogen will still want to work with me?' Lorrie asked petulantly, his shirt collar ringed with a coating of sweat.

'I don't know,' Suzanne said honestly. 'Her life's changed now. She might not have the time.'

'But –'

'Don't ask me,' Suzanne interrupted. 'Ask her. I can't speak for Imogen.'

'But you're her . . . her. . . .' He paused, wondering just *what* Suzanne was. She wasn't her mother, or her aunt. So what was she? Imogen's guardian? Imogen's keeper? *What?*

Noting his hesitation, Suzanne turned and looked over the top of her sunglasses.

'Well, *what* are you?' Lorrie asked.

'Her ally,' Suzanne said simply. 'And she is mine.'

The flat in Kensington was overcrowded even before Imogen and Rowan brought in their possessions. Everywhere Tom had amassed books, plants, figurines and sports equipment. The kitchen spilled over into the lounge, and the lounge spilled over into the bedroom. Raising her eyebrows, Imogen looked at the wardrobe.

'This is too small,' she said, glancing at the piles of clothes.

'We've got the house in Southport,' he said quickly. 'There's plenty of cupboard space there.'

Grimacing, Imogen stepped over a pair of tennis racquets. 'Didn't you ever have a cleaner? Or is this supposed to be cleaned?'

He looked shamefaced. 'It's crowded. She did the best she could.'

Imogen walked over to him, stretching up to kiss him. 'I love it here. It's horribly male,' she said, unfastening his shirt and pulling him down on to the bed. 'Positively *gamey*.'

'We can have it any way you like.'

She smiled seductively. 'I was hoping you'd say that.'

'I was talking about the flat,' Tom said, returning the smile. 'You do what you want with it.'

She pulled off his shirt with a flourish. 'Only after I've done what I want with you,' she said, laughing.

Tom had a certain amount of money, but he wasn't the type to throw it around, and before long Imogen realised that the improvements she wanted would run beyond his means. So she adapted her ambitions; she redecorated and let him see the bills for the necessities, but the mirrors and the pictures came from her own funds – and from Suzanne's.

'Take what you want,' she said loftily. 'I can't use all of it. I was thinking of selling up anyway.'

'Selling up?' Imogen asked, stunned. 'You love this place.'

'It's too big for one –'

'Since when is it only for one?' Imogen countered. 'Michael's always here, and you hold God knows how many parties. You need this place.'

'I need this place like I need to put my face in a fan,' Suzanne said shortly. 'I asked Elizabeth to come and live here, but she wouldn't hear of it.'

'She's better off up north,' Imogen said tactfully, picking up a framed photograph of Giles she had found in her old room. 'Look.'

Suzanne stared at it: 'Shall we have a ceremonial burning on the patio?'

Imogen kept looking at the picture. 'I can't believe I was ever married to him.'

'He always had trouble with that too,' Suzanne retorted,

sitting on the radiator and looking at the mass of objects on the bed. 'Is Rowan still as keen on Tom?'

Imogen turned, smiled. 'He can't believe his luck. Tom takes him to football, cricket, you name it. You know, sometimes I look at him and it seems as though Rowan could be his child. They even look alike.'

'Apart from the beard.'

'Give it time,' Imogen said drily. 'Giles is still sulking, though.'

'I'm always convinced that Giles took a degree in sulking,' Suzanne said drily. 'He's getting a very *slack* look now, a kind of weariness round the gills.' She paused, picking her words carefully. 'Is he still with Terry?'

'They broke up,' Imogen said, surprised how little it hurt. For years she had found it agonising to talk about Giles and his lover, but now, married and secure again, she could talk easily about it. Even sympathise.

'Terry left him a few months ago.'

'Oh, poor Giles,' Suzanne said sarcastically. 'I bet that hurt. I *hope* that hurt.'

'I don't wish him any ill, you know,' Imogen said sincerely. 'Perhaps if we hadn't had Rowan, I would have done. But having to see him all these years and keep contact – well, the hurt faded after a while.'

Suzanne stood up. 'Forget him. He's in the past. You've got a new husband now and a better father for Rowan. Make the most of your chances, you've deserved them.'

Imogen knew it, and made it work for her. Tom's life was hectic, his hours long, appointments filling many evenings. Another woman would have found it hard to adapt, but Imogen didn't. She had lived on her own long enough to be able to bear her own company, and made the most of the time they spent together. Besides, she had her work, and continued to deliver caricatures for Lorrie and for Dickie Bedlington. Both magazines were doing well, the yuppie readership growing, the circulation extending to Europe. Her work was seen and admired, the celebrities she targeted often requesting the originals, her status as an MP's wife making Imogen all the more collectable.

There was no rivalry between her and Tom. Imogen's work was no threat to his, especially as she now caricatured media people rather than MPs. He was proud of her achievements and prouder still when Rowan showed real sporting prowess. Tom had the life he wanted, the wife he wanted, and the son he wanted. No man was luckier, and a new confidence entered him. His speeches, before rather brusque and factual, suddenly began to improve. Humour never having been his strong point, the dry comments Imogen injected into her husband's orations made a real impact. People listened more intently, and while listening for the witticisms, they also heard the pertinent points Tom Wrigley had to make.

His career began to pick up, his intelligence, coupled with his newly discovered confidence, marking him out. He changed his appearance too. Out went the sports jackets and the brown suits, in came the dark navy pinstripes and the silk ties. Surprised, he looked in the mirror and saw an elegant man he had never suspected, a man at ease with himself, a man set to change things. He didn't see the old Tom Wrigley – he saw an imminent cabinet minister standing there.

Away from the House he was happiest in jeans, playing football with Rowan, or driving up north to visit his constituents. He listened carefully to what they had to say, suddenly understanding the little domestic irritations which mattered so much to people. Before he had listened, but not understood; now he listened and identified with them. He was now a family man, and could take on the burdens of other family men, the difference being that he was in a position to change things.

As Tom altered, Imogen backed him. She had seen his potential all along, admired his ambition and was relieved to find that he made time for her and Rowan. At first she had waited for the honeymoon period to fade, for the novelty to wear off, dreading the day he would resume his old ways. But he never did. He had wanted to be married, and enjoyed marriage. It was that simple.

It was simple for Imogen too. After years of uncertain finances, after years of bringing up Rowan alone, it was a profound relief for her to share her problems.

'You know something,' she said to Suzanne over the phone. 'When you live alone you don't confide in people. And do you know why? Because even if you're breaking your heart, in order to talk to someone you have to go and see them, or phone them up – and then they might be out, or if they do pick up the phone, you have to go through polite small talk before you can really say what's on your mind, and by that time it doesn't seem such a good idea, after all. There's no emotional spontaneity when you live alone; no way of just turning round and speaking to someone in the same room. If you want to talk, you have to make an *effort*, and that's just what you don't want to be bothered doing.' She paused. 'So in the end you don't pick up the phone – instead you get through it on your own.'

'I phone you if I'm pissed off,' Suzanne said thoughtfully. 'But then I was never the type to suffer in silence. That's more your line.'

'That's exactly what I'm saying,' Imogen replied. 'Now I'm with Tom I can just talk naturally. Turn round and say, what do you think of this? Or how dare she say that to me! It feels good, Suzanne, really good. It feels like home.'

Knowing them already she soon made friends among the Tory wives and girlfriends, Penny being her favourite as they shared the same sense of humour and frankness. She liked Maxie, and pitied Claudine – who didn't? – and she thought that Danielle had hidden qualities. Well hidden, admittedly, but there nevertheless. The only one she truly disliked was Sarah, seeing her a dry, angry woman with little love for her husband. Or her child. That worried Imogen. She could understand falling out of love with a man. But a child? Never.

Driven into each other's company by force of circumstances, the women lunched together, dined together, went to the cinema together and gossiped together. There were dozens of MPs' wives, but they all found their little cliques and clung on to them. More like a gaggle of schoolgirls than a privileged group of women. But it worked because they understood the life, and commiserated with each other. They knew about the long absences, the foreign trips, the cancelled dinners. When one of them was let down, it was more than likely that the others had been too, so understanding was quick and complete.

The girlfriends lived the same way. Maxie was, to all intents and purposes, married to Harry, and was a glorious prize on his arm at functions. Only Danielle felt that her position was rocky. Trevor wouldn't marry her, and although he wasn't an MP, but a lawyer, she found herself drawn more and more towards the Tory women as he became more and more involved with the party.

'I can't imagine why Jimmy married Sarah,' Imogen said to Penny one day. 'I mean, he's so full of life, so typically, charmingly, the PR man. And she's so –'

'Tactless,' Penny finished. 'Yes, I know. We've been waiting for years to see when, and how, she finishes him off. But the grandees in the party like Jimmy, so unless she does something drastic, he'll survive.'

'Is he good at his job?'

Penny nodded. 'Sarah had the money, and Jimmy the tongue. She was crazy about him the first time I met them. . . .' Imogen thought of the bushy-eyebrowed Jimmy Bentley, finishing people's sentences, standing flat-footed, solid, ready to laugh. '. . . then they started to argue and Sarah got into feminism. She went over to New York and talked to all those crazy bitches who were "enobling womanhood" and when she came back she was pressing all of us to go to seminars with her, and to stop waxing our legs because we only did it because we were "under male domination".' Penny burst out laughing. 'She was wrong, of course. We did it *in order* to get under male domination.'

Imogen laughed.

'What about Claudine? How did she meet Arnold?'

Penny smiled gleefully. 'Rumour has it that her uncle paid Arnold to marry her.'

'What!'

'Yes,' Penny said, nodding. 'The uncle apparently told Arnold that he would put up the money for his campaigning if Arnold married his niece.'

'I don't believe it!' Imogen said firmly. 'That's too feudal for words. Anyway, I can't see Arnold Miles letting himself be told what to do.'

'Oh, but that's because you didn't know the Arnold of old,' Penny confided. 'You know him now, but fifteen years ago it was very different. He was thin and whippety then, down from Gateshead, with an accent thick as a bowl of suet. He had brains, but no class, and worse, no money. So when Claudine's uncle came up with the shekels, he went for it.'

'And *he* looked down on Ira,' Imogen said thoughtfully.

Penny put down the wire she was shaping and leaned over her workbench.

'Incidentally, what's happened to him since you married Tom?'

What happened to Ira? Well, Imogen thought, the first thing he did was to go away. For over a month, somewhere hot, with a girl or maybe even two. She didn't know where he was, and neither did the office. They just told her that Mr Mazan was abroad and would contact her when he got back.

He did, of course. Took her to lunch at Claridges, his deep tan making the black eyes even darker. He looked more foreign than ever.

'If you tan any more the National History Museum will put in a bid for your hide,' she said, kissing him on the cheek.

'Sit down,' he said, patting the seat next to him. 'Put your *tuchis* here.'

Obediently, she sat down.

'So, how goes it?'

'Good,' she answered. 'How's things with you?'

'I went on holiday –'

'*No!*' she said, with mock surprise.

' –I swam a little, sunbathed a lot, played some roulette.'

'I take it it wasn't Blackpool.'

He smiled. 'Nice.'

'Very.'

He smiled again.

'I had fun.'

'Did you go alone?'

He gave her a slow look. 'I took a lady . . . do you mind?'

'Ira,' Imogen said gently, 'why should I mind? Is she nice?'

He paused, picked up his fork and began slowly to draw lines on the tablecloth.

'My type.'

His reserve alerted her. This was no fling, no bimbo.

'Who is she, Ira?'

He stopped playing with his fork and broke off a piece of his bread roll, buttering it lavishly.

'An old friend.'

This doesn't sound like a friend, Imogen thought, suddenly anxious. She stared hard at him, studied the side of his face and the way a muscle moved in his cheek as he chewed. He seemed uncomfortable, almost sad.

'Sorry, Ira . . . I didn't mean to pry.'

'It's Simone,' he said simply.

'Simone!' Imogen repeated, aghast, then dropped her voice. 'But you said it was over between you two. You said she was always hassling you.' Her hand moved over his. 'Oh why *her*, Ira? Why?'

He turned his head.

You've got older, Imogen thought with surprise. I don't remember so many lines around your eyes, or the way your lips press together. You had fuller lips before, Ira, and a nice mouth. A good mouth. Not a hard one.

'She and I go back a long way.'

It wasn't enough.

'But Ira –'

He picked up her hand and kissed the palm, smiling. 'Enough, enough already. *Kvetch, kvetch, kvetch*.'

'I'm not nagging,' she said, smiling back. 'I just want you to be happy.'

'Only the dead are happy. You want miracles?' he asked, trying to keep the mood light, but failing.

The holiday had been a success of sorts, Simone had been attentive, clever in bed and intelligent out of it. A skilful woman, without heart. . . . Oh yes, he had telephoned her, after all. Had hung back for a long time, resisted the siren call, resisted the pull back into the person he was, the person he wanted to escape. He even thought in the end that he'd beaten it; that he would never contact her again; that she had lost her grip on him.

After all, why should he want to be involved with a woman who was the female version of himself? It was unhealthy. You looked for good in a partner; for the missing parts in yourself. Not for a carbon copy. Unless that was the only way you felt comfortable, knowing that you were with someone on the same level as you. From the same litter; feeding from the same trough.

'Why, Ira?' Imogen repeated.

Why? he thought. Well, why not?

'I thought you didn't like Simone any more.'

I didn't.

'I thought you weren't going to call her any more.'

I wasn't.

'I thought it was over.'

It was.

'So what happened?' Imogen asked again. 'What happened?'

'I used to have a dream,' he said finally. 'I would go to sleep and dream that I looked in the mirror . . . and for years I saw you standing there. Standing next to me. You . . .' he paused. 'Then the night after you got married I had the dream again, only this time Simone was standing there.' He touched the end of Imogen's nose gently with his fingers. One, two, three, four. 'Now choose.'

She touched the end of his index finger and he smiled.

'That's for luck.'

'From your lips to God's ear,' she said softly. 'From your lips to God's ear.'

Chapter Twenty-Five

'The bitch is back.'

'Who?' Imogen asked.

Penny looked at her hard. 'Eve Miller.'

'And who is she?'

'The lady who wanted to be in your shoes,' Penny replied. 'She's five feet six and all muscle. Works for a fashion magazine, travels a lot, has an expense account like Onassis and a mouth like a Dyno-rod pipe. Watch out for her, she's lethal.'

'Did she go out with Tom?' Imogen asked warily.

'Only for a short time. Then she moved on to Arnold, then moved on and out into the publishing world. Rumour has it that she can do things with a bar of soap that would make your eyes water.'

Imogen put down her coffee cup and glanced out of the window. Tom was in the garden with Rowan, teaching him the finer points of tennis, the boy tall and athletic, Tom beginning to show the slightest paunch from a run of working lunches.

'Was Tom keen on her?'

'Oh, you have nothing to worry about,' Penny said eagerly. 'She was far keener on him than he was on her. She just hoped, that's all.' She picked up some of Imogen's caricatures on the kitchen table. 'These are good – and very funny.'

'They're for Lorrie,' Imogen said, still watching Tom. 'I have to take them over to him later this afternoon.'

Penny laughed behind her. 'I like this one on Holly Norton, she'll go ape when she sees it.'

Imogen glanced over her shoulder, pitching her voice into

a perfect imitation of the woman's: 'I *do* so want to have a copy, dear, to show my friends. You have such an eye, such a talent.'

Penny laughed. 'You've got her off to a tee, and that's a fact. Don't any of them ever complain about the drawings?'

'Only once. One tycoon said that I made him look ugly, and that his wife was embarrassed.' Imogen shrugged. 'Otherwise, no, the caricatures aren't malicious, just accurate. Nothing important.'

'Oh, come on!' Penny chided her. 'You know how much attention they get. Plenty of people mention them to me when they know we're friends; someone even said that one of your caricatures was worth a whole page of editorial.'

Imogen was unimpressed, her thoughts elsewhere.

'Hey, you're not worried about what I said, are you?' Penny asked anxiously. 'I mean, about Eve Miller? She's not in your league.'

'I'm pregnant,' Imogen said simply.

'Oh.'

Her hand moved across the table to take Penny's. 'Will you be the baby's godmother?'

Penny nodded, unusually subdued. 'Congratulations,' she said finally.

'Thanks, Penny, I know this is hard for you.'

She put up her chin defiantly: 'It shouldn't be. Women are entitled to have children, even if I can't.' She stopped, her tone impatient. 'God, how bloody selfish! How can I think about *myself*?'

'We all do, sweetheart,' Imogen said evenly. 'It's the way of things.'

She had told Tom the previous night, waiting until he had finished a long recital of his speech, her knees drawn up under her chin, her hair brushed back from her face. He wasn't to be the first person to know, Rowan had had that honour, and had listened carefully as his mother told him the news.

'A baby?' he said, incredulously. 'Oh Gawd!'

She smiled. 'Sounds good, hey?'

'Sounds *weird*!' he countered, putting his head on one side. 'Boy or girl?'

'Too soon to say, yet,' she answered. 'I just wanted you to be the first to know. You always come first, you know that, Rowan.'

He blushed, his narrow face with its angular bones looking older than his eleven years. He's not going to be a boy much longer, Imogen thought, he's almost grown. Quite a brother for the newcomer; quite a shock for him.

'How do you feel about it?'

He blew out his cheeks: 'Wow!'

'Yes, that's pretty much how I felt,' Imogen replied drily.

Rowan laughed, then banged his hands on the table. 'Have you told Giles?' he asked.

Not 'Have you told my father?' she noticed. Now it was Giles. Dad no more. To all intents and purposes Rowan thought of Tom as his father now. He was more like him than Giles: more sporty, more similar in temperament. Odd how children manage to sort out their own lives.

'No, not yet.'

'And Tom? What about him?'

'I told you – you're the first to know.'

He smiled, pulled a goofy face. 'Well, it'll keep all my friends talking for a bit,' he said easily. 'I suppose you'll give it some poxy name?'

Imogen stared at him in horror. 'Why should I do that?'

'Well,' he said simply, 'Rowan's a real beauty, isn't it?'

'It was your father's idea,' Imogen said, her tone injured. 'Take it up with him.'

After what seemed an interminable length of time, Tom finally finished his speech. Imogen told him then, watching as he undressed, his back turned to her. She knew he heard her, but for an instant he didn't respond.

'Tom?'

He turned then, walked over to the bed and sat down.

'You're having a baby?'

She nodded.

'A baby?'

'Yeah, you know, they're small, pink, and they cry a lot.'

He kissed her hard. 'I know what a baby is!' he said,

286

delighted. 'Oh God, Imogen, this is the best news I've ever had.'

'What about the time you got a hole in one?' she asked, teasing him.

'It makes everything perfect,' Tom went on, hugging her to him. 'Perfect.'

'Yes,' she said softly, 'it does, doesn't it?'

But she shivered when she said the words, a sudden anxiety slipping over her skin like a cold draught. Maybe she was *too* lucky, too complacent. Maybe things couldn't be this good. Relax, she told herself, enjoy it, you've worked for it . . . but the feeling wouldn't budge. I have the man I wanted, I have Rowan, and now I am having another child, Imogen thought later, when sleep wouldn't come. Why can't I enjoy it, why?

She lay awake for much of the night, hearing Rowan get up and go downstairs for something to eat, hearing the cistern flush at one-thirty. And still she couldn't sleep. Tom moved, turned over, snored three times, then lapsed into the dark of the small hours. His body was only a shape in the bed beside her, his features blurred. It will all be fine, Imogen told herself. It will all be fine. . . .

But her mind wandered, drifted from London to the North, and it took root in the dark streets of Little Lever and a Manchester hospital ward.

Chapter Twenty-Six

The first months of Imogen's pregnancy were uneventful. Tom was a thoughtful and loving – if distracted – partner, his speeches calling him away from home more often now that there had been a Cabinet reshuffle. He had hoped, almost counted on being promoted, but in the end the longed-for post went to an old starwart of the party. They told him that it was nothing to do with his work, or his image, but more to do with experience. He argued; they held firm; he threatened to resign; they suggested that he think about it – after all, reshuffles happened all the time.

But the incident left Tom shaken, and irritable. It was no good Imogen telling him to be patient, to wait his turn. He was still young. Hang on, don't queer your pitch, she said, it will all come in time. . . . But he wasn't comforted and brooded, became moody, striking out at his family in response to the imagined slight. All his old feelings of inferiority came back, full-blown. It was the old boy network, he insisted, the bloody old school tie.

In the seventh month of pregnancy Imogen found herself relying less on Tom and more on Rowan, her son taking on some of the household chores as her husband took more frequent trips abroad.

'I think he should stay home more, Mum.'

Imogen rubbed her back, the ache at the base of her spine dragging on her. The weather was sultry, freak weather for October, the days short and steamy. It was a bad time to carry a baby.

'I know, but he's busy trying to prove a point,' she explained, kicking off her shoes and sitting down in the kitchen in Kensington. The dishwasher door opposite reflected her image: a woman shiny with heat, her belly extended. Unsettled, Imogen turned away. 'Tom wants to show them that they made a mistake by not promoting him.'

'But he'll get another chance, won't he?' Rowan asked, pouring them both some orange juice.

'Of course he will,' she replied, taking the drink gratefully. 'But he doesn't see it that way. He's in a hurry, and he wants everything *now*.'

Her voice took on a sharp edge, impatience under the surface. She had been disappointed for him, *with* him. They had both wanted him to be promoted, but the way he overreacted was childish, petty, and it lowered him in her eyes. His ambition had always been obvious, but it was dangerous now; he wanted to brag, to strut his stuff, and he had been held back, curtailed. So now everything else in his life was wrong. He didn't like the Kensington flat, it was suddenly too crowded with Imogen and Rowan and the baby coming. He didn't like having to drive up north every weekend to see his constituents. It was a bore, a hassle.

Time was when they had all gone up to Southport together, taking the opportunity to enjoy the weekends as a family. The house there was large with a fine landscaped garden, the neighbourhood quiet, unlike the fuggy blast of London. Time was when Tom loved the cool air up there and took Rowan to the beach to play cricket on the white sands. They had spent much time together there, grown to know each other, an affection developing naturally.

Time was – but not now. Now, only two years after their marriage, Tom had altered. There was still a powerful love between them, but the lure of ambition was stronger, and Imogen recognised it regretfully. She had even expected it, had become inured to it; but it still hurt when she realised that in the pecking order of Tom Wrigley's life, she came second. The Mother of Parliaments, Imogen thought sourly was a bitch.

Soon the trips to Southport became less frequent. Imogen was heavily pregnant and the journey tired her. She argued that Rowan could go, but Tom was against it. I'll go alone, that way I'll come back quicker. . . . Only he didn't, he stayed on, sometimes returning on Monday mornings and going straight to the House. It was easier that way, he reasoned, wondering what the fuss was about. I used to do it that way before. . . .

'You weren't married then, Tom,' she said coolly.

'I can't run my life round a family!' he snapped, without thinking.

Stunned, Imogen turned away.

'Sorry, I didn't mean that,' he said hurriedly glancing at the clock and wondering why all women got unreasonable when they were pregnant. 'I'll be home about eight, okay?'

She knew better than to wait for him. Instead, Imogen phoned Ira and chatted for a while about nothing in particular and then she and Rowan watched a Sylvester Stallone film, her son hooting loudly at the romantic parts. The film ran in front of her eyes without Imogen even seeing it; her thoughts were elsewhere. Oh well, I suppose it had to happen in the end, she thought calmly, he's a busy man and an ambitious one. That was one of the reasons I fell in love with him. He only has so much time to spare, and I'm not looking my best at the moment.

The baby kicked at her side and Imogen reached out for her son's hand. Rowan turned, allowing her to lay his palm against her stomach.

'It's the baby.'

'I didn't think it was a rabbit,' he said, smiling.

She laughed; always laughed with Rowan.

His fingers rested against the swell of his mother's belly. 'Is it a boy?'

'You know that I didn't ask,' Imogen chided him. 'I want it to be a surprise.'

'I suppose Tom wants a boy,' Rowan said, getting up and sitting next to his mother on the settee.

'Why?'

'To call his son,' he answered simply.

'But he calls you his son,' Imogen replied, staring into Rowan's face. 'Tom loves you very much.'

'I know, but it's not the same,' Rowan said emphatically. 'I was just a rehearsal for the real thing.'

Lightly Imogen swatted him on the head with the *Radio Times*. 'God, you do talk some rubbish.'

But later she thought about what her son had said, and wondered, and realised that he had, inadvertently, recognised a real truth. Tom had married a ready-made family, he had overnight obtained a wife and a child; but now there was to be a new baby. A son of his own . . . but what if it wasn't a son? Imogen wondered. Would it matter? These days, with women doing everything men could, would it matter what sex the baby was?

She would have asked him about it, but they never had the time. As the weeks crept further and further towards the birth, Tom was called away to Brussels and then to New York. Surprised by the lack of interest and by the lack of any physical contact between them, Imogen tried to talk to him.

'Tom, can't you stay home one weekend?'

'I'm busy, for God's sake.' He paused, knew he had gone over the top. Turning, he saw Imogen standing by the fridge in bare feet, a spoon poised above a carton of yoghurt. She's so pretty, he thought suddenly . . . and so pregnant. 'Sorry, I didn't mean to snap.'

She laid down the yoghurt. The heat was making her listless, the baby a heavy drag on her. She felt unlovely and unloved.

'I just want to see a bit more of you, Tom. I love you, surely that's not too much to ask?'

He moved over to her, bent down to kiss the top of her head. But she didn't move him sexually; the bulge of her stomach was solid between them, forcing them apart.

'I'll try and get back on Sunday,' he said, smiling half-heartedly. 'There's nothing wrong with you, darling, it's always like this. Ask the other wives.'

She did. They commiserated. They called Tom names and said he was crazy and sympathised with Imogen. Which wasn't what she wanted at all. She didn't want sympathy, she wanted her husband.

'It's a bad time, especially since they've got that important vote coming up –'

'Since when haven't they got an important vote coming up?' Imogen countered irritably, leaning across Penny's work table, her back aching constantly. 'God, I feel lousy. I never remember feeling this bad with Rowan.'

'You were younger then.'

Imogen rolled her eyes heavenwards. 'Thanks, that was all I needed.'

'Oh, do stop it!' Penny replied heatedly. 'You still look wonderful.'

'I look like Pavarotti.'

'No!' Penny replied shortly. 'He's a brunette.'

They both laughed, the tension lifting, Penny laying down her tools and sitting opposite Imogen.

'So where are you having the baby?'

'The Portland.'

'Same date?'

She nodded. '16th December.'

'A Christmas baby. Some present.'

'Yes,' Imogen said thoughtfully. 'Let's hope Tom thinks so too.'

She went into labour early, on 14 December. Tom was busy at the time so Imogen left an urgent message for him at the House. Rowan was calm, funny as usual, and went with his mother in the ambulance, holding her hand. Blind with pain, Imogen clung on to her son – but she went into the delivery room alone.

'Let me come with you,' Rowan said, his narrow face drawn into an unaccustomed frown.

'No, sweetheart, you wait for Tom outside.' She winced, rolling on to her side. 'Go on, please. . . .'

Obediently he went outside and waited. He waited and started every time the phone rang or the door opened. He listened and watched the entrance of the delivery room and tried to catch the eye of every passing doctor. Nurses came and gave him drinks, Suzanne phoned and told him she was coming up to London, and he remembered to telephone Elizabeth in Little Lever. But Tom didn't come.

In the delivery room Imogen had her baby after being in labour for ten hours. She pushed the child out into the world alone and gripped fiercely on to the side of the bed, wondering why her husband wasn't there with her. Alone she gave birth, and alone she cradled the little dark-haired daughter they handed to her. The room was white with lights, steel and tile, inhuman, impersonal. Cold. Gently Imogen stroked her child's head, a nurse finally glancing round the door. 'Your husband's here,' she said, smiling.

Imogen glanced up, her heart banging.

The doors swung open, a voice coming loud into the room. But not Tom's voice, Ira's.

'Will *I* do?' he said simply, sitting down on the side of the bed.

Tearful, Imogen glanced down.

He saw that she was close to breaking down and peered at the baby. 'Is she okay? I mean, has she got everything she should have?'

'Everything except a father.'

He touched Imogen's hand.

'Tom's busy.'

'You're busy.'

'Yeah, well . . .' he glanced around the delivery room, smiling wryly. 'I suppose there'll be hell to pay when they realise I'm not your husband.'

'They'll throw you out.'

'Well,' he said easily, 'I've been bounced from better places than this.'

Imogen's voice was low, timid. 'Thanks, Ira.'

He nodded. 'Like I said – what are friends for?'

Tom had not been pleased to find Ira Mazan with his wife and new baby. Not pleased at all. In fact, he tackled Ira and they had a sharp exchange in the corridor outside, their voices raised loud enough for Imogen to hear them through the closed doors. Tom's blustering tones were easy to follow, but Ira kept his voice low, cold. Then there was a sudden silence. She stared at the doors, waiting, but a few minutes ground on before Tom finally put in an appearance.

'That bloody Mazan!' he snapped. 'Why did you let him in?'

Amazed, she stared at him. 'What the hell are you talking about, Tom? We've been trying to get hold of you for hours.'

'He had no *right* to be here. He isn't your husband,' he paused. 'Unless you'd rather he was.'

Incensed, Imogen glanced at the baby in the cot next to her bed. 'Tom, stop it. Please.'

He knew he had gone too far and sighed, walking over and glancing down into the crib, then touching his daughter gently on the cheek. His face was drawn: too many late nights, too many speeches, too many dreams chased without rest. Tom Wrigley, Imogen thought blindly, what's happening to you?

'She's lovely,' he said at last, although the pleasure in his voice was subdued. Had he really wanted a boy so much? Imogen wondered.

The door opened again. Rowan walked in and looked curiously at the newcomer. 'A girl – I knew it!' he said happily. 'What are you going to call her, Mum?'

In that instant Imogen made her choice. She looked at her husband and then at her son; at the boy who had been with her and cared for her when Tom had been too busy to spend time with his wife. She looked at them both and then finally turned to Rowan.

'You choose.'

Tom flinched, the wedge coming between them in that instant. It was an act of defiance on Imogen's part, a way of striking back. He knew it and felt belittled – and ashamed.

Rowan grinned. 'I can choose? Really?'

His mother nodded.

The boy stared at the new baby and then glanced up: 'Can we call her Joy?'

Steadily Imogen and Tom looked at each other, their minds going back to that day in Little Lever, the day of the funeral, the day Tom had waited in his car outside and made up his mind to marry Imogen. THE BEST IS NOW, the poster had said, and for an instant both of them knew how close they had come to losing everything.

'Joy is a good name,' Tom said finally, touching Rowan on the shoulder. 'And a hopeful one.'

There followed nine months of mutual effort. Imogen recovered her figure and returned to her old glory, Tom spent more time at home, and at the weekends they went up to Southport *en masse*, Tom holding his surgery and seeing his constituents there. Congratulations, they said, a new baby. Well done. We like to think that our MP's a family man. . . . He revelled in the compliments and the attention, liked to talk about his home life and his daughter. Joy was Tom's doll, his little miracle, and he spoiled her, picking her up and resting her on his chest, her tiny body lying happily against his heart. He gushed over her and took photographs, bought toys and even got up in the night to comfort her. But he had the sense to fuss over Rowan too, taking the time to make sure that the boy didn't feel excluded.

He was, in those months, the ideal father and husband. Too ideal, too perfect to last. It was as if Tom had taken on a role, a position. He had been promoted in his own private domestic Cabinet and was taking his responsibilities seriously. Seriously, but not *naturally*, Imogen thought, watching him. He was trying too hard, being too ambitious, wanting everything to run perfectly, smoothly – and it never did. Especially when it came to children.

She tried to keep the atmosphere relaxed, but Tom was already writing off for information on the best schools for his daughter and things became so intense that even Rowan noticed.

'I suppose she'll have to end up as Prime Minister?' he said drily.

'Oh, give it time, the novelty will wear off,' Imogen responded evenly.

'He's gone all gooey,' Rowan said with disgust.

'It gets fathers that way sometimes,' Imogen said, teasing him. 'You wait until you're a father.

'Oh, I'm not even going to get married,' Rowan replied. 'I don't like children.'

Alarmed, she studied him. 'You will, in the end,' she said, thinking suddenly of Giles. 'Honestly, it'll all seem perfectly natural when the time's right.'

'Yeah . . .' he replied, unconvinced.

By the time the following August came round Tom was travelling again, and by the time the House was recalled, he was back to his usual ways. He didn't stop loving Joy, but he found home life restricting, the trivia of day-to-day domesticity boring him. Imogen knew that he longed to return to his travels, to hear the applause again and receive the adoration of his constituents. They might hound him, bore him, weary him, but they also *looked up to him* – and he needed that above everything.

The flaw in his make-up was too obvious to ignore. Tom's feeling of inferiority damanded respect, adulation, applause – and a family did not offer that. To Joy, Rowan and Imogen he was the man in jeans, the father who fixed things intermittently, the man who padded to the bathroom in bare feet and worried about his weight – he wasn't the MP at home, his status didn't count there, didn't matter. They just loved him – but it wasn't enough.

I can't give you what you want, Imogen thought helplessly, no woman can. There is no glamour in the school run and the shopping at Sainsbury's – I can take as much as possible off your shoulders in that way, but you'll always be *real* here; not the man in the pinstriped suit, the man on *Newsnight*, the man on Radio 4. You can't deliver speeches to us, or demand that something be done about the drainage system in Moss Side. We are your family, your bolt-hole, your anchor. We are supposed to be the people with whom you can relax. Stop trying to *impress* us, Tom, she thought helplessly, we love you anyway.

Sex, which had previously been frequent and lusty, flagged. The baby cried at night and Rowan's forays to the kitchen prevented many spontaneous moments. Soon Imogen and Tom became tense around each other, careful, wary, and before long Imogen saw her husband's diary fill with evening engagements, her own days spent at home or with the Tory women.

'Keep working on your own career,' Ira advised her. 'Then you've got something else to think about.'

'I don't have the time – what with the baby and Rowan, and the houses to look after –'

'You shouldn't let your talent slide,' he insisted. 'Keep Lorrie sweet and Dickie Bedlington, keep your contacts going. It's good for your confidence, Imogen.'

'Listen, Ira,' she snapped. 'I never wanted to be famous, that's not my style. I wanted to have a family and to help a husband get on . . . I'm very working class that way.'

'Ouch.'

'Sorry,' she replied, ashamed of the remark, 'it's just that my talent lies in loving, in making a home. I'm not the ambitious one.'

'That's a shame,' Ira said tartly, 'because you're three times smarter than Tom's ever going to be.'

'I just want the marriage to work –'

Ira frowned: 'And it isn't?'

'In its own way – but not in mine,' Imogen admitted. 'Tom's losing interest, I can feel it.'

Impatiently Ira waved away his secretary and waited until she had closed the door behind her before speaking again.

'It's just your imagination.'

'No, it's not,' Imogen said fiercely. 'We aren't relaxed in each other's company. We don't laugh any more.'

'Which reminds me,' Ira said suddenly. 'Have you heard the one about the Jewish woman who wou!dn't have a colostomy because she couldn't get the shoes to match?'

'That's disgusting!' Imogen said, grinning.

'Always leave 'em laughing,' Ira countered, then paused, suddenly serious. 'If you need me, just pick up the phone. Okay? If there's trouble, call.'

Chapter Twenty-Seven

Eve Miller. Five feet six and all muscle. Wasn't that what Penny had said about her? Amongst other things. . . . Imogen looked at the pile of vegetables in front of her, ready to be prepared for dinner, a knife lying alongside the chopping board. In the bedroom down the hall, Joy was sleeping, Rowan still at school. The flat smelt cool, winter coming into the walls, the ceiling still marked from where a champagne cork had hit it. Champagne, Imogen thought coldly, we celebrated in champagne when the baby came home.

Methodically she began to chop the carrots, then peeled the potatoes. Joy slept on. Imogen chopped loudly, wanting the baby to wake, wanting to have a reason to go in and pick her up. But the baby didn't wake and the pile of vegetables grew. Inch by inch. She kept chopping, slicing, dicing, cutting. The winter sun shimmered against the knife blade, the board smeared with juice. Chop, chop, chop, came down the blade, Imogen cutting faster and faster, the vegetables tumbling over and falling to the floor. Ugly clumps now, wet slabs of raw food dropping to the ground around her.

And she kept chopping, too fast, far too fast, cutting into her finger, the blood coming quick and easy over the white slivers of potato. Chop, chop, chop. . . . The pile grew, stupidly high, too much for one family, too much for one meal. But she didn't stop and before long she couldn't; her only sanity was in the knife, in keeping busy, in doing all those little housewifely duties that a woman did to keep her home and her man. Keep cutting, keep cutting. Her hair fell over her forehead, her eyes blurring, the knife awkward in her hand, her wrist aching. Chop, chop, chop, went the blade, Imogen rocking on her feet – then suddenly and violently she swept all the cut vegetables on to the floor.

Sick with distress, she howled drily, trod the food underfoot, then raised the knife and, with all her energy, plunged it into the wooden board.

'No, I don't believe it! Not Tom.' Douglas's face was ashen, staring at his wife.

'Neither do I,' Penny said, rinsing a scalpel in the white enamel sink. 'Can you believe he would be so stupid, so bloody stupid?'

'Eve Miller,' Douglas said, aghast. 'After all these years.'

He said the same to Harry Taylor later at the House, and then to Trevor Rowe-Thorne at a dinner engagement the following day. He even felt it his duty to pass it on to Arnold Miles, who looked completely uninterested. Only Jimmy Bentley was really surprised to hear about Tom's adultery.

'Sarah doesn't know about it,' he said, his bushy eyebrows drawn together, his stocky frame leaning against the bar. 'I'd have heard all about it if she had. You know how she bangs on about men cheating on their wives.'

Douglas looked round. 'I don't want to gossip,' he said, smoothing his red hair over his bald patch. 'But it does look bad. I mean, Imogen's a lovely woman, what *can* he have been thinking of?'

'Sex,' Jimmy said flatly, finishing his pink gin and ordering another. Douglas watched the stocky PR man, wondered if he knew that his nickname summed up his love of alcohol. 'Pink Jim'. . . . Oh, if only you knew. 'It always comes down to sex,' Jimmy went on blithely. 'She can't have been any good in the sack.'

Douglas thought the remark was tasteless. 'So that's why you and Sarah stay together, is it?' he asked acidly. 'Rampant lust?'

Jimmy was immune to sarcasm, and smiled professionally. 'It was just an observation,' he said, 'Who's Tom supposed to be screwing?'

'Eve Miller.'

Jimmy started violently, but regained his composure with remarkable speed.

'Eve Miller, hey? But I thought she was abroad.'

'Came back,' Douglas said, taking a handful of peanuts and putting his head back to swallow them. He chewed for several minutes before answering, Jimmy waiting patiently. 'She's working in publishing now. Some magazine or other. *Health and Beauty*, I think Penny said.'

Jimmy glanced over Douglas's shoulder, and smiled as Harry Taylor approached. He walked quickly, as short men do, taking hurried strides, his hair as immaculately groomed as ever. Douglas looked at the layered bouffant admiringly.

'So, what's news?' Harry asked, immediately taking a bar seat to avoid looking up to the bulky Jimmy.

'Tom's affair,' he replied, shooting a glance at Douglas. 'Apparently Eve Miller is back.'

Unimpressed, Harry ordered a whisky. 'Now you know why I don't get married. Maxie's very broad-minded.' Jimmy and Douglas exchanged glances. 'Wives get so bloody serious about things. I mean, Tom probably just wanted a bit on the side. What's the harm, hey? I think it's unreasonable to expect any man to be faithful to one woman.'

Douglas thought of Penny and of the scalpel she used to take the hide off her carcasses. She was nifty with it, he thought uncomfortably, and very accurate. He'd seen her skin a rabbit in a couple of minutes. He sat down on the stood next to Harry and instinctively crossed his legs.

'Well, I still think it's just a storm in a teacup,' Jimmy went on. 'It'll blow over . . . after all, Imogen's on to a good number with Tom –'

Wryly, Douglas nodded. 'Women just don't realise that sex isn't important to a man.'

'Unless you're not getting it,' Jimmy said woefully.

'Sarah being a little *difficult*?' Harry said, his smile wolfish. 'I can't say I ever have trouble with Maxie. Can't get enough of it.'

Douglas coughed, grimly embarrassed. 'Well, I think it's a shame.'

'We all do,' Jimmy said, downing his second pink gin. 'But that's life. After all, what can you do about it? What can poor Imogen do about it?' he smiled, his bushy eyebrows raised in an expression of benevolence. 'She's a clever girl, you'll see, she'll take it in her stride. I mean, she can't really do anything else, can she?'

He was out and the office was empty. Impatiently Imogen paced the white-carpeted floor, walking past the stark, modern black furniture, the glass tables and the impressive view over the Thames. Several vast glass sculptures threw prisms of winter sunlight over the white walls and a bunch of Arum lilies stood to attention in a heavy Lalique vase. The afternoon was dying, slipping into dusk, the traffic moving slowly on the street below; slowly but noiselessly, the sounds obliterated by the double glazing, the street lamps coming on.

Imogen sat down and crossed her legs, then stood up again. The previous day she had phoned and told Ira what she intended to do, but she could tell from his voice that he didn't believe her. It was too out of character for her to behave in that way. Imogen never took revenge. Not on Giles, not on Tom. She always played fair. Stood on her dignity. . . . Idly Imogen flicked at the heads of the Arum lilies, watching as they rocked gently in the vase. Everyone thought they knew how she would react; everyone had her off to a tee. Good, she thought fiercely, that'll count in my favour now. No one will suspect me – not Imogen, not the good little wife and mother. Not her. Oh no, Imogen wasn't going to play dirty. . . . Like hell, she wasn't!

A moment later Ira came in, kissed Imogen on both cheeks and then noticed the bandage on her hand.

'Not a suicide attempt, I hope?'

She smiled grimly. 'No, just a little domestic accident.'

'Anyone killed?'

She slammed down the papers she was holding on Ira's desk. 'I'm not going to let Tom get away with it. . . . No man is going to make me feel this bad – without suffering for it.' She pushed the pages over to Ira, waiting for him to sit down and look at them.

He laughed loudly after reading only the first few lines. 'This is outrageous. Dynamite! . . . Imogen, you can't really want me to publish this?'

'Why not? It's the truth.'

'Well, apart from the fact that accuracy has nothing to do with journalism, Tom will go ape when he reads it. *If* he reads it.'

'Everyone reads your magazine, Ira, you know that. Even Tom sometimes. And even if he misses the piece, his friends will see it and they always talk about the articles – he'll find out one way or another. He's bound to.'

Ira carried on reading, mesmerised: ' "In a jock strap with a pair of cricket stumps . . ." ' he could hardly speak for laughing. 'Bloody hell, Imogen, the poor bastard will be laughed out of court.'

'No, he won't, because only Tom and his friends will know it's about him. No one else will have a clue.' She paused. 'Well, perhaps a few other women will know it's Tom, but that's not the point. What matters is this – I'm doing this to frighten him, to throw a scare into him. Once he realises that someone's on to him, and that the whole affair could become public, he'll be so scared of the publicity that he'll come home in a flash –'

Ira was still reading, incoherent with mirth: ' ". . . and a bottle of whitener . . .".'

Imogen snatched the pages out of his hands. 'Oh, concentrate!' she said furiously. 'It's not a joke to me, Ira . . .' her voice faltered. 'Tom's cheated on me, just like Giles did. How do you think that makes me feel? Am I supposed to think that it's *funny*?'

'Hey,' Ira said softly, 'come on, kiddo, don't get upset.'

Imogen pushed her hair back from her face, struggling to keep her composure. 'I'm going to make this marriage work, Ira, I swear it. I'm going to get my husband back – whatever it takes.'

He nodded slowly. 'Okay. But what if Tom finds out that it was you who wrote the piece? If he does you really will have blown it.'

'He won't!' she said adamantly. 'Tom doesn't think I'm capable of doing something like that. He'll just read it and know that someone's found out about the affair – then he'll get windy and dump Eve Miller. In fact, if he suspects anyone, he'll suspect *her*, not me. After all, she's in publishing, she has the contacts.'

'Yeah, and I know her,' Ira admitted grimly. 'Are you sure Tom's sleeping with her?'

Imogen nodded.

'Crazy bugger,' he said thoughtfully, picking up the article again. 'I'll put it in the next issue, Imogen. I just hope it does the trick.'

She smiled warmly at him.

'Thanks, Ira. Thanks. . . . If there's anything I can do for you –'

'There is, actually.'

Imogen looked at him questioningly. 'What?'

'Just tell me – where do you get a bottle of whitener?'

Tom was quiet, guiltily so. He had felt miserable about the affair for weeks, Eve becoming a bore, phoning him at the House and writing to his party offices. She had even discovered the number of the house in Southport and rung him there. He didn't like it. It was supposed to be a fling, a one-off. After all, they went back a long way, they knew the set-up.

But Eve wasn't the old Eve. She was cunning now, not quite so much the 'In bed, out, Thank you, scout' type she used to be. Europe had hardened her, made her ambitious. What had once been an uncomplicated woman was now a woman with big ideas, and those ideas included Tom Wrigley. She didn't want to marry him; didn't want domestic security; she wanted to be his mistress. Sex offered, washing done elsewhere.

He had been a bloody fool, Tom thought to himself, glancing over to where Rowan sat on the settee, Imogen's newspaper lying under his feet. He had a good home, a handsome family, and an enviable wife. Why had he endangered it? Why? – for sex, for flattery, for attention. Eve had flirted with him, made him feel important, puffed up his wobbly ego, and in bed she had moaned at the right times, and made more than favourable comments about his physique and his performance. She remembered what he liked too. . . .

But a greasy little affair wasn't enough to risk his marriage for, Tom thought, no way. He had been a fool, but he had been lucky. Other men had been caught out, their careers ruined, for just this kind of indiscretion. Tom leaned his head back against his seat. I must put it behind me, he thought, it wasn't fair on Imogen and it could be disastrous for me. Oh God, he mused, what if the papers found out? What if Imogen heard about it? What if the Prime Minister heard?

He was sweating and loosening his collar. Calm down, everything's fine. It was a stupid thing to do, but no one's any the wiser. Yes, thought Tom, he was going to be okay. He was going to be one of lucky ones.

He was wrong. The following week *S'expression* hit the news-stands and the first person to read it was Harry Taylor. He saw the piece entitled 'Private Members', and, drawn by the title, began to read. Maxie was asleep next to him, her breathing deep and slow. Harry's accelerated rapidly as he read on:

> *A man who finds pleasure in the sporting life. A very adept and athletic gentleman who prefers stirring his stumps in Chelsea to an evening in the House; a man known to put a bottle of whitening to an exacting use. . . .*

'*Eeek!*' Harry shot up in bed, Maxie stirring beside him.

'What is it?'

Frantically Harry pulled on his custom-made, built-up slippers, and hurried to the phone. Then he changed his mind, raced back into the bedroom, brushed his hair, and then made the call.

'Jimmy,' he gasped, 'have you seen the new *S'expression*?'

'Shut up!' Jimmy snapped, turning over in bed. 'Sarah doesn't even know I read it.'

'Oh God, Jimmy, it's about Tom,' he stammered. 'No names are mentioned, but it's obvious. It could ruin him.'

Recognising a crisis when he heard one, Jimmy hurriedly pulled on his dressing gown, Sarah waking up and frowning at him.

'What's the matter?'

'Nothing, my dove,' he said, smiling wanly and covering the mouthpiece. 'You go back to sleep –'

'I don't want to go back to sleep! I want to know who's on the phone.'

'*Jimmy!*' Harry called down the line. '*Jimmy!*'

Still smiling, Jimmy put the phone in his other hand. 'It's nothing important –'

'Now, listen, you bushy-eyed slug,' Sarah said meanly. 'Either tell me who's on that phone –'

He needed no further encouragement. 'Harry's on the phone.'

Sarah was still frowning. 'What does that sawn-off runt want?' Realisation came quickly. 'Okay, Jimmy – so *who* has done *what* to *whom*? Somebody's up to something or they wouldn't be ringing their PR man at seven in the morning.'

Jimmy kept smiling grimly and turned his attention back to Harry. 'Listen, I'll phone you back when I've seen a copy. Bye.'

Then he turned back to his wife.

'There's a piece about Tom Wrigley in a magazine called *S'expression*,' he explained blithely. 'I can't comment until I've seen it, so I'll have to go out and get a copy.'

She smiled coldly. 'Why bother, Jimmy? It's in your briefcase – under the *Evening Standard*.'

Penny saw it too, after Trevor Rowe-Thorne had seen it and declared that legally there was nothing they could do. No names had been named, he said, so it was better if they just sit it out. He explained the situation to Danielle over lunch, his right cheek developing the nervous tic it always did when he was under pressure. He took off his glasses and closed his eyes as he talked, Danielle staring at the fine veins in his temples and thinking of the marbled fat on the side of a piece of beef.

'Of course, Tom's been a fool.' He opened his eyes

momentarily in order to get a grip on his wineglass. 'Adultery is such a messy business.'

Danielle lit a cigarette; Trevor winced.

'Darling, it's such a bad habit, do you have to?'

She ignored the remark, thinking of Tom and wondering why, if he had to have an affair, why didn't he pick her?

'I mean, the tar will clog up your lungs and cause all kinds of horrors. . . .'

She inhaled, her thoughts elsewhere. God, poor Imogen, what a chump she must be feeling. But still, at least she was Tom's *wife*. At least she had *that*.

'. . . cigarette smokers shorten their life by up to 20 per

her hand, her wrist aching. Chop, chop, chop, went the blade, Imogen rocking on her feet – then suddenly and violently she swept all the cut vegetables on to the floor.

Sick with distress, she howled drily, trod the food underfoot, then raised the knife and, with all her energy, plunged it into the wooden board.

'No, I don't believe it! Not Tom.' Douglas's face was ashen, staring at his wife.

'Neither do I,' Penny said, rinsing a scalpel in the white enamel sink. 'Can you believe he would be so stupid, so bloody stupid?'

'Eve Miller,' Douglas said, aghast. 'After all these years.'

He said the same to Harry Taylor later at the House, and then to Trevor Rowe-Thorne at a dinner engagement the following day. He even felt it his duty to pass it on to Arnold Miles, who looked completely uninterested. Only Jimmy Bentley was really surprised to hear about Tom's adultery.

'Sarah doesn't know about it,' he said, his bushy eyebrows drawn together, his stocky frame leaning against the bar. 'I'd have heard all about it if she had. You know how she bangs on about men cheating on their wives.'

Douglas looked round. 'I don't want to gossip,' he said, smoothing his red read it!' he said pompously, turning over on to his back and pushing the magazine under his pillow.

Maxie shrugged, all compliance. 'Okay Harry, whatever you say,' she said, pouring some baby oil on to his chest, her fingers working lovingly at his skin. 'But it's very funny,' she said, before pausing and adding softly, '. . . and *very* accurate.'

'It reminds me of a joke,' Penny said to Douglas in the basement when she had read the article. 'This man comes in with his two dogs and wants them stuffing. So the taxidermist says, Do you want them mounted? Oh no, says the man, they were just good friends!'

She laughed hugely at the joke, Douglas watching her balefully.

'I feel sorry for Imogen,' he said. 'I thought she was a friend of yours.'

'She is,' Penny agreed, 'but if I know Imogen, she won't take this lying down. You'll see, that is one smart lady.'

'It's a pity,' Douglas continued. 'I thought they were well matched.'

'It's not the end of the marriage – just a hiccup.'

He looked at his wife in open astonishment.

'D'you mean to say that if I had an affair you would see it as "just a hiccup"?'

Penny regarded thoughtfully for a long instant. 'Don't be silly, Douglas. It would be the end for us.'

He swallowed: 'So why isn't it important for Imogen?'

'I didn't say it wasn't important,' Penny said, with more than a little exasperation. 'I just think that Imogen has her head screwed on, that's all. She wants the marriage to work, and unless I'm very wrong, she'll do everything to hold on to Tom. Besides,' she said confidently, 'that Eve Miller's nothing but a scrubber. She has no class; she's not in the same league as Imogen.'

'But who wrote the article?' Douglas asked, his forehead shiny under the overhead light. 'Who would *want* to write it? And for what purpose?'

'To get their own back,' Penny said flatly. 'Maybe it's a little farewell gift from Eve Miller. Maybe Tom dumped her and she's taking revenge. It would be just up her street, *and* she knows everyone in publishing, including Ira Mazan.'

Douglas stared at the stuffed badger in front of him, his expression woeful. 'I just hope that Imogen doesn't find out, that's all.'

Tom was thinking the same. He had heard about the article and rushed out to buy a copy of *S'expression*, hiding it between the covers of *Which Car?* until he got back to his office. He read it quickly, then read it again, then groaned. Who in God's name had written it? Okay, the rag belonged to Ira Mazan, but someone else had written the piece. But who? Eve?

His temper accelerated rapidly. Something like this could ruin him. Admittedly there were no names in the piece, nothing concrete, but someone might guess. After all, hadn't Harry, and Jimmy and all the others? He struggled against panic, trying to steady his nerves. He knew he had been a fool, but had thought he had got away with it.

His secretary walked in suddenly; Tom stuffed the magazine into a drawer, smiling nervously. Mystified, the woman gave him some messages and then left. Tom gazed at the cover glassily. Who would know it was him? Only a woman who had slept with him would know such details, and none of them would expose an old affair. Not Maxie certainly, nor any of the other women he had known. Unless . . . the thought came to him suddenly, unpleasantly. Eve hadn't been too pleased when he told her to cool things, to back off a little. She had seemed to take his rejection well, but there had been a certain chilling coolness about her the last time they had met. Could she have written it to pay him back? *Could* she?

The idea took hold. Who else? Tom asked himself. She knew Ira, and she was the only one who had nothing to lose. Oh God, Tom thought, if Imogen ever gets to hear about this – but then again, how could she? She wasn't likely to read *S'expression*, was she? *Or was she?* Perhaps Ira would show her a copy, have a good laugh at Tom's expense. He loved Imogen, what better way to get his own back? What better way to try and split the marriage up?

Tom suddenly regretted the way he had spoken to Ira, and the numerous slights he had inflicted on his rival.

People had said that Mazan was dangerous, but he hadn't listened. *He* had won Imogen and had been delighted to rub the publisher's face in his triumph. And now Ira Mazan was taking his revenge. Either by design or accident, Tom's affair had been made public and unless he was very careful he would lose not only his wife, but his career.

Imogen mustn't find out, Tom thought frantically. He would make more time for her, cherish her, act like a proper husband and father. No more affairs for him, no more involvements with dangerous women like Eve Miller. He had learnt his lesson. He had been lucky after all.

Chapter Twenty-Eight

'Very clever, very clever indeed,' Suzanne said admiringly. 'Did it do the trick?'

Imogen nodded. 'It worked like a charm. As I thought, Tom suspected Eve Miller and dropped her so quickly she must have got a nosebleed.' She smiled, savouring her victory. 'You won't believe how attentive he's been lately, full of presents and surprise dinners, coming home early and taking us all up to Southport for the weekends. He thinks he's got away with it, and that I don't suspect a thing. Oh yes,' Imogen said, 'it threw such a scare into him that he's not going to wander again.'

Suzanne's voice was cold. 'He shouldn't have done in the first place.'

'I agree – but you know men, they can't help themselves.'

'I think he's been a bastard –'

'Let it drop,' Imogen said warningly. 'I wanted Tom back and he is – that's all that matters.'

'Are you sure?'

'Do you mean, have I forgiven him?' Imogen asked. 'Not really. I'm angry, but I *won't* have another failed marriage. Tom is very attractive to women, I understand that. I suppose I even suspected that something like this would happen one day, but he's too careful of his career to risk a further affair. Honestly, believe me, he won't cheat on me again.'

'If he does, God help him.'

Imogen sighed. 'What's done is done, I can't change the past. Tom is clever, Jaco, but he's not as clever as I am. I have a home and family to protect and I aim to do just that.' Her voice was calm, determined. 'No woman is going to take what's mine.'

'But if he ever found out that it was you who wrote the piece –'

'I wrote about his adultery. He was the one who committed it.'

'Men don't see things that way,' Suzanne warned her. 'Tom would see it as a betrayal if he found out that you'd been the one to expose him.'

'He *won't* find out,' Imogen insisted. 'He never suspected me for an instant; in fact, I can tell from the way he talks to me that he thinks I know nothing about it. My dear husband would never believe I had it in me. That his *wife* would write a piece for a soft porn magazine – impossible! Believe me, I know Tom, it would never enter his head.'

'Well, if you're sure –'

'I am. Trust me.'

The months passed, the piece slowly forgotten, Tom and his friends heaving a collective sigh of relief. Their concern was not merely for Tom, they could all imagine how they would feel if their liaisons came to light, and not one of them wanted to go through his experience. So as the dust settled they forgot – and soon the hideous event began to fade from everyone's mind.

Except Ira's. The article had been too close to home not to make a salacious read and he had received many approving letters about the piece. The public had apparently enjoyed 'Private Members' and wanted more – a fact Ira passed on to Imogen the next time they met.

'You could write a regular column, you know.'

She pulled a face. 'I don't think so. The piece was a one-off, and it achieved its objective – why would I want to keep writing about Tom? It would be dangerous if I pushed my luck, and besides, next time the wrong person might guess – and that would ruin his career *and* my marriage.'

'I don't mean write about Tom,' Ira said smoothly, 'I mean, what about the other husbands and boyfriends? As you said, who would suspect you, Imogen? No one. You're the last person they would think of.' He leaned towards her over his desk. 'It would be sweet revenge for all the affairs, sweet revenge for the Tory ladies. . . .'

Imogen frowned, but the idea appealed to her. Arnold Miles, if exposed, might decide to spend more time with his family, and as for Douglas – if what she heard was true – wouldn't Penny just love to get even in print? She mused on the idea, then shook her head.

'No, let sleeping dogs lie.'

Ira nodded, prepared to let the matter rest. Knowing Imogen he realised that she would think about it and possibly be tempted . . . but only in her own time. Let it stand for a bit, he told himself, just let it stand.

It would have stood for all time had not Sarah discovered that Jimmy, who apparently had been called to a meeting in Copenhagen, was in fact spending a weekend in Lyme Regis. It had been a fluke, a mixed message from his secretary that had tipped her off, and when she bumped into Imogen that afternoon on Kensington High Street she was too furious to be cautious.

'Hi, Sarah,' Imogen said warily. 'How are you?'

Sarah turned to look at her, blinked, her eyes hard, her low voice rigid, dark.

'I need a drink.'

They went to the nearest hotel. Sitting in the lounge, Sarah ordered two Martinis. Thinking one was for her, Imogen was astonished to see her companion down both of them in a matter of seconds. Swallowing hard, Sarah leaned back in her seat, her neck flushed, spotted red with rage.

'That bushy eyebrowed toe-rag is sleeping with his ex-researcher in Lyme Regis,' she said bitterly, taking out a handkerchief and blowing her nose loudly. 'Bastard.'

Imogen glanced around, motioning for Sarah to keep her voice down.

'I don't care!' she said fiercely. 'Why should I worry who knows?'

'Keep it down,' Imogen warned her. 'You don't want everyone to know what's going on.'

Sarah stared at her, the grey eyes piercingly mean.

'Don't preach to me,' she said spitefully. 'Your husband's no better.'

She had expected a shocked reaction and was

disappointed. 'You *knew*!' she said, her tone hovering between surprise and curiosity. 'You *knew* about Tom all along. You sly little bitch.'

'Don't call me names!' Imogen said sharply. 'Don't take your temper out on me.'

Sarah hung her head. She looked bulky in the small lounging chair, her drab suit doing nothing for her figure. On the third finger of her left hand was a large emerald engagement ring – vulgar, out of place and out of character. Imogen watched her tap her foot, then saw with horror that she was fighting hard to stop herself from crying.

'Pig . . .' she said brokenly. 'We have a son . . . oh, all men are the same. You can't trust any of them, not one, they all have their brains in their trousers. He said he would never leave me.' Sarah slumped further down the seat, her jacket bunched up behind her. Imogen was astonished to find that she pitied her, even began to like her a little now that she could see something of the real woman behind the butch exterior. 'He said that he was forced to go – *forced!* – I'll give the bugger forced!'

'Sarah, keep your voice down,' Imogen warned her again. 'You don't want everyone to know your business.' Her voice dropped. 'If you want to get your own back on Jimmy, do it quietly.'

'You can't divorce someone quietly.'

'You don't really want to divorce him,' Imogen replied calmly. 'Do you?'

'No,' Sarah agree, signalling for another Martini. 'I don't want to lose the fat bastard. I actually *like* him.' She took the glass from the waiter and drank half the cocktail in one gulp. 'Jimmy and I got drunk on these once. We were in Oxford and got completely smashed. We made love in a bus shelter. It gave a whole new meaning to the word layby.' She smiled drily. 'A bus shelter! God, now he wouldn't go anywhere that wasn't on an expense account. Oily sod. . . .' Her eyes fixed on Imogen. 'He fancies himself as a real hot shot. Hot shot, hot shit!'

Imogen pressed her lips together, trying hard not to laugh.

'Said he was going to be the "power behind the throne" –

and I believed him! Power behind the throne, hah! the only throne he's got power over is the one marked "Armitage Shanks".'

'People are looking at you,' Imogen said, clutching Sarah's arm. 'Don't let them see the state you're in. Brazen it out, Sarah. You won't keep Jimmy this way, you know that.'

He eyes cleared slowly, her heavy jaw coming forward. 'You kept quiet, didn't you? I have to hand it to you for that. No one realises that you know about Tom. I admire you for keeping your nerve.' She looked Imogen up and down, then smiled, one side of her mouth rising lopsidedly. '*You* wrote that piece in *S'expression*, didn't you? Don't bother to deny it, I know you did.'

'Sarah, listen –'

'God, that was smart!' she said honestly. 'It was really clever, Imogen. . . . I've underestimated you, I thought you were just a good-looking walkover.'

'Not quite,' Imogen said drily. 'I just took my revenge quietly.'

'Sneakily.'

'If you like.'

'Oh, I do,' Sarah said, grinning. 'I *do* like. So,' she said, leaning towards Imogen and supporting herself with one hand flat on the table. 'How do we go about it?'

'About what?'

'Don't act dumb! You wrote that piece, I know you did, and Tom came running home because of it. You got him back because you scared him back into his trousers – now I want you to do the same for me. Write something about Jimmy. Please, Imogen, I can give you the works, every-thing you need to know. Everyone will read it –' she laughed. It was more of a bark – 'and he'll go crazy.'

Imogen frowned: 'It might not work a second time.'

'*It will*!' Sarah shouted, then dropped her voice conspira-torially. 'Jimmy will never know who wrote it. No one ever thought of you before, so why will they now? You have the perfect cover. You're a respectable wife and mother – not the kind of woman who would write for a porn magazine.'

'But I know Ira. Someone's bound to put two and two together.'

Sarah shook her head, then blinked, the Martinis taking effect. '*Everyone* knows Ira Mazan. . . . In fact, we all thought Eve Miller had written that article, she's more the type. Believe me, Imogen, no one will suspect you. Besides, why would you write an exposé on Jimmy? You've no axe to grind, and we aren't exactly bosom chums. To all intents and purposes, there's no connection between us.'

The idea was tempting. Imogen hesitated, looking at Sarah and thinking of 'Pink Jim' laughing and echoing his way around the MPs. The PR man would soon be in need of a PR man, she thought wryly, her mischievous streak pushing her on.

'Anyway, what makes you think it would make good reading, Sarah?'

She smiled knowingly, then fell back into her chair. 'How about a man who wears a corset when he makes love? Is that interesting enough?'

Ira was luminous with mirth. 'A corset! No, don't tell me, it's got suspenders, hasn't it?'

Imogen waved the article under his nose, grinning. 'Jimmy Bentley has spent his life covering up other people's indiscretions; now we'll see how well he manages his own affairs.'

'If you'll pardon the expression,' Ira said evenly, taking the paper from her. 'My, my, I must say that I admire your crusading spirit, Imogen. You have turned into quite the little warrior, taking on all these big bad men.'

'Don't be snide,' she said, sliding into a seat opposite him. 'They have it coming –'

'And they are going to get it,' he said admiringly.

'They're all cheats, Ira. They should be stopped,' Imogen said, adding more softly, 'It hurts when you find out that your husband's fooling around. I mean, really *hurts*, especially if you've got children.'

'But Sarah Bentley is hardly the timid type, is she?' Ira countered, 'Rumour has it that she once hurled a man over a walnut table at the Garrick Club.'

'It was oak.'

'Well that makes all the difference,' he said drily.

'The man was being objectionable –'

'She *makes* men objectionable,' Ira replied. 'It's what she's good at. It's her purpose in life.'

Imogen raised her eyebrows. 'Listen, whatever you say, Jimmy's cheating on Sarah and that's not fair. He's always so bloody smug, so patronising about everyone else, it's about time he got his come-uppance. Besides,' she said coolly, 'I don't know why you're being so sensitive all of a sudden, you were begging me to do more when you saw the sales figures for the last issue.'

Ira smiled winningly. 'Well, I suppose the public *do* have a right to know. . . .'

She nodded, her tone sarcastic. 'Oh, absolutely. It's only right.'

'. . . and the idea of the Tories' PR man wearing a corset *does* have a certain fascination.'

'I knew you'd see it my way.'

Ira nodded. 'So we'll aim for the next issue?'

'Fine,' she agreed, smiling and rising to go.

'Imogen,' he said lightly. 'You couldn't get pictures too, could you?'

She shot him a warning look and walked to the door, Ira opening it to find Simone standing there. From the look on the Frenchwoman's face it was obvious that she had overheard their conversation – and it was also obvious that she was incensed to see Imogen.

'So,' she said bitterly, 'I see your little friend still comes to see you.'

Ira was quick to react. Simone was a dangerous eavesdropper, and could be treacherous when crossed.

'Calm down, Simone,' he said lightly. 'Imogen and I were just catching up on the gossip.'

She leaned against the door frame, ignoring Imogen, her jealousy coming like a heat from her.

'I warned you, Ira,' she said coldly. 'This has to stop. You have to stop seeing her.'

He faced her, his mood switching from genial charm to real dislike.

'Don't tell me what to do –'

'I think I should leave,' Imogen said, throwing a worried glance at Ira. 'I have things to do.'

'I can imagine,' Simone said savagely, watching Imogen as she passed and walked to the lift. She looked untroubled, cool, but her stomach was tight and a low buzz hummed in her head. She didn't know about the call girls, but she knew about the casinos, and knew also that Simone had many influential friends. If she talked, if she repeated what she had heard. . . . Damn it! Imogen thought furiously. Why had she been tempted into writing another article? She had achieved what she wanted with the first, why had she pushed her luck? Why had she endangered herself? . . . The lift doors opened slowly, indolently, Imogen walking in and turning just in time to see Ira and Simone arguing in the office beyond.

But her fears seemed to be groundless. Nothing happened – except that Tom was even more attentive and spent much of his spare time playing with Joy; and it seemed that the life Imogen had longed for and fought so cunningly to maintain was secure. She lived happily, even forgot about the next issue of *S'expression* and the article on Jimmy – until the day it came out.

Then the phone started ringing: Sarah, dark with triumph. 'Jimmy's taken a week off,' she said gloating. 'A virus, he said when he called the office. A virus, my arse!'

Imogen laid down her shopping the phone tucked under her chin. 'Did he see it?'

'*Did he see it!* All Parliament saw it – mind you, what do you expect with the title "Private Members"? The phone's never stopped ringing all morning. Harry was on first, then Douglas, then Arnold. The old fart.' She paused for breath. 'Naturally Jimmy's pretending that nothing's wrong and walking around with that professional smile slapped on his face – you know, that desperate look he always assumes when something diabolical has happened.'

'But he's said nothing directly to you?'

'God, no!' Sarah hooted. 'He's just praying that I know nothing about it.' She dropped her voice. 'I heard him talking to Trevor Rowe-Thorne though, but it sounds as if he's saying the usual thing – "Just keep quiet and let it blow over". I have to say, Imogen, that your Mr Mazan must be delighted, his circulation's got to be soaring over this!'

Imogen smiled and pushed back her hair. Ira *was* pleased, very pleased. He wanted more articles on the 'Private Members'. You can do it, he said; talk to the Tory women, let them get their own back in print. People love the pieces, love to guess who the member is this month. . . . And in the meantime raise your circulation? she countered. . . . Yeah, he agreed, why not?

'Listen, Sarah, never tell *anyone* what I did, will you?' Imogen asked. 'It's the last time –'

'Oh no!'

'*Yes*!' she snapped. 'The last time. I've got Tom back and Jimmy should be sufficiently terrified to stay home for a while.'

'But Imogen, it's such a good idea. A blow for women everywhere –'

'Forget it,' Imogen said warningly. 'I'm no feminist. I did what I did for my own reasons, but other women can fight their own battles.' She fingered the handle of her shopping bag, glancing over to Joy sleeping in the pushchair. It had been fun, a lark, but she had too much to lose to risk any further exposés. It was over. She and her family were safe again, enough was enough. 'Promise me, Sarah, promise me that you'll never tell anyone that it was me.'

'Oh, all right,' she said reluctantly. 'I owe you that much, at least.'

'Not a word. Ever.'

Sarah nodded wearily. 'Trust me. Not a word shall pass my lips.'

> IF YOU WANT TO KNOW WHO WROTE THE
> ARTICLE ABOUT YOU IN *S'EXPRESSION*,
> YOU SHOULD LOOK CLOSE TO HOME.
> VERY CLOSE. YOUR WIFE.

Tom read the anonymous note three times. At first he had dismissed it, thrown it into the waste-paper bin. Then he had wondered about it, about the person who had written the note. So the connection had been made, had it? An outsider knew that the first exposé had been about him. But *which* outsider? Tom smoothed out the crumpled sheet and stared at the words. No, it was just malice. There was no possibility of Imogen having written the piece. He and his cohorts had decided that Eve was responsible. . . .

And yet Eve had been outraged when he suggested it, and even more furious when he dumped her for her treachery. *Her* treachery. No, he thought again, not Imogen. She had too much class, too much style to do something like that. She wouldn't risk humiliation. . . . But she had already been humiliated, he thought guiltily, *he* had humiliated her. . . . Tom stood up, nervously walking round the office. Nearby Big Ben chimed the hour, the sound lapping over the riding Thames. . . . The piece had had him scared, he had to admit it. He had been terrified that the article might lead to a full exposé in the tabloids – and then what? To the Prime Minister's ear? To his constituents? To disgrace?

His career would have folded. No more chance of a ministerial job, no more chance of his ambitions being fulfilled. He would be out on his ear, relegated to the back benches, or to a career in business. What an end – but surely Imogen wouldn't have risked that? Surely she was as ambitious as he was? If *he* was disgraced, *she* was. . . . Which was why the piece was anonymous, he realised suddenly, his hands banging against the wall in fury. Oh, it was clever, bloody clever. She had exposed him enough for him to be scared and for his inner circle to be amused, but not enough for him to be publicly disgraced.

Come to think of it, Tom realised, it was *very* like Imogen. Eve would never had had the style to think up such a ploy; she would have reacted immediately, not plotted a distant and pertinent revenge. Imogen had been cheated, not once, but twice, Tom thought. First by Giles and now him – she wasn't the type to take that kind of betrayal lying down. For a moment he almost admired her – until he thought of his career and the risk she had taken.

He could have been ruined. Instead of facing him and having it out with him in private she had run off and

319

embarrassed him in public – Tom thought of the bottle of whitener and cursed under his breath. No one had forgotten that little detail. . . . The bitch! Tom thought violently. How could she risk everything for revenge?

Another thought crept up on him – she had worked with Mazan to do this! Mazan, of all people! He must have helped her, must have encouraged her. He had always been jealous of him, Tom thought furiously, always been a sore loser. How he must have loved hearing all the details, poring over their love life in his dirty little magazine. . . . I'll kill her, Tom thought, enraged, I'll get my own back on her for this. No one makes a fool of me. No one.

Tom did not come home that night. Imogen had made dinner and then bathed Joy before putting her to bed, then she had played Scrabble with Rowan. Finally, around eleven, she hurried her son off to bed and picked up the phone, dialling the House and asking for Tom. There was no reply, so she left a message and went back into the lounge.

The night was heavy with stars as she opened the curtains and looked out. A blank, bald feeling of dread welled up in her, a sense of impending disaster. You're okay, she willed herself, you're home safe. But where was Tom? Lately he had been so attentive, always ringing. Lately he had been the perfect husband. No, she said to herself, he can't know, I'm just panicking, that's all. He's delayed somewhere, that's all.

The phone rang. Pick it up, she thought, be normal, be natural.

'Tom?'

His voice was distant, violent. 'How *could* you do it, Imogen?'

'Do what?' she asked cautiously. He's found out, someone's told him. But who? The Frenchwoman's face slid in front of her eyes. Simone had heard, and had taken her revenge. What goes round, comes round. She wanted Imogen off the scene, away from Ira, and when she found out they were still friendly and, worse, working together, she had reacted by telling Tom. She knew it would ruin Imogen's marriage – and that was exactly what she wanted.

'Don't lie to me!' he shouted. 'You wrote that piece on me, and the one on Jimmy. How could you?'

She tried to reason with him, calm him.

'Tom, come home, we'll talk.'

'*No!*' he snapped. 'If I saw you at this moment I'd bloody kill you.'

Her panic was real, terrifying: 'Tom –'

'I don't know what we're going to do,' he went on, 'I have to think. How *could* you threaten everything, Imogen?'

'*How could you?*' she shouted. 'You had the affair, not me. You slept with that woman. Did you think about me then, or about the children? You're angry. Well, so am I!' she howled, beyond reason. 'You asked for it, Tom, and you got it.'

'You betrayed me –'

'*You betrayed me first!*' she hissed. 'I was your wife, and you thought nothing of cheating on me, on risking our marriage. You're only angry now because you think your career was threatened.'

'It was!'

'It's a career, Tom. It's not flesh and blood. Not family,' she said helplessly. 'Did you really think I wouldn't retaliate?'

'We could have talked –'

'Like we're talking now?' she countered. 'You didn't *want* to talk, you just wanted to have the best of both worlds. A wife and family *and* a mistress. Well, I don't want a man who doesn't put me first. I expect to be treated with respect –'

'So do I.'

'*Then earn it!*' she bellowed. 'I didn't cheat on you –'

'What about Mazan?'

Her face paled. 'I'm not sleeping with Ira. I have *never* slept with him.'

But Tom was beyond reason. At that moment he would have preferred to think that Imogen *was* having an affair, it would have lessened his own guilt.

'You humiliated me.'

'No. You humiliated yourself.'

Tom's anger flared, her criticism and refusal to mollify him making him strike out: 'I won't be home.'

'Oh, Tom,' Imogen said coldly. 'You haven't really been home for months.'

Chapter Twenty-Nine

Penny was sitting beside Claudine's bed, her hand resting on the cover. She seemed asleep and only turned when she heard the door open and Imogen walk in.

'Hi.'

'What happened?'

'She took an overdose,' Penny said, her voice listless. 'Arnold was fooling around again. She found out and just flipped . . . they say she's going to recover, though. She was lucky, the daily found her in time. Lucky . . . well, that's what they think anyway.'

Stiffly Imogen sat down. 'But Claudine loves her children, I can't imagine her doing this. She *couldn't* have wanted to leave her kids.'

'It was the last straw,' Penny said flatly. 'Arnold provoked her once too often.' She looked over to Imogen, whose eyes were puffy, dead.

'What's the matter with you?'

'Tom and I split up.'

'Oh, God.'

'Yes . . .' Imogen said simply, turning away and watching Claudine's face, waiting for any sign of movement. There was none. She looked different, her fringe smoothed back from her forehead, her face untroubled, unaged. She was almost a pretty child again.

'Why did you split up?'

Imogen forced herself to answer. 'I wrote those pieces in S'expression –'

'You did *what*!'

'. . . and Tom found out. Someone tipped him off, and he went crazy. He said I'd betrayed him.' Her voice faltered. 'It was supposed to be a lark, Penny. A joke, a way of getting my own back without him ever finding out it was me. I thought it would bring him home, and then everything would be the same as it was before.' She drew in her breath slowly, painfully. 'Well, he did come home, but then he found out – and now he's gone again. For good.'

'No,' Penny said reassuringly. 'He'll be back.'

Imogen said nothing in response. There was nothing she could say; the thing she feared most had happened. She had lost her husband. She had been too clever, too clever by half, and now Tom had gone. The realisation bit into her, her eyes fixing on the sleeping figure in the bed.

Adultery kills, she thought suddenly. It kills people. If Claudine hadn't been found in time she would have died. Arnold's infidelity would have killed her as surely as if he had cut her throat. He has no real love for her, or for his children. He wanted gratification and was prepared to risk everything for it. His wife and his family. Imogen put her head back, her eyes following a dry crack in the ceiling. This is no joke, she thought, this is deadly.

'She'll live,' Penny said with conviction, as much to reassure herself as Imogen.

'Yes, she will. But in a while Arnold will have another affair and rub her nose in it again,' Imogen said, her voice white with anger. '*Why* do they do it?'

'I don't know,' Penny said honestly. 'Ego? A need to be the big shot?' She scratched her knee. The noise grated against the worn walls. 'Douglas cheated on me once.'

Imogen frowned. 'Why?'

'He said that he wanted to feel young again.'

'Did it work?'

'Not when I'd finished with him.'

They laughed bitterly. The room was cool, without sun. Sad.

'I want Tom back,' Imogen said quietly.

'Yes, I'd want him back too.'

'*Why* do they do it?' Imogen asked again, her voice thin, without substance.

'Because we're the wives, the ones always at home, waiting. Because they're sure of us. Because they know that

324

we'll say what you've just said – *I want him back* – whatever they do.'

'It isn't fair,' Imogen said brokenly.

'No, and d'you know something? If you try getting your own back by going out and having an affair yourself, it doesn't help.'

Imogen looked up. 'Did you do that?'

'Oh yes, I got in touch with an old flame and we had a fling,' Penny admitted. 'I even told Douglas afterwards, but he didn't believe me. Thought I was making it up.' She sighed. 'You see, my animals aren't the only things that have been stuffed.'

Imogen laughed, but her thoughts were already running on. 'There *has* to be a way of getting Tom back,' she said, her voice hard. 'I know who tipped him off, a woman called Duchamp – Simone Duchamp – and I intend to pay her back, measure for measure, for what she's done to me.'

Penny winced: 'Oh God. Be careful, don't do anything reckless.'

Imogen stared at her in amazement. 'I want revenge.'

'So did Claudine,' she said coolly. 'And she was prepared to kill herself to get her own back.'

'No man is going to kill me *or* beat me,' Imogen said emphatically. 'And no woman either.'

Ira smoothed down the front of his suit and then crossed his legs, admiring the hand-stitched loafers he was wearing. He couldn't look at Imogen, felt too inadequate, too biased to offer advice. The words which leapt to his lips were the wrong ones – dump the bastard, we could try and work something out together – but he wasn't going to say them. Imogen belonged to Tom Wrigley's world, just as Ira belonged to his. There were too many differences between them; inescapable; unbridgeable. Oh yes, Imogen might have been brought up by a remarkable woman, might have a working-class background followed by a wealthy upbringing; might be able to move between several strata of society – but she was, in the end, what her spirit dictated. And her spirit dictated a home and family – and a husband like Tom Wrigley.

Imogen wasn't mistress material. She might be broad-minded, but that wasn't the kind of life she would have picked for herself. She had been to Cannes, Rome, Florence, New York – Suzanne had taken her. To Imogen, there was nothing glamorous about such places. They were intriguing, but what else? So what *could* a man offer her? Money? She had it, and would inherit from Suzanne a great deal more. Travel? She'd done it. Culture? She'd seen it. Fun? She grew up with the kind of people who fill the Diary pages of the tabloids.

All *any* man could really offer Imogen was security and love. That was all she lacked and all she wanted. But both of her husbands had failed her. Both Giles and Tom had turned out to be incapable of giving from the heart. Ira felt dry-lipped with despair, inadequacy making him unusually silent. He didn't even look at Imogen, sitting in the seat next to his, he didn't *want* to look at her, because it hurt, because every time he saw her he knew could never have her.

'It was Simone, I know it,' she said quietly, her hand lingering around the stem of her wineglass. 'I want to see her, Ira. Where is she?'

'Are you sure it's her?'

'Positive. She heard us talking that day about the piece on Jimmy . . .' she trailed off.

'I'm behind you. You know you've got my support.'

'Yes.'

Ira frowned: 'If she *has* told Tom –'

'She has.'

'Okay,' Ira agreed. 'Well, you know that I'll never forgive her for it. Never. She's broken up your marriage because of her jealousy.'

Imogen looked helplessly at him. 'I want to get my own back on her – and I want you to help me.'

'How?'

'I want to know everything about Simone Duchamp,' Imogen continued. 'Everything.'

'She runs casinos –'

'And?'

'Call girls.'

Imogen's hand stopped fingering the stem of her glass. 'Call girls?'

326

He nodded. 'She has done for years. The casinos are a cover. Only the people who use them know – Arnold Miles, for example.'

Imogen studied Ira's face. We are worlds apart, aren't we? she thought. To you there is nothing so remarkable in this, you had an affair with this woman, loved her once. Knowing what she did, you *loved* her . . . and why not? Imogen thought, why should I expect you to live by my rules? I've cared about you for years because I was fascinated by you; intrigued by the girls and the magazine, fascinated by the world in which you moved. I never wanted to be a part of it, I just liked to watch it, to imagine it . . . so what right have I to be shocked?

'Is she at the Paris casino now?'

He nodded again. 'Listen, Imogen, let me handle it –'

'*No!*' she snapped. 'It was my marriage she ruined, not yours. She wants you, Ira, so much that she was blinded by reality. She *must* have known that you would find out it was her. She must have. How did she think you would react?' Imogen paused. 'Or maybe she never thought of it – just struck out when she could and never considered how it would alienate you.'

'It's over between Simone and me,' he said flatly. 'I can forgive most things, but treachery, no.'

Imogen breathed in deeply. 'I'm going to see her, you know.'

'Yes, I thought you might.'

'Have you got any message for her?'

He shook his head, deeply angered. 'No. Nothing that could be repeated, anyway.'

The following afternoon Imogen flew over to Paris after calling Suzanne up in Brighton. She explained only that she and Tom were having a trial separation and that she would be back the following day. Cold with fury and despair Imogen refused to confide further, and for once Suzanne did not push her.

Imogen arrived in Paris at around six in the evening, immediately going to the George V hotel and changing into her most expensive outfit. Blindly she looked at her

327

reflection in the mirror and then ordered a taxi to take her to the casino. She did not ring to warn Simone of her arrival – she wanted to keep the element of surprise – and when she walked into the plush entrance of the Longville Club she was brittle with nerves.

In French she asked for Simone, giving a false name and waiting several minutes before a male secretary finally ushered her into a suite of rooms behind the gaming area. Simone's taste was dark, the walls ebony panelled, the floor marbled, the colour of soot. As she walked, Imogen's heels clicked on the smooth surface, her figure reflected eerily under her feet. Simone was sitting at a Louis XIV desk, her sleek dark head bent over a ledger. Hearing the approaching footsteps she looked up, then winced.

'So . . .' she said evenly, her composure awesome. 'Mrs Wrigley.'

'Get up,' Imogen said simply.

'Why?'

'Because I want to talk to you,' she replied, walking over to the desk and standing by the side of it. The room was heavy with lamps, the deeply fringed shades casting a suffocating gloom over the gilded furniture.

Indolently, Simone rose to face her.

'Well?'

'You're smaller than I remembered you,' Imogen said disparagingly, turning away and then immediately turning back. Her hand rose quickly, and with all her force she struck the Frenchwoman straight across the face. Simone rocked, took in her breath, then sat down heavily.

'What was that for?'

'For ruining my marriage,' Imogen said icily. 'You're lucky I don't kill you.'

The blow reddened the Frenchwoman's face but she had too much pride to show any pain.

'I'm going to pay you back,' Imogen said, her voice deadly. 'I'm going to ruin you and your business, and your call girls –'

Simone refused to react.

'. . . and I'm going to make sure that Ira never sees you again. Never speaks to you, or makes love to you, or even *thinks* of you. I'm going to make you *suffer*, and I'm going to enjoy every minute of it.'

Simone flinched. The threat about her business had had little effect, but the realisation that Imogen could – and would – keep Ira away from her made her panic, her defences toppling.

'I didn't mean to do it –'

'Oh yes, you did! You meant to hurt me all you could,' Imogen contradicted her, 'and now I'm going to return the compliment. You've wanted Ira for years, longed for him, dreamed that you'd get him in the end.' She paused, her face a chalk relief. 'Well, you won't. He despises you now. Loathes you, and I will make sure that he continues to hate you.'

'You can't!' Simone said anxiously.

'Oh, but we both know that I *can*, don't we?' Imogen countered. 'You were right to be afraid of me, very wise. You thought I had some influence with Ira, and you were absolutely right. He'll never see you again. You are, to all intents and purposes, dead to him.'

Simone's eyes were brilliant with anxiety, hysteria creeping into her voice.

'You can't do that!'

'I *can*,' Imogen replied evenly, 'and I *will*. Tit for tat. You ruined my life and now I intend to destroy yours.'

The Frenchwoman was breathing quickly, her face flushed with anger and fear. She had gone too far; she knew it almost as soon as she had written the letter to Tom Wrigley, but she had wanted to hurt her rival, to injure her. Ira loved Imogen; after everything Simone said or did, his first thought was always for Imogen. She had hated her for that, loathed her, plotted against her and then struck when the time was right. But Simone had not given the matter enough thought, and the triumph was fleeting. She might have damaged her adversary, but in doing so, she had destroyed herself.

'I love him . . .' Simone said dully.

'I love Tom,' Imogen replied, 'and it hurts when you lose them.' She leaned over the desk, her expression intimidating. 'It gets worse, too. After a while you can't *stop* thinking about them, longing for them, but it's no good, they're gone. You've lost them. The way you're feeling now is nothing to the way you'll feel tomorrow or the day after. All this wealth –' Imogen gestured round the room dismissively – 'will mean nothing. All your businesses and all your power will be *less* than nothing. You'll go to sleep thinking of the man you lost and you'll wake up knowing that there will never – *never* – be anyone to replace him.' Her voice was hoarse. 'Ira despises you now and I'll make sure he keeps despising you until the day he dies.'

Slowly Simone rose to her feet and walked to the window, drawing the shutters with shaking hands. The room was tomb-like, closed off, dark with dread.

'Please don't do this,' she said finally, turning back to Imogen. 'I'll talk to your husband – say that what I wrote was a lie.'

Imogen shrugged. 'Tom won't believe you, it's too late now.'

'But there must be something . . .' Simone insisted. 'There must be something I can do to make it right again.'

'No,' Imogen replied coldly. 'Nothing.'

Frantically Simone paced the floor, her long skirt sliding over the cold marble, her shadow huge against the far wall.

'Why did you come?' she said suddenly, her thoughts clearing. 'You're a clever woman, Mrs Wrigley, you didn't come all the way to Paris just to gloat. There's another reason, isn't there?' Imogen said nothing, but Simone knew she was on to something and pursued her line of thought relentlessly. 'You wrote that first article to get your husband back, and it worked. It was clever. *You* are clever.' The Frenchwoman stopped pacing, stared at the impassive blonde woman who faced her. 'You came here to threaten me, to tell me that you knew about the agencies, but why? *Why* did you do that? . . . If you'd simply wanted to get revenge you could have informed on me long distance.' Her voice rose with certainty. 'You came for another purpose. What?'

Calmly Imogen leaned back against the desk, her ankles crossed, her voice firm.

'I know a way for you to get Ira back.'

'How?' Simone asked breathlessly.

'He loves his daughter – adores her, in fact.'

'Tusha?'

Imogen nodded. 'Yes, Tusha. Ira thought she was running wild in London so he sent her back to her mother –'

'Go on.'

'– unfortunately her mother had even less control over Tusha than he did. She's joined a religious group –' Imogen laughed ironically – 'in Los Angeles; given them all her money and her possessions and gone to live there.'

Simone was sharply curious: 'How do you know?'

'I know most things, Madame Duchamp,' Imogen said coldly. 'I just wait until the time is right to *use* what I know,' she continued coolly. 'Ira is a Jew, a strict Jew, he would be *enraged* to know what his daughter has done. He would do anything to get Tusha away from a place like that – and he would be very grateful to anyone who would help him to get his daughter back.'

The Frenchwoman's eyes widened, understanding coming quickly.

'Go on.'

'I could see to it that you were the person who managed to get his daughter back.'

'Why?' Simone asked warily. 'Why would you do that for me?'

'Because I want your help,' Imogen answered impassively. 'I need your contacts and your assistance. I want my husband back, and I want to make sure that this time he stays.' Her face was rigid, unreadable. 'You were right, I *did* write those articles. I wrote them for a joke at first, a way of poking fun from a distance. But circumstances have made me realise just how serious it really is.' She paused, thinking of Tom, of Claudine's suicide attempt, and of the men she knew. Slowly, Imogen smiled, the old light of mischief flickering in her eyes. 'I'm tired of being used; of being cheated on. I don't like it – no woman does. The difference is that most women take it – whereas *I'm* prepared to do something about it.'

Simone was listening carefully, her mind running on. She wanted Ira above everything and was quite prepared to

331

consider anything the Englishwoman had to say. She also found herself unexpectedly impressed by Imogen – and slightly fearful. This was no ordinary woman; this woman played rough.

'What do you want me to do?'

Breathing in deeply, Imogen picked up her bag, her hand gripping the dark leather.

'My patience, Madame Duchamp, has run out. I have two children and one broken marriage behind me. I do *not* intend to make it a second.' She walked towards the door, then turned. 'I feel for you. I despise what you've done, but I *do* feel for you. We all love our men, we all care too much. Women make a habit of it. Look at you: for all your power and money, you're crippled at the thought of losing Ira. Well, I've decided that I'm going to give the men a run for their money, and if you're sensible, you'll help me. I intend to even the score a little, level the ground a bit. I want Tom back, you want Ira back. . . .' Imogen thought of the women in London, and of their men. 'We all want what is rightfully ours, and I think I know a way that we can all get it.'

'I'll help you,' Simone agreed hurriedly. 'What do you want from me?'

'I'll let you know when I'm ready,' Imogen said coldly, 'but if you back out, if you try to go back on your word, God help you. If you think you're suffering now, you've no idea of how much you'll suffer if you ever cross me again.'

Chapter Thirty

Meticulously Imogen laid the table in the Kensington flat, then stood back to gauge the effect. The meal was to be special, a way of celebrating Claudine's recovery. She was out of hospital and back home with her children after several weeks of counselling and many visits from her friends. She came back to life gradually, her embarrassment increasing as she realised the full enormity of what she had done. Why? she asked, I have children, I must have been mad. It was Arnold fooling around like that. It was the last straw. . . . Imogen had listened and sympathised, although she and Tom were still estranged and rumour had it that he was seeing Eve Miller again. She heard the rumours and she waited, marking time.

The meal smelt superb, the wine was chilled, the table set for six. It was a Saturday and Suzanne was looking after Rowan and Joy down in Brighton so the place was peaceful, quiet; the women would not be interrupted, or over-heard. . . . Imogen had given the plan much thought over the previous few weeks. She had considered her marriage and decided that although Tom was unfaithful he was still the man she wanted. Their love for each other was recoverable; it was only his roaming which needed curtailing. It could be done, Imogen told herself, it *must* be done. After all, it was bad for his career, and it was damaging for the children.

She had brought Rowan up singlehandedly, but there was no way she was going to do the same for Joy. Her daughter needed a father, and she needed her *real* father. Instinct told Imogen that Tom wanted to return. He had been angry, bitterly so, but his temper always gave way to remorse, and when Imogen refused to take his calls Tom found himself bewildered, unexpectedly excluded from the family he had so recklessly endangered. He wanted to come back, but she would not relent. So instead he turned to Eve Miller – and Imogen, keeping her nerve, waited.

With impressive composure she went over the plan in her head. She would have liked to tell Ira, but even he would have been shocked. And Suzanne would have talked her out of it. No, Imogen thought, this one she did alone. It was a risk, but if it worked it would bring Tom home. And it would bring the other men into line as well. . . . She smiled to herself, suddenly excited, the thrill tingling against her skin.

Penny was the first to arrive. She glanced at the table appreciatively: 'Oh, wonderful. This *is* a good idea.'

She turned, Danielle walking in hurriedly and throwing her briefcase on to a side table. 'Bloody women!' she snorted. 'Why can't they make up their minds about what colour paint they want?' She lit a cigarette and then sniffed the air. 'Umm, chicken . . . Trevor's favourite.'

Maxie and Claudine arrived soon after, Sarah coming in last, her deep voice strident.

'Well, you look okay now, Claudine,' she said loudly. 'Suicide obviously agrees with you.'

Ignoring her, Imogen began to serve the meal. They chatted as they always had; six women in an expensive flat, eating good food and discussing their work and their children, and finally their men.

'. . . Harry's gone off to vote,' Maxie said, sucking the end of her spoon.

'They're all voting tonight,' Penny replied, running her hands through her short hair and then checking her reflection in the mirror opposite. 'Douglas said that it's very important. You know, one of those "vital votes".'

'I suppose that means Arnold will be late home,' Claudine said timidly.

'Well,' Sarah replied snidely, 'he'll be late home, vote or no vote.'

'Dry up!' Danielle snapped, grinding out her cigarette. 'You're so bloody tactless,' she said hotly, then glanced over to Claudine. 'You don't know how lucky you are. I only wish Trevor had a *reason* to come home late. He just makes up stupid excuses about legal dinners.'

There was a lull at the table, Imogen breathing in deeply and then leaning forwards.

'Tom's seeing Eve Miller again.'

Penny's luminous eyes widened: 'Oh no!'

'They can't stop, can they?' Danielle offered, wiping some cream from the side of her mouth. Her hair was newly done, the set stiff with mousse. She had made an effort, but looked uncomfortable rather than glamorous. 'I'll swear that Trevor's having an affair.'

'Harry cheated on me once,' Maxie said suddenly, her face a study of disbelief. 'I mean, just because he's an MP he thinks he can screw around.' The other women studied her: the immaculate profile, the lush V of her cleavage. 'I bet he sleeps with other women when he goes on those trips abroad.'

'So,' Imogen said evenly. 'Arnold's repeatedly cheated on Claudine; Jimmy's cheated on Sarah; Harry was unfaithful to Maxie and apparently now Trevor is starting to roam. Tom we all know about,' she said flatly, turning to Penny. 'You seem to be the only woman who got a faithful man.'

She hesitated. 'Well. . . .'

'Go on!' Sarah hissed, her broad face animated.

'Douglas doesn't sleep around. He *talks* around.'

Five pairs of eyes fixed on her.

'What?' Imogen asked finally.

'He told me once – confessed – that he once paid a woman to listen to him.' She paused, her dark eyes wide with irritation. 'Well, don't all look so bloody astonished, I was *furious* – I mean, he never gave me so much as 50p for listening to him whinge all night.'

They all laughed, Danielle lighting up another cigarette. Her hands were functional, the nails unvarnished, although her figure was tight from frequent workouts.

'Trevor will never marry me, will he?' she said.

Imogen touched her hand. 'So what made you say that?'

'Well, if he'd wanted to, he would have done so already. . . . I just keep hanging around and waiting.' Her breathing accelerated, as it always did when she was nervous. 'He doesn't seem to want me enough to marry me, but he wants me around.'

'Harry's like that,' Maxie offered. 'As long as I'm massaging his back, he's fine, but there's only so much I can take. Besides,' she said sulkily, 'baby oil softens the nails, I broke two last week.'

Sarah's expression was indescribable. 'Don't we realise, they've all cheated on us –'

'Exactly!' Imogen said. 'That is my point.'

They looked at her curiously.

'What makes a man stay home? Apart from comfort and love. I mean, what makes a man stay home permanently?'

'Shackles?' Penny offered.

Imogen raised her eyes heavenwards. 'Fear.'

The word slipped over them all.

'Fear,' she repeated. 'They are all important men. Tom, Harry, Douglas and Arnold are MPs, Trevor is the Tory Party's lawyer, and Jimmy is their PR man –'

'We know all this,' Sarah said abruptly.

Danielle's expression was hostile, 'Let her finish!'

'. . . as I said, our men are all high profile, important. They would have a lot to lose if they were caught in an embarrassing situation. They would lose face, but worse, their careers.'

'So?' Sarah asked, yawning. 'I mean, the meal was good, Imogen, but you're getting boring now.'

'No, she isn't!' Danielle replied. 'I want to hear what Imogen has to say.'

'Me too,' Claudine said softly, her support surprising everyone at the table.

'If our men were exposed in a scandal, discovered sleeping with prostitutes, for example –'

'*I would kill Jimmy!*' Sarah hollered.

'Shut up!' Danielle warned her. 'Let Imogen finish.'

'. . . they would be terrified, thinking their careers and reputations were finished. But just suppose. . . .' She paused, knowing that they were all listening now. 'Just suppose that they had been duped. That they had been set up. *They* would think it was real and be terrified of being discovered, but we would know it was just a scam. The result would be that they would be so scared of fooling around that it would teach them a lesson they'd never forget. They'd come back home as quiet as lambs.'

'Who's the "we"?' Penny asked sarcastically, staring at Imogen.

'Ahhh.'

'Well, go on, Imogen!' Penny insisted. 'You can't stop now.'

'I just want to know one thing before I continue,' she said. 'Do you all want your men? I mean, do you *really* want to keep them?'

The five women nodded.

'So you wouldn't mind taking part in a plan which might be . . . unusual . . . but which would mean that you'd *keep* your men for ever?'

Penny was watching Imogen carefully. 'What kind of plan?'

Imogen took in a deep breath to steady herself. 'I know a woman called Simone Duchamp. She has casinos, and she runs a call-girl agency. I also know that Arnold –' Imogen glanced over at Claudine. 'Sorry, but I have to explain. . . .'

'So explain,' she said softly.

'. . . Arnold has used some of the girls in the past. And I think Harry has too, and Tom.' Imogen ran her tongue over her dry lips. 'You have to realise that Simone's girls are very upmarket, not even recognisable as call girls. They look and sound like well-educated women, and they are employed to act as escorts – in and out of bed.'

'Go on,' Penny urged.

'All our men are going on that trip to Paris next month. I know for a fact that there is going to be a dinner party at the George V, and that Arnold is thinking of getting one of Simone's girls to amuse him afterwards.'

'What!' Sarah said hoarsely. 'The son of a bitch!'

'Sarah, calm down,' Imogen said firmly, turning to Claudine. 'I wouldn't have told you this unless it was necessary. Do you trust me?'

She nodded, pale with misery.

'Okay, well, I've talked to Simone and I got her to suggest

to Arnold that it would be a nice idea if he organised a girl for each of them –'

Danielle leapt to her feet, tipping over her ashtray. 'Jesus, are you mad! I don't want Trevor sleeping with some whore. He could *catch* something, for God's sake –'

'Not from us.'

Penny turned her head, stared at Imogen. 'From *us*?'

'Yes,' Imogen said calmly. 'We're going to stand in for the call girls.'

'Jesus . . .' Penny said.

'Never!' Danielle snapped.

'Oh . . . what a hoot,' Maxie said, smiling glossily.

Claudine paled, her head low. 'I couldn't, Imogen.'

'You're bloody crazy! A disgrace to feminism!' Sarah said forcefully. 'That any woman in this day and age could even think –'

Imogen held up her hands for silence.

'I know it sounds incredible, but just listen to me –'

'I don't want to listen!' Danielle said hysterically, still standing. 'You must be mad!'

Penny leaned back in her seat, her eyes dark. 'Just let me see if I understand what you're saying, Imogen. You want the six of us to go to Paris, pose as call girls and sleep with our partners –'

'Not *our* partners,' Imogen replied. 'Each other's.'

Danielle sat down heavily and reached for the bottle of wine.

'*Each other's?*' Penny echoed. 'Why would we do that?'

'All right, here's the plan,' Imogen said calmly. 'Arnold will, with Simone's help, arrange for each man to have a girl in Paris. Simone will arrange for those girls to go to the George V and visit each man's room. The men won't see *who* goes to *whose* room. So,' Imogen paused, knowing that each woman was listening, 'when we turn up they will be incredulous –'

'They won't be the only ones,' Penny said drily.

'Hear me out, please. Say I go to Douglas's room. At first he'll be taken aback. He'll think I'm working on the side, secretly. He'll get a kick out of the situation and if I tell him to keep the matter quiet – because I don't want anyone to find out – he will keep it quiet. After all, it wouldn't be in

Douglas's interest to tell anyone. But Douglas won't realise that the six of us have banded together in this.' Imogen took in her breath, keeping her voice steady. 'While I'm with him, Maxie will be with someone else, Danielle with someone else. . . . Think of it, the men won't be able to resist, and they'll be tickled pink to think that they're sleeping with someone else's woman.'

Penny's eyes narrowed. 'Even if anyone considered your bloody crazy idea seriously, what the hell is the point? We sleep with them – so what?'

Imogen looked at her steadily. 'The point is that we all want our husbands back.'

Penny pushed her: 'But how do we do that by sleeping with someone else?'

'Oh God,' Danielle said simply, refilling her glass again.

Imogen continued evenly. 'After we've slept with them, we'll all make notes about what they did. Their sexual inclinations, preferences. . . .' Imogen paused again, 'Then each of you will give me your notes – and I'll do the rest.'

Penny's voice was steely: 'What's "the rest?" '

'I want that to be a surprise,' Imogen answered calmly. 'You have to trust me.'

'Trust you!' Sarah retorted, her mouth hard above her heavy chin. 'If Jimmy found out that I had slept with someone else –'

'He won't!' Imogen said firmly. 'And he won't be able to tell anyone what *he's* done either. How could he? Who could he tell? He won't want his indiscretion airing, and as sure as hell, he won't want it to come out that he's slept with one of his wife's friends. Can't you see the headline – Tory PR Man Sleeps with MP's Wife in Paris.'

Sarah lapsed into silence; Claudine slowly lifted her head and said, 'Imogen, I *do* trust you, but I couldn't do it to Arnold.'

' "*Do it to bloody Arnold*"!' Sarah repeated disbelievingly. 'He's been doing it to you for years. You ought to jump at the chance to pay that bugger back.'

Imogen studied her carefully. She had been worried about Sarah, knowing her feminist views. If she could get this woman on her side, the rest would be easy.

'Arnold *needs* a taste of his own medicine,' Sarah went on, hotly angry, 'and come to think of it, it wouldn't do Jimmy much harm either. I'm sick of him thinking he can do what he likes.' Her mind was shifting, she was sliding towards agreement, and Imogen knew it.

'Will you do it?'

Sarah's face was hard, her hands resting flatly on the top of the table. 'Okay. Yes, yes, I'll do it.'

Danielle looked at her incredulously. 'You can't!' she screeched, her voice unnaturally high. 'It's a hideous idea. I feel dirty even thinking about it – besides, what would they think of us? We'd be no more than sluts to them.'

Imogen sighed. 'I've told you, *they won't know*. It will work out perfectly if you leave it to me. After the deed is done,' Imogen said, smiling, 'I'll make sure that each man is so scared that he'll return to his proper partner faster than the speed of light – and he'll *stay* with her too.' She watched Danielle drain her glass. Her make-up was slightly shiny now that she was warm, and her hair was not as perfectly coiffed. She looked softer, prettier. 'Listen, Danielle,' Imogen continued, 'you want Trevor to marry you, don't you?'

She nodded, her eyes wary.

'Well, I can't promise that he'll do that, but after this little episode, when he sees what's in store for him, he *might*. Isn't that enough reason to go through with it?'

She hesitated, Maxie chiming in enthusiastically, 'Oh, go on, Danielle, it can't hurt. Besides,' she said slyly, 'I'm more than a little curious, aren't you?'

'I'm for it,' Claudine said quickly.

In unison they turned to look at her in surprise. She was sitting perfectly still, her eyes shadowed by her fringe, her hands dug deep into the pockets of her voile dress. Smaller than the others, and dressed in a Laura Ashley print, she seemed the most innocent and youngest of them all. The one least likely to agree . . . or so they had thought.

'Well done!' Maxie said, hugging Claudine quickly. 'You're a revelation.'

A slow tapping started, then increased at the end of the table. Each woman's head turned to the sound: Penny was banging her fork in a rhythmic beating until she had everyone's attention. Then she stopped and leaned forwards, the short dark hair glossy under the overhead light.

'So Maxie, Claudine and Sarah are in agreement with you, Imogen,' she said. 'Only Danielle and I are against you.'

'Well . . . actually I think we should do it,' Danielle said, closing her eyes and leaning her head back. The wine was making her dizzy, reckless, all she could clearly think about was what Imogen had said – Trevor might marry her. If she did this, it might force his hand. She was tired of waiting; she might be waiting for ever unless she took a gamble. What was there to lose, really? Hardly her virginity – only her self-respect, and what was *that* worth in the end? She could turn out to be a proud, but lonely, old maid. No, Imogen's plan was worth a try. It *had* to be.

'Are you sure?' Penny asked her.

Danielle nodded.

'So it's only you, Penny, who's against it,' Maxie said blithely. 'What's the problem?'

'I don't fancy any of them,' she replied bluntly.

'Oh, is *that* all!' Maxie replied, laughing darkly. 'Well it's only for one night. I mean, we don't have to keep them.'

Imogen smiled, then leaned towards the group. 'All we have to decide now is who sleeps with who.' She looked around. 'Has anyone any preferences?'

'I'd like Tom,' Danielle said quickly. Too quickly.

All six women laughed, Imogen regarding her steadily. 'Why not? You've always wanted him.'

Danielle kept her head down, flushed from the wine and from embarrassment.

'Well . . . he's . . . oh, you know,' she said, folding her arms defensively over her chest.

Imogen looked down at the list of men, the bloated, arrogant Arnold heading the names.

'What about Arnold?'

There was a chorus round the table. 'Not Arnold!'

Claudine looked mortified. 'He's very good in bed, actually,' she said, her tone shy. 'Very inventive. . . .'

'He's had plenty of practice,' Sarah said drily.

341

'. . . he can be a bit rough, though.'

Sarah's face lit up. 'Rough, hey?' she said, with an ominous tone in her voice. 'Well, perhaps he needs someone who can stand up for themselves.'

'So you'll take Arnold?' Imogen asked, watching Sarah nod before glancing at the other women. 'Who wants Jimmy?'

Sarah's voice was acid: 'I warn you, you'll need the best Janet Reger camiknickers to kick-start him.'

'Oh God,' Penny moaned. 'I can't wear those things.'

'You don't have to – he wears them.'

Claudine's head jerked up. Maxie laughed softly. 'Well, I suppose it *would* be a laugh.'

Imogen raised her eyebrows. 'So you'll take Jimmy?'

Maxie shrugged. 'Why not?'

Hurriedly Imogen wrote Maxie's name against Jimmy's, then she looked up again. 'Who wants Harry?'

'What's he like?' Penny asked Maxie suspiciously.

'Heavily into baby oil,' she replied, laughing again. 'Oh, Harry's very sweet really, but very sensitive.' She studied Penny for a long moment. 'He's also very touchy about his height – so wear flat shoes.'

'In bed?' Penny countered wryly.

'Oh, you'll be okay. . . .' Maxie went on cheerfully. 'Just let him read you his speeches and nod at the right moments and you'll be fine.'

'So I buy a quart of baby oil, wear flat shoes and have my ear bent all night?' Penny said drily. 'Will we have time for sex?'

Imogen watched her. 'Are you on?'

Penny nodded, her eyes dark. 'I can't believe I'm doing this. But yes. Okay, put me down for Harry.'

'That leaves Trevor and Douglas,' Imogen said thoughtfully. 'And that leaves you and me, Claudine.'

Claudine glanced nervously at Danielle. 'What's Trevor like?'

'Fine, if you don't touch his hair,' she replied, swirling her remaining wine round her glass. 'He can't *stand* anyone touching his hair.' She paused. 'Also he's not very . . . you know . . . very. . . .'

342

They all leaned forwards.

'. . . *interested*,' Danielle finished, then rushed on. 'He's always worried about his work, or some court case or other, and sometimes he can't –'

'Perform?' Maxie offered.

Claudine smiled with relief. 'I'll take Trevor,' she said happily. 'He sounds fine for me.'

Cautiously Penny turned to Imogen, looking at her handsome profile and the fall of blonde hair to her shoulders. There was only Douglas left. *Her* Douglas. And now she was about to agree that Imogen should sleep with her husband. Good-looking, funny Imogen, exciting Imogen – what if he fell in love with her? Penny flinched mentally. Douglas Fairbane, MP for Essex East, her husband of ten years. Douglas, of the lugubrious face and the lank red hair, Douglas, who wrote his speeches in the basement on the table next to her. Douglas, the man she knew had been intermittently unfaithful and yet the man she adored. Douglas, the husband she wanted to keep – whatever the cost.

'You get Douglas then.'

Imogen held her gaze. 'Do you mind?'

'Yes,' Penny said truthfully, 'but on the other hand, I'd rather it was you than anyone else.' She glanced round the table. 'No offence, ladies, but Imogen's a good friend and I trust her.' She looked back at Imogen; her eyes were honest. 'He likes to talk –'

'I heard.'

Penny nodded. 'If he tells you things . . . personal things . . .' she swallowed. '. . . then I'd like to know afterwards. I mean, in a way I don't mind you sleeping with him, but I do mind it if he *talks* to you. That's friendship, isn't it? That's real communication. People who talk often grow to love each other.' She glanced away suddenly, her voice shaky. 'He doesn't talk to me, Imogen. Not enough. It's something I've been trying to change, trying to draw him out, trying to understand what he thinks and what he feels. . . .' Her oblique eyes were dark with warning. 'You can have him physically, Imogen, but don't take him mentally, please. Leave me that . . . please.'

Chapter Thirty-One

'Have you got it all organised?' Imogen asked Simone Duchamp over the phone that night.

'Everything's fixed.'

'It has to run smoothly,' Imogen insisted, her tone cold. 'This plan has to run like clockwork.'

'I've arranged it with Arnold,' Simone said evenly, fully aware that her hopes for the future rested with this Englishwoman, and fully aware that if she failed, she would lose Ira. 'Each man will go to his hotel room after the dinner and then the women will go to them. They are all on different floors, so the likelihood of any of them bumping into each other is remote –'

'It might have been better if they'd been booked into separate hotels.'

'I mentioned that to Arnold,' Simone explained. 'But he wouldn't alter the arrangements. The meeting had been planned for a long time, it would have looked suspicious if I'd pursued the matter.'

'Yes, you're right,' Imogen said thoughtfully. 'And you're sure that he suspects nothing?'

'Nothing,' the Frenchwoman replied firmly. 'Arnold Miles expects a call girl to visit him, and he expects the same for the other five men.'

'Good,' Imogen said, waiting for Simone to speak again, to ask the vital question. She wasn't disappointed.

'What about Ira?'

'*What* about him?'

Her voice had a catch to it. 'You said you would help me.'

'And I will,' Imogen said calmly. 'I told you about Tusha, well, you have to get her back to her father. He knows she's with that sect in Los Angeles – apparently his ex-wife told him yesterday, so he's running around frantically thinking of a way to get Tusha out of there.'

'Go on,' Simone said urgently.

'Logic won't work with Tusha, she's headstrong and manipulative, she doesn't give a damn how much she hurts anyone – and that includes her father. In order to get her out you have to bribe her out.'

'What?'

'Pay her to leave,' Imogen said coolly. 'Money is the only thing Tusha understands. If you go to her and offer her enough, she'll leave Los Angeles. And if you tell her that you'll give her a further payment when she returns home to her father, she'll do exactly what you say. Then the rest is easy. In order to keep Tusha home you have to keep her in funds, but on one condition – that she sings your praises to Ira, and convinces him that you are the right woman for him. Tusha has to tell him a story – that you came to Los Angeles and convinced her that she was being stupid and that she was hurting her father. Tusha isn't stupid, she'll go along with it.'

Imogen paused, her voice metallic, sharp with warning. 'I'm doing this because I believe that you really love Ira. I don't like you, Madame Duchamp, I don't like your greasy little businesses either, but that's your concern. The only thing that interests me is Ira. I love him. I always have,' Imogen said openly, honestly. 'He's been a constant in my life and he's been trustworthy and genuine – there are very few people I can say that about. He comes across as a real smooth operator, but he's a good man, and good men have feelings.' Her tone was black. 'You hurt him – a month from now, a year from now, ten years from now – if you *ever* hurt that man, I will personally destroy you. I will make it my duty, I swear it.'

'I won't hurt him,' Simone said hurriedly. 'I love him.'

'Then keep loving him,' Imogen replied, 'and remember you can't fool me or lie to me – Ira tells me everything.'

'Not again!' Suzanne said over the phone. 'My bloody weekends aren't my own, what with your kids over here every ten minutes.'

'So what went wrong?' Imogen countered drily. 'A bad haircut or a cancelled dinner?'

Suzanne sighed dramatically. 'If you must know, I went blonde –'

'Oh God. . . .'

'Exactly,' Suzanne continued. 'I can't think why I did it, it just seemed like a good idea at the time. . . . Anyway, I can't go out until the hairdresser comes round to fix it, and he can't get here until tomorrow. So I'm walking about incognito like Lawrence of bloody Arabia.'

Imogen laughed loudly. 'The kids won't mind, Suzanne. You know how tactful Rowan can be . . . oh, come on, say you'll take them for a weekend. It's important.'

'Why?' Suzanne countered, sitting in front of her dressing-table mirror and rubbing cream into her neck. 'What are you up to?'

'I'm off to Paris –'

'Paris!' she exploded. 'With whom?'

'Tom,' Imogen said, wincing. Well, it wasn't really a lie, Tom *was* going to be there.

'Oh, that's great, darling,' Suzanne said. 'A romantic weekend.'

'You could say that.'

'Wine and candlelight, the Eiffel Tower and sex. You might discover a whole new side of him.'

Imogen's breathing was accelerating rapidly.

'. . . you two should get back together again. You were perfectly matched – I mean, look at all those mismatched couples. God makes them, and the Devil pairs them.'

She can't know, Imogen thought, she *can't*.

'Besides, what's a bit of infidelity, really? A marriage should be strong enough to withstand the odd fling.'

'Suzanne,' Imogen said hurriedly, 'I have to go. I've got a million things to get ready.'

'Oh, fine, darling. Don't worry, I'll have the kids,' Suzanne said cheerfully. 'You just get over to Paris and save that marriage of yours.'

'I intend to.'

'Yes,' Suzanne said, a wily note creeping into her voice. 'I also know that you are up to some of your old tricks –'

'Suzanne, what *are* you talking about?'

'About you, darling,' she replied, vastly amused. 'You can't con me. I don't know what you're up to, but I know you're up to something. Well, whatever it is, good luck.'

Imogen was all injured innocence: 'I don't know what you're talking about.'

'No, sweetheart, of course you don't,' Suzanne replied smoothly. 'But remember – I know you.'

Claudine was sick on the plane. She sat next to Maxie, who was reading a copy of *Vogue*, and suddenly threw up into the paper bag provided. Wincing, Maxie guided her to the toilet, standing guard outside the door as several men stared hungrily at her.

'Are you okay?' she asked when Claudine finally re-emerged.

'I don't think I can go through with this,' she said brokenly.

Maxie helped her back to her seat and ordered some mineral water. 'Of course you can. You've only got Trevor. Think of Sarah with Arnold.'

Claudine made a strangled cry into her handkerchief.

'Oh, sorry,' Maxie said, glancing round the plane. 'Sorry. . . . I haven't seen any of the others, have you?'

'Imogen said that she and Penny were going on an earlier plane and that Sarah and Danielle were following us.'

Maxie sighed, stretched out her legs into the aisle and smiled at a man sitting opposite. 'It's quite a lark though, isn't it?'

'No,' Claudine said plaintively. 'It's horrible.'

'I packed my most spectacular underwear,' Maxie went on, crossing her long limbs and feeling the man's eyes on her skin. 'Something *really* unnerving.'

'I never thought about that,' Claudine wailed. 'I just brought my M & S stuff.'

Maxie leaned her head back against the seat. 'Do you think it will work?' she asked. 'I mean, what exactly is Imogen going to do afterwards? She seemed so confident that the plan would work. . . .' Maxie sighed, 'I only hope it does. I mean, Harry's short, but he's sweet. I don't want to lose him.'

There was a quick retching noise next to her. Raising her eyebrows, Maxie led Claudine back to the loo.

In her suite at the George V, Imogen was pacing the floor. It was six o'clock in the evening and all the women had arrived and gone to their different rooms, only Penny remaining with her. They had avoided each other on arrival, careful not to attract notice, and one by one had phoned Imogen to report in. Carefully she ticked their names off the list and then slid the notepad back into her briefcase, glancing over to Penny.

'Not long to go now.'

Penny leaned forwards, her elbows resting on her knees. 'Harry, of all people!' she said. 'If Douglas ever finds out about –'

'He won't. Stop it,' Imogen said firmly, her nerves close to the surface.

'Do you think they'll all go through with it?'

Imogen nodded. 'They've come this far, they won't turn back.'

'Maxie said that Claudine was sick on the plane. Twice.'

'She'll be okay,' Imogen replied emphatically. 'We only have another five hours to go.'

'Five hours,' Penny repeated, running her fingers through her hair. 'I'm going for a bath.'

'That'll take five hours?'

'It will if I have it in London,' Penny countered drily.

'Listen,' Imogen said quietly, sitting in a chair next to Penny. 'I know it's difficult, but desperate times require desperate measures.'

'And they don't get more desperate than this.'

'Are you okay?' Imogen asked softly.

She shrugged her shoulders. 'Not bad, it's just the waiting that gets to you.' Idly Penny glanced over at the bed. 'What are you wearing?'

'Armani.'

'For Douglas?' Penny asked, aghast. 'He wouldn't know Armani from C & A.'

'Do you want me to wear something else?'

'You brought a *change*?' Penny asked incredulously. 'Jesus, you are thorough.'

Gently, Imogen stretched out her hand and took Penny's. 'Listen, it'll be difficult, but it'll be worth it. You want Douglas, I want Tom. All the others want their men back; this is the only way of making sure we keep them.'

Penny's fabulous eyes turned on Imogen.

'You're sure this will work?'

'Yes,' she said firmly, 'it *will* work.'

'If you even *think* of keeping him –'

Maxie was all docile amazement: 'Who would want to *keep* Jimmy?' she asked, looking down at Sarah as she walked into her room.

'He's *my* husband, you just remember that.' Sarah's glance suddenly fell on the underwear on the bed. 'Eekkkkk!'

Hurriedly Maxie picked up the lingerie. 'It was just an idea. . . .'

'Listen, bitch,' Sarah said fiercely. 'I would like Jimmy to *live* through this night. He isn't used to too much sexual excitement. I don't want to have to come in here in the morning and scrape what's left of him off the walls. . . . Do I make myself clear?'

Idly, Maxie tucked the underwear back into her case. 'It was just a thought. . . .'

'Well, think again!' Sarah snapped, walking out and banging the door behind her.

'Just try to eat some scrambled eggs,' Imogen said gently, leaning over Claudine and wiping her forehead. 'Your tummy's empty.'

'I couldn't . . .' she stammered pitifully. 'This is wrong, Imogen. All wrong.'

'You told me you wanted Arnold –'

'I do!'

'Then you have to go through with it,' Imogen said, sinking to her knees next to Claudine's chair. 'No, you don't . . . not if you don't want to.'

'I *don't*?' Claudine said, suddenly brightening. 'You mean that?'

Imogen nodded. 'I'm not going to force you to do anything against your will. I couldn't do that, Claudine.'

'Even if it *was* your husband who organised the whole idea of the call girls,' Penny chipped in, leaning against the bed with her arms folded. 'I mean, Arnold's not such a bad man. He sleeps around, he has whores, he doesn't give a stuff about his wife or kids. Let's face it, Claudine, you've got a beauty there. And you know you have, after all, what happy woman *doesn't* try to commit suicide?'

'Penny!'

Claudine laid her hand on Imogen's shoulder. 'No, don't shout at Penny, she's right. Arnold *is* a pig – he made me so miserable that I wanted to die.' Her voice wavered. 'I have three kids, three lovely children, and yet he made me feel so bad that I'd have left *them* . . . it seems incredible now, but he caused me so much pain, I just wanted it to stop. . . .' She smiled apologetically. 'He's not worth much, but he's my husband and I want to stay married. I couldn't cope alone . . . not with the kids . . . I just couldn't.'

'So you'll go through with it?' Penny asked her.

Claudine nodded. 'Yes.'

'Well, look at it this way,' Penny said cheerfully. 'Trevor's libido is somewhat limited, and with any luck after dinner he'll be so smashed he won't be up to anything.'

Claudine nodded half-heartedly then turned to Imogen. 'How long do we have to stay?'

'As long as it takes,' Imogen replied.

'Hard luck, Claudine,' Penny said drily. 'It looks like you're going to be there all night.'

Penny glanced into the mirror, studying her reflection. She appeared boyish, slim, only her heavily shadowed eyes giving her a powerfully sensual look. Carefully she re-applied her lipstick, and then turned when the phone rang.

'It's time.'

She nodded, and then walked out.

Maxie was delighted with the effect and stood back to look at Claudine. She had made her face up skilfully, her natural childish prettiness coming to the fore, her simple voile dress tied tightly around her waist.

'Oh no, not those shoes!' Maxie said sharply. 'Haven't you got any others?'

'Only some high heels – but I can't wear them, they make me wobble when I walk.'

Maxie helped her into them, ignoring her protests. 'Walk slowly – that way you'll manage.' She glanced at Claudine's reflection in the morror. A pretty peasant, innocent. 'You look wonderful.'

'You look *incredible*,' Claudine said, staring at the beauty next to her. Maxie was dressed in white to accentuate her tan, her hair piled high on top of her head. She looked sleek and lazily predatory, and was smiling with pleasure when the phone rang.

'It's time.'

Maxie turnd to Claudine and winked. 'It's time.'

The same message went to Danielle and Sarah, catching the latter off guard as she struggled to zip up the side of her skirt.

'I can't do it up!' she hissed to Imogen over the phone.

'Why did you bring it if you couldn't fit into it?'

'*I could fit into it yesterday!*' Sarah shouted. 'It must be the Mars bars.'

'Mars bars,' Imogen repeated patiently. 'How many did you have, Sarah?'

'Only four –'

'Four!'

'I always eat sweet things when I'm nervous,' Sarah replied shortly. 'Anyway, Arnold is hardly a sylph himself, is he?'

'But he has to be attracted to you,' Imogen replied hotly. 'I'm coming to your room. Wait for me.'

She was just crossing the end of her corridor when she saw Danielle by the lift. She saw her, did a double-take, and then walked back staggered. Danielle had not seen Imogen; she was looking mistily at the elevator board, her well-honed body poured into a yellow sheath dress, her hair curled and falling around her face. For an instant Imogen nearly choked, but before she could do anything the lift arrived, and Danielle stepped in.

She's going to sleep with my husband! Imogen thought disbelievingly, her feet pounding down the corridor to Sarah's room. My husband! And *I* organised it. . . . Her mouth dried. This plan had better work, she thought, suddenly panicky. Dear God, it had better work. . . . Loudly she knocked on Sarah's door then walked in.

'What a bloody sight!'

Sarah was red in the face from exertion. 'I've been trying to get the zip to close.'

'Sarah, you couldn't get that zip to close unless you had your hip removed.'

'What a bloody mean thing to say!' she howled furiously. 'It's all right for you, you're good-looking, any man would fancy you. No one's going to want me, not even that hideous Arnold.' She sat down on the edge of the bed, close to tears.

Contrite, Imogen sat down next to her. Sarah was so warm that a heat came from her, her skin flushed, her embarrassment palpable.

'I've never slept with any other man apart from Jimmy,' she confided shyly. '. . . I've always been afraid of men.' Her hand toyed with the half-closed zip. 'Look at me! I'm ridiculous. I'm too fat, too plain – no man would want to sleep with me.' Her eyes were pink-rimmed as she looked at Imogen. 'All of you are attractive in your own ways, but I'm not. I'm so afraid, so scared that he'll laugh at me. . . .'

Imogen slid her arm around Sarah and hugged her, feeling her head resting heavily against her shoulder.

'Hey, come on, you're the feminist, the one who's always telling us we're as good as the men,' Imogen said, her tone warm. 'You *can't* be afraid of a man – especially Arnold, that fat buffoon.'

'He might laugh at me –'

'He will in *that* outfit,' Imogen agreed, getting to her feet and looking round. 'Come on, let me get you ready.'

She worked for nearly fifteen minutes, dressing Sarah in a plain suit and lending her a blouse. The make-up was light, careful, but when Sarah looked into the mirror, she glowed.

'Now come on, we're late,' Imogen said finally. 'It's time to go.'

Sarah held back.

'*Come on.* Arnold won't laugh – and you'll keep Jimmy.'

Together they walked out and got into the lift, Sarah leaving at the fifth floor, her anxious face staring at Imogen until the doors closed.

'Oh God . . .' Imogen said, leaning back against the wall. 'Let this work, please . . . please. . . .' She regulated her breathing, checking her reflection in the mirror. Come on, keep calm, keep calm. She ran her tongue over her lips, thinking of the women in the various rooms scattered around the hotel. Sarah with Arnold now; Harry with Penny; Maxie with Jimmy; Trevor with Claudine; Danielle with Tom. . . . Imogen's eyes fixed on the lighted board above her head: five, four, three – then the lift stopped at the second floor and she stepped out.

On shaking legs Imogen walked down the corridor to Douglas's room. Her mouth dry, her heart pumping so fast that she felt light-headed. Go on, she willed herself, go on. . . . The door number was written in gold, No. 45, and for an instant Imogen couldn't knock. Her hand moved upwards, but she couldn't knock. She tried again, then suddenly thought of Giles and Tom – and knocked.

The door opened immediately. Obviously Douglas had been waiting for his visitor and was impatient to meet her. He was smiling, then his head jerked forwards curiously, his left hand rummaging for the glasses in his top pocket.

'*Imogen?*' he said incredulously.

She put her finger up to her mouth to motion him to be quiet, then glided past him into the room.

'*Imogen?*' Douglas repeated, closing the door and walking tentatively towards her. 'Is it really you?'

She nodded. 'Yes.'

'But I thought . . . I was expecting a . . .' he trailed off, suddenly smelling a rat. What if Imogen had found out about his little visitor and was coming to confront him? What if she was going to tell Penny. . . . He was clumsy with fear.

'Listen, Imogen, I've never done anything like this before.'

'Like *what*, Douglas?'

'It was Arnold's idea,' he said frantically. 'I don't want Penny to find out. . . .' He thought of the stuffed animals at home. 'Please don't tell Penny what I was going to do.'

'What you were going to do?' Imogen repeated softly. 'Does that mean you're not interested in me? That you're disappointed?'

Douglas's lugubrious face altered from blank terror to quizzical hope.

'*You're* the call girl?'

Imogen nodded.

Douglas sighed, then poured out some champagne for both of them. 'Well, this *is* a surprise.'

You'd better believe it, Imogen thought wryly.

'You a . . . call girl. Wow! Don't worry, I won't tell Tom.' He sipped eagerly at his drink, eyeing her furtively.

'This really is a surprise,' he laughed, but his features remained doleful. He couldn't believe his luck. Of all the women to get. God, it was a dream. . . . Douglas looked at her, and kept looking, longing for her and yet curious.

'It's amazing to find you doing this. You, of all people . . . but why, Imogen? I mean, why do you do it? You could get help, advice. You don't need to live this kind of life. So why do you do it?'

She sighed to herself. Penny was right. Sex was one thing, but friendship was quite another. Talk to me, Douglas was saying, talk to me.

Leaning across the bed and sipping at her champagne, Imogen looked deeply into his eyes and said: 'Well, you see it all began like this. . . .'

Chapter Thirty-Two

The following morning

The first knock on Imogen's door came just before six, Maxie walking in and handing her a couple of pieces of paper. She then sat down, picked at Imogen's croissant and yawned.

'So how did it go?'

'Imagine Jimmy in a corset –'

Imogen put up her hands. 'Enough,' she said, carefully reading what Maxie had written. 'He did *that*?' Maxie nodded. 'And then did . . . *what*?' Maxie nodded again, flicking the crumbs off her linen jacket. 'God, I don't believe it.'

'It's all true,' Maxie swore. 'I couldn't have made it up. I couldn't have *thought* it up.' She opened the window and glanced out. Paris was hot with early sun. 'Why do you want those details, Imogen?'

'Because it's the most important part of the whole plan,' she replied calmly.

Maxie shrugged, and leaned further out. 'Jimmy looked stunned when he opened the door and found me standing there. He asked if Harry knew.' She giggled softly, 'I think it turned him on, making love to someone else's girlfriend.' She turned round slowly, her golden face questioning. 'How did it go with Douglas?'

Imogen glanced up. 'He talked.'

'All night?'

'Well . . . most of it.'

Maxie's expression was sly. 'But when he wasn't talking?'

'He was trying.'

'Oh . . .' she said with immediate understanding. 'Poor Douglas. I suppose he was terribly upset?'

'Much more than I was,' Imogen answered truthfully, walking to the door and letting Danielle in. She looked horribly happy. Almost smug.

'Well, here you are,' she said, handing Imogen the notes she had made. 'But I suppose you know everything there is to know about Tom already.'

Imogen took the notes and put them with Maxie's.

'I can see why you want to hold on to him,' Danielle went on. 'He makes Trevor look pretty sick by comparison.'

Resisting an impulse to slap her, Imogen turned to Maxie. 'Can you let the others in?' she asked, then greeted Sarah, Claudine and Penny as they walked in. They all seemed oddly triumphant, curiously calm, and gave Imogen the notes without hesitation.

'You've all written down *everything* they did?' she asked.

There was a hum of agreement.

'But why?' Penny asked. 'I think we should know now.'

'No, not now. You'll know it's worked when you all get your men back – *then* you'll know it worked.'

Sarah stared at Imogen fixedly. Imogen had been kind to her the previous night and she was grateful, too grateful to push.

'Arnold wasn't rough at all – in the end.'

Claudine gave her an anxious look. 'What did he say when he opened the door and found you standing there?'

' "Jesus wept!" was his precise reaction.'

'Harry kept asking if anyone had seen me,' Penny said grinning, 'then he asked me to take off my shoes.' She turned to Maxie. 'Did you know about the toilet paper?'

'What!' Maxie said, aghast. '*What* about the –'

'Is it in the notes, Penny?' Imogen asked, deftly cutting into the impending argument.

'Every word and every deed.'

Sitting alone on the side of the bed, Claudine said softly, 'I like Trevor.'

'Pardon?' Danielle said. '*What* did you say?'

'I said I liked Trevor . . . he was very kind.'

'Kind?' Danielle echoed disbelievingly.

'Yes,' Claudine said, her voice sweet, 'and he doesn't really mind having his hair touched. Not really.'

Sensing a nasty turn in the conversation, Imogen moved in swiftly. 'Listen, everyone. We can't squabble amongst ourselves or the whole thing will be a failure. We have to forget what we did and you all have to go home and await the prodigals' return.' Her voice was firm. 'No one is to think about last night. It's over. Just concentrate on the future, and forget everything else –'

'It'll be hard,' Danielle crooned.

'All right, try to imagine living the rest of your life without the use of your limbs,' Imogen said icily. 'Because that's how it's going to be unless you shut up.'

Cautioned, Danielle slid into immediate silence, Penny turning to Imogen.

'Did you say that we have to leave now? It's so early.'

'I know,' Imogen replied, 'but you have to go before they're all up and about. I'm staying on for a while, I'll follow you later.'

Sarah was impatient, eager to know what was going on. 'But why –'

'Trust me,' Imogen said quickly.

'Yes, yes, I do.'

They left one by one, not acknowledging each other if their paths crossed, and only when they reached the airport did the women meet up again. They were alternately guilty and exhilarated, and very, very impatient to know exactly what Imogen was going to do next.

Bathed and dressed, Imogen took out her briefcase, and on a tiny portable computer began to type. It took her nearly an hour and a half, as she read the women's notes and then adapted what she read into the short synopsis of an article. She hadn't the time to write a full piece, just a few paragraphs outlining exactly what the man had done the previous night – and with whom. The information was lethal, and when she finished, Imogen entitled each piece 'Private Members' and pinned it on to a copy of *S'expression*.

She knew the effect it would have. Horror, followed by real terror that they would be exposed. For an influential, powerful man to be caught having an affair was bad

357

enough, but to be caught having an affair with his colleague's wife or girlfriend – the publicity would ruin him. They all knew about the previous exposure articles in *S'expression*, but those hadn't named names; this time it was to be made obvious that their names would come out – together with the name of the woman they had slept with.

The beauty of the plan was simple. Imogen would put the information into plain brown envelopes and then slide them under the men's doors – the magazine with the article affixed, and a note saying, GO HOME AND STAY HOME, OR THIS WILL BE PUBLISHED. It was a warning. And she knew that every one of them would take it as such. The men would never risk their careers and families again. They were being given the chance to escape punishment – and not one of them would refuse it.

Calmly she finished typing, then put the computer back into her briefcase and walked to the lift. Cautiously she went to each man's room and slid the relevant envelope under the door, then returned to her own room. Only one man did not receive the same package. Oh yes, Tom received the article, and the warning note, but it wasn't pinned to a copy of *S'expression* – but to a copy of the *Sun*.

Preoccupied, Tom stepped into the lift, a hand coming round the door as Trevor prevented its closing and hurried into the elevator beside him. A jumpy smile crossed Tom's face instantly, a nervous tic starting around his left temple as he looked at his colleague. He had spent the previous night with Danielle, *Trevor's* Danielle, the woman who was supposed to run an interior design studio in London, but who was, in fact, a call girl on the side. It had given Tom a certain *frisson* to make love to Trevor's girlfriend, but in the cool morning the previous night's incident looked more than a little shabby. If Trevor found out. . . . He was a lawyer, for God's sake, Tom thought, panicking; he could ruin him.

So could the *Sun*, he thought, sweating and thinking of the package he had received. Tom didn't know who had sent it, only that it too could ruin him. But he had ruined himself, he thought blindly. Why the hell do I sleep around, why don't I just go home to Imogen and make everything all right with her again? I have a family, a good career – why risk it?

'Morning,' Trevor said half-heartedly, thinking of the ominous package he had in his briefcase.

Oh God, he was a prominent lawyer, the Tory Party's adviser, if this came out he was finished. He had slept with Arnold Miles's wife, Arnold was supposed to have organised call girls for them, and Trevor had laid his wife instead! God, if Arnold found out about Claudine. If the Prime Minister found out about *him*. What had he been thinking of? Why hadn't he resisted? Because I drank too much, Trevor thought balefully. Because I thought it was all a bit of fun. . . .

'Morning,' Tom replied, staring straight ahead, guilt burning into him like a branding iron.

'Did you sleep well?' Trevor said, then immediately regretted asking. Who the hell had *Tom* slept with?

'On and off,' Tom squeaked, then cleared his throat. 'I actually went to bed early.' He kept sweating. 'I mean, not that early. Not for any particular reason either . . . I was just tired,' he added lamely.

Trevor was too locked into his own misery to notice Tom's discomfort.

'Are you going home now?'

Tom nodded frantically. 'Straight away!' he replied, then smiled loopily. 'I mean, there's no place like home, is there?'

'Absolutely not.'

'Absolutely not,' Tom echoed dimly.

'It's good to have someone to go home to,' Trevor said inanely. 'Danielle's a fine woman.'

Tom swallowed drily.

'Quite.'

'And Imogen's great,' Trevor went on limply. 'We don't value them enough.'

'No.'

'No,' Trevor echoed.

Both men stared at the lighted board over their heads – 5th floor, 4th floor, 3rd floor – both willing the lift to reach the foyer.

'I'm going back to Imogen,' Tom said firmly, sticking his finger in his collar and loosening it around his neck. 'A good home life is worth a lot.'

'I might marry Danielle,' Trevor volunteered woodenly.

'Great,' Tom said, his eyes still burning into the board. 'That would be great. She'd make a fine wife . . . I mean, I'm sure she would. . . . Not that I'd really know anything about it . . . about Danielle, I mean.'

Trevor turned slowly and stared at Tom. 'Are you all right? You seem jumpy.'

Tom grimaced, his teeth clenched in the parody of a smile. 'It's just that I slept badly,' he said.

'Oh God,' Trevor said brokenly, 'didn't we all?'

While Imogen flew back to London, Simone Duchamp spoke to Ira over the phone. He was ringing her to say thank you for helping him with Tusha. He appreciated it, he said. It had been a real worry to him, and she had been a great help.

'Think nothing of it,' Simone replied, even though Tusha had cost her over £40,000 so far. She was going to succeed, and £40,000 wasn't much to pay for Ira Mazan.

'It was good of you, Simone,' he went on. 'Tusha means a lot to me. I'm glad that you get on with her.'

They didn't; they hated each other, but that didn't matter. Tusha would sell Simone to her father in return for some impressive pocket money. As to the future, well, who knew what would happen to any of them?

'We should have lunch,' Ira said finally, reopening the relationship as easily as he would have opened an oyster.

'I would like that.'

'Yes,' he said simply. 'I know.'

Rowan was sitting in the back garden at Brighton, sunning himself and thinking of the girl who lived two doors away. She was very tanned, so he decided he would work on his tan too, decided that maybe he could impress her with a real California cool look.

'You're going red,' Suzanne said, touching his shoulder and making a hissing noise.

'Red!' Rowan repeated, horrified, leaping up on long, athletic limbs.

Smoothly, Suzanne slid into his place and then looked up. 'You fall for it every time, Rowan,' she said, laughing. 'Don't worry, you look wonderful. That girl will be panting after you.'

He towered over her, his hair falling over his forehead.

'Sun makes you wrinkle.'

'I know, darling,' she replied evenly. 'But the best thing about getting older is that you don't give a damn.' Her eyes glanced over to where Joy sat by the fishpond. 'I wonder what she'll be doing at my age?'

'Probably pushing you around in a bathchair,' Rowan said drily.

Suzanne laughed and turned to him. 'You are *so* like your mother, and not a bit like your father.' She paused. 'How is Giles?'

'Fine. He doesn't go out much any more. Just works, really.'

'No new "friend"?'

Rowan shook his head, his eyes screwed up against the sun. 'No. He doesn't seem to want to be bothered . . . he wants me to join him in the business though.'

Suzanne rubbed some oil into the tops of her arms. 'And what do you think about that?'

'I think I might,' Rowan replied. 'I like the idea of keeping it going. I think Mum would like it as well.'

Pleased, she studied the boy. No, not a boy any longer, almost a young man. So many years go by, Suzanne thought, so many people come in and out of our lives. She thought of Elizabeth, of Julie in the Manchester hospital, of Giles, of Ira, and then of her beloved Imogen – and then she thought of Tom.

She didn't know what Imogen had been up to in Paris, only that she was plotting something. Suzanne had seen the look too often and heard the tone of voice too often not to suspect that Imogen was planning some strategy. She wanted Tom back, and by God, she was going to get him back. . . . The Brighton sun beat down on Suzanne and on Imogen's children, it fell over the flagstones and basked

361

along the white-painted walls. I always knew you were special, Imogen, I always knew you would succeed. You brought me such joy, and later you brought me your children, and all your dreams were mine too. No woman ever wanted children as much as I did, and no woman ever was luckier to be sterile.

An act of God? Maybe, Suzanne thought. I never gave birth to you, darling, but you *are* mine and you've stayed mine all these years. A natural child might have left me or disliked me; you loved me and stayed with me out of choice. No mother on earth could ask for more.

'Gran?'

'Imogen?' Elizabeth's voice was faint, old now. 'How are you, love?'

'Just fine,' she said warmly. 'Tom and I are back together. It's all going to be okay.'

Elizabeth smiled down the phone. 'I thought it would be in the end. I had a hunch.' She was tired, breathing slow, laboured. Oh, it would be nice to sit down, but there was still the shopping to do later. 'I'm glad you're happy, really glad.'

'Are you all right?'

'I'm old, love,' Elizabeth said laughing. 'There's no cure for that.'

Imogen was immediately anxious: 'Do you want me to come up?'

'No, I want you to stay with your husband and your children. I'm fine, just fine.'

'I wanted . . .' Imogen paused, struggling to find the words. 'I wanted to say thank you, Gran.'

'For what?'

'For bringing me up, for being there when I needed you. For helping me, and listening, and for all the things you sacrificed for me.'

'I never gave you anything I didn't want you to have.'

Imogen nodded. 'I know, but you had so much to worry about for so long. What with Grandad and my mother. It must have been so hard for you.'

'You'd have done the same,' Elizabeth said honestly. 'It

was nothing remarkable. I did what I thought was right. All my life that's all I ever worried about – doing what was right. I never wanted to get on, or be rich – I couldn't have done it even if I'd tried. But I could see promise in you, I had enough sense to see it in you. You had quality, love, and that sets a person apart. Quality and goodness.' She paused for a moment. 'When I die –'

'No!'

'Now hear me out,' Elizabeth countered. 'When I die, love, don't get upset and fretting about burials and head-stones and all that nonsense. Just put me by Graham and Julie and then stop grieving . . . I'll always be there, you know that. You won't be able to pick up the phone to talk to me, but I'll hear you nevertheless. I don't believe much in God, Imogen, but I know that rightness, goodness, never dies.'

Imogen could hardly speak: 'Gran. . . .'

'Enough, I don't want to talk about it any more,' Elizabeth said firmly. 'Thank you for what you said, love, and thank you for what you are.'

'I love you,' Imogen said quietly.

'Thank you for that as well, love,' Elizabeth replied. 'I love you too. Always and always.'

Chapter Thirty-Three

They came home one by one. Little lambs, all of them, coming back to the fold. Arnold to Claudine, Douglas to Penny, Harry to Maxie, Jimmy to Sarah, Trevor to Danielle and Tom to Imogen. They came home anxious, willing to please, their briefcases carrying the damning details of their Paris trip. Some put the envelopes in security vaults, some burned them. But none of them forgot any of the blistering words. They each thought that they had been the only one to be duped, and each dared not confide in the others. Because how *could* any man forgive a friend for sleeping with his wife or girlfriend? And how *could* any man condone such stupidity?

A couple of them thought of tackling Arnold, asking him about the call girls he had laid on, trying to ascertain if he knew that one of the Tory women was a working girl. None of them realised that *all* the women had been in on it. It never occurred to any of them to imagine that all six women had plotted the thing together. If they *had* swapped notes, they would have realised. The warning in the package had been clear – GO HOME AND YOU'RE OUT OF THE WOODS, or words to that effect. All they had to do was to return to their proper partner and everything would be okay.

It was a small price to pay, even for the bachelors. Harry and Trevor might not be married to Maxie and Danielle – but if it came out that the top Tory lawyer and a Tory MP had been sleeping with other MPs' wives, their careers were as good as dead. They had had their fun, and had paid for it in nervous anxiety and many startled glances at the telephone. By the time all six of the men returned to London, Arnold was close to collapse and Douglas was mute with shock.

They tried to put a brave face on things, but every time Harry saw Douglas, or Jimmy bumped into Harry, they began to blather uncontrollably. Luckily all of them were in such a state that they hardly noticed the condition of their colleagues and when they returned to London each made a dive for the only place he felt safe – home.

And each woman was waiting. Some found it hard to hide their feelings, but they all remembered only too well what Imogen had said. They'll come home. That's what you want, isn't it? That's what we did it all for. Trust me, she had said, it will work. Forget everything that happened that night and just think of the future.

But some found it difficult.

'How was your trip, darling?' Penny asked, kissing Douglas on his mournful cheek.

'Fine,' he said, avoiding her eyes. 'I'll just go up and change.'

'You do that, sweetheart,' she agreed pleasantly. 'I thought I'd invite Imogen and Tom round at the weekend. How do you feel about that?'

There was a loud thud, a bag being dropped upstairs. Smiling grimly, Penny walked back to the kitchen.

Tom came back in a peculiar mood, flinging open the front door and bellowing for Imogen. She came out, frowning, her hands wet from preparing a salad. Without any explanation he picked her up and carried her upstairs, tossing her on to the bed and then kissing her vigorously, his beard rubbing against her cheeks and neck. When he paused for breath, she smiled at him.

'This is very Rhett Butler,' she drawled in a Southern accent. 'What do you think you're doing there, boy?'

Hurriedly Tom pulled off her dress, kissing her shoulder hungrily. 'What I should have been doing for the last few months,' he said darkly. 'Now shut up.'

Harry, of all people, suffered the most. He came back to his Holland Park flat and skulked in, Maxie hearing him and coming out of the drawing room.

'Hell fire! Don't creep about like that!'

365

She jumped. 'What's the matter?'

He shrugged, moodily petulant. 'Nothing.'

'How was the trip?' she asked, walking over to him and helping him off with his coat.

'Lousy,' he said sullenly. 'I need a drink.'

Together they walked into the drawing room, where Harry poured them both a stiff gin. He couldn't forget what he had done – and with Penny, too! He didn't even like dark women, and he couldn't *stand* short hair.

'You look tired,' Maxie said languorously. 'Come and sit by me.'

He moved over and perched on the edge of the settee uneasily. Maxie was a hell of a woman. Better looking than anyone, sexy, not *that* stupid. . . .

'I missed you.'

'That's nice,' she said, sliding her hand up the back of his jacket. 'But all the Parisian women are supposed to be so chic.'

'They couldn't hold a candle to you,' he said hurriedly.

Maxie frowned. 'Your hair looks different,' she said, touching the back of his neck.

Harry felt dizzy. He had risen after Penny had gone and had panicked when he found the package. Almost hysterical, he had set about dressing and then doing his hair, only to find that his hand shook so much he could hardly hold the comb. After ten minutes of hard manual labour he looked in the mirror – and saw a member of the Tufty Club looking back.

'I had trouble with it,' Harry said, self-consciously touching his hair. 'It wouldn't go right.'

'I'll do it for you,' Maxie purred. 'You're home now, you just relax.'

He leaned back against the settee gratefully.

'I think the world of you, Maxie. You know that.'

'I know, Harry,' she said, her voice gentle. 'You show it in everything you do.'

The biggest triumph was Danielle's. After waiting for six years, Trevor proposed and the happy couple threw a celebration – with all their friends attending. It was a lively evening, although most of the men couldn't look each other in the eye and most of the women kept smiling at each other in that knowing way women have.

'Well done,' Imogen whispered to Danielle.

'He's not Tom,' she replied. 'But he's the best I'm going to get.' She squeezed Imogen's hand. 'I don't know how you pulled it off, and I don't want to – but thanks for what you did.'

'It was a pleasure.'

Danielle winked, suddenly full of life. 'Well, I don't know about yours. But mine certainly was.'

'But if you had to say what was the *best* thing that ever happened to you,' Imogen said, glancing over to Suzanne, '– with a man, I mean. What would it be?'

Suzanne tapped her front tooth with her index fingernail. 'I think this capping's loose.'

'Suzanne!' Imogen snapped. 'Didn't you hear what I said?'

'Yes, that's why I thought of my tooth. You see, Michael paid for these to be capped. About ten years ago, when he had that part in the film that was never released because the director fell out with the –'

'Spare me any more details,' Imogen said. 'So having your teeth capped is the best thing a man ever did for you?'

'No,' she replied shortly. 'My ex-husband died. That was nice.'

'You are *unbelievable*,' Imogen said, shaking her head. 'I asked Gran what was the best thing she ever got from a man, and she said – a memory. She said the best of Grandad had been the memory he left. Of those last good years.'

'Sex.'

'Pardon?'

'Sex,' Suzanne repeated. 'That's the best thing I got from a man.'

'It's not very profound, is it?'

Suzanne bristled: 'Listen, you want culture; buy a book. You want the truth; ask me.' She studied Imogen for a long moment. 'So go on, tell me. What was the best thing you ever got from a man?'

'I don't know, I haven't got it yet.'

'You ambitious little sod,' Suzanne said, smiling. 'You really are quite something, Imogen. I only hope that Tom can live up to you.'

'So do I,' she said, grinning, 'so do I.'

Chapter Thirty-Four

London,
Two years later

'We could lose,' Tom railed. 'We could lose.'

'I don't think so,' Imogen replied calmly. 'You just have to keep your head, and don't believe the opinion polls.'

She stopped drawing and pushed aside the caricature she was preparing for Lorrie. Her work had increased, as had her name, but she put her family first. As she always had, preferring to push Tom, to back up his ambition. He had progressed quickly, become well known, his comments used as sound bites, his face cropping up more and frequently on the television. Time had changed them all: Rowan was apprenticed to his father in the school holidays, and Joy was almost four. And now the biggest challenge of Tom's career was coming up. There was to be a general election – if the Tories won, he might well get a coveted place in the Cabinet. If they lost, it meant years in the wilderness.

For months Imogen had helped him to campaign. She was a tireless worker and a good-looking woman – both attributes counting greatly in her favour. She walked the northern streets with him, and stood by him, and spoke up for him, and her sense of humour injected many meetings with spirit. They liked her, up north; she was one of them. They liked her in London too; she was one of them. She enlisted everyone's support, calling up old friends, asking Ira for contacts – which he gave willingly. He had watched her rise with amusement and some pleasure; now living with Simone he was as glossily immoral as he liked, and resigned to his way of living.

'It suits me, I was always a *shlep*.'

'Sure,' Imogen said smiling. 'Just tell me, is Simone good to you?'

'Like a mother.'

'Then God help you.'

He laughed loudly.

'Tom's worried that the Tories might lose.'

'Never.'

'If they do, he'll never get over it,' Imogen replied. 'I want him to win, Ira. He *needs* to win.'

'As Allah wills,' he replied. 'As Allah wills.'

'You're a Jew!' Imogen said, laughing. 'So what's with the Allah business?'

The polls looked bad as the weeks progressed, Labour pulling ahead, Tom spending more and more time on the hustings. His voice faltered; sipping honey and hot water he carried on, but his energy began to dip at the beginning of the last week, and he was losing weight quickly.

'You've fought a clean campaign,' Imogen said. 'Whatever happens, you should be proud of that.'

'Which is more than can be said for my Labour opponent,' Tom said bitterly. 'Read that.'

It was a piece in the *Evening Standard*, which hinted at Tom's past. It was a lie, easily discredited, about fundraising – but mud sticks, and Imogen knew it.

'How dare he!'

'I don't know,' Tom said wearily, 'but the damage is done.'

'No,' she said calmly. 'You fight fire with fire, Tom. I refuse to let anyone get away with this. If you don't care about yourself, think about your family. This man has to be stopped. He's a liar and worse. You don't want to fight dirty, fine. I admire your morals. But sometimes you have to put the boot in. Especially with a man like that.' She paused. 'He isn't fit to be an MP, *you're* the man for job. Not him. If you give up, I'll never forgive you. Defeat isn't what we've fought for and worked for. I wasn't brought up to admit defeat in *anything*. If you want it, you fight for it. You're the right man – and you have to make sure that everyone else knows that too.'

Tom looked at her, stunned by the cold fury in her voice. 'How?'

'Your rival has a past.'

Tom frowned: 'He *has*?'

Imogen nodded, then walked over to a side table and began to write. She wrote about the Labour MP, about what she had heard and been told by his ex-girlfriend. She wrote, and her mind went back to a morning in Paris, and the pieces she had written then. She had been fighting to keep her husband that day; now she was fighting to defend her husband and obliterate his rival. Calmly she wrote, and calmly she passed the paper to Tom a few minutes later.

He read it, stunned, and then burst out laughing. 'Oh, no,' he said, delightedly. 'Not a poodle, tell me it wasn't really a poodle.'

'A standard,' she said, raising her eyebrows.

'You know that we could discredit him with this, and then win,' Tom said, his voice rich with excitement. 'We could win, Imogen, win!'

'From your lips to God's ear,' she said, 'from your lips to God's ear.'